In the Wake of Ashes

Also by Lorrieann Russell

By Right of Blood
My Brother's Keeper
Fortcoming:
Passages
The Ballade of Amelia White
Farewell Arcana
A Man Named Logan

Lorrieann Russell

In the Wake of Ashes

Edin Road Press

❁

IN THE WAKE OF ASHES

ISBN: 978-0-61582038-5

Published by Edin Road Press
1508 Continental Square
Lexington KY 40505

publisher@edinroad.com

Peprint edition: March 2015
©2013 by Lorrieann Russell
First edition ©2001 by Lorrieann Russell

Cover Artwork by L.A. Russell
Book design and production by the author

On the Web:
lorrieannrussell.wordpress.com
www.facebook.com/lorrieannrussell

Chapter 1

September 1612
Port Edin Settlement, An Island off the Coast of New France

WILLIAM OPENED HIS eyes and breathed in the early autumn crispness of the fresh sea wafting through his bedroom window. *Another beautiful morning.*

The sun had barely peeked over the horizon, yet the sky already held the promise of a warm, clear day. He lay in bed listening to the gentle rolling of the ocean and the call of the seabirds. *Such a lovely song.*

He closed his eyes for a moment, content to just listen to the sounds of life and, as was his custom, offered a silent prayer of thanks for the sunrise.

A gray tabby hopped up onto the bed and chirped to him in greeting.

"Shall be a diamond day by the looks of that sunrise, Dragon." He scratched between the cat's ears and allowed her to walk on his chest and rub her head against his face. She folded her paws and hunkered down on his shoulder, purring. "Yes, I agree. 'Tis far too early to be rising but it would be a sin to waste such a morn as this laying about, wouldn't it." In reply, the cat closed her eyes, resting her chin on her paws. He chuckled and stroked her back. "Fair enough, another moment or two, then."

Next to him, Mehlyndia stirred and rolled over, dropping her arm across his chest and upsetting the lounging cat. Dragon made an insulted snort, stood and stretch, then sauntered, tail up, to the far end of the bed.

William brushed the hair away from his wife's eyes. "Good morning, Melly."

"Hmm?" Mehlyndia blinked then yawned and looked at her husband. "You're awake with the dawn again. Trouble with your sleep?" she asked, nuzzling up to him.

"Who could sleep on such a morning?" He smiled, giving her a squeeze. "Especially today. Come on. Help me up. We have a busy day ahead. The men shall be here soon. It won't do for me to be still abed when they raise the beams, will it?"

"I'm sure they're all still firmly asleep, my love." She gave him a quick squeeze and sighed before reluctantly pushing herself up to sit. "But, I suppose you are right. The ladies will be here far ahead of the men, I'm sure. We have a grand feast to prepare. While all the men are busy raising the house, we'll be raising the bread to feed them." She drew on her dressing robe, stretched and yawned, then walked around to William's side of the bed. "I'm sure I will be on my feet most of the day," she said, as she pulled his chariot-chair close to the bed. "Ready?" She held both hands to him.

"Ready." William threw the covers aside, reached for her hands, took a long breath and pulled himself up. He held onto her, one arm around her shoulders, the other persuading his right leg, then the left, to dangle from the edge of the bed. He sat for a moment, recovering his breath. "You must be tired of this," he muttered, as he did every morning.

She gave him her traditional reply and then kissed him.

"Not yet." It was a ritual played out almost every morning since they arrived in Port Edin. She positioned the chair alongside the edge of the bed. "The wheels are beginning to wear. They hardly roll properly anymore. You really should have Ian mend them for you."

"Ian?" William laughed. "I think not. He's talented with his flute and quick with his herbs and poultices, but he's hopeless in the wood shop. He'd make the wheels square and then where would I be?" He reached up and locked his hand around Mehlyndia's shoulders as she locked hers under his arms behind his back. "Now," he said and shifted his weight forward to allow her to ease him into his chair. William always took care to keep this little bit of morning business cheerful, though he hated every minute of it.

"It's getting harder to do this," she said, taking a breath once he was settled into his chariot.

"Does it hurt?" he asked, concerned, placing a hand on her expanding middle. "I don't want you to risk—"

"No." She patted his hand on her belly. "We're fine, love. But it won't be long before I'll need Elinor to help me." She walked behind him and pushed the chair closer to the window so he could look toward the road.

"Don't wait too long to ask for help," he said, looking up at her over his shoulder. "You and the little one should not have to be lugging about the likes of me." He sighed and then turned away from her, resting his elbow on the windowsill, his chin in his hand. "I'm not quite the husband you expected, am I."

"Am I complaining?"

"You never do." He half smiled, but his cheer had left him.

"No gloomy moods today, Mr. Philbrick." She turned him to look at her, with a gentle hand on his shoulder. "It's going to be a glorious day. There'll be friends and family about, and plenty of food. We're long overdue for a happy event, I'd say." She put her hands in the small of her back, and arched, stretching again. "We're to have a new home, at last, to make room for this growing clan we've started."

"Aye." He smiled at her finally, and then gave her tummy an affectionate pat. "This little one will have a proper roof above him well before he arrives."

"Are you so sure it's a son then?" She laughed as she went around behind the dressing screen to change her clothes. "There's the remotest possibility I could provide you a daughter, you know."

"Now that would be pleasant," William mused, looking out the window, "a Fylbrigge daughter."

"Philbrick," she corrected him as she came out from behind the screen, fully dressed. "I know you're not fond of that name, but it's the one we must use now."

"Philbrick," he repeated with a sigh. *The one thing I'm sure of about myself— my name –and you make me change it.*

Seany, their five-year-old son, interrupted their conversation. "Papa?" he called, standing in the doorway, blanket in hand, rubbing his eyes.

"Seany? Come here, lad." William held his arms out as the tyke went to him and climbed up onto his lap for a hug. "Did we wake you up too early, son?"

"No. Is it time to build the house yet?" Seany asked, his face stretching into a yawn.

"Almost." William laughed. "As soon as Ian and the rest

come. Are you ready to help with the heavy lifting? I'll need you to carry my hammer for me."

"William, you shouldn't tease the boy," Mehlyndia said, holding a hand to Seany. "He's too little and will only be in the way."

"I am not too little," Seany protested as he took his mother's hand and hopped off William's lap. "I'm big enough to carry Papa's hammer. See?" He bent his little arm to show off his muscle. "I'm strong!"

"That you are." William mussed the child's hair. "I should think we can find a job for you today. We'll need all the hands we can find to get the frame up by sunset."

"We?" Mehlyndia raised a brow to him. "Surely you're not planning to—"

"We." William shot her a quick look. "You don't expect me to just sit and watch all day, do you?"

"No, I expect you'll be in the thick of it and scaring me to pieces, as always. I suppose it's too much to ask you to be careful?"

William chuckled. "I'll be as careful as I ever am."

"That, sir," she rolled her eyes heavenward, "is exactly what I was afraid you'd say." She laughed as she kissed him on the forehead. "Come on, Seany, let's leave Papa to his thoughts now and get you some breakfast." She patted the boy on the bottom and scooted him across the room.

"Breakfast!" Seany burst into giggles and trotted away, dragging his blanket behind him.

"I'll bring yours to you, my love," Mehlyndia called over her shoulder as she chased after her son.

"Take your time," William said, watching them go. *I'm*

not going anywhere. He sat quietly, enjoying the breeze on his face, half dozing while he listened to the sounds from the kitchen, the scrape of the spoon on the mixing bowl, the shuffling of the dishes as Mehlyndia went about getting Seany's breakfast.

"How many cakes would you like, darling?" she asked.

"Fifty-eleven." Seany spouted with a giggle.

"Oh, you'll not eat more than fifty-ten," Mehlyndia said, laughing. "We'll save that last one for Papa."

Seany's laughter echoed throughout the little cottage and as it always happened, the simple sounds of his family and home filled him with a feeling of peace. He closed his eyes for a moment, and offered another silent prayer of thanks, knowing how fortunate he was to experience this lovely morning. He should not have been alive.

William Mastin Fylbrigge— now called Philbrick— had spent the last four or so years bound to his chariot chair, with precious little recollection of his life before he was put there. He knew he had been whole and strong before he had come to this shore, though he could scarcely remember his old home across the sea. He remembered nothing of the circumstances that had brought him here, or how he came to be in such a sorry condition.

On rare occasions, Mehlyndia would speak dreamily about a place called Stonehaven on the eastern shore of Scotland, and the castle she called 'Drumoak'. She would ask him if he remembered the time they had done this or that, or the party for so-and-so from wherever. Did he miss the grandness of nobility? He would nod, and smile, perhaps laugh as if the memories were clear. He hated to admit to her that he could barely recall Stonehaven, let alone the details of the events she described. She humored him by laughing along, however he knew she was not fooled when he pretended to remember.

He did know that they'd left Scotland rather abruptly, not quite five years ago and not long after they married. Most of his waking memories of the place were shady at best but in his dreams, he saw clearly— images of a large hall with a grand stairway, colorful glass windows, and endless corridors lined with gleaming stone pillars. The dreams of this place were comfortable and familiar, and at times seemed so real he believed them to be true. In his dreams of Drumoak, he was always whole, able to walk, run, and do fine woodwork carvings with his hands. Most times, he would see himself as though watching from the side. He could watch himself performing simple tasks without difficulty or ascending the great stairs two at a time, then sliding down the wide polished granite banister. He would see his own face cheerful, young, and unmarked rather than scarred and lined at the eyes as it was now. His hair would still be black as a raven, free of the rebellious white streaks that framed his face now, belying his twenty-five years as far older.

In his dreams, he traveled the corridors and rooms, knowing how they looked, felt, even how they smelled, knowing every stick of furniture, every drapery. He would walk the castle, inventorying each painting, vase and statue.

And there would always be music. Sweet, clear music that he believed was of his own making somehow, yet he could never see how he was creating it. His life in this castle had been one of privilege; he was certain of that much.

Along with images of the castle, there were also memories

of faces. He would see Elinor, cheerful in her kitchen, busily preparing a meal or organizing a feast. Mehlyndia would be there, as well, dressed in elegant silks and intricately embroidered gowns, quite unlike any she had ever worn in Port Edin. He remembered an elderly gentleman with a graying beard and a warm winning smile. Edward? Was this man his own father or was he Mehlyndia's? Truthfully, he was unclear on that but in his dreams, he called the man 'Father'. In one dream, Edward called him 'son' and had given him a horse he named Star. *He must have been my father.*

On occasion, he would encounter a young lad not much older than Seany, with chubby cheeks and mischief in his eyes. He carried a little wooden sword with twining for the hilt and adorned with an elaborate carving of a dragon on the blade. The boy charged about the castle, sword raised, eager to vanquish the vandals of his imaginary game.

But the two figures William saw most often, he could never find names for; a young woman, with large brown eyes and long chestnut colored hair, and a man close to his own age, with stern but gentle eyes colored the same deep green as his own. They would stand together as though watching him, as he walked the corridors, always present, never farther than the nearest door or window, yet never close enough for him to touch. He was always greatly pleased to see them, though they seldom spoke to him. They would wave, smile, and if they did speak, their voices would come from a place just behind his ear, rather than from their mouths. He knew he had loved them. In his most recent dream-visit to Drumoak, the woman's name had been on the tip of his tongue and he was certain he had spoken it. But when he awoke, her name, face and her companion, faded back into the misty place in his memory that stubbornly hid away from him during his waking hours.

His dreams of Drumoak came often. At times, he would awaken from them with a warm, content feeling as the visions faded. But most often, they would leave him with a sad sense of loss, more profound than he could express. He knew he had once been happy within those castle walls and suspected that whatever had brought him to his current physical malady had happened away from there, though he could not for the life of him imagine what it had been.

Aside from his useless legs and the premature white streaks in his otherwise black hair, he carried a goodly number of scars. Most of the marks— the ones that encircled his wrists and ankles, and the hook shaped crease on his left cheek— were still fairly prominent, though they had softened a bit over the years. He had only limited use of his hands, as his fingers were somewhat gnarled at the joints and he could not straighten them completely. He could grip and hold his woodworking tools well enough, but he lacked the dexterity to do any of the fine carving he had seen himself doing in his dreams. Even holding his quill was a challenge and his nightly journal entries were written in large block letters instead of the careful tiny script he once used.

He sat idly examining his fingers, tracing the scars on his left wrist with his right hand, wondering again how he had come by them. He was certain Mehlyndia knew but she refused to speak of it. In fact, whenever he would ask her of it, she would become so upset she would almost swoon, and William hated to cause her distress, so he would not prod her for details. He was certain that Elinor knew the truth as well, but like Mehlyndia, she would grow pale and turn away at his questions. He reasoned that eventually he would come to know the truth on his own and there was no gain in causing Mehlyndia and Elinor distress.

His reverie was interrupted when Dragon hopped up onto his lap. "Ah, are you ready to begin your day then?" He chuckled as the cat made herself comfortable, kneading his knees with her front paws. "Is that it? You believe I'll allow you to sleep on my lap all day? I don't think so." He laughed as he picked her up and set her on the windowsill. "Go on, earn your keep, you hairy beast." With a gentle nudge, he persuaded the cat to jump out the window to the front yard. As he watched her disappear in the grass, he saw a tall man with a cheerful smile and a lighthearted lilt in his step approaching the cottage.

"Good morning, Ian." William called from his window.

Ian looked up and waved. "Hello, Will." He walked directly to the open window and rested his arms on the sill. "How does the morning find you?"

"I'm well enough, I suppose." William reached a hand in greeting to Ian. "Melly's getting breakfast, have you eaten?"

Ian shook his head and frowned, "I'm fasting today."

"Fasting? With the feast that—"

"You're too easy, Will," Ian laughed. "You believe anything I tell you."

William shook his head, suppressing a grin. "No wonder you left the clergy. You're evil."

"Did you only now puzzle that out?" Ian grinned, giving William a pat on the shoulder, "Let me come 'round. I'll see you in a moment." He walked away from the window, still chuckling.

I don't know what I'll do if that man is not cheerful one day. William smiled as he waited for his friend to join him.

Ian Proctor had sailed with William and Mehlyndia when they had left Scotland aboard the *Lady Anne*. William was not certain but since Ian was never present in his dreams of Drumoak, he assumed they had met aboard the ship. But then, he did not remember the ship journey except for the few days when they had anchored off shore. Ian's had been one of the first faces he had seen when he woke up after spending months lost in some sort of delirium. His face seemed vaguely familiar, but he assumed that was because Ian had helped Elinor and Mehlyndia care for him during the crossing.

All William really knew about Ian's life before Port Edin was what the man had told him. He had once been a cleric— priest or a monk of sorts— and had chosen to leave his calling to make his way in the New World as an apothecary. William had a difficult time imagining Ian as a cleric. His sense of humor was quick with a sarcastic bite to it, and no one enjoyed bawdy tales and laughter more than Ian. Even in the dreariest of times, there was a clever twinkle in the man's pale blue eyes. His cheerful disposition and friendly nature never failed to lift William out of a cheerless mood. Ian was a good friend, one he was grateful to have in his life, though he often got the impression that Ian may have been harboring secrets of his own. For all his sunny smiles and cheerfulness, there were times when William noticed a lost and wistful look in his eyes. Ian also bore the ghosts of scars on his wrists, not terribly unlike William's, though they were far less visible. Many times he had wanted to ask Ian about them, wondering if it would help him remember how he came by his own scars, but he could not bring himself to ask.

"Look what I found in the kitchen." Ian entered the room carrying Seany, giggling and upside down over his shoulder. "The rascal was stalking your breakfast." He plopped the lad down onto the bed.

"Was he?" William gave his son a wide-eyed look of mock reproach. "I hope you saved a crumb or two for your wretched father."

"No, Papa I ate it all." Seany patted his stomach, laughing as he rolled around in the big blankets.

"He certainly did but I've made more." Mehlyndia chuckled as she carried William's breakfast tray into the bedroom. "Ian, would you care for some breakfast? I've made enough cakes to feed the whole of Port Edin."

"That would be lovely, madam. Thank you." Ian smiled, then took the tray from her. "Didn't you make any for him?" He motioned with his head toward William.

"Him? Is he to eat today? I thought we fed him yesterday?" Mehlyndia teased.

William made a comical moan. "Alas, I shall starve."

Seany stopped rolling and gave his mother a disapproving scowl. "You made Papa sad, Mum."

Mehlyndia winked to her husband. "Have I?"

William reached his arms out to his son, "Oh, we're just playing, Seany, I'm not sad. See?" He grinned as wide as his face would allow. "Ian's got my breakfast." He motioned for Ian to set the tray on a little table in the far end of the room.

Seany climbed up onto William's lap and gave him a hug. "Good. You need your breakfast. That was mean."

William held Seany tight for a moment, then let him slide off to the floor. "Thank you for your concern, son," he grinned at the lad. "Go on now, get your breeches and shoes on, and go see if Elinor needs any help."

"All right, Papa." Seany smiled and ran back through the door.

"I'll bring you something in a moment, Ian." Mehlyndia said, as she followed Seany.

"He's a good lad, Will." Ian said, as he went around behind William. "I see a naturally kind heart in him. He'll make you right proud one day." He pushed William's chair to the table in front of the breakfast tray.

"Aye," William said. "He makes me proud now." He reached for the kettle on the tray, poured some of Mehlyndia's spiced cider into his cup, and took a drink. "And so shall his little brother or sister." He smiled at the thought. "I find it so wonderful to know there is another bairn on the way and that I'm not a completely useless man. It's overwhelming, Ian."

"I'm sure it is, Will," Ian said, quietly. "You're a lucky man." He pulled a stool up to the table and sat down, then rested his chin on his hand and looked at William closely for a moment. "So what's troubling you?"

William looked up over his cup. "Nothing, why d' ye ask?"

"You've got that look about you." Ian's face grew serious. "Dreams plaguing you again?"

"When are they not?" William made a halfhearted chuckle. "No, it's not the dreams." He pushed the cakes around on his plate idly with his fork. "I'm worried for Melly. With the little one coming, and Seany to look after and me—" He dropped the fork and sighed. "Ian, the least I can do is to find a way to get out of bed on my own. It's not right that she should have to put herself and the child at risk just because—"

"I'm not complaining, William." Mehlyndia interrupted, bringing in a tray for Ian. "And I've told you when I can no longer lift you on my own, I shall call Elinor to help me." She placed the tray on the table in front of Ian.

William looked at her, embarrassed that she had heard him. "It's not right. A man should not burden his wife with—"

"Hush." Mehlyndia placed a hand on his lips. "You are not a burden." She leaned down and kissed him. "You're my husband. Now, eat your breakfast."

William leaned back in his chair. "Some husband," he muttered.

Mehlyndia shook her head, ignoring William's comment. "Ian, could I ask you to clear away when you've finished? I need to see to the preparations for the feast."

"My pleasure."

"Thank you. I'll leave you two to talk then." Mehlyndia gave William an affectionate pat on the shoulder, smiled at him, then left the room.

"So, do you think you can help me?" William asked.

"Help you what?" Ian asked, between bites.

"Get out of bed," William answered, as he picked up his fork.

Ian froze, his fork halfway to his mouth. "You want *me* to come and do it, instead of your wife?"

"No, lunk." William rolled his eyes. "I want you to help me

find a way to do it myself."

"Ah." Ian took another bite and creased his brow in thought. "I see." He set the fork down and looked over toward the bed. "It shouldn't be too difficult to rig up something. I expect all you really need is something to grab on to."

"Aye, that's what I thought too." William nodded. "A handle of sorts that I can hold to pull myself up. Then Melly won't have to lift me."

Ian stroked his chin. "Let me think on it, but yes, I'm sure there's something we can do." He made a crooked grin and leaned close to William. "Perhaps we could put one in the privy as well?"

William blushed, but could not suppress a grin. "Absolutely."

By mid-day, the little cottage was teaming with activity. Elinor, ever the organizer that she was, saw to it that each of the ladies who had come to help cook had a proper job and a proper spot to do it in. Since Mehlyndia's kitchen was quite small, most of the preparations took place outside on worktables the baking bread filled the large stone oven adjacent to the barn. Kettles of steaming vegetables and soups bubbled away, suspended over open fire pits, and for the main course, a whole calf roasted slowly on a on a spit that turned by means of a leather strap borrowed from the lathe in William's workshop. Elinor mourned the huge efficient kitchen she once commanded at Drumoak, with its acres of work tops and the colossal stone oven and iron cook stove — a rarity in Scotland, especially forged on Edward's order — making the Drumoak kitchen the envy of the highlands. She missed her own cozy quarters and the company of the other maids as well, though she was careful never to mention it to anyone.

Prior to Port Edin, Elinor spent the majority of her fifty-four years in service to Mehlyndia's father, Lord Edward, Duke of Stonehaven. She had enjoyed keeping the castle in proper working order, managing the household staff, and had taken pride in knowing everything that took place within its walls. Edward often shared his thoughts with her or sought out her advice on small matters. When his wife Anne of Sutherland passed away, it was Elinor that Edward turned to for comfort. She never expected she would have ever left Drumoak but the choice had really not been hers. Edward had implored her to stay with William as he was in sore need of her healing talents, and she would never refuse to go where she knew she was most needed. Besides, she felt responsible for William's misfortune and felt she owed it to him to stay with him. It wasn't a terrible burden for her, however, she truly loved the young couple as her own children, and now that she was accustomed to the more primitive conditions of Port Edin, she was content to manage the workings of this far smaller household.

Elinor was in her glory this day. The last festival she had presided over were the preparations for William and Mehlyndia's wedding five years earlier. Of course, the wedding banquet was far more elaborate than this peasant's feast they were planning today, but she was enjoying the task all the same.

The Blessed Mother grant this feast end on a far happier

note than the wedding, she prayed silently. *Grant that this celebration be the beginning of good and better times, as they've so earned it.* Dragon came by and brushed against her leg, and she finished her thought aloud to the tabby. "After all, there's no reason anyone would be sending assassins to a house raising, now, is there? This day shall end peaceful and merry with a fine dinner had by all."

Dragon sat and looked up to her.

"They're well deserving of the peace they've come to know here, I say." She squatted to pet the cat. "It's long overdue."

"Elinor?" Mehlyndia said, entering the kitchen with her apron laden with carrots. "Who are you talking to?"

Elinor blushed and chuckled to herself. "A silly habit, I suppose, but I was talking to Queen Dragon here. She's quite the listener, you know." She stroked the cat and straightened up again. "Let me help you with that, dear." She picked up a large basket.

Mehlyndia emptied her apron into the basket and sat down on the workbench with a sigh. "You're not alone in your silly habit," she laughed. "I believe William speaks to Dragon on a regular basis. No wonder the creature believes she is in charge of the running of this house." She bent and stroked the cat, then took a long breath.

"Are you feeling unwell?" Elinor set the basket on the table and sat next to Mehlyndia. "You're flushed."

"It's warm outside in the sun, I'll be fine."

"You've been on your feet all morning, you just sit here now. Let the other ladies handle the rest of the cooking. And I'm sure Prissy won't mind keeping an eye out for Seany."

"Thank you, Elinor, but I've had a hard enough time

convincing these women that I'm made of no lesser stock than they." Mehlyndia sighed and wiped her face with her apron. "I grow so weary of the whispers and snickers behind my back. Is it my fault I was not raised on a farm? Josephine Ashcrofte practically fell all over herself to hurry and tell Prissy how uneven my rolls were."

Elinor watched Mehlyndia's face turn redder as she spoke. She knew it had been a difficult adjustment for her to go from being Lady Sutherland, the future Duchess of Stonehaven, to Goody Philbrick, common housewife and mother. Elinor admired Mehlyndia's determination to fit in and felt equally irked by the snobbishness of the other wives. As pompous and self-admiring as noble women could be, at least they did not belittle each other by comparing bread rolls and the whiteness of their linens.

"There now, dear, don't let them bring a pall on your day. They don't intend to be unkind." She patted Mehlyndia's hand. "After all, they've no idea where we've come from, and that you'd had no reason to learn to cook as a girl." Elinor gave her a warm smile, then glanced through the open kitchen door. "See, out there? Prissy will have none of Josephine's waspish gossip. She's giving the old biddy a bit of a tongue slapping."

Mehlyndia followed Elinor's gaze, then made a smug smile. "That's because Prissy's rolls are even more uneven than mine." She laughed out loud and caught herself. "Shh, she's coming in."

"Do you need help with the chopping?" Prissy asked, pointing to the carrots Mehlyndia had carried in.

"No, I think I can handle it, but I'd be grateful if you'd

keep an eye on Seany. He's been wanting to join the men in their building all day. I've had a devil of a time keeping him out from underfoot."

"My pleasure," Prissy beamed. "I'm glad to have an excuse to get away from Josephine." She put her hand to the side of her mouth and leaned close to Elinor and Mehlyndia. "She's been into the sacramental wine again and is running at the mouth. She just called the vicar a dried up old goat!"

"Oh my!" Mehlyndia covered her mouth and giggled into her hand. "Well she is his wife, so she would know how dried up he is."

"Melly! You're wicked!" Prissy giggled.

"Aye, I've learned to adapt, haven't I." She winked at Prissy. "Thank you for minding Seany, Prissy, you're a dear."

Prissy winked back and trotted out of the kitchen.

Elinor watched her go. "That lass is such a joy. Always cheerful, that one. Simon married well."

"Aye," Mehlyndia agreed, "she's a dear. She reminds so much of..." She cast her eyes down and picked at her apron.

Elinor nodded and finished Mehlyndia's thought. "Laurel?"

Mehlyndia looked up. "Aye. Laurel. Prissy's got the same streak of mischief in her." She shrugged, stood and went to the door to look out. "I find I've been thinking about Laurel often lately. I miss her so."

"It's the time of year," Elinor said quietly, then stood and retrieved a cutting board and a large knife from a shelf. "It will be five years come the end of this month."

"Five years." Mehlyndia nodded, then wiped the perspiration from her face and joined Elinor at the table. "At times, it seems more like fifty, and others, it feels like only five days. It's not right that she isn't here with us. She would have loved taking care of Seany." She picked up a carrot and the knife, and began chopping. "I'm sure she'd be quite amused to see me chopping carrots." She raised the knife a little higher with each chop. "I'm sure she'd be pleased to see how well William is coping." She brought the knife down hard and sent the tops of the carrots sailing onto the floor. She stood frozen, then burst into tears.

Elinor put an arm around her, and coaxed her to lean on her shoulder. "Hush, now. What brings this about?"

"He spoke out in his sleep, again, Elinor. He's still trying to remember." Mehlyndia cried onto Elinor's shoulder. "He called her by name this time."

Elinor held Mehlyndia at arm's length, looking her in the eye. "Does he remember her at last?" she asked.

"No, only in his sleep." She took a breath and blew her nose. "Elinor, why must we keep it all from him? He loved Sean and Laurel. It seems cruel not to allow him those memories."

"I know, dear, but it's best." Elinor gave a quick glance over both shoulders, being sure there was no one to hear her. "After all, the moment he learns of Laurel, he'll remember how she died, and then *why* she died the way she did—"

"She saved his life," Mehlyndia argued. "Would that be so wrong for him to remember?"

"Not in itself, dear, but think." Elinor put her hands on the sides of Mehlyndia's face. "If he remembers Laurel, the memories of his trial will soon follow and all that came before it." She fought a shudder that crept down her spin.

"And what brought him to trial in the first place. Dear, we've had peace here since we've come and he's come such a long way. It's best he not remember his former talents with the herbs and... charms." She whispered the word, giving another quick glance over her shoulder.

"That is the last thing I want him to recall." Mehlyndia sighed.

"And what gain would there be in him remembering all he could do before, if he cannae do it now?" Elinor said, wiping Mehlyndia's cheeks with her apron. "Would only pain him all the more."

"You mean the music, don't you?" Mehlyndia said flatly. "It was the most important thing in the world to him to be able to sit and play his lute and lose himself in the tunes. Do you think he honestly has forgotten it? I don't. Watch him when Ian plays his flute. He enjoys it well enough, but I can see it his eyes, he's missing his own music terribly." She shook her head impatiently, turned back to her carrots, and resumed her chopping.

"Aye, I've seen the look, dear, but there would be no sense telling him about his lute. He couldn't possibly play it now. Why pour salt in the wound?"

Mehlyndia looked up with a sudden, guilty blush in her cheeks. "Salt in the wound? You're probably right. Now I wish I'd waited to speak with you before I..." She shook her head, turning away.

"Melly?" Elinor asked. "Before you did what, dear?"

Mehlyndia forced a smile, waving her hand as if to dismiss the thought. "Oh, 'tis nothing, Elinor. A silly notion I had last spring. Remember William's birthday in May, when Ian played that lovely tune on his flute?"

Elinor nodded.

"You see, while William was listening, he seemed quite taken with the music, and you know how he gets that faraway look when he's daydreaming."

"Oh, yes." Elinor smiled.

"Well, I happened to notice that he was keeping time with the music with his hand. It was as if he was strumming the air. I'm not even sure he was aware of it, but it made me feel sad just the same."

Elinor placed her hand on Mehlyndia's cheek, wiping away a stray tear.

Mehlyndia continued, looking to her hands as she spoke. "I mentioned it to Ian and he said he'd noticed it too, and we agreed that perhaps there was an alternative to his lute— something simple to play. So, when Father's ship arrived in June, I wrote him asking that perhaps he could send something musical back on the next ship. I thought perhaps Geoffrey would have an idea of what to send. I've been looking forward to the next ship to see what comes... but now, I'm not even certain I shall be able to give it to him. Oh, Elinor, I feel just awful! You're right, it will hurt him more to remember what he's lost..." She buried her face in her hands and cried. Elinor pulled her to her shoulder in a motherly embrace.

"Oh, child, what could I possibly know? I think that was a splendid idea and I'm an old fool for my fear. We shall give him back his music and it will be a balm for his spirit, something to chase those gloomy winter blues away from him." She rocked Mehlyndia on her shoulder for a moment, the stood back, turning the young woman's face up, persuading her to smile.

"Do you really think so?"

"Aye, I do," Elinor assured her with a kind smile, then turned to the chopping block and scooped up the carrots into a small pot. "Besides, he's remembered some things on his own already, eventually it may all come back in its own time. I just pray he's prepared for it when it does."

"Melly, Elinor, come on out," Prissy called excitedly through the kitchen door. "They've raised the frame! It's time to nail the bough to the peak."

"So soon?" Mehlyndia set her knife down, and wiped her hands on her apron. "Where is Seany, is he out of harm's way?" she asked, hurrying to the door.

Seany peeked out from behind Prissy's skirt, and held a hand up to his mother. "I'm here, Mum."

"Thank goodness, I was worried you were in the way." Mehlyndia sighed as she took his hand. "I wouldn't want you to get stepped on or squashed under a log, after all."

"But Papa said I could help." He stuck out a lip, and frowned. "He said I could carry his hammer."

Elinor joined them in the doorway and leaned down, resting her hands on her knees to speak to the boy. "I'm sure your Papa wants you to stay where it's safe while they raise the frame. That's dangerous work and they won't be able to watch out for you, little one."

"Can I ride up with Papa then?" he asked, pointing toward the construction.

"What?" Mehlyndia gasped and followed Seany's gaze. "Good God in Heaven! Has he lost his mind?" She ran out of the kitchen toward the men, leaving Seany with Prissy and Elinor.

"What is—?" Elinor looked to see what had sent Mehlyndia running. "Blessed Mother, some things never change," she sighed, shaking her head.

"You don't suppose he's planning to let them hoist him to the peak?" Prissy asked, wide-eyed. "It's at least twenty feet or more!"

"That's *exactly* what he's planning, Prissy." Elinor held Seany's hand tight, then followed Mehlyndia to the construction.

William sat in the sun watching the construction of the frame that would eventually become his home. He had spent months planning the structure on paper, and having the logs hewn and notched. It would be a fine home and would be large enough, if the need arose, to serve as one of the garrison houses in the settlement. It would have two stories with a half floor for an attic. The second level of the house would protrude ten feet over the first on one side and be fitted with removable panels in the floor to allow for quick exit or strategic defense should they ever find themselves under attack from the native people. William thought the likelihood of an attack remote, as the natives he had come to know were quite pleasant and peaceful. He assumed the more likely function of the openings would be the disposal of wash water.

The lower level of the house would include a large kitchen he was sure Elinor would appreciate more than Mehlyndia, a sitting room, a bed chamber for Seany and one for Elinor, and the master bed chamber for himself and Mehlyndia. He had made last minute changes in the design to include a small nursery off the master's chamber. The second level would have four more bedchambers, each with a proper fireplace. The rooms to the front, where the escape panels would be, would also include built-in bookcases that would conceal passages to other parts of the house. It would be a safe and warm place indeed for him to raise his family.

One of the unique features he had put in his design had been a suggestion from, and worked out by, Ian. For all outward appearances, it resembled an empty closet. But next to it, behind yet another hidden panel, would be a series of pulleys, cantilevered weights, and ropes that when pulled, would lift the entire closet to the second floor. This was how William was planning to be able to enjoy his entire home. Though he was skeptical that the contraption would actually work and that he would be far too heavy for Mehlyndia to hoist, Ian assured him that with enough pulleys and weights, that even Seany could lift a draught horse to the second level.

Though he would have rather been helping with the construction, William sat in his chariot-chair, plans in hand, amazed as he watched his design become reality. When the last of the construction beams had been notched and fitted together properly, the frames were raised, one wall at a time. Deep pits had been dug and then half-filled with rammed earth and stone to serve as footings for the huge beams. The frames were lifted by bulls, pulling large chains attached to what would be the highest crossbeams while the men lifted from underneath. The bottoms of the beams would slide into the ditches and, if the planning had been right, they would stand straight. This was the most dangerous part of the job, and the one William was most worried would go wrong, but after the first, then the second wall was raised, he became more confident in his foremanship. When the last wall had been raised and the crossbeams set, William sat, marveling at the skeletal structure of his home. *I'm not as dull-witted as I thought. It worked. It all actually worked!*

When the frame was complete, the men let out a wild cheer, then sat in the grass to rest. William had known most of these people for only a short time. Some had only arrived to Port Edin in the past months on the latest ships that had come from France. Each family was eager to build for themselves, though most of their homes would be far smaller. Among the men were Ian, and the only other person, besides Elinor, that had come across with him from Stonehaven, Simon MacHenry.

Simon had actually gone back to Scotland after the initial crossing and William assumed he had only come with them that first time to see that he and Mehlyndia were safely settled. He vaguely recalled that Simon had once been a friend of his in Drumoak and he was not sure, but it seemed that Simon might have been a soldier. William and Mehlyndia were surprised but pleased, when Simon returned to Port Edin the following year, with his new bride, Pricilla, who preferred to be called Prissy.

"I told you it would work." Ian clapped William's shoulder. "That was a fine bit of engineering you worked out."

"He worked it out?" Simon scoffed. "It should have fallen afoul before it started, then." He crossed his arms over his chest, grinning.

William turned the plans over in his hand and gave Simon a confounded look. "That's odd. The peaks are pointing the wrong way, look." He held the upside-down plan out to Simon.

Simon burst into laughter and shook William's hand heartily. "Congratulations, Will. 'Twill be a fine home."

"Thank you." William rolled up the plans and took another gander at his masterpiece. "I'm as surprised as you are, Simon. It's better than I expected. I'm amazed that the frame is finished so quickly."

"It isn't finished yet." Ian shook his head, looking to Simon. "Is it, Simon?"

"Why, no, Ian." Simon stroked his chin thoughtfully. "There's something missing."

William gave Ian and Simon a suspicious look. He unrolled his plans to see what could possibly be missing. "What are you two talking about?" he asked.

Ian winked at Simon with a grin. "Won't be finished without that last touch, will it?"

"Not at all," Simon answered.

"All right, what are you two up to?" William rolled his plans again.

"Why, the blessing of the bough, of course." Ian extended a hand to the peak.

"The bough?" William looked where Ian pointed. As part of the construction preparation, a large iron arm, with a pulley on the end protruded from the peak. A rope had been threaded through and was attached to a workman's bench, meant for hoisting building materials. "What bough?"

Ian gave William a mischievous smile, then nodded a

signal to Ephraim Ashcrofte, the new vicar, and Charles Blackwood, the blacksmith of the village, who were sitting on the grass nearby, both wearing the same look of smug conspiracy. They stood and went to the workman's bench and set it across two barrels. Charles held up the evergreen branch that, as part of the traditional builder's blessing, would be attached to the peak of the frame and remain there throughout the rest of the construction. Ephraim held up a hammer.

"So... who is to place the bough then?" William asked, with a slight sense of trepidation.

"The bough is always placed by the master of the house, of course." Simon said, resting a hand on William's shoulder.

"What?"

Before he could protest, Ian and Simon flanked William, and lifted him off his chair, each taking one arm and leg, and carried him to the workman's bench and sat him down.

"You're not serious..." William laughed, looking back and forth at his friends. "Are you?"

"Aye." Ian and Simon spoke together, as they handed him a long length of rope.

"Strap yourself good, lad, you're going up," Ian said with a comical seriousness in his eyes.

"Absolutely!" William grinned as he wrapped the rope back and forth around the bench and across his lap as many times as the length would allow. He looked up to Ian, then to the peak. "It is safe. *Right?*"

Ian leaned close to William. "Yes, but if you don't want to do it, tell me. Truly, Will, it's up to you."

William looked again at the peak, thinking it over. "How

high is it?" he asked quietly.

"It's a bit more than twenty feet to the ground from up there," Ian said, still speaking quietly. "If you like, I'll go with you, if you're afraid," he offered.

William grinned and raised a brow. "Afraid?" He took the hammer from Ephraim. "I think not. Hoist me, lads!"

The men around him cheered as Charles handed William the evergreen bough. It was no more than a yard in length and an inch in diameter. William threaded it under the rope on his lap, along with the hammer.

"Ready?" Ian asked, as he checked the safety rope.

William wrapped his left arm around one of the supporting ropes. "Ready."

Slowly, Simon pulled the rope hand over hand, lifting the bench toward the peak.

Twenty feet to the ground. Twenty feet? For a moment, William had an odd feeling he'd heard someone tell him that before, then the thought passed as finally he reached the peak of the frame. He glanced down to the ground. *Wrong thing to do.* He closed his eyes for a moment to steady a strange trembling that began worming its way from the pit of his stomach up through his chest. *Fine time to discover that I'm not fond of heights. Just hammer the bough and be done.*

"You're doing great, Will!" Simon called up from the ground.

"Just drop it in now," Ephraim added his encouragement.

William tightened his grip on the support line, then reached for the bough with his free hand and slid it out from under the rope. A U-shaped bracket had already been placed in the beam and all he had to do was slide one end of the bough into it, then give it one or two taps with the hammer and he would be done. *Easy enough. Just hold on tight and lean out a bit—*

"William!" Mehlyndia cried out. "What are you doing?"

William jolted violently as the sound of her voice startled him and for one terrifying moment, he was certain he was going to fall off the bench. His brief panic was echoed by a chorus of startled gasps from below him that quickly settled. He clutched the support rope as tightly as possible and took a long breath, then looked down, nodded to the people that all was well. He looked to where Mehlyndia's voice had come from. She was running toward the construction from the cottage. Elinor and Prissy, with Seany in tow, ran close behind. Ian ran to meet Mehlyndia half way, and stopped her from getting any closer. She argued with him for a moment, a mixture of panic and anger on her face. *Oh, I'll catch it from her later, I'm sure.* Elinor caught up to them and put a motherly arm on Mehlyndia's shoulder.

"Be careful!" Mehlyndia called up to William as Elinor persuaded her to sit in the shade. "That's a long drop!" She settled on a rock beneath a large oak tree and watched him through her fingers.

"I'm always careful." William answered, forcing a smile he hoped appeared more confident than he was feeling after being startled. When he turned his attention back to placing the bough, he discovered, to his dismay, he would have to lean out farther than he expected to reach the bracket. He instinctively wrapped his left wrist one more time around the support rope, which tightened, almost painfully so, as he leaned out, holding the bough with his right hand. Another strange echo flashed in his head, *the drop is twenty feet to the floor.* He froze, bough midway to the bracket, as the tremble in his middle made its way to his hand. *Ground, not floor, there's no floor under me. It's the ground.*

"Will?" Ian called up, from directly under the bench. "Is something wrong?"

William did not answer. He sat still as a stone.

"Can you answer me?" Ian called again, a concerned urgency in his voice.

William wanted to answer, but found himself unable as the strange echo in his ear came and went. *Answer the question, yes or no.* For the briefest instant, the recollection was clear to him, then gone again, leaving an uncomfortable tremble he did not understand. He closed his eyes for a moment. *It's only the height that's shaken me. That's all.* He sat, still waiting for the unpleasant sensation to pass.

"Simon, help me with the ladder."

William looked down to see every face staring silently up to him. He had not realized until then, that all the cheering and conversation had gone silent. *How long have I been sitting here?* He still held the bough in his outstretched right hand, and his left was becoming numb as it clung to the support rope.

"Will?" Ian spoke calmly as he climbed to the highest rung on the ladder, almost eye-level to William on the opposite side of the beam. "Are you all right?"

William closed his eyes for a moment and repeated the half-memory. "It's twenty feet to the floor." He opened his eyes and looked at Ian.

Ian kept his voice steady, though the concerned look in

his eyes belied the calmness. "Place the bough, Will, then they'll lower you down, slowly—"

Answer the question and we'll lower you gently, all it takes is one word—yes or no. William glared at Ian, then with a sudden and inexplicable anger, he forced the bough into the bracket. He picked up the hammer and gave the bracket one furious whack, securing the bough to the beam, setting the bench to swinging, and banishing the echoes in his mind all at the same time. The people on the ground burst into cheers. William took another long heavy breath as the wave of unexplainable anger passed. "I did it."

Ian exhaled loudly and nodded, a slow grin spread across his face. "You certainly did." He looked down toward the ground. "Bring him down, Simon."

"Gently!" William added, feeling slightly giddy.

At sunset, Mehlyndia rang the beckoning bell, calling her guests to the barn to enjoy the feast she and the other ladies had spent the entire day preparing. All gathered around the large table that was set in the shelter of the communal barn. The roasted calf was carved and set out on several platters, surrounded by bowls of steaming squash, carrots, and green beans, breads, and pots of butter and cream. With Ian's help, William took his place at the head of the table with the men seated on his right and their ladies across from them, on the left. The older children sat at a smaller table that had been set especially for them, while the toddlers and very young sat with their mothers, except for Seany. William insisted his son sit with him. When all had found their place, they stood and joined hands.

William realized he was expected to offer the Thanksgiving prayer as the 'founder of the feast' but was never comfortable in speaking prayers in public. He never recited any of the common prayers that were offered at Sunday meeting, as the chant-like, unthinking quality of them left him feeling somewhat unfulfilled. The way the prayers droned automatically, without inflection from the congregation, only heightened his resistance to speaking them. So, for his own comfort and true to his own faith, he kept his prayers to himself, and the words were never the same, coming to him as the spirit led him.

With all his neighbors now standing around him, holding hands, waiting for him to say something, he decided on the most graceful and inconspicuous solution to his dilemma. "Please forgive me for not standing." A polite chuckle made its way around the table in answer to his jest. "Since we are honored with the presence of Reverend Ashcrofte, I believe it appropriate for him to lead us in the prayer."

"My pleasure." Ephraim nodded solemnly bowing his head. "Thank thee, Father in Heaven, for the food you hath provided. Amen." He looked up. "Let's eat."

William chuckled quietly. *I could have done, at least, that well.*

"Ephraim, really." Josephine scowled at her husband. "The poor man suffers enough in his infirmity, the least you could offer is a proper blessing and a word for healing—"

"Thank you, Ephraim," William interrupted her. "The blessing was perfect." He smiled, politely, at Josephine, camouflaging the irritation he felt at her well-intended, but unthinking words. "I'm not suffering more than a ravenous appetite at the moment, Goody Ashcrofte."

Josephine pursed her lips and blushed but said no more, much to William's relief.

"Everyone sit down, please. The work is done. It's time to enjoy ourselves."

Mehlyndia sat to William's left, Seany on his lap and Ian to his right. Next to Ian, Simon. Elinor sat to Mehlyndia's right, Prissy next to her. As far as William was concerned, they were his family, and he was well pleased to have them all close to him.

"Now, Mr. Philbrick, would you care to explain yourself?" Mehlyndia asked, stern brow raised, as she prepared a plate for Seany. "What, in the name of God, moved you to ride to the peak as you did?"

"Ian and Simon moved me," William answered with an innocent smile. "I was kidnapped."

"Us?" Simon placed his hand on his chest in mock astonishment at William's accusation. "It was your idea, Will." He looked to Ian for support. "He begged us to hoist him up, didn't he, Ian?"

"Aye!" Ian nodded comically, then looked at Mehlyndia wide-eyed. "He overtook us and forced us. He's a nasty one, your husband is."

"Nasty he is for scaring me to death." Mehlyndia, finally, relented and laughed at Ian. "I suppose you'll next try to convince me he overtook Ephraim and Charles as well?"

"Of course I did." William said, straight-faced, "Pass the bread, please, Elinor."

"Here you are, dear." Elinor passed the breadbasket, smiling. "It's nice you haven't lost your sense of humor. But in all seriousness—" She leaned forward and wrinkled her brow to him. "—what *were* you thinking?"

"That's the trouble, Elinor, he wasn't." Mehlyndia said, taking the bread from William. "You could've fallen you know; then where would Seany and I be?"

"I was careful—"

"And you two!" Mehlyndia shook her head toward Ian and Simon. "You should know better than to allow him to talk you into—"

"Melly," Ian held up the palm of his hand to quiet Mehlyndia. "William was right the first time. Simon and I kidnapped him." He lowered his hand and sighed. "It was completely our plot, he had no idea what we were about. It's just that we both knew how badly he wanted to be part of the building and we thought—"

"Ian," William tapped Ian's shoulder. "It's all right, no need to explain." He looked at his wife. "I'm sorry I scared you, Melly. But as you can see, I'm well and fine, no harm done. Please, let's just enjoy this glorious dinner you've worked so hard to organize."

Mehlyndia shook her head, and gave up the argument.

The rest of the meal was passed with polite conversation and Ian's lighthearted quips. The ladies discussed plans for a quilt they would sew together to pass the coming winter months and the men spoke mostly of the rest of the construction of the house.

"You'll want it all closed in before the snow flies, Will," Simon said, sitting back with a cup of after dinner ale. "The bricking has to come next though."

"That'll go quick with enough hands to the task," Charles said, as he pulled up a chair next to Simon. "I've done a fair bit of masonry work in my day. We'll have the hearths and chimneys up in short order. I'll be glad to oversee the job."

"Thank you, Charles, I'd much appreciate it," William said, extending a hand to the man to seal the agreement.

"My pleasure." Charles smiled as he shook William's hand. "I may even find need for this lad as well." He reached out and mussed Seany's hair.

"For me?" Seany looked up wide-eyed and pleased.

"Are you stout enough to carry a bucket of water, lad?" Charles asked.

"I'm strong enough to carry two," Seany said, holding up three fingers. The men laughed heartily and Seany buried his face on his father's shoulder.

William motioned the men to quiet with a wave of his hand. "I know you're a good strong lad." He gave his son a tight squeeze. "The other children have gone to play tag in the moonlight, would you like to go?"

Seany lifted his face and nodded.

"Go on, then. Don't wander far, though."

"All right, Papa." He gave his father a quick hug, then slid off his lap and trotted out of the barn toward the other children.

William watched his son join in the children's game, merrily dancing about in the moonlight. His thoughts strayed to the new child who would arrive early in the New Year. *Perhaps I'll build a cradle then? I can do that much now.* He had not been able to build a proper cradle for Seany and the child had been bedded in a sea trunk for his first months. But then, he had not had the opportunity to prepare at all for Seany's birth as Mehlyndia had carried him through what

William had come to regard as his 'dark time'; the months of the crossing that he had spent ill, lost in the dark of his own mind, after whatever the event had been that put him off his feet. He'd come back to the living, as Ian had put it, only a couple of months before his son's birth and was hardly able to hold a quill, let alone build a cradle. But he'd grown steadily stronger since he woke up, and decided at that moment that he would indeed build a proper cradle for his new little son or daughter.

Lost in his thought, working out the plan for the cradle, he hardly noticed that most of the guests had wandered away from the barn to enjoy the exceptionally warm September evening. The ladies were busily clearing away the remains of the meal on the far end of the table when Ian interrupted his thoughts.

"I don't suppose you'd care to talk about what went on today?" Ian asked leaning his elbows on the table.

"Hmm?" William looked up to him. "What do you mean?"

Ian kept his voice low. "Something happened at that peak. That was more than a simple reaction to the height you had up there."

"Oh." William sighed and sat back in his chair. "You noticed that? I suppose everyone else did as well?"

"Well, it was fairly obvious you didn't like it up there. My guess is Ephraim and Charles attributed it to the height. You must have noticed neither of them volunteered to do any of the high work." Ian laughed lightly but his eyes grew more serious. "But they don't know you as well as I do. Something else drained the roses from your cheeks, and I wondered if you wanted to talk."

William sat silently for a moment, thinking over the sensation that had overcome him just before he placed the bough. He could not recall exactly the echoes that had come to him, only that they seemed familiar. What he did remember was the all-encompassing sense of anger that he felt. As he sat thinking, his right hand idly found its way to his left wrist and he began working slow circles on his scars. He winced, surprised that it hurt him to do so at that moment. "I hadn't realized I'd done this." He held his wrist out to show Ian.

Ian examined William's wrist. "A bit of rope burn. I'm not surprised, given the way you lashed yourself to the safety line."

"Ah, that was probably it." William rubbed his wrist again, tracing the lines of the scars. "Ian?" he began, then sat quietly, not quite knowing what he wanted to ask.

"Aye?" Ian raised a brow and leaned forward.

"It was almost there. But I couldn't get my fingers around it."

"The bough? It was farther to lean than we thought."

"No." William shook his head. "Something... I'm not sure what but something about that bench, or maybe it was the rope, I'm not sure..." He knew he wasn't making sense, but Ian had always been easy to speak to, letting him ramble if he needed. "It reminded me of something..." He looked Ian in the eye. "I almost remembered it, Ian. But it was gone in an instant."

Ian drew a long breath and rested his chin in his hand. "Your accident? Is that what you remembered?"

"Accident?" William scoffed. "I stopped believing that long ago. You don't come by these sorts of marks by accident." He held his wrists out. "You should know that," he said quietly, looking at Ian's wrists.

Ian self-consciously folded his hands on his lap, concealing the marks on his wrists. "What do you think it was then?"

"I think," William began slowly, "I came by these marks the same way you came by yours." He looked Ian in the eye. "And when you finally come to accept that I'm not as fragile as the robin's egg you and Mehlyndia and everyone else believes I am, you will share with me how you came to own them."

Ian looked away. It was the first time William had known him to be speechless.

"I'm right, aren't I?"

"Will, I can't answer—"

"Seany!"

William looked up to see Mehlyndia running out of the barn door.

"Seany! What are you doing up there?" she cried frantically.

William looked through the doorway, but could not see Seany. "Ian, go see," he said, fighting a rising panic at Mehlyndia's reaction to whatever Seany was doing.

Ian jumped up and ran out of the barn. He stood in the doorway, looking to the place Mehlyndia had run. He relaxed, a wide grin on his face, he waved to William. "All's well."

"Thank God." William exhaled as the panic passed. "What's happening?"

Ian stood in the doorway, smiling, watching something. In a moment Mehlyndia appeared, a contrite Seany in tow. She led him into the barn and sat him on a bench near William.

"Your son has inherited your talent for scaring me to death!" she said, an angry scowl on her face.

Seany sat pouting.

"What has he done?" William asked, not knowing if he should laugh or be angry.

"He managed to climb the scaffold nearly to the peak! Thank goodness Charles's boy Kevin was close by." Mehlyndia dropped herself heavily on the bench next to Seany.

"You could have fallen, little man," William said, suddenly as frightened as Mehlyndia had been. "Why did you climb up there?"

"I'm sorry Papa." Seany dropped his little chin to his chest. "I wanted to help build the house."

"You scared us to death," William said, trying not to raise his voice to his son. "Where on earth did you come by such a bold streak?"

Mehlyndia gave William an incredulous look. "You need to ask?" she said, drumming her fingers on the table. "I'd say he is, indeed, his father's son. The both of you should be sent to bed early."

William finally allowed himself to laugh. "Yes, ma'am." He held his arms out to his son. "Come over here and sit with me, Seany. We'll keep each other out of trouble."

Seany hopped off the bench, climbed up happily onto William's lap, and snuggled in. William smiled at the boy and finally relaxed completely. It was then he remembered the conversation he had been having with Ian and that he had finally asked about the marks on his wrists. He was not surprised that Ian had chosen not to come back into the barn with Mehlyndia. *Ah, well,* he thought, *I'll ask again some other time. It's not as important as this.*

"How would you like to help me make a present for the new bairn?" he asked Seany. The child remained quiet. William looked down to find Seany had already fallen asleep in his arms. "Sleep sweet, lad."

Chapter 2

December 1612

THE PROGRESS ON the house moved along far quicker than William could have hoped. Luckily, the last of the hammering was finally complete just in time for the first snowfall which came early during the late days of October. The summer had been kind, and thanks to the help from the Mi'kmaq—the native people of New France—for the first time, they would face the winter with a fully stocked cellar. William had taken a liking to the strange hard-shelled vegetable they called 'squash' and the sweet sugar that was extracted from the trees. In return, the Mi'kmaq had taken a liking to the bannock cakes and the yeast breads the settlers made, and both settler and native had enjoyed the exchange of cultural recipes.

With luck and prayers, the fevers would be fewer this winter than they had been in the past. The first winter the Philbricks had spent in the cottage had been the hardest and spring had not come a moment too soon. Both Elinor and Mehlyndia suffered a spell of sickness that had put them abed for weeks, and though William was spared the fever that year, he had had to rely on Ian to help him care for Seany and for his own special needs.

That was a terrible time but even through Mehlyndia and Elinor's illnesses, the Philbrick household was far luckier than many of the other families in the settlement. They were the only household in Port Edin to suffer no deaths that first winter. No less than twenty souls were lost among the settlement that winter, and far more among the Mi'kmaq. Though the sickness was less severe in subsequent winters and even with the ample food and fuel wood they had coming into this one, the arrival of the first snow so early in the year was a foreboding omen indeed.

As with the raising of the frame, moving day was an equally exciting community event. The men came to help move what little furniture William and Mehlyndia owned into the new house. It looked woefully lost in the big empty rooms, but William had plans to build new furniture during the winter months.

By mid-November, winter settled full and heavy. More snow than the three previous winters combined covered the settlement and it was a blessing to be in the new house with its warm thick walls, and comfortable hearths. Simon and Prissy, out of necessity, took up temporary residency with the Philbricks when the thatched roof of their own little cottage could no longer hold the weight of the snow.

Seany took great delight in showing Simon how to work William's magic closet, demonstrating how to lift people to the second level of the house. The closet was the most anticipated part of the project, and when it was finally finished—and proven to actually work—it became the most popular source of entertainment in Port Edin. William never minded the company. He reveled in his friendships and indeed, was well thought of by the rest of the community. He grew accustomed to the curious side-glances and looks of pity he would receive from the new settlers and paid them little attention. The majority of the population came to know him, and learned to look past his limitations, which suited him.

By the time December approached, Port Edin was ready for another feast, and the Philbricks were more than pleased to oblige. The ladies came bearing gifts of baby clothes and blankets to welcome the bairn, and a covered hot dish of their own creating. The men gathered in William's workshop.

Charles Blackwood marveled at the way William had rigged up his lathe. "How on earth d' ye make it run without a foot pedal?"

"Pull that lever, there," William said, proudly. "The one next to the lathe."

Charles pulled the lever, which lowered a gear through the floor that was turned by a paddle that took advantage of a fast flowing underground stream. As the water pushed the paddle, the gears began to turn a convoluted network of belts and pulleys, which operated not only the lathe, but a drill and a bow saw as well.

"Well done, lad!" Charles exclaimed, watching the belts turn, fascinated.

William had earned quite the reputation as an inventor but modestly shrugged off the praises he would get for his innovations. After all, he only came up with solutions out of necessity brought about by his own shortcomings. *Nothing miraculous in that*, he reasoned.

The most important of his recent inventions, in his opinion, was actually quite simple; a railing next to the bed, which allowed him to get in and out on his own, and similar railings in the necessary house. Simple in their design as they were, once he got used to supporting his weight on his hands to move himself to and from his chariot, they were monumentally liberating.

On Christmas Eve, William presented Mehlyndia with the new cradle he had spent the past two months working on in secret. It was made from maple and he had taken pains to see the wood was sanded as smooth as silk to avoid any possibility of splinters to the babe. He had even managed to carve a rough and simple ivy design on the side. Crude as it was, it was the first intricate carving he had done with his bent-up fingers and he was quite pleased with the result.

"Do you like it?" he asked, as Mehlyndia marveled at the little cradle.

She looked up with happy tears forming on her eyelids. "It's beautiful. William, this must have taken you months." She ran her hand over the ivy carvings, tracing the vines with the tips of her fingers. "I didn't realize you were able to carve again. It's almost as you used to..." She left her thought unfinished, and went to him and leaned over him for a hug. "Thank you, my love."

"You're welcome, Melly. The carving is rough, but I'm glad you like it."

"It's lovely, darling." Mehlyndia took a seat next to the fireplace, still admiring William's handy work. "The wee one shall have a proper bed and fine warm blankets. We've been truly blessed these past months."

"Aye, we have." He smiled and drew the lap blanket up around his arms to stave off a slight shiver. "I think we need to refill that wood box. It's going to be a cold night." He looked around the sitting room. "Where is Seany hiding?"

Mehlyndia made a tightlipped grin, then answered, "Oh, he's around."

"What are you up to?" William asked, amused with the sudden twinkle in her eye.

"Me?" she asked, wide-eyed, feigning surprise. "Nothing. It's Christmas, William, allow me my secrets for a little bit."

"Ah, is that it?" William laughed, then shivered again. "Melly, could you stoke that fire a bit, it's cold in here."

"The fire is warm enough here," she said and got up from her chair to push him closer to the fire. "Better?"

"Thank you." William answered, pulling the blanket up even further. "Are you tired of me yet?" he asked as he stared into the fire.

"Terribly," she said, with an exaggerated sigh as she sat back in her own chair. "I shall have to put you out soon." She winked at him and picked up the knitting she kept in a basket next to her chair, a half-finished bootie dangling from the needles.

"Just checking." He smiled, watching her skillful hands whirl the yarn around her knitting needles. Though he was closer to the fire, the warmth of it didn't seem to reach him and he shivered again, but said no more about it. Truth was, he never seemed to feel quite warm enough no matter how many blankets he put on his lap. It was always a mystery to him that even though he had no real sensation in his legs they always seemed to feel cold. He always felt the winter in his shoulders and arms, and some days his joints ached him badly enough that he never left the spot by the fire. He hated those days and considered them wasted.

He sat quietly, watching Mehlyndia's knitting, coming close to nodding off when a jubilant Seany bound into the room. "Papa, wake up," he giggled, tugging on William's blanket.

"I'm awake," William said. "What's all the excitement? Has Father Christmas come?"

"Not yet!" Seany put his chubby hands over his mouth and laughed, then turned to his mother. "Ian is here, is it time?" he asked.

"Is Elinor ready?" Mehlyndia asked, with a smug smile.

"Yes!" Seany said.

"Good, go on and tell Prissy and Simon to come down, and then we shall all be ready." Mehlyndia gave him a pat on the bottom to scoot him along.

"Ready for what?" William asked, trying not to smile.

"It's a surprise, Papa, I'm not s'pose to tell," Seany said, all a-giggle as he trotted out of the room.

"Aha!" William laughed. "A conspiracy under my own roof."

"Do you believe yourself to be the only one capable of keeping a secret?" Mehlyndia said, pointing with the tip of her knitting needle to the cradle.

William gave her a curious look, bemused with her teasing.

The quiet of the sitting room was soon filled with the sound of laughter and music as Ian led the way into the room, playing a tune on his flute. Elinor followed behind Ian bearing a tray laden with steaming mugs of mulled ale and honey cakes. Prissy entered behind Elinor, holding Seany by the hand. They followed Ian in a serpentine march around the little table in the middle of the room, singing a raucous rendition of 'Good King Wenceslas', Seany's voice rising above the rest. Elinor put her tray on the table and finished the final chorus with gusto.

William applauded them eagerly, laughing. "Music worthy of angels." He smiled, then looked around, a bit confused. "Where is Simon?" he asked, craning his neck to look past Ian to the door.

"I'm here." Simon called from the other room. "Is everyone ready?"

"Ready?" William asked.

Mehlyndia seemed about to burst with giddiness. She set her knitting aside and then stood beside William, and leaned down to speak in his ear. "I've a gift for you." She looked up, and gave Seany a wink. "Now, Seany."

Seany cupped his hands around his lips, "We're ready, Simon!"

Simon entered the living room, dressed head to toe in furs and evergreen garlands, carrying a bough of holly entwined with an ivy vine in one hand and a package in the other.

"Look Papa, it's Father Christmas," Seany giggled as Simon put the evergreens on the mantle above the hearth.

"I am indeed." Simon chuckled, "I believe I'm to deliver this to the lord of the manor." He held up the package, which was about an arm's length long and vaguely triangular shaped, wrapped in burlap and tied with twine. "Would that be you, my good sir?" he asked, with a comically serious expression.

"I suppose I am." William answered, with a polite bow of his head.

Simon placed the package on William's lap as the rest

gathered round him. He untied the twine and pulled away the burlap. "Oh my." William stared wide-eyed and swallowed back an unexpected lump that formed in his throat as he looked at Mehlyndia's gift— a beautiful ornately carved stringed psaltery. He ran his hand across the strings, they sounded for all the world like heaven to him. "It's wonderful, my love."

Mehlyndia crouched next to him, and spoke quietly. "You used to play the lute for me. Do you remember that?"

"A lute?" William looked at her closely, forgetting the other people in the room. "Is *that* what it was?" He knew there had been music in his dreams, but just how it had been created was one of those mysteries he could never completely grasp; yet he was certain it had been himself playing it. He brushed the strings again with his right hand and let them ring. "Did I play well?" he asked quietly.

"Aye, like an angel. And you shall again."

The others moved back quietly, allowing William space, finding seats around the table. He sat, eyes closed as, for the first time, he was able to pull a memory out of the dark and hold on to it. *I played a lute.* Images of a morning, long ago found its way to him...

He was in one of the grand rooms of Drumoak— his room, he was certain— in a comfortable corner next to the fire. The instrument in his hands was elaborately carved with impossibly fine details. It was his own work. He plucked the strings as quietly as possible, not wanting to awaken

Mehlyndia, who was sleeping peacefully as the first light of dawn shown through the window, the sunlight playing on her face. The music he played, the same he had heard in his dreams, filled the corner where he sat. He played a plaintive melody and hummed quietly at first but soon, before he realized it, was singing to the morning. In his memory, he watched his un-marred left hand dance deftly along the neck of the lute. When his song ended, he allowed the strings to ring until their vibrations came to a natural end.

"What lovely songbird has blessed me with such a sweet tune this morning?" Mehlyndia smiled at him from her pillow.

"I had not meant to wake you. A thousand pardons for disturbing your sleep." He bowed in jest. "I am at your mercy for penance, m' lady."

"Well then, good sir," she sat up and held out her hand for *him to kiss. "As penance for such a crime, you are hereby required to provide like tunes each morning to greet my day."*

"I remember," William said, looking up into Mehlyndia's eyes, no longer caring to keep his emotions from showing as a single tear found its way down his cheek. "I played for you in the mornings."

"Every morning." Mehlyndia brushed the tears from his face and kissed him. "Ian helped me think of a suitable replacement for your lute that we thought you might be able to manage, and this is what we decided on. I wrote to Father last spring. It's been difficult for me to keep this hidden since it arrived on the last ship. Geoffrey, the luthier in Stonehaven, made it especially for you. Do you remember him?"

"Geoffrey?" William felt a smile growing, pleased with himself that he was able to bring to mind the face of the elderly luthier who had taught him how to play and how to carve. "Yes. Yes! I do. He made this? That's wonderful... thank you, Melly."

"You're welcome, my love." She kissed him softly, then crouched on the small stool next to his chair, taking his right hand in hers, gently stroking his knuckles. A ghost of a frown crossed her face. "Do you think you'll be able to play it? I know your hands are not what they once were."

William positioned the psaltery properly on his lap with an innate knowledge of how it should be played. The instrument was little more than a triangular wooden box, with a flower shaped hole cut under the stringboard. The strings could be sounded by plucking or strumming with his right hand, while the left would dampen the strings to produce different chords. It would require far less dexterity than needed for lute playing, and the music would be just as sweet. "I shall need a lesson or two, but yes," William smiled broadly. "I should be able to play this."

"This calls for a toast!" Ian said, raising a mug of the mulled ale.

He had been so taken with the psaltery and the memories it had brought to him, that William had completely lost the fact that his adopted family was there to share Christmas Eve. "Yes! Elinor, if you would..." He motioned to the mugs. Elinor handed one to him and one to Mehlyndia before picking one up for herself. William raised his mug, "A toast then, to family and friends and blessings on us all."

"Amen!" Ian clinked his mug with Simon and Prissy, then gave Elinor a quick kiss, raising a blush to her cheeks.

"May I have some, Papa?" Seany asked, trying to get a sniff at William's mug.

William indulged the boy with a grin. "Just a sip, it's a bit strong for a little one."

Seany took a sip then wrinkled his nose and shook his head.

"Don't you like it, son?"

"No! It's awful."

William laughed heartily, "Good for you, lad, keep yourself that honest!"

"Have you decided on what you'll call the bairn?" Prissy asked Mehlyndia, as she made herself comfortable on a cushion by the fire.

"I've not thought about a name for a lass, but if it's a lad," Mehlyndia said, looking at the little cradle. "I should like to name him William. If that suits you, darling."

"If that's your wish. I've never had any complaints with the name." William smiled, pleased with the idea. "So long as you don't call him Willie," he added, with a comical shudder.

Simon burst out laughing. "Aye, I made that mistake only once." He took a swallow of his ale and leaned forward, resting his elbow on his knee. "I called you Willie but one time. I think it was the year before we left Scotland, when we were touring with Edward. D' ya recall?"

William had no idea what Simon was talking about, but he nodded and grinned. "Tell them about it, Simon."

"Aye," Simon chuckled, "we were camping somewhere north of Lothian County. As it happened, it was Will's birthday and he was wanting to celebrate. So he asks Sean and Isaac to go with him to the nearest town to scare up a keg or two from the tavern." He laughed for a moment. "He didn't have a coin in his pocket, and neither did Sean, as I recall, so Will picks up his lute and musses up his hair, and says 'no worry, tonight I'm a bard and shall sing for my ale'."

William listened carefully, not wanting Simon to stop, as he tried to remember the event on his own.

"I can just imagine it." Mehlyndia smiled politely, looking at William. "You could sing the miter off the bishop in those days."

I could?

"He could at that!" Simon roared with laughter. "Anyway, he jumps on his horse, trots off in the dark, Sean on his back as always, though barely able to keep up behind him, Isaac not doin' any better, and they're off to the first tavern they can find."

Sean was on my back? That seems right, why can't I remember his face?

"They're gone a good five hours," Simon continued, "when I hear the horses coming back. I looks out, and here, all by h'self, no rider, I see Cirrus, Will's stallion coming into camp."

William leaned forward, "Where was I?"

"Well I got nervous when I saw Cirrus comin' back alone, and I nudged Ewan, who was keeping watch with me, to wake up. Then I hear the other horses and this God-awful caterwauling coming out of the woods. I think something terrible has happened, as it sounded like a wounded she-wolf caught in a snare. I'm on my feet, got my sword raised, and I see the others coming out of the dark and they're laughing. Sean is singing to the top of his lungs, Isaac's got the lute— and *he* was no musician I can tell ye—and there he is,"— He extended a hand toward William. "— draped across Sean's saddle, like a sack of grain; he'd already fallen off three times and Sean was tired of pickin' 'im up."

"Simon!" Mehlyndia gasped and motioned to Seany, who held a look of utter dismay on his face. "That may be all we need to hear of this tale."

"Ah, sorry about that," Simon blushed. "I'll save the rest for another time."

"No, finish," William protested, then laughed. "It's a funny story." *I'd like to know how it ends.*

Simon looked at Mehlyndia for approval.

She sighed then grinned. "Go on then."

With a twinkle in his eye, Simon leaned on his knee again and resumed his oration. "Well, it seems he'd hoisted his age in pints that night, and was feelin' a little..." Simon glanced at Seany, "... under the weather. Sean calls out, 'Lads, we're back, the finest musical troupe to ever grace the highlands' and I says, 'Look Ewan! 'Tis Willie Fylbrigge and his famous trained monkeys!' Sean almost fell off his saddle, laughing, and gives Will a shake. He says 'Ye hear that, Willie! Simon's called ye a trained monkey!' Will looks up and drops off the horse like he's made o' burlap."

Simon started to laugh and was soon joined by Ian. Elinor too shook head to toe with laughter.

"As he's tryin' to get his feet under him, he comes up to me, and says, quite seriously, stickin' his finger in m' face," Simon closed one eye, and crossed the other. "Will says, 'You can call me a trained monkey, but don't ye ever call me 'Willie'!' Then he falls flat in the grass, finger still in the air, and slept it off 'till morning." Simon slapped his knee, roaring with laughter.

William had chosen the wrong moment to take a sip of his ale and almost choked on it when Simon finished his story. The room filled with laughter as they made toasts to the holiday and to each other's health, and William could not resist a toast to the trained monkeys, which evoked even more unbridled laughter for several minutes. Seany curled up on a cushion not far from the fire as the adults enjoyed conversation and music. Ian managed to show William the basics of how the psaltery was to be played, and it was not long before he was able to pick out a melody and keep up with Ian's flute playing.

William could not imagine a finer gift than the psaltery and to be given back something precious that had been lost to him; his music. But even in the sweetness of the memories brought back by the instrument, he felt a twinge of bitterness that the simple fact he had once been a musician had been kept from him, and he wondered what other pieces of his life his family kept hidden from him and why. Specifically, he wanted to know more about Sean. Mehlyndia had named their son for this man and Simon had said he had been on his back 'as always', yet William could not for the life of him conjure his face or voice in his mind. He resolved that he would finally sit Mehlyndia down and ask her, face to face, about this fellow named Sean. But, for the sake of the gathering, he would not ask tonight.

"A few days of practice and you'll be ready to play for the entire village." Simon smiled, sitting back with his ale.

"I appreciate your confidence, Simon." William laughed as he fumbled about, picking out the melody of 'Greensleeves'. "But I think it will take me months to figure this out." He found the notes he required and plucked out the tune. To his astonishment, it wasn't too far afoul from what he intended to play and allowed himself a smug smile.

"That's not bad at all, Will." Ian gave him an impressed grin, then picked up his flute and played along.

"Do you remember the words?" Elinor asked, as she rocked to the music.

William closed his eyes, already beginning to feel comfortable with his playing, he began to sing, full-voiced and sweet, for the first time in more than five years. "*Alas my love, you do me wrong, to cast me off discourteously, for I have loved you for so long, delighting in your company...*"

When he had finished he sat back, pleased with himself for remembering the song. He looked up to Mehlyndia in time to catch her brush a tear from her cheek.

"You still sing like an angel."

"That was lovely, Will," Prissy said, with an astonished look on her face. "I didn't know you could sing."

William tilted his head and chuckled. "Neither did I!"

It was close to midnight when Mehlyndia asked Simon to carry Seany to his bed and the good nights had all been said. Ian had been invited to stay in his customary guest-room, and after pushing the 'lord of the manner' to his bedchamber and helping him settle in, he too retired for the evening.

"Could you stoke up that fire before you come to bed?" William asked Mehlyndia as she changed into her bedclothes. "I still can't seem to feel warm tonight."

"After all the mulled ale you had, you should be asking for an open window instead of a fire," she said, as she placed another large log in the fire. "There, that should serve us for a while. I find the room quite warm to be honest, but I'll bring out the extra quilt for you if you're still cold."

William nodded, as he began to drift off to sleep. "Thank you."

Mehlyndia spread the quilt over him and climbed into bed, snuggling up close. She suddenly sat up and threw the quilt aside. "Why didn't you say something?"

"What?" he asked, shivering.

"You're burning with fever."

"Father?" William called to the man he saw standing at the top of the grand stairs.

"Come up here," the man replied, then turned away.

"But you know I can't climb the stairs."

"Come now, it can't be as bad as all that, my boy, come up here," the man said, his voice dying away as he vanished into the shadows.

"Wait, don't go." He waited for an answer but heard only the echoes of his own voice. He looked around to see where he was. The room was familiar and large with gleaming white marble floors and a tall ceiling. The great hall in Drumoak. *It's a dream,* he thought then looked back toward the stairs. *If I'm dreaming, I can climb them.* He looked down, surprised to find himself, as always, sitting in his chariot with one of Mehlyndia's quilts on his lap. Confused, he tossed the quilt aside, and tried to rise from his chair, but found he was as unable as always to move his lower limbs. *But if I'm dreaming, I can walk. I've always been able to walk here before.*

"Will." Another voice, a young woman this time, spoke from somewhere in the darkness around him.

He turned his body as far as he was able, searching. To his left, on the far wall, a door swung open. A light shown in from the open threshold, almost blinding him. A young woman stood, silhouetted black against the light in the doorway, one hand raised, beckoning him.

"I can't reach you— "

"Come up here!" The voice from the top of the stairs called again.

William looked up but could not see anyone. "Why can't I see you?"

Another voice, gruff and guttural, came from somewhere behind him, sending a violent shudder of dread and half-recognition down his spine. "Open your eyes. You know the rules," it said, with a groaning growl and laughed.

Behind him, William heard the sound of metal against metal, then a click. A key turning. He tried to look behind him but found his movements even more difficult than usual, as now his arms too, seemed as heavy and numb as his legs.

"Run away, little one." A new voice, a woman, echoed from his right; the hearth wall of the great hall. He followed the sound of her voice, as suddenly the smoldering embers ignited into furious spears of fire. The hearth began to grow and soon took up the entire wall, the flame growing with it. The woman stood in front it, calling to him. "Run away, little one, run away."

"I can't run away, I can't even move." He stared, transfixed by her face. *I know her.* She took a step backwards and melted into the fire, just as her name came to him.

"Rebecca! No! Why can't I move?" he yelled, struggling to move. He looked down, horrified to find his chariot chair replaced by a rough-hewn wooden chair and his wrist held fast with iron manacles. He struggled furiously, looking back up to the top of the stairs, crying out in a terrified voice that he barely recognized as his own, "Father, please come back! I need your help." No reply came. "Why do you stay silent!" His cry echoed throughout the hall around him.

As he struggled, he felt himself lifted from the sides, though he could not see anyone near him. The chair turned in mid-air to face the large ornate wooden doors of the main entry to the hall. He was raised a few feet then dropped, the chair painfully impacting the floor. Behind him, the growling laughter continued and he heard another clicking turn of a key. Slowly, the doors began to swing open. He looked frantically to the side, to the lighted doorway where he had seen the woman's silhouette, hoping she was still there, and was relieved to see her shadow still in the doorway.

"Lass, please! Will you help me?" he cried out to her. "I can't move!"

She glided silently toward him, moving away from the light and stopped. "Say my name, Will." Her voice did not come from where she stood, but from the space just behind his ears.

"I don't know your name." He squinted against the light, trying to see her face more clearly.

The sounds of a crowd and a clamor of joyless laughter took his attention back to the great doors, as they suddenly burst opened. Beyond the doors, hundreds of distorted, grotesque faces laughed and jeered, pointing toward him with gnarled and twisted fingers.

Blessed Mother, please wake me from this dream!

"Say my name, Will!" The young woman called to him again. He turned to look at her. As she moved further from the light of the doorway, he began to discern her features; large brown eyes, and long chestnut colored hair that fell freely about her shoulders. Small and fragile looking, she held her right hand, palm up toward him. "I have something for you." A silver object appeared in her palm.

The crowd began a slow and rhythmic chant, and though William could not understand their words, the sound terrified him. The fire on the hearth flared suddenly, sending angry licks toward him, keeping time with the chanting of the crowd. He began to tremble and his wrists ached terribly as he struggled against shackles on the chair. "Why won't you help me?"

"You've forgotten me," she said, and William could see she was crying.

"No, I just don't know your name... please, they're coming in." He looked away from her to the crowd. They were getting closer, pointing, and droning their mysterious chant. He closed his eyes against them but could not block the sight as the heat from the fire seared his face and arms. Sweat rolled from his forehead into his eyes and mouth. "Please, help me. I can't move!"

"Look away from them, Will," she said. "They have no power over you now."

William forced himself to look away from the grotesque throng of chanters, and concentrate on the young woman. She took a step closer. "Please, help me," he said, on the verge of dissolving in his panic. "It's so hot, please, move me away." The fire licked closer to him, creeping snake-like across the floor. The chanting grew louder, echoing throughout the hall.

"I have something for you," she said, palm outstretched toward him, the silver object catching the light from the fire. "This will give you my name." She walked to him, finally closing the space between them. She wept silently. A single tear rolled down her face and dropped from her chin. She caught the tear in her palm, wetting the silver. William could see the object clearly now, it was a badge, adorned with an image of an eagle. He knew what it was. It was kept in a wooden box in his dresser in Port Edin. *How could she have it?*

She placed the anointed badge on his shoulder and leaned forward to kiss him lightly on the forehead. "It is because I love you."

She stood slowly, allowing her hand to rest on his shoulder. Her touch calmed him. As he looked into her eyes, from somewhere in the depth of his mind, he finally found her name and spoke it quietly, "Laurel."

The instant her name left his mouth, the chanting silenced, leaving only a waning echo that quickly died away. The doors closed. He relaxed for a moment, until again he felt the heat of the flame lapping at his face. He looked up to her, pleading, "I'm so hot, please, Laurel, move me away."

She stood silently, smiling at him through her tears and reached out to him.

To his profound relief, he found he was no longer shackled to the chair as he took her hand.

"Stand up," she said.

He gripped her hand tightly and stood. He embraced her, and the two stood sobbing in each other's arms until the heat once again sent a threatening caress down his back. He turned to look at the flame and saw it take the shape of an animal with a long neck and tail, and sharply taloned claws. "The dragon has come for me again."

"No, Will. She's not here for you this time." Laurel squeezed his hand and turned him to look at her. She reached up and wiped away the perspiration that had matted his hair to his brow and smiled sadly, "Give the eagle to your son." She released him and began to walk backwards toward the fire-dragon.

William tried to follow, but found that though he could stand, he still could not move his feet. He watched in horror as Laurel turned from him and ran into the midst of the dragon. It folded its fiery tail around her and shrunk back into the hearth, and disappeared.

"No! Laurel, come back," he cried out and fell to his knees, then collapsed completely to the floor.

He lay still, shivering on the marble for what seemed like days, unable and unwilling to move. Every so often, he heard voices around him, speaking in hushed, low tones.

"It's been so long. How much longer can he last?"

"He's stronger than he was. I worry more for her."

"She's sure to follow if we lose them both."

Who has been lost?

For hours— or was it days?— he didn't move, until at last he felt a soothing breeze waft across his face. He heard another voice— a man's voice, familiar and comforting— carried in the breeze that touched him. "It's time to wake up, Will."

"No, it was my fault," William argued, keeping his eyes

closed, still believing himself to be on the marble floor. His left hand found its way to his shoulder, closing his hand around the badge. "Laurel took the fire from me again. It's my turn to die."

"Not yet. I'm here to prevent that. Same as always, I'm on your back, Will. You need to stay with the living."

"Sean?" William opened his eyes slowly, his hand still at his shoulder. He found he was not lying on the floor of Drumoak, but in his own bed in Port Edin. He blinked back the light until his vision cleared and looked up to see the concerned faces of Ian and Elinor looking down at him.

"Welcome back," Ian smiled, his eyes betraying a profound relief as Elinor removed a damp cloth from William's forehead.

"We were beginning to think you'd decided to leave us for good this time," Elinor said.

William glanced to his shoulder, surprised to find the eagle pinned to his bed shirt. "I thought I'd dreamed this. How did it get here?"

"Oh, you'll think me silly really." Elinor smiled shyly as she took his hand from his shoulder and held it gently. "But it was me who pinned it there. Ye see, m' mum used to say that wearin' silver on the full moon is supposed to ward off a fever... silly old wives tale, to be sure. But I thought if there were any truth at all, it couldn't hurt."

"Fever? I've been ill?" William asked, finding his throat too dry to speak clearly.

"Aye, for close to a week, dear," Elinor explained. "You gave us a terrible scare."

"A week?" William reached for his railing, but lacked

the strength to move more than an inch or two. Ian helped him sit up while Elinor propped up the pillows behind him. "Where is Melly?"

Ian and Elinor exchanged nervous looking glances and did not answer him.

"What's wrong? Where's my wife?" William asked, beginning to feel the panic return. "Where's Seany?"

"Seany is fine. He's staying with the Simon until you're well." Ian took a long breath and sat on the edge of the bed. There was no trace of his usual good humor on his face. "Melly's abed in the room above us."

"Is she ill?" William asked, trying to pull himself up, again. "Help me, I need to see her."

"No." Ian placed his hand on William's shoulder, gently persuading him to lie back against the pillows. "She's sleeping, Will. She needs her rest."

"What's wrong with her?" he asked, and began to cough from the dryness in his throat.

Elinor gave William a glass of water. "She'll be fine, dear. She's good and strong. Prissy is with her. Don't worry now. You need to get your own strength back."

William drank slowly, looking back and forth between Ian and Elinor. The uncharacteristically solemn expression in Ian's eyes and the distress on Elinor's face brought a terrible understanding. "We've lost the child, haven't we?"

Ian nodded. "I'm sorry, Will," he said, quietly.

William sank down into the bedding. The room seemed to turn at odd angles and grow dim as a sudden wave of vertigo assaulted him. He closed his eyes tight, waiting for it to pass. *I'm still dreaming... that's all this is... a dream.* His hand drifted to his shoulder again, folding over the badge, it felt cold against his palm. *Not a dream, this is real... Oh, God.* After several moments of silence, he asked quietly, "Was it the fever?"

"No, dear, 'twasn't the fever," Elinor told him, dipping the cloth in a basin of water. She wrung it out and placed it back on his head. "The bairn just came early. She was too small and weak."

"She?"

"Aye, a little lass," Elinor sighed.

"When?"

"Two days ago," Ian answered for Elinor.

"What happened?" William impatiently pushed the cloth from his head. "She was fine the last time I saw her."

"Calm down, you'll bring back the heat," Elinor said, replacing the cloth. She dropped herself heavily on a stool beside the bed, with a sigh. "It was the stress that brought the pains early. She refused to leave your bedside for days—"

"It was my fault. I knew the burden was too much for her," William cried as he tried to sit up again and immediately regretted the action as his vision dimmed into dark blotches.

"Lie down." Ian pushed him back. "It was not your fault. Don't carry guilt where you haven't earned it," he said softly.

William stared at Ian, certain he had heard him say those words to him once before but as always, the recollection passed before he could fully call it back.

"I don't think you realize how close you were," Ian said, pulling the blankets up. "We had even called Ephraim to stand ready to administer rites."

"Rites? For me?" William asked, astonished.

"Aye," Ian answered, in a falsely calm voice that William suspected was for his benefit. "When it seemed you were to leave us, Melly was beside herself with grief and it brought her labor early. The child was born in the small hours, and lived only long enough for Ephraim to baptize her."

"Baptize? She was named then?"

Elinor and Ian exchanged glances again, then Ian continued. "Ephraim asked Melly if the name you had called out in your fever was the name you had chosen for your child. Melly told him it was, and the babe was baptized—"

"Laurel?" William asked before Ian could finish.

"Aye," Ian answered. "Do you remember calling out?"

William shook his head and closed his eyes, allowing the darkness to creep over him again. *The dragon didn't come for me, she came for the baby instead. For Laurel.*

In the days that followed his fever, William stayed abed, lacking the strength or desire to rejoin the rhythm of everyday life. He lay staring idly out the window at the snowy landscape beyond, wondering what he could have done to prevent the loss of his child. No matter how often Ian or Elinor reassured him the baby's death had nothing to do with him, he felt in his heart that it was his malady that caused Mehlyndia to suffer the early birth and loss of her child. *His* child. After all, Mehlyndia routinely worked herself to exhaustion, lifting him, moving him around, and seeing to personal needs that no wife should be asked to do. She shouldered more than her fair share of Seany's needs as well. The night he came down with the fever, he felt it coming, yet he ignored the symptoms because of his own selfish desire to hear Simon's story and to stay up playing the psaltery. Had he done the wise thing and taken to his bed early and asked Ian for a powder to stave off the chills, he believed he could have avoided the fever all together. If he had done that, he was convinced they would still be happily anticipating the arrival of the little one instead of mourning her loss. He wondered if he could bear to look his wife in the eye ever again after all he had done to her.

On the fifth morning, Mehlyndia quietly entered their bedchamber for the first time.

"Are you awake?" she asked in a gentle whisper, brushing his face with her hand.

William opened his eyes and looked up to his wife for the first time in nearly two weeks. He tried to answer her with words but found he had no voice to speak. He held out his arms and the two embraced. Mehlyndia cuddled down on the bed next to him, and they lay together silently.

As she held him, William's feelings of guilt lessened as her warmth brought him to his senses. *No, it wasn't my fault. It was just bad timing. She still loves me.*

"Do you feel better?" William asked.

"A bit," she said. "You?"

He hugged her as close as he could, "Yes."

"I'm sorry, my love," she said, as the tears began.

"Sorry?"

"I wasn't careful. I thought I had lost you and I gave no thought—" She buried her face on his chest and sobbed.

"Shh. It wasn't your fault. It's I who should beg your forgiveness. I should have told you I wasn't feeling well."

"It wasn't your fault you took ill. The fever has run

rampant throughout the settlement."

"Has it?"

"Yes," she swallowed hard and squeezed him. "You're the first to recover. I was so frightened, William. After the others died so quickly, I had lost hope you would come back to me—"

"Others?" William asked startled. "Who has died?"

Mehlyndia sat up, and looked at him with a surprised look on her face. "Elinor hasn't told you?"

"No," he said, beginning to feel the tremble in his middle as a terrifying notion settled on him, realizing he had yet to see his son. "My God! Where's Seany? Is he all right?" he asked, reaching for the railing.

"Calm down." Mehlyndia put her hands on his shoulders. "Seany's fine!" she said quickly. "He's staying with the Ashcroftes until you're well."

"Thank God." He exhaled loudly and relaxed. "Tell me then. Who've we lost?"

Mehlyndia took a breath. "When the fever took the others, it was swift. Young Kevin Blackwood succumbed in only a day."

"Oh no," William said, wiping his cheeks with his hand. "Charles must be devastated. He lost Rachel just last winter, now Kevin?"

Mehlyndia nodded. "Charles is holding up well, from what Ephraim says, but I'm sure he's heartbroken."

"Who else?"

"Clive's wife, Ellen."

William closed his eyes, remembering the heavyset woman who had presented Melly with a beautifully quilted baby blanket on Christmas Eve. He didn't know her well, but felt sorry for her loss just the same.

"She lasted two days," Mehlyndia said, staring past him to the window, fidgeting with the blanket. "There have been others as well."

"How many?" William asked, watching her face carefully. He was beginning to wonder if she was keeping more from him.

"I'm not sure," she said then looked away. "I was getting my news from Ian."

"I'm sure it's kept him busy—" William stopped and looked at her quickly. "Where is Ian? He hasn't been to see me for days."

Mehlyndia looked away from him and sighed, twisting the blanket in her hands. "He's upstairs."

"Oh no," William said, echoes of the panic he had felt returned as understanding came to him. "Ian has the fever?"

Mehlyndia nodded, then got up from the bed and walked away to the window. She looked out, speaking in halted breaths. "He took it two days ago. The dear man has cared for everyone else in the settlement, and now... Elinor has been tending to him. That's why Seany is really still with the Ashecroftes."

"How bad is he?" William asked, feeling the trembling rise in his chest.

"As bad as any." Mehlyndia turned to look at William. "I worry he shan't be as fortunate as you."

"I need to get upstairs." He reached for the railing at the side of his bed, and pulled himself up to sit.

"No, William, you're not strong enough yet." Mehlyndia pushed him back down.

"It's been days, 1 need to get up there." William said, determined to get himself out of bed finally, he pushed her hand aside. "Melly, please, bring my chariot around."

She hesitated for a moment, looking from William to his chair, then pulled it up to the edge of the bed for him. "I'm afraid 1 can't lift—"

"1 know," he said, raising one hand to quiet her. "1 can do it myself." He reached for the arm of the chariot with one hand while grasping the railing with the other. Prior to his fever, with lan's help, he had learned to balance his weight on his arms just long enough to swing himself around into the chair. He'd met with disaster a couple of times while perfecting this maneuver and landed on the floor, which he took in stride while lan was there to help him up. Halfway into his attempt, it became obvious that he had yet to regain enough of his strength to complete his swing. In his determination to see his friend, he was willing to risk dumping himself on the floor, but for Mehlyndia's sake and because he promised himself he would never ask her to lift him again, he stopped himself and settled on the edge of the bed. Frustrated, catching his breath, he abandoned his attempt to get into his chair.

"Do you want help?" Mehlyndia asked, reaching her hand out to him.

"No!" William answered in an unintentionally sharp manner, scowling at the chair in front of him.

Mehlyndia stepped away and turned her back.

"Melly... I'm sorry. 1 didn't mean to..."

"1 know." She took a breath and turned back to him with a forced smile. "Sit still and I'll fetch Simon to help you."

Reluctantly, William agreed. "Thank you."

She wiped her eyes on her apron and left the bedchamber, closing the door behind her.

How many times has Ian come between disaster and me, and I can't even get out bed while he's dying in my own home. He sat, fighting to keep hold of his emotions, waiting for Simon to come. *Always relying on someone else.* A terrible fear settled on him that Ian would be taken and William was dismayed with himself to discover a good part of that fear was completely selfish. He had come to depend on the ever-cheerful apothecary with his wry sense of humor, not only for friendship but also for his help. Ian had never treated William as an invalid nor looked upon him with doe-eyed sympathy for his malady. Ian had always looked on William's mobility difficulties as a puzzle to solve rather than the mournful circumstance of the village cripple, and William had come to appreciate that approach more than he had ever realized until that moment.

Pushing aside the selfish feelings, he admitted to himself that Ian was more to him than a means to his independence. He was his friend and he owed him his life. Of the few memories he had of the crossing, the one that was clear to him was that it was Ian who had encouraged him out of the dark with his music. In fact, his first memory of this new life was waking up aboard the *Lady Anne* to the sounds of Ian's flute. Everything before that was a complete mystery. It was the music that had brought him back and Ian had played it. The least he could do was to get himself to the second level of his home to sit with his friend, and tell him 'thank you'.

"Will?" Simon said, standing in the doorway.

"Come on in, Simon."

Simon came around to William's side of the bed. He looked at him with an expression William could not remember seeing on his face before, a mixture of sorrow and joy.

"Melly said you was up at last," Simon said, as he pulled up a stool to sit by the window. "I'm glad to see ye are. Are ye feeling better?"

William was astonished to see Simon's eyes sparkling with the threat of tears. "Yes, thank you. I hear I gave you all a bit of trouble," he said, trying to lighten the moment.

"Aye, ye did," Simon said, smiling. "I'm glad you're back, Will." He looked at the chair in front of William and tipped his forehead with his hand. "Melly said ye needed me. And here I am just sittin'."

"I need to get upstairs," William said, reaching for Simon's hand. "I want to see Ian."

Simon grabbed William's arms at the elbows and guided him gently into his chariot. "I had a feeling that's what this was. I was just telling Elinor that you'd move heaven and earth, if you had to, to get upstairs."

"Fortunately, all I need to move is my own arse," William said, with a false chuckle. "But it seems I can't even do that. Hand me that quilt there, please."

Simon gave him the quilt, then went around behind him to push the chair. "Are you sure you're feeling up to this? I mean..." He paused for a moment. "He's right sick, Will. I'd hate to have you catch it again."

"Yes, I'm sure." *The next thing I work on is a way to move this confounded thing by myself.*

As he was pushed from the bedroom through the sitting

room, William's eyes fell on the psaltery, propped up against the chair by the hearth. In a moment of inspiration, he motioned for Simon to stop. "I want that."

"Now?" Simon asked, an incredulous look on his face.

"Indulge me."

Simon shrugged and retrieved the psaltery, and handed it to William. "I don't think Ian's up to playin' but if ye want it, ye got it."

"Thanks." He brushed the strings lightly as he took it from Simon. "You'd be amazed at what a little music can accomplish, my friend."

Simon pushed him into the kitchen and opened the door to his 'magic closet', then pushed the chariot in. "Ready?"

"Go ahead."

Simon opened a slender panel on the wall next to the closet and pulled on the large rope. Slowly and steadily, the closet rose. The convoluted array of pulleys and cantilevered weights allowed for a smooth ride up. Once the closet reached the second level, the rope was secured with a long-handled clamp that prevented it from crashing back to the first level. When it was time to return to the kitchen, the clamp would be eased open with the handle, providing an equally smooth ride down. The only flaw to the design, as far as William was concerned, was he could not reach the rope himself. *Ian and I should work on that,* he thought idly, while riding up, then swallowed the lump that formed, remembering how ill his friend was.

When they reached the second floor, Mehlyndia and Elinor were waiting to meet him.

"How is he?" William asked, as Elinor pushed the chariot to Ian's room.

"He's sleeping for the moment," Elinor said, quietly. "Ephraim is in with him."

"Ephraim? Has it gone that far?"

"I'm afraid so," she whispered, looking down.

"William, are you sure you want to go in there?" Mehlyndia asked, with one hand on the doorknob. "It won't be pleasant."

"I'm sure it won't be." William reached for Mehlyndia's free hand and gave it a squeeze. "But I need to see him, Melly."

When Mehlyndia opened the door, the first sight of his friend, pale and motionless on the bed, sent a shudder through him. He glanced at Ephraim, then back to Ian, startled to see that Ian's wrists had been bound to the headboard with linen strips. "Why have you done that?"

"To prevent him falling from the bed when the thrashing takes him," Ephraim answered as though it had been a foolish question, then softened his tone. "No different than was done for you, son."

"You tied my wrists to the bed?" William asked, in disbelief.

"Yes, only for your own safety," Ephraim answered, calmly.

I wasn't shackled to a chair, I was tied to the damned bed. Images from his dream flooded back to him and with them came the horrible waves of panic. "Untie him, Ephraim, he's not thrashing now."

"He's unaware—"

"Untie him!"

"William!" Mehlyndia snapped. "I warned you it was not pleasant."

"You don't understand, it'll hurt him, I know—"

"We've not hurt Ian." Ephraim left Ian's bedside and stood in front of William, putting a hand on his shoulder. "He doesn't even know he's tied."

William pushed Ephraim's hand aside. "He does! Ephraim, please." He spoke through his teeth, and began to tremble as the images from his dream came back to him. "It brings it all back. Please, you need to untie him."

"Calm down, Will." Ephraim said, replacing his hands on William's shoulders. "Brings what back? What are you talking about?"

"This!" William thrusts his wrists out, displaying his scars to Ephraim.

Mehlyndia gasped and put her hand to her mouth, then turned away from her husband.

Ephraim stared at William's wrists, an expression of understanding softening his eyes. "My God." He closed his hands over William's and spoke gently. "I'm sorry, I never knew you... you're right, he's not thrashing now, there's no need to tie him." He looked to Elinor and nodded.

Elinor went to Ian and released his wrists from the headboard.

He knows how I got these scars. William decided he would have a talk with Ephraim when a more suitable moment arrived. He took a long breath and relaxed. "I'm sorry I raised my voice, Ephraim; that was uncalled for. I know you're only here to help." He looked to his wife, who still stood with her back to him, silently sobbing into her hands. "Melly? I'm truly sorry."

She wiped her face and turned to him. "Has it all come back to you? Truly?"

"No. I simply overreacted to a bad dream," he answered and pulled her to him. "I didn't mean to upset you."

She crouched down, resting her head on his arm, and idly brushed the strings of the psaltery on his lap. "I'm just tired, William, I should like to go lie down for a while."

"Yes, do that," he said. "I'll be down soon."

"Do you need something to help you sleep?" Elinor asked her, still standing next to Ian.

"No, thank you, Elinor, I'll be fine." Mehlyndia straightened up, then leaned over to kiss William lightly on the side of his face before she left the room.

"Is she truly well?" William asked Elinor when Mehlyndia had closed the door.

"Aye, it's normal for her to tire easily. She's still recovering."

William nodded, then looked up to Ephraim. "Could I have some time alone please?"

"Of course, I won't be far." Ephraim patted William's shoulder. "If you need to talk, I'm willing."

"Thank you."

When Ephraim left, Elinor pushed William's chariot close to the side of Ian's bed. "Do you wish me to stay or go?"

William reached for her hand and gave it a squeeze. "Stay."

She stood next to the bed, dipping a cloth in the water basin, and as she had done for William, she placed the damp cloth on Ian's head. "I'm surprised it took as long as it did to catch up with him," she said as she sat down on a stool next to the bed. "He's taken the burden of the entire village on him and refused to rest when he should have. But that's his way, I suppose. I've never known him to shy away when he feels he can be of help. Even in Stonehaven, he was right ready to jump into the fray—"

"Ian was in Stonehaven?" William asked, surprised.

She gave him a curious look. "Of course. I thought you remembered that much. We met on the street that same day—" She stopped in mid-thought, shook her head, and looked away. William got the impression he had just stepped into forbidden territory again.

"I don't remember," he said, struggling with his desire to learn more of his past but not wanting to upset Elinor. And certainly it wasn't the time to dwell on himself when Ian was so ill. He let the subject pass. "You're right though, I've not known him to shy away either."

Ian began to stir slightly in his sleep, but still lay silent.

"Let me warm some broth for us. I'll be back in a bit," Elinor said, then stood and gathered up her basin and cloth.

William watched Elinor wring the cloth and dump the water out the window. When she reached for an empty mug on the nightstand, something vague but certain started coming to his mind. Before she could move too far from him, William reached out and put a hand on her forearm. "A moment, Elinor," he said, staring past her and trying to bring shape to the notion that was coming to him. "Broth?" he said, more to himself than to her, then looked up at her.

"What is it, dear?"

He closed his eyes for a moment, squeezed her arm before he opened his eyes again. With no understanding of why or how, he said, as though reading directions from some unseen page, "Make a brew, a strong one, with equal parts of feverfew, white willow bark, and lavender, but be sure to boil the water separately. Then, infuse the brew until it's the color of dark amber."

Elinor dropped the basin as though it were suddenly too hot to hold on to. She clasped her hands to her mouth and stared at him. "Blessed Mother!" she gasped, then picked up the basin.

William looked at her, startled by her reaction and confused with his own innate intuition of what Ian needed to recover. "What? Am I wrong?"

"No," she said, catching her breath. "You're exactly right!" She smiled nervously and added quickly, "I should have thought of that myself. That's why I jumped, dear, I feel a complete fool."

William was skeptical of the explanation of her reaction but didn't push her. "Do you have all those ingredients?"

"Yes, yes, I'll take care of it." She hurried out of the room, muttering, "Feverfew! Of course, that's what's called for..."

I'll wonder how I knew that some other time.

"Ian?" William spoke softly to his friend. "Can you hear me, lad?"

Ian made no direct response, only turned his head in his sleep and moaned slightly.

"I hope you're not having the dreams I did," William said, as though idle conversation would bring Ian back. Truth was, he spoke more for his own comfort than for Ian's. "Nasty dreams those were. When you're well, I'll paint in all the details for you and you can tell me how demented I truly am." He chuckled, not feeling the least bit cheerful. He looked down to the psaltery that still rested on his lap and began to pluck the strings lightly, randomly until he found a pattern that pleased his ear. "This is a lovely instrument, don't you agree?" He played a little louder. "I can't thank you enough for helping Mehlyndia get it for me." The random pattern worked its way into the more recognizable melody of his favorite tune. He closed his eyes, losing himself in the sound of music as he hummed along to 'Greensleeves'.

"Welcome back," William said, smiling at Ian as he finally opened his eyes with the dawn.

"Hmm?" Ian blinked and turned his head toward William. He opened his eyes fully and gave him a curious look as though he had just woken from a catnap rather than days of fever. "Was that you making all that noise? Or was it one of your trained monkeys?"

William laughed in relief at Ian's quip. "I confess, 'twas me." He took the cool cloth from Ian's head and placed it in the basin then turned back to his friend with a more serious expression. "I think we're even now. You scared me to death."

"Did I?" Ian pushed himself up with the heels of his hands. "How long have I been asleep?"

"Three days," William said and yawned. "Your fever finally broke about two o'clock this morning." He gave Ian a grin and extended his hand. "You beat it, my friend."

Ian smiled and took William's hand. "So did you. I guess that makes us kin survivors."

William glanced down at the scars on Ian's wrists and his own as they shook hands. *So it seems.*

"Do I hear voices?" Elinor opened the door and peeked in. "Ian, you're awake!" She joined the two men by the bed, then systematically examined Ian's eyes, felt his forehead and neck, then stood back and smiled. "No fever left in ye, dear, thank goodness." She reached to the nightstand, retrieved the empty teacup and looked inside. "The brew did the job then."

"What was it?" Ian asked looking at the cup. "One of your powders? It must have been a good one, I feel much better."

"You have him to thank. 'Twas his idea and a right good one." Elinor gave William a smile.

"Him?" Ian raised a skeptical brow and looked oddly at William. "What was it?"

"Feverfew, white willow bark, and lavender," William said, allowing himself a smug smile. "Pushed the fever right out of you." He scratched the back of his head and laughed to himself. "Although how I knew to fix it for you is a mystery to me."

"It come to me when I was brewin' it, how you must have known of the feverfew," Elinor said, as she gathered up the basin and cloth. "Do you recall when you were sixteen?"

William sighed, "No."

"I'm sorry, I forget myself sometimes." Elinor blushed and continued, "The winter you were sixteen, you fell ill with a terrible fever, not any better than this last one. Poor Edward was beside himself that time."

"It was a bad one as well then?" William asked.

"Aye, you were down four or five days as I recall." She opened the window, dumped the basin, and quickly closed the window, sending a chilly breeze through the room. "I remember I used the feverfew for ye then and it broke the fever in short order. Why I didn't think of it sooner this time around is a wonder. I must be getting old and feeble-minded." She placed the empty cup in the basin and headed to the door. "I'll tell everyone you're up, Ian. Simon and Prissy have been askin' on you. Blessed Mother, it's good to see you smilin'." She grinned at the both of them and left the room, closing the door behind her.

"Feverfew," Ian said shaking his head. "Of course. I should have thought of that as well. You put the apothecary to shame, Will." He sank down into the bedding and pulled the blanket up under his chin.

"I suppose," William said, staring past Ian. *Elinor is covering again. It wasn't from that fever I knew what to do. How could I have known the proper proportions and how to prepare it?* He shook aside his thoughts and turned his full attention back to his friend. "I should let you get your rest."

"I am still tired," Ian admitted. "How are you feeling? You look as though you've spent the night right there where you sit."

"I did," William said, stifling a yawn.

"That's no way to get over a fever, young man," Ian said, pointing his finger, a stern scowl on his face. "Go to bed."

"Are you going to push me back to my room?" William said with a comical grin?

"Good point," Ian yawned as his eyelids began to droop. "So long as you're stuck here... be a good little monkey and make more noise."

William smiled and began to play the psaltery softly, as Ian drifted back to sleep.

Chapter 3

Port Edin, Late May 1613

THE ARRIVAL OF spring did not come a moment too soon. With the first glorious breath of warm air, the women were eager to open the windows and purge the houses of the winter and all the ills and demons left in its wake. Rugs were hauled out and beaten, draperies taken from the windows and set out in the fresh spring breeze. It seemed every quilt in Port Edin found itself decorating a clothesline, alive with the stiff sea wind. The quilt that Mehlyndia, Prissy, and Elinor had labored over during the endless winter months received its last stitch as the March winds died away and after a good airing, was carefully stored away to await the following winter. The quilts and bedding that had covered William and Ian, as well as all the others who had taken the fever, were burned as a precaution against any lingering sickness. When the fever had run its course, the population of Port Edin was only half of what it was the previous autumn— only forty people in all remained.

When fully recovered from his own bout of the fever, Ian carried the recipe for the feverfew brew to every household in the settlement. Though it had been too late to save the early victims, those taken anew were quickly remedied. William decided early on that he would prefer the people of Port Edin believe the remedy had been discovered by the village apothecary, rather than himself, and after an animated argument on the subject, he finally convinced Ian to take the credit for the cure. In the end, it made no difference where the recipe had come from, it was considered a Godsend by all.

In early April, a memorial service was held in the little wooden church in honor of all those souls lost during that terribly long winter, little Laurel Anne Philbrick among them. The wooden grave marker her father carved displayed her name as Philbrick in bold block letters at the top. Further below, camouflaged within an elaborate filigree of carved ivy, William had rebelliously concealed the name Fylbrigge. No one seemed to see it and if they did, did not mention it.

Soon after landing in Port Edin, Ian had taken it upon himself to establish a rapport with some of the native people, among them, Akonni—a Shaman elder of the Mi'kmaq. Ian and Akonni developed a fast friendship, learning from each other, trading knowledge of herbs, lore, and even soup recipes using the indigenous plants of New France. Unfortunately, there was also the inadvertent sharing of illnesses between them as well. Though he seldom visited Port Edin during the winter, when his people started showing signs of the settler's fever, Akonni came through the snow seeking Ian's advice on how best to treat it. Ian was pleased to share Will's feverfew and white willow bark brew with the Shaman. Akonni embellished the recipe with a bit of honeysuckle and peppermint for taste, and had equal success in relieving the fevers.

When the snow finally cleared, Ian proposed a trip to

visit Akonni's village. Much to Mehlyndia's objection, Ian invited William to accompany him, assuring her the native village was only a mere half day's ride to the north of Port Edin settlement. She vehemently protested the idea of her husband going off into what she referred to as 'that God awful wilderness'. But William was more than eager to leave the confines of Port Edin for a day or two and after promising upon his life, her life, the sun, the moon and all the stars that he would be *careful*, she relented.

"You best keep him out of harm's way, Ian Proctor!"

"Of course!" Ian promised, placing his fist to his chest.

When the vicar, Ephraim Ashcrofte, learned of Ian's planned visit to the Mi'kmaq, he eagerly asked the two if they minded his company on their journey, citing his mission of scoring a baptism or two among the natives. His position of vicar had been granted to him with the contingency that he baptize and convert as many of the Mi'kmaq as possible, however, Ephraim did not put a great deal of effort into this particular aspect of his role, much to his wife's consternation.

"Ephraim, it's your duty," Josephine scolded him one day, in the middle of the square for all to hear, "to save them from their savage ways. You don't want the governors to arrive only to find you've not converted a single savage do you?"

"I've baptized four in the last year, that's surely enough to appease the governor." Ephraim had argued. "But if it will keep you from jabber-jawing me to death, then I'll make a special effort come spring to get up to their village."

She had been appeased.

Ian and William were more than pleased to have Ephraim along on their trek. William secretly believed Ephraim's desire to join them had more to do with a chance to spend time away from Josephine than it did in fulfilling his mission of 'scoring baptisms', and said as much to Mehlyndia.

"Well frankly, William, I cannae say as I blame the man," Mehlyndia laughed, "I know *I'd* be perfectly ready to *swim* back to Scotland if I had been cooped up with Josephine all winter."

On the first day of May, Ian loaded up the little one-horse wagon with his herbs, blankets, enough provisions for four days, and some breads and cheeses for Akonni and his people. William brought along a wooden box containing his carving tools, planning to pass the time carving wooden animals for an ark he was making for Seany's approaching sixth birthday. Ephraim packed his prayer book and a bottle of holy water, and, with a wink to his two traveling companions, slipped three extra flasks of 'sacramental' wine under the seat of the wagon.

Ephraim nudged Ian with his elbow. "For ceremonial purposes only, you understand."

"But of course," Ian said, straight faced. "You cannae have a baptism without wine, after all."

"I should say not," William chimed in, as he waited in his chariot aside the wagon for Ian to finish loading it. When all was secured, Ian helped him up onto the long driver's seat, which had been fitted with a back and arm rests specifically for him.

With one final check of the inventory, Ian proclaimed them ready to roll. With mock sincerity, Ephraim blessed their provisions, the wagon and the horse for luck, and the three were ready to travel.

"Why can't I go with you?" Seany pouted, as he scampered up onto the seat and plopped himself down next to William.

"Because it's a long trip up to see Akonni and you'll be bored to tears," William said, giving the boy a hug. "Besides, you need to be the man of the house and stay here to take care of Mum."

"She's a big grown up lady, Papa. She can take care of herself." Seany scowled and crossed his arms.

William could not resist a chuckle at his son's insight. "I'm sure she can. But you still need to stay here to take care of Elinor."

"She's even bigger!" Seany argued.

"Dragon?" William said, raising a brow. "Surely you're bigger than the wee cat. I know *she* needs you."

Seany narrowed his eyes and drummed his little fingers on his chin. But before he could find an argument for leaving Dragon too, Mehlyndia arrived with an extra bundle of blankets that she placed in the back of the wagon.

"Where is it you believe you are going, little man?" she said, hands on hips, looking at Seany.

"To feed Dragon." Seany laughed, then gave his father a quick squeeze around the neck before blithely hopping off the cart. "She needs to be taken care of, you know," he informed his mother as he trotted off toward the barn, calling over his shoulder, "Dinnae worry, Papa, I'll take care o' Mum for you."

"Good, lad." William laughed as he watched his son disappear through the big barn doors.

"Lucky for you, Mr. Philbrick, you've not decided to take him with you off to God-only-knows where," Mehlyndia said, with feigned anger before she stepped up on the wagon to sit next to him.

"And risk being skinned alive by his vicious mother?" William grinned and kissed her. "I don't think so."

"You will be careful, won't you?" she asked, giving him a hug.

"As careful—"

"Don't say it." She covered his mouth with her hand and laughed. "I know. As careful as you *ever are.* I should know better than to even ask by now."

He took her hand in his and kissed her palm. "Yes, you should. But, I promise I've no desire for adventures on this trip. We are simply going to see Akonni and see how his people fared over the winter. With luck, I may even bring back some furs or some of that sweet brown sugar they make from the trees."

"And a pet bear for Seany," Ian added as he climbed up onto the wagon.

"Yes, and a pet bear," William grinned.

"So long as it's a clean bear." Mehlyndia laughed and shook her head. "I love you."

"I love you too."

Mehlyndia kissed him and climbed down, and stood aside allowing Ephraim to take her place

"Don't worry, Melly," Ian called to her as they moved away. "Ephraim and I won't let him wander off."

"See that you don't, Ian Proctor!" she called back, her hands cupped around her mouth. "Be careful!"

William chuckled and waved. When safely out of Mehlyndia's ear range, he turned to his companions with a wry grin. "I feel like I've just run away from home." He motioned to the reins. "May I?"

Ian started to hand William the reins, then stopped. "I see that look in your eye."

"Oh, let him have some fun," Ephraim snickered, matching William's mischievous grin.

William cocked his head and held out his hands for the reins. "Please?"

Ian sighed, then laughed and handed William the reins.

"Grab hold," William said and shook the reins hard with a shout, "Yah!" and set the horse into as much of a gallop as the beast could manage while towing the cart.

Ephraim let loose an enthusiastic hoot as William urged the horse to run.

Ian grabbed the seat, just in time to keep from tumbling off. "You are a madman!" he yelled with a gleeful grin.

"Absolutely," William agreed as he thoroughly enjoyed the closest he had come to a gallop through the woods in years. "Whoa, boy, settle down."

He brought the horse to a slow walk after only a few minutes of running. The horse complied with a snort and a bob of his head.

Ian loosed his death grip from the driver's bench, exhaled and then released a loud and hearty laugh as he retrieved the reins. "I hope you enjoyed yourself," he said, making a quick visual inspection of the inventory in the back of the wagon.

Ephraim reached under the seat and grinned as he held up one of the wine flasks, then placed it back under the seat. "Precious cargo is unharmed."

William only made a tightlipped grin and sat back against the makeshift seat back. Putting his face to the sky, he drew in a long breath of fresh clean air of the forest. "This feels wonderful." He stretched his arms and laced his fingers together behind his neck. "I cannae remember the last time I ran a horse a through the woods."

"It was five minutes ago," Ephraim quipped with a chuckle.

"I suppose it was," William said, allowing Ephraim's remark to pass. He took another deep breath and relaxed in the seat, then turned to Ian. "Thank you."

"For what?" Ian asked.

"Suggesting that I come along."

Ian shrugged. "We all need the fresh air now and then." He made a clicking sound with his tongue and shook the reins to pick up the horse's pace slightly. "It's good for you. Puts the roses back in your face. As your physician, I highly recommend it. As your friend..." He gave a quick side-glance to William. "I thought you'd enjoy some time away from home."

William nodded, but said nothing, watching the scenery pass by. As usual, Ian's insight was on the mark. He did feel ready to burst from his own skin lately. Though he knew she meant well, and he loved her no less than he ever did, Mehlyndia's constant hovering since his fever was beginning to feel like a slow suffocation as she barely allowed him out of her sight for more than an hour or two. The day he finished the grave marker for Laurel, he desperately wanted to be alone, just to gather his own thoughts and be free to release his grief privately. But Mehlyndia had chosen that, of all days, to stay on his elbow, asking if he was warm enough, did he want another lap blanket, did his joints hurt, and did he need to rest. He'd lost his temper finally and yelled at her to leave him alone and stop treating him like an invalid child. She ran away crying and he thought himself the world's biggest lout for the remainder of the day. Since then, she had relaxed her vigilant watch over him somewhat and he had done his best to keep his temper in check but still, he longed for the freedom to just go off alone once in a while.

A trek through the pines and the anticipation of spending a night or two under the stars was far too enticing for William to refuse and, in a rare display of authority, he told her he was going and that was that. After all, invalid or not, he was still the man of his home and no man should allow himself to be coddled and smothered by his own wife.

"How did you convince Mehlyndia to agree?" Ephraim asked.

"Hmm?" William said, coming out of his reverie. "Agree to what?"

"Your mind does wander, my friend." Ephraim chuckled. "How did you convince ye wife to let you come along with us?"

"She didn't *let* me come," William answered, somewhat defensively. "I *told* her I was coming."

"Put your foot down did you?" Ian said with a grin.

"So to speak." William laughed in spite of himself. "I'm sure she won't mind a day or two to call her own. I know I'm more than ready for a change of scenery."

Ian nodded and kept his eye on the path in front of him. "I can imagine you must be. When was the last time you left the settlement?"

William thought for a moment, then answered, "Three years, come June. And that was only for a few hours. It's a wonder I haven't lost what's left of my mind from simple boredom."

"Three years?" Ephraim shook his head, giving William a fish-eyed stare. "With no break from your wife? No wonder you were ready to come along." He shuddered. "God grant I never go three years without a break from my wife!"

William laughed. "God grant I never go three years without a break from your wife!"

"Amen to that!" Ian piped in and burst into laughter.

Ephraim turned insulted looks to the both of them in turn.

"Uh... I'm sorry." William cleared his throat and nudged Ian with an elbow, who bit his lip against a stifled laugh.

"So am I, son, so am I," Ephraim sighed, looking down to his hands, idly twisting the ornate gold wedding ring he wore, the engravings resembling a chain around his finger. "But then, had I as fair a bride as you, three years would be a treat."

William nodded. "Thank you."

"You know, Will," Ephraim began, still looking to his hand. "I've always wondered, just how did ye manage to catch such a sweet *young* wife?"

"What?" William asked, not sure if he was amused or insulted by the question.

"Well after all, she can't be more than twenty-four at most and you're, what, forty? Forty-five?" Ephraim asked.

Ian snickered under his breath. "You're far off that mark, Ephraim."

"You certainly are." William smiled amicably but was taken aback by Ephraim's assumption. He knew the white streaks in his hair made him look a *bit* older but still, he did not believe they aged him *that* much. After all, his hair was still *mostly* black.

Ephraim blushed, clearly embarrassed by his mistake. "Thirty-five?" he ventured, with a sheepish grin.

Ian guffawed so loudly a small flock of birds fled from an overhead tree. "You'd best stop while you're ahead, Ephraim." He held his stomach laughing until he caught William's stare. "You must admit, Will... it's funny— ahem... ." He affected a stern look, scowling. "Ephraim, tell him you're jesting with him."

William kept his eyes on Ian, fighting to keep the grin from his face. *Let him squirm out of that one,* he thought, bemused while Ephraim fumbled for his words.

"Surely you're older than... I mean, you must be at least..." Ephraim narrowed his eyes, scrutinizing William's face, then threw his hands in the air. "Well if I've offended you, son, it wasn't my aim. My most humble apologies. Just how old are you?"

"I'm not offended Ephraim." William smiled. "I'll be twenty-six at the end of this month," he said, unable to conceal his amusement as Ephraim tried, and failed, to hide his astonishment.

"Is he having me on?" Ephraim reached over William and nudged Ian.

Ian, took a breath, halted his laughter, and shook his head. "No, he's quite serious, Ephraim."

The humor drained from Ephraim's face as he took another close look at William. "I'm sorry, lad," he said and turned his face abruptly.

"No worry, Ephraim, most folks think I'm older," William assured him. In the year since he had come to know Ephraim, he had never known the vicar to turn a doleful eye of pity to him and he hoped that would not become the case now. "I hope you don't think less of me for my youth," he said, with a crooked grin he hoped would bring back the lighthearted mood they had shared only moments ago.

Ephraim smiled and nodded. "No, I don't think less of you," he said, gently. His eyes fell on William's wrists and he casually pointed toward them. "I suppose that would have turned my hair white too."

William looked quickly at Ephraim's face, "What would?"

"Being tor—"

"Whoa!" Ian abruptly called the horse to a halt as the wagon began to list severely to the left. "Hold on! The path has washed out."

The horse whinnied in protest at Ian's sudden jerk of the reins as its forelocks sunk into a muddy pit in the path. The left wheels groaned as they became bogged down in the mire nearly to the axle.

"Damn!" Ian growled, looking over the edge of the wagon. "We won't be going any further for a while." He hopped off the cart and stood, hands on hips, scowling at the damage. "The wheels are wedged fast."

Impeccable timing, Ian, William thought, suspicious that Ian had intentionally run the cart into the mud as a diversion against whatever Ephraim was about to say. *Just as I was going to learn something.* He considered, for a moment, asking Ephraim to continue but thought better of it. The vicar had been clearly uncomfortable with the subject and seemed more than eager to leave it and focus on the problem of the mud. He made a note to bring it up again, later— perhaps when Ian was not present.

Ephraim hopped off the wagon on the right and made his way around to Ian, scrutinizing the problem as he went. "We're too heavy for this foot path. That's the trouble."

"Aye," Ian agreed. "I should have thought of it. The Mi'kmaq dinnae pave roads to their village with cobble stones." He scratched the back of his head and looked up to William. "You're the engineer among us, why didn't you think of that?"

"Me? I'm just along to provide ballast." He laughed and gestured to Ephraim. "Blame him. He only blessed the horse, not the cart."

"True enough." Ian nodded. "It's his fault then. Ephraim, you should have blessed the entire cart."

"You sound like Josephine." Ephraim chuckled and sloshed through the mud to get a closer look at the front wheel. "It's in good all right. We'll have to unhitch and then back it out to firm land." He dug some of the mud away from the wheel with his hand but it was so wet, it oozed back down quickly, refilling the hole and sucking the wheels down even deeper. "It won't be easy for just the two of us, Ian."

"Will we be able to continue?" William asked, leaning over the seat to see for himself.

"Not in the cart," Ian sighed, looking toward the sun now lowering in the western sky. "There's not enough daylight left to get back to Port Edin today, even if we could get it out."

"How much farther is it to Akonni's village?" William

asked.

Ian looked at the trail ahead, then to the sunken wheels. "It's only another four miles or so... I think. But the path doesn't get any wider." He trudged through the mud and climbed back up to sit next to William. "I could go ahead on foot and bring Akonni back with me, if you're willing to wait here with Ephraim."

"That sounds logical. What do *you* feel about it?"

Ephraim straightened up and wiped the mud from his hands onto his trousers. "We're apt to be here for the night, Will. We'll be sleeping in the open air instead of in one of those cozy bark huts as we had planned. Are you up to that?"

"I've camped before," William answered with a shrug. "One night won't be so bad."

Ephraim trudged out of the mud and stood looking at the path ahead, then from where they'd come from, and turned to Ian. "Will you be all right walking alone? Do you want me to go with you?"

"I'll be fine," Ian answered. "I'll take a pack and a lantern. I should be able to make Akonni's village by sunset and we'll be back for you in the morning."

"No, wait. Ephraim's right," William said, pushing himself back into a proper sitting position. "You shouldn't go off alone."

"I see no alternative," Ian said. "The way that wheel is wedged, it'll take more than Ephraim and I to winch it out. I either go on ahead to get Akonni to help us or back to Port Edin and bring Simon or Charles. Either way, Will, you're not going anywhere. I'm not about to leave you alone. You'd be an easy treat for the wolves. Ephraim will be able to keep the fire going to keep them away."

"I hadn't thought of the wolves," William admitted, then sat back, brooding. The joy he had felt at the beginning of the trip steadily soured into trepidation at the thought of Ian off alone in the woods with night falling. And why should Ephraim have to spend the night tending a campfire, all because he could not be left alone? He looked around behind in the wagon and saw what he was hoping to see, the extra blankets. *Thank you Melly!* "Ian, you don't have to go alone."

"We've already gone through that," Ian protested, waving a hand. "There's no way you are staying—"

"Exactly, I'm going with you."

"What?" Ephraim and Ian spoke together, both looking equally confused.

"Hear me," William began, then turned as far as possible and attempted to stretch toward the bundle of blankets. "Ephraim get that bundle for me."

Ephraim handed the blankets to William.

"Thank you." William took the bundle and unwrapped it, giving a tug to one corner. "Yes, this is good and stout." He looked up at his perplexed companions. "I'll need two long narrow branches to act as poles. Twelve or fifteen feet long should do, and some rope."

"What the devil are you planning?" Ephraim said finally.

"A litter." Ian grinned. "Of course."

"Yes." William nodded, pleased with himself. "Make the poles long enough to be hitched to the horse and drag behind far enough to stretch the blankets between the two, and that will give me a place to sit. That way, we all stay together and Ephraim won't have to stay up all night defending my sorry arse from the wolves."

"Next time anyone calls you dull-witted, I will most definitely strike them." Ian laughed.

"I'd appreciate that."

Ian rooted about in the back of the wagon until he found the toolbox. He removed a small hand-ax and found a length of rope. He gave the ax a swing in mid-air, then tipped his forehead with a smile, and headed off toward a grouping of pine saplings. William stayed on the wagon supervising while Ian cut and stripped the branches and brought them to Ephraim, who laced the ropes between them, creating a netting that would act as a support under the blankets. When the construction of the litter was complete, the long ends of the poles were lashed to the pack on the back of the horse. With the blanket in place over the netting, Ephraim and Ian helped William off the wagon and into his new traveling arrangement. He assumed he would be able to sit on the thing, but it became apparent, quickly, that the angle and the lack of back support would make that impossible. Stubbornly, he attempted several ways of securing himself at either the knees or ankles, but when his last maneuver caused him to tumble into the mud— much to Ian's delight— William relented and just lay on the thing.

"Look on the bright side, lad," Ephraim said, sitting on a log, wiping sweat from his head. "At least, you can keep your dignity and not be dropping into the mud every five feet. And you've got a lovely view of trees from there."

William looked up toward the treetops. "And a fine view it is!" He crossed his hands over his stomach, to get more comfortable, and to make the best of his situation, he kept his irritation at having to lie down like a helpless invalid to himself. "I'll be sure to call out if I see anything falling from the trees." He looked up directly over his head and burst out laughing. "And you're sure to hear me holler if I see anything falling from that!" he said, pointing to the horse's backside.

Ephraim slapped his leg and roared in laughter. "I'm sure we will!"

Ian came around and inspected the riggings of the litter. "This was a good idea, Will, you're far enough off the ground to stay dry," he said, not sharing the joviality of the others. He looked again toward the west and shook his head.

"What's wrong, Ian?" William asked, concerned with the serious expression on his friend's face.

"We've lost too much daylight," Ian answered, still looking toward the sunset. "I think it would be foolhardy at best to set out now. We should make camp here for tonight. Then go on in the morning."

Ephraim looked to the west and nodded. "Well, if we're to camp, we'll need a fire. Give me that ax and I'll get us what we need."

"Right," Ian, said handing the ax to Ephraim. "I'll break into the provisions for supper. Akonni will just have to do with one less loaf of Melly's bread."

"I'm sure he won't mind," William said, then yawned. Whether it was the fresh air, the excitement of being away from the village, or the fact he was lying down, he wasn't sure, but he soon realized he was quite tired. He closed his eyes for what he thought was a moment but when he opened them again, the sun had set fully to the west, the stars were bright against the black night sky and Ephraim and Ian were conversing, while something he assumed to be rabbit meat was roasting above a roaring campfire.

Ephraim was speaking in quiet tones. "Why didn't you tell me that before? I would never have brought it up."

William lay still, not letting on he was awake.

"It's not something I care to talk about, Ephraim," Ian said as he pushed a log into the fire with a long stick. "We decided long ago that it was best left to rest. It can do no good to bring it all out now."

Best to leave what to rest? William wondered, suspecting they were discussing him by the side glances he was receiving from Ian. He kept his breathing as steady as possible and listened, watching the two men through his half-opened eyes.

"I don't see what the harm in telling him would be," Ephraim scoffed. "It's not as though they're looking for him here. You said, yourself, they believe him to be long dead and buried."

Dead and buried?

"I admit, I've wrestled with it myself. Many times." Ian shrugged. "But it's mostly for her sake that I've kept my promise. She's scared to death he'll go back to his charms and chants, and bring it all down on himself again. I suppose I harbor that fear as well."

Charms and chants? William caught his breath, hoping he had not been heard.

"It's still hard for me to believe," Ephraim said, shaking his head. "I'd never have guessed it of him that he practiced the old religion and to be skilled in the way of the charms and folk magic. Not that it makes a difference to me..." He looked up at Ian and pointed with his thumb toward William. "Has he been baptized?"

What? What kind of question is that?

"Oh, I'm sure he has," Ian answered with a nod. He tilted his head and narrowed his eyes to Ephraim, then said, "I thought it made no difference to you."

"It doesn't," Ephraim said, defensively and checked the meat on the sticks. "I know a good man when I meet one and don't hold his convictions of faith against him. Perhaps he's got enough magic left in him to get that wheel free." He laughed, then stopped when Ian did not share the humor of his quip. He cleared his throat and assumed a more serious expression. "Truth is, I was going to offer him a baptism if he wanted it, just so I could add him to my tally. A purely selfish act on my part. The governors are due soon, and I'm way behind in my 'converting of the heathens', you know."

"He's in no need of conversion." Ian grinned and looked closely at Ephraim. "You don't believe the Mi'kmaq to be heathens, do you?"

"No." Ephraim turned the meat on the stick. "They've struck me as good folks, Akonni's people. They know God sure as we do. They've simply given Him a different name."

Ian nodded and chuckled. "A philosophy like that could get you as roasted as that rabbit where I come from."

"Unfortunately it's likely to get me roasted by my own wife. So I'd best tally me at least *one* baptism on this trip," Ephraim noted, laughing. "I wonder if the horse would count."

Ian joined the laughter, then looked toward William. "We should wake him. The rabbit is almost done."

William opened his eyes fully at the change of subject. The suspicions he'd long tried to ignore had finally been confirmed; Ian did know fully well what had happened to him and had been keeping it from him. Then again, the idea that charms and chants were involved, and Ephraim questioning whether or not he was even baptized confused him greatly, and he wondered for a moment if they were actually talking about him or if he were just being paranoid. Was it really himself that Ephraim was referring to when he said *they believe him dead and buried?*

"I'm awake." William stretched and yawned. The smell of the rabbit caused a grumble in his stomach. "What's cooking? It smells good."

"Ah, you've decided to join us then?" Ephraim said, checking the meat. "We've got roasted rabbit and a bit of bread." He winked. "And nice sacramental wine."

"Sounds good." William pushed himself up on his hands and finding the position awkward, laid back down. "I don't suppose anyone would care to help me up?"

Ian got up, retrieved the chariot from the back of the sunken wagon, and brought it close to the fire before going to William. "Do you need to visit the forest before supper?" he asked quietly.

"I thought you'd never ask," William answered. Such business had become commonplace between he and Ian, and it occurred to him how glad he was now that he was not left alone in the forest with Ephraim after all. He liked the man well enough but there were certain aspects of his life he did not relish burdening on people outside his family circle. This was certainly one of those things.

With his sundry needs taken care of, Ian brought William to his chariot and rejoined Ephraim, just as he was taking the rabbits off the sticks. Ephraim plopped one down onto a wooden plate and handed it to William.

"Thanks," William said, accepting the plate. It was not lost on him that Ephraim seemed to be avoiding eye contact. He wondered if Ephraim suspected that he had caught part of his and Ian's conversation, about the mysterious *charms and chants.* "I interrupted you when I woke up, Ephraim, please go on with your conversation. It sounded interesting."

"Hmm?" Ephraim looked up. "Oh, wasn't anything important." He cast a quick glance to Ian.

The glance Ian returned and the quick shake of his head told William, he was right. They had been discussing him.

Proceeding carefully, feigning ignorance of their previous discussion, William asked, "So, how many Mi'kmaq have you baptized?"

Ephraim shook his head and laughed lightly. "Only four." He seemed relieved at the subject William had chosen to ask him about. "I'm way behind."

William smiled and nodded. "I'm not surprised. They're proud people and they take their faith seriously. Why it matters to the governors that they be baptized is a puzzle to me."

"Oh, it's the same old business," Ian said, with a dismissive sigh. "Keep the church happy, keep the monarchs happy, and business goes on as usual. The governors see the settlement as a business, after all. The fact that we've taken pains to establish a good rapport with the Mi'kmaq on their own terms is meaningless to the church. They'll want the heathens to bend their knees to *their* altars, regardless of the damage it will cause to our relationships if we try to force it."

"I've argued that myself, Ian," Ephraim said, pointing with a rabbit leg. "The whole reason France set up this settlement was for trading and such. The English made their settlements in Virginia with the 'convert or be conquered' approach and look where it led them— attacked and starving behind their own barricades. We have no fear of the Mi'kmaq attacking for the exact reason Ian points out. We've left them to their own ways. And they've been nothing but friendly and helpful to us in return. Forcing them to convert, and come to be baptized seems... counterproductive in that light."

"So, why did you agree to take the post to begin with, Ephraim?" William asked.

Ephraim looked away and answered quietly, "It was a way to leave England and all the politics of religion and bickering between the Protestant movement, the Catholics, the king's ideas on it all..." He shook his head and sighed. "Josephine and I left England when the Protestants were faring no better than the country folk during the hysterics of the witch hunts a few years back." He gave a quick glance to William, then looked away.

Witch hunts? An odd tremor found its way into William's middle at the word. The same tremor he had felt while sitting on the raised bench when he was about to place the bough on his newly constructed house. *Charms and chants? They believe him dead and buried?* He glanced up at Ian and was taken aback to see the intent stare his friend held on him. Ian averted his eyes quickly when William met them with his own.

"We went to France," Ephraim continued, "where Josephine has family. We wanted to start fresh, to be able to practice our faith in peace."

"I fully understand that sentiment," Ian said, tossing the bones of his eaten rabbit into the flame. "Those were trying times."

"We saw the opportunity to move to this settlement as a God-send," Ephraim explained. "A chance to set up our own congregation without the ever-watchful eyes of the hierarchy looking over my shoulder. I accepted the conditions of the appointment merely as a means to get us away. But I'm afraid Josephine takes it far more to heart."

"So you're tallying baptisms for her sake?" William said, picking the rabbit apart. He had yet to eat any.

Ephraim nodded. "There's a lot to be said for keeping peace under your own roof."

"I'm sure," William remarked, chuckling, and looked down on his plate. He found his appetite less than it had been. He sat staring, unable to shake the tremor, and the questions that were swimming around in his mind. *Ian's kept something from me, he said, 'more for her sake'. Melly's sake? He said she's afraid of the charms and chants. What charms?* He pushed the meat around on his plate as though the movement would bring him the answers. *Ephraim said, 'they believe him dead and buried'. Who believes that? 'They're not looking for him here'. Looking for who? Me? What could I have done that anyone would presume I'm dead?*

Another conversation worked his way into his thoughts; *Philbrick, William. I know you're not fond of that name, but it's the one we must use now.* Melly had told him on more than one occasion he was not to use his own name. As a revelation took form in his mind, the tremor wormed its way to his shoulders, as he suddenly pushed the meat off the plate with his hand, sending it flying into the fire. "Why must I use a false name?" he blurted, not intending to speak aloud but was somehow relieved he did.

"What?" Ian said, looking at him quickly.

"My name. Why must I call myself Philbrick?"

"Isn't that your name?" Ephraim asked, with a slight twitch to the side of his mouth.

"No. It isn't." William looked from Ephraim to Ian and then back. "He's told you, hasn't he?" he asked bluntly.

"What are you talking about, Will?" Ian said, quietly.

"You know," William said, more angrily than he intended then lowered his voice. "I heard you talking. You told him more than you've told me in five years."

Ephraim held up a hand, "Settle down, Ian's not told me—"

"Hasn't he?" William argued, raising his voice anew. "You're wondering if I've even been baptized! Why is that, Ephraim? Is there something about me to make you doubt it? And who is it that *they*—" He made a wave to the space about him. "—whoever *they* are, believes is long dead and buried?" He looked up quickly at Ian before Ephraim could answer, gripping the arm of the chariot to forestall the trembling he felt in his hands. "Is that why I must use a false name? Is it William Fylbrigge who is believed to be long dead and buried?"

Ephraim began to answer but Ian held a hand up to him, "Will, you're jumping to conclusions—"

"Ian, tell me, damn it!" William hollered, sending an echo through the forest. "Does the Old World think me dead?"

Ian stared, tight-lipped and lock-jawed. He stood and walked over to where William sat in his chariot and crouched next to him. He took a long breath, looked William in the eye, and began slowly, "Before I answer, please tell me something, do you remember anything of Scotland at all?"

"I remember Drumoak," William said and looked into the fire, as though speaking to the flame would make it easier to recall. "I can describe every detail of the place to you. Every room. Every painting. And I remember some of the people I knew there. My father, Edward. A young lad named Duncan, I think it was. An older woman, a servant... her name escapes me, but I see her clearly in my mind, always sad... crying." He looked up at Ian. "Then, there are the other two. A man close to my age, and a young woman with long hair and brown eyes," he spoke quietly, almost to himself. "The two I loved."

Ian nodded. "Sean and Laurel."

William looked at Ian, suddenly finding it difficult to speak. "Yes. Did you know them?"

Ian glanced up at William, then looked back into the fire. "I met Sean only briefly, in fact it was only a day before he passed on."

"He *is* dead then," William said and felt a catch in his throat. "I suspected that much."

"Yes. I was still a monk in those days. I performed the Last Sacrament for him," Ian repiled softly. "You were with me when I did. I can't really tell you much more about him, except you were quite close. As close as brothers."

William looked away, fighting a sudden unbidden wave

of emotion. *As close as brothers. And I cannot even bring to mind his face or his voice?* He swallowed hard and asked, "And Laurel? Did you know her as well?"

"Aye. I did," Ian answered quietly, looking down at his hands. "Though only for the last few days that she lived."

He said nothing more for several moments, and the look in his eyes told William that Ian had probably known Laurel far better than he had Sean, and the memory seemed a sad one to him. He wondered how Laurel had touched Ian that would leave such a hollow look in his eyes. And though he was unclear of the details of who she was or what part in his own life she shared, Laurel's memory touched a sad place inside him as well. He wrestled with the notion of asking for more details about her but chose to allow Ian to keep his memory of Laurel to himself for the time being.

After a moment, Ian broke the silence. "So your memories are only of images of the people?" he asked. "Do you recall any details of the town?"

"No. It's as if nothing exists outside the walls of the castle. Even in the dreams, I can't see beyond the windows, and the one time the doors did open, all I could see..." William shook his head, and made a dismissive wave of his hand. "But that was only a dream."

"What?" Ian asked, looking up. "What did you see?"

"Demons," William answered in a low whisper, then laughed it off, even though the memory of the chanting crowd from his dream still sent shudders through him. "I told you, it was only a dream."

"One I'd not like to share." Ian half smiled and stirred the embers with a stick. "What do you remember about the inside of the castle?"

"I remember little Duncan, running about with his wooden sword, in and out of the kitchen doors and up the grand stairs." William said and closed his eyes, capturing the image in his mind of the cheerful little lad and his imaginary dragon hunts through the corridors of Drumoak. "It seems to me that I was actually the one who made that sword for him, though the carving I remember on it is far more detailed than anything I've done here."

"That's possible," Ian said. "You were well known for your wood carving."

William opened his eyes and looked at Ian curiously. "Was I? Is that how I earned my trade then as well?"

Ian laughed lightly under his breath before he answered. "No, you had no need to earn a living by trade, my friend. You were a nobleman."

"A nobleman?" William said, stunned. "Me?"

"Him?" Ephraim echoed William's astonishment.

"Aye." Ian made a cross with his finger on his chest. "When I met you—" He leaned forward, idly poking at the fire as he spoke. "—you had only recently been named heir to Lord Edward, Duke of Stonehaven upon your marriage to his daughter. You were named Earl of—"

"Sutherland!" William finished as the title came to him suddenly, like a flash of light out of the dark place in his memory. He looked wide-eyed at Ian, as for the first time in years he recited in an almost inaudible whisper the designation that had been bestowed on him: "I was Lord William of Drumoak, Earl of Sutherland."

Ian nodded.

"What?" Ephraim gawked at Ian. "*He* was William of Drumoak? *The* William of Drumoak?" Ephraim sat back, staring saucer-eyed at William, he slapped his knee and shook his head. "My God!"

Ian dropped the stick and gaped at Ephraim. "You've heard of him?"

"Heavens, yes! His tale is the stuff legends are made of." Ephraim answered, looking at William as though he had never seen him before. "No wonder they've given you a new name, lad; you're famous!"

"Famous?" William almost rocked from his chariot leaning forward toward Ephraim. He caught himself by grabbing the arms of the chair in time to keep himself from falling. "Ephraim, what tale?" He looked to Ian, who seemed equally astounded at Ephraim's proclamation. "Do you know what he's talking about?"

"No!" Ian said, shaking his head. "Perhaps you should tell the both of us, Ephraim."

"You mean you've not heard your own..." Ephraim began then threw his hands in the air and slapped his own forehead. "Of course you've not heard it, how could you? You've been here since it all happened, haven't you. Well, I'll be pleased to tell you the tale as I've come to know it. Of course, you understand it may be far astray from the actual truth." He looked at Ian with an incredulous grin. "You be sure to set me straight on the details I have wrong. If someone were to tell me I'd be sharing a campfire with William of Drumoak, the Demon of Stonehaven, I'd call them daft."

"Demon?" William froze, the trembling he felt earlier suddenly returned to his chest and his arms, causing him to lose his grip on the chair and his weight to shift to the front of the seat. Ian was on his feet in an instant and managed to catch him before he fell from the chariot and tumbled into the campfire.

"Settle down, Will, you're going to hurt yourself." Ian turned an angry eye to Ephraim. "Vicar, I think you've had too much wine. I'm sure you've mixed your rumors... with some other—"

"Was there another William of Drumoak named Earl of Sutherland in 1607, that were put to trial?" Ephraim took a swallow from the flask and wiped his mouth with his sleeve.

William could barely find his breath to speak and he looked from Ian's dumbfounded expression to the smug wine-induced smirk on Ephraim's face. *He's drunk... that has to be it.* He looked down to his wrists, and the scars that ringed them and to the gnarled joints in his fingers. *Charms and chants?* Idly, he traced the mark on his face with his left hand, trying to mentally put the pieces together. *The Demon of Stonehaven?* "No... no, this is insane. I'm no demon. I realize there are large pieces of my past that I've forgotten and, for reasons I have yet to understand, it has been clear to me for some time that you and Melly and everyone else have been deliberately keeping those pieces missing, but... did I truly stand trial? Surely you would not keep something like *that* from me... would you?"

Ian shook his head, making a scoffing sound from behind his teeth. He waved his flask toward Ephraim, then leaned close to William and said, "He's muddy-minded, Will."

Ephraim snorted indignantly and took another long swig of his wine. "My mind's as clear as yours, Ian Sproctor."

"Proctor," Ian corrected him and pointed a thumb to the vicar, whispering to William, "See?"

William narrowed his eyes skeptically to Ian and nodded to him in half-belief. "Yes, Ephraim, you must have it wrong—"

"I do not!" Ephraim argued. He took a long slurping guzzle from his flask. "You'd have to be a demon to survive all they did to ye, lad; just look at ye scars there and tell me I'm wrong."

William glanced to his wrists, then back to Ephraim.

"Will—" Ian began.

William raised a hand. "Let him finish. What caused the scars, Ephraim?"

"The tortures!" Ephraim rolled his eyes, as though it were a foolish question. "The beatin', 'n the burnin', 'n the droppin', 'n the flailin'." He shuddered and drank some more, "'N all the cuts... oh 'tis a horrible tale."

"Ephraim!" Ian growled at the older man.

William fought to keep the growing panic under control, as Ephraim rambled off what he had heard by way of legend. *He's drunk and he doesn't know the real story.* "Ian? How much of that is true?"

Ian scowled at Ephraim, averting his eyes away from William, "You're potted, old man!" he spit out, then took a large gulp from his own flask.

"Says you!" Ephraim grunted. "The way I rem'ber the tale, the monk— and my money says that monk were you, Sproctor—" He waggled an unsteady finger and winked. "—that monk gave 'im the Last Sacrament before they did the test with the poison. Were the Sacrament what drove out the demon. An' when it lef' ye body, ye died right there in the witness chair." He knotted his brow and looked at William, befuddled. "So how's it then that ye not be dead aft' ye died?"

Ian rolled his eyes and shook his head. "For pity sake, Ephraim, shut up! You've obviously been had, the man never died!"

"Enough!" William raked his fingers through his hair, dropped his elbows to his knees, and rested his head in his hands. His mind was swimming with questions and vague memories that he mistrusted as imagination, conjured by the wine he had drunk, himself. He fully distrusted Ian's assertions that Ephraim was merely confused in his rumors, his own instinct telling him there was a bit more than a grain of truth to the tale the vicar told. Yet, though he was clearly addle-minded from the wine, if even *half* of what Ephraim had declared was true, there was a trial of some sort involved— *skilled in the way of charms? Witchcraft? Is that what it was?* "I've heard all I can stand for one night. And you both have had more wine than you need." He looked from one man to the other and sat back in his chariot, frustrated that even Ian did not have the sense to stay sober.

"When you are more clear-headed, I'll ask you for the truth, Ian. I know there's far more to this than you're telling me."

"Will, please..." Ian groaned and rested his head on his knees. "Enough for now. You're right, my brain is far from clear."

"So I noticed." William said and slouched back in his chair. A grumbling snort from Ephraim's direction took his attention. "Well, it's obvious he won't be keeping the camp fire burning tonight," he said, as Ephraim's head nodded to his chest, his hands protectively crossed over his wine flask. "I guess it will be up to the two of... Ian?"

Ian responded with a light snore.

"The least you could have done was stoke the fire first." William sighed, watching his companions sink further into their stupors and sleep.

A cool spring wind rustled through the forest sending a chill down his back. He, instinctually, reached for the lap quilt he generally had, but soon remembered it was still back on the litter. His irritation with Ian slowly transformed into anger and then trepidation when the wind whipped through camp, diminishing the flame of the campfire even further. He glanced around to see what was within his reach that may be helpful. The stick Ian had used as a poker was lying next to the chariot, just within his reach, and though it was a bit of a stretch, he managed to wrap his fingers around it and grab. He examined it, considering its usefulness, and frowned. It was barely three feet long, and only an inch or so around, but the only other means of defense they had brought with them, a musket, was tucked under the seat of the wagon. *I suppose I can beat the wolves on the head with this stick—for about a half a minute before they devour me.*

"Ian!" He shouted, trying to poke his snoring companion with the stick, but it was too short to reach him. "Wake up, you sodden lunk!"

Ian mumbled and sank down onto the ground next to the fire. He folded his arm and rested his head on his elbow, facing away from William.

"Ephraim?"

Flanked by his snoring companions, as a rebellious gust of wind stole away the rest of the campfire, William resigned himself to the reality that he had been left alone in the forest after all.

"All right, Will, think." William spoke aloud as he surveyed his predicament. "You either sit here and freeze, or get your sorry arse to where the blankets are." He craned his neck, looking over his shoulder to where the litter, still attached to the horse, held his quilt. He thought of beckoning the animal but realized the tether Ian had looped over a branch was too short. "It's not more than ten feet. Too far for you, but that's not so far for me, aye?" He shook his head, chiding himself for the ridiculous notion. "Might as well be ten miles." He sighed and jammed the fire-poking stick he held angrily into the ground next to him. The force of the motion caused the chair to rock slightly. "This stick may not be so useless after all." He raised it with both hands, as though he was about to deliver a deathblow with a sword, and thrust it into the earth just in front of the chair. He inclined it toward himself and leaned over. Summoning all the strength in his upper body, he pushed against the stick. The chair rolled back a few inches. Encouraged, he repeated the motion, gaining another half-foot.

"If I can't walk, then I'll row," he said, plunging the stick into the earth and pushing himself a third time. He sat back to catch his breath, looked again toward the litter to judge his progress, and frowned. He looked at the marks in the earth where he had pushed and realized he was fooling himself. "It will take all night to get there at this rate." He slouched back in the chair, disgusted with himself for even trying.

"Wake up!" he yelled, as loud as he was able to his companions. Neither man responded with more than an inebriated snore and a shift in their position. He shouted again, but his only reply was his own voice echoing back to him. "Next time you invite me into the woods, remind me to cut my own throat first!" He grumbled and tossed the stick in Ian's general direction, hoping to hit him. He missed. "Lucky for you, my aim is foul!"

The wind whirled in about the trees, raising swirls of duff about him. He wrapped his arms around himself and glanced up to the sky. The moon was near full and provided a good amount of light though the motion of the trees in the wind. The clouds that drifted across it made it difficult to discern objects more than a few feet away. He sat silent, staring into the mottled shadows of the forest, listening to the constant moan of the wind through the pines. He heard a muffled snort behind him. Startled, he turned to look and relaxed, recognizing it was the horse nickering in his sleep that had made the sound. He jumped again when somewhere above him, the furious sound of wings taking flight, and the mournful call of an owl took him by surprise. "You're going to make yourself mad if you don't relax," he scolded himself, rubbing his palms on his upper arms for warmth. "It's only forest sounds. You've heard them before."

"Mmmm."

A low groaning came from somewhere to his right.

"Ephraim?" William turned to the sleeping vicar. "Was that you? Are you awake?"

"Mmmm."

The sound came to him again, but William could see now that it was coming from beyond where Ephraim lay, from someplace in the woods but not far outside the circle of the camp.

"Is someone out there?" he called into the darkness, then listened. The sound did not repeat. He reached for the stick again, annoyed with himself when he remembered that he had just flung it at Ian. "Fool." He looked beyond Ephraim, squinting into the dark. The moon-cast shadows of the swaying trees made it difficult to see clearly. Within the dappled shadows, William thought he saw something large and solid, moving slowing between the trees in the same direction from where the moaning sound had come.

"Mmmm."

The sound was definitely growing louder and to William's ear, it definitely did not sound human. He watched the looming mass of the shape lumber between two pines as though it were tethered, while it continued making the strange low moaning sound. "Mmmm."

"Ian!" William called in a strangled whisper, not taking his eyes from the shape. Ian lay, no more than twelve feet away, blissfully sleeping, curled up next to the log. "Ian Proctor!" he called through clenched teeth.

The moaning thing in the woods stopped at the sound of William's voice and seem to freeze in its position. William thought better of calling to his friend again, fearing he had just called unwanted attention to himself. He stared, unblinking, at the hulk as the moaning started anew. The wind again sent a chilling swirl, picking up leaves and tossing them about. The trees swayed in response to the increase in the wind and with it, the moaning became louder still, as though it wished to be heard above the ear-splitting crescendo of an impending storm.

William gripped the arms of his chariot and, without giving more than a half-second of forethought, launched himself off it, landing with a thud on his chest in the dirt, losing his breath and gaining a mouthful of dust in the process. He lay face down, gasping and spitting, as the howling echoed around him. He covered his head with his arms until the wind died down, taking the howl with it. He lay still for a moment, listening, before raising himself up on his elbows to look again toward the woods. The wind parted the clouds and the moon at last, shown steady on the thing, revealing its identity.

William laughed out loud in relief as the unmistakable form of a moss covered, hollowed out log became clear in the moonlight. The mournful moan had been nothing more than the wind through a hole in the side of it, and the movement a mere trick of the moonlight as it danced on a drapery of moss covered pine limbs. "You're truly hopeless, Fylbrigge. You must have been one pathetic nobleman." He dropped his head down onto his folded arms, laying on his belly, feeling completely foolish that not only had he let his fear get the better of him, but now he was stuck on the ground.

"I might as well make the best of it." He pushed himself up on his elbows again, and dragged himself closer to where Ian lay snoring. Had he landed on his back, he would have had a more difficult time maneuvering his weight around. As it was, it was more work than he had anticipated to cross the few feet between himself and his friend.

"Ian, damn it, wake up! I swear, if I ever see you bend your elbow to drink again, I'll knock your head off!" he muttered, as he trudged along on his elbows. "None of this would have happened if you'd kept the cart out of the mud. And don't argue with me, I know you dumped it deliberately. Well, look where it got you! Drunk in the forest and your secret spilled just the same. Most of it anyway. Don't think I'll forget to get the rest of the details."

He rested to catch his breath. Only another four feet or so and he'd be able to reach out and grab Ian's ankle. He dropped his head onto his arms for a minute, and wondered what damage, if any, he might be causing to his legs. If he cut himself on a rock as he dragged along, he'd never even know about it and could bleed all over the place before he even reached Ian. He laughed mirthlessly to himself, thinking of the irony. "Here I am, the *Dreaded Demon of Stonehaven,* probably about to freeze or bleed to death like a slug on my belly." He lifted his head and shouted in Ian's direction. "And all because the apothecary passed out!"

Ian muttered in his sleep and swatted away a fly that landed on his nose, but remained in his unperturbed slumber.

William shook his head, sniggering under his breath. "Well, my fate will be far more pleasant than yours, Ian Proctor. I'll just lie peacefully right here in the dust, but you'll be the one who'll have to face up to Melly." He laughed wearily into his arms and lay quiet.

He had but only those last four feet to go, but the six or so he'd already dragged himself had taken most of the strength from his arms, and his shoulders were beginning to stiffen with painful spasms. He shuddered for a moment as the pains reminded him of the conversation he'd been having earlier in the evening, and the revelation Ephraim had made to him about how he'd come to own the body he was burdened with—*'the beatin', 'n the burnin', 'n the droppin', 'n the flailin', 'n the cuts... oh 'tis a horrible tale—*

"A horrible tale. That's all it is. A tale." He took a breath and propped himself up on his elbows again before he collapsed down immediately, relenting to the protesting pains in his shoulders. He forced himself to relax and draw his breaths slowly to calm his jangled nerves before attempting to go further. He closed his eyes and waited for the spasms to pass.

The wind again began to build and though this time he knew what was causing the sound, the moaning from the hollow stump was unnerving. *It's a log, for pity sake, Fylbrigge, have you no mettle left in you?* It seemed to answer his thoughts by sending a wind-devil of duff and ash from the campfire, whirling about his face. The dust choked him for a moment and he buried his face on his arms until the wind moved it away. The whirling debris seemed drawn to his head and shoulders; had he not known better, William would have thought that the flurry of leaves was consciously examining him as it moved methodically along the entire length of his body. *Wind has no mind about it, and mine is barely thinking clearly, so forget it. It's wind. Plain and simple.*

He lifted his head again when the dust had settled and squinted in the moonlight to see how much farther he had to go to reach Ian. Four more feet. The clouds had finally given way, affording him a better, if not perfect, view of his friend. He gathered his breath and pushed himself up on his aching arms, eyes fixed ahead of him on Ian's ankle. He pulled himself another foot. Something below his waist, possibly at his thigh, though he could not be sure, had snagged on a root that stuck out of the ground, and torn away at his leather leggings. If it was enough to tear the leather, he worried, he had probably just tore into his leg as he had feared would happen.

He stopped his forward effort and collapsed onto his belly. Rolling over was a challenge when he wasn't exhausted and paranoid; in his current state, it would be near impossible for him to roll onto his hip, allowing him to check his upper legs for cuts. He rested for another moment, then locked his jaw and harnessed the last strength he had in his shoulders and arms. He twisted his left shoulder under and pushed against the ground with his right hand. He stretched his left arm out straight for leverage and managed to hold the position long enough to reach his upper leg with his right hand for a couple of seconds. As he feared, his hand came away wet, sticky with blood.

"Damn! Ian, wake up!"

It was then that the shadow crept over him. He froze, not looking around, sensing the shadow was caused by something physical and was not a trick of his mind played on him by the forest. He felt it hovering over him, large and looming, and black as night. The wind whipped into another temper tantrum, swirling up the dust around him. "Ian, wake—"

He never finished his call, as he felt himself suddenly swallowed within a blanket of oppressively heavy blackness.

"Are you hungry?"

"Your leg."

William looked down at his left leg to see a long gash from the middle of his thigh to just above his knee. A large piece of leather was missing from his leggings, apparently torn away when he'd cut himself. The wound had bled quite a lot by the looks of it, though it was now caked with dried blood and debris from the forest floor.

The man brushed away the debris and looked closely at the wound. Then seeming content, he nodded, "It will heal."

William glanced at his leg, it did seem to only *look* worse than it was and he dismissed his former worry of bleeding to death in the forest.

The man resumed his original seat, retrieved the rabbit, and once more held it out to William. "You really should eat something. It may be a long time before you have the chance again."

William reached hesitantly to the stick and froze, hand midway between them.

The man rolled his eyes impatiently. "Go on. Take it."

William took the stick and slowly brought the rabbit to himself, giving it a sniff. It certainly smelled real and his stomach responded with a hungry grumble. He gave a wary glance to the man, then tore a small piece of meat from the rabbit, and put it in his mouth. He chewed slowly, swallowed, and then looked up, astounded. "It's real!"

"Of course it's real. What else would it be?" The man chuckled, placing another skewered rabbit over the fire. William wondered where the second one had come from. He was sure he had only seen the one.

Allowing his hunger to overrule his rising trepidation,

William picked another piece of meat and ate it, admitting to himself it was good. He nibbled a bit more, then looked up to his curious companion. "So, who are you?" He glanced from side to side, startled to realize there was nothing but complete blackness around the circle of fire light. He found no trace of the wagon, his chair, the horse, or his two companions. The sky was no longer illuminated by the full moon. Even the trees seemed to be missing. "And where are we?"

"Who am I?" The man made an indignant snort, then laughed. "I should think you'd know who I am by now. As for where we are?" He shrugged, palms up. "We're right here, of course."

William frowned and stopped eating. "I'm not fond of guessing games. Especially when I'm at a disadvantage."

The man grinned and snickered under his breath. "No, you never were." He pulled the second rabbit from the fire and examined it, and speaking more to it than to William, he said, "So I winnae keep you guessing. I must say though, 'tis a grievous thing to me that you've forgotten so much. It will make this all the more difficult." He placed the rabbit back over the fire, then looked up. The smile the man had worn softened into a look William could only interpret as true grief. "Ye truly don't know me, brother?"

"Brother?" William's eyes widened and he caught his breath. The tremble that had plagued him earlier began to make its presence known again. "I don't remember having a brother."

The man lowered his eyes to his hands and spoke in a softer, sadder voice. "You did, Will. Two in fact." He looked up again with a strange, cynical looking smile. "But you're not likely to receive a visit from that other sot. He'd sooner place a dagger in your back than stand up to protect it... as I always did. I was always at your back."

Always on my back. Him? That's impossible! Brother? No one ever told me he was my brother. William's breaths started coming in short staggers as a terrifying recognition settled on him. "Sean?"

The man nodded.

William shook his head in disbelief, still unconvinced the man was not a dream, though everything around him conspired to the contrary. The trembling in his middle increased and found its way to his voice. "You can't be Sean. Sean is dead. You're not here. *I'm* not here, this is only a dream." In his agitation, he thrust the rabbit away from him, it landed in the embers of the campfire. He rocked forward, attempting to move himself toward the man. "Why are you lying? You cannae possibly be Sean!"

The man tossed aside the rabbit he was roasting and scooted on his knees toward William, catching him under the arms before he fell completely onto his stomach again. Pushing him back to a proper sitting position, he placed his hands on William's shoulders and looked him square in the eye. "Will, I never told you a lie my entire life. Look at me. It's me. Your brother. Your friend."

William silenced himself and stared into the intent green eyes of the man. The hands resting on his shoulders were definitely solid. He swung his own left hand up and rested it on the man's— *Sean's*— shoulder. In that instant, William was overcome with a torrent of conflicting emotions. His heart beat rapidly at the joy of being with and recognizing his lost brother; at the anger he felt that his memory had been stolen from him; confusion at not knowing if he were dreaming or awake; and most disconcerting, he felt an all-encompassing sense of fear that this *ghost* was with him and he had no idea where Ian and Ephraim had vanished to.

"Breathe," Sean said, then pulled William to himself.

William did not resist. Embracing his brother, he surrendered briefly to his emotions, joyfully accepting Sean's presence as genuine. They remained locked for several moments while William brought his breathing under control. When they broke, Sean sat down next to him. "It's good to see you."

William could not suppress the smile he felt coming as he looked at Sean's face, no longer caring whether he was dreaming or not because it didn't matter. What *did* matter was that he remembered his brother. A flood of images rushed to his mind, bubbling out of the dark place of his memory and into the light, that he felt were far to vivid to be inventions of his imagination. As if watching a player's performance, he saw himself as a child of twelve, disheveled and thin, with the haunted look of a caged animal on his face, accepting a hand of greeting from another young man who was saying, "My name is Sean. I'm to welcome you to Drumoak. This is your home now."

He watched the play in his mind as the scene changed. They were slightly older, his own face far more animated and happier than his earlier memory. They rode horses through a field set with obstacles of hay bales and log piles. "Keep up, Sean!" William was hollering over his shoulder, as he pushed the horse to his limits to jump the bales. Sean galloped fast up behind, and the two raced the course laughing. He saw them as they aged, always together; Sean teaching him the proper way to hold a sword, and how to fight, and then later, he saw them laughing as Sean helped him don the elaborate suit of clothes he had worn for his wedding. He watched the images change rapidly through his memory until one image came and struck like a stone, taking the smile from his face. He saw Sean, ashen faced and still, a gaping wound across his chest and forehead, and he saw himself keeping vigil beside at the deathbed.

"I watched you die," William said quietly.

"Aye," Sean said, matching William's quiet tone. "Ye stayed with me until it was over. 'Twas only then that I learned you were my brother. When you said goodbye."

He died. This is a dream then. The thought brought a lump to William's throat. *Well, if it be a dream, so be it. I'll enjoy my brother's company for as long as God grants me this bit of sleep.* "I wanted to tell you before then that you were my brother. But... I never had the chance. I'm sorry."

"No apologies necessary," Sean said. "I know now and that's all that matters." He smiled and reached for the rabbit he had abandoned, and resumed cooking it. The one William had dropped into the coals was now far too burned to be eaten. "You'll have to eat this one. I've no need for it anyway."

William nodded absently, only half-curious about why Sean was being insistent that he eat. "Sean, there's still so much I don't remember. You said I had *two* brothers. I can't for the life of me remember another. What is his name?"

Sean handed him the now fully cooked rabbit. "No reason that you should remember *him*," he said, hissing the word 'him'. "I'd call it a blessing that you don't." Sean's voice suddenly held an angry edge to it. A dark shadow crossed his eyes, as he continued. "But if you must know, his name was Thomas, Earl of Aberdoir. He was a loathsome snake and that be all I care to discuss of him." Whether it was the mention of the name or the scowl on Sean's face, or both, he was not sure, but the answer filled William with an overpowering sense of dread.

"Was? He's dead as well then?" William asked.

"Long dead. Best forgotten," Sean answered curtly, with a flair in his eye that told William to ask no more about Thomas, 'or else'. "He's not why I'm here." He pointed to the rabbit. "Eat Will, please. I've not got long and you haven't eaten."

William thought better of arguing, and began picking at the rabbit. "Why are you here then?" he asked and ate another piece of the meat.

The scowl vanished from Sean's face and he grinned. "To cover your back. Same as always."

"Why?" William asked, confused, as he absently ate the rabbit.

"That's my job," Sean explained with a shrug. "I don't mean to brag, but I've always been fairly good at it, too. I've kept you in one piece so far... more or less." He nodded toward William's legs, then lowered his eyes apologetically.

"What are you talking about?"

"I did the best I could back there. But you must admit, I've done far better since."

William shook his head, confounded with what Sean was saying. "You did your best back *where?*" He looked down at the gnarled joints of his left hand and held it up, as though to display it to Sean. "Were you with me when this happened?"

Sean sighed and patted William on the shoulder. "There'll be time for all those questions later. But right now, there's something more important we need to discuss." He held up a hand to forestall the argument William was about to make, then shook his head, the sadness returning to his eyes. "I've got very little time, Will, and when I'm gone, you probably will only remember half of what I tell you, so please, just listen." He gestured to the half-eaten rabbit William still held. "And please, finish your supper."

William nodded, feeling the lump return to his throat. Unthinking, he obediently began to pick at the rabbit. He tore the last few bits of edible meat from the carcass and ate them, leaving only bones and grizzle on the stick.

"Good." Sean sat back and took a long breath. "In the beginning, you always knew when I was with you." He made a half-hearted chuckle, with look of mock accusation in his eye. "Though you doubted my existence as much then as you do right now."

William couldn't resist a smile at that.

"But I've been with you right along, making sure you stay with the living."

Stay with the living? That was a familiar echo to William's mind that sent a shudder through his shoulders down his arms and revealed itself to Sean as the carcass of the rabbit shook on the end of its stick.

Sean reached over and took the rabbit away from William and tossed it into the embers, sending a column of sparks skyward. "You're shaking," he said as he put a brotherly arm around William's shoulder. "No wonder. You're freezing. Let me get that blanket." He stood without waiting for an answer, took a single step backward, and vanished into the blackness, only to step out of it almost within the same heartbeat, holding the quilt William customarily draped on his lap. Sean wrapped it around his shoulders and sat back down next to him.

William pulled the edges of the quilt around himself. *It is a dream. This was too far away for him to retrieve it so quickly. Calm down, let him have his say. It's a dream. Only a dream...*

"Why do you always assume I'm a dream?" Sean asked, as though in answer to William's unspoken thoughts. A trace of glee brightened his face that quickly darkened back to seriousness.

William stared stupidly on his companion before finding his voice to ask, "Why are you here?"

"I came to give you a warning."

"Warning?"

"It's not over, Will. You've not left it all behind you, dead and buried in Scotland. It's coming again, brother."

"What's coming?"

"You need to give the eagle to your son before the dragon comes for it. She's readying her fire again, only she doesn't know where to hunt; she's searching."

"Dragon? Eagle? I don't understand. *What* eagle? Sean, you're not making any sense."

Sean stood and turned his back. "Give the eagle to your son. He'll need it to stand against them."

When Sean turned back, he had changed, and William gasped at the appearance of the gash across his forehead and the wound on his chest, the chalky paleness that stole the color from his face. Sean placed his right fist across his chest in a gesture of respect and bowed his head slightly. "I kept my promise." He lowered his arm and smiled sadly. "You must keep yours. Give the eagle to your son."

Before William could find his voice to answer, Sean turned on his heel and the blackness took him in.

"Sean, don't leave... I don't understand, please...," William called into the dark. No answer returned to him. He pulled the quilt tightly around, and allowed himself to collapse to his side. He buried his face in his arm and cried like a child, feeling the full burden of the loss of his brother all over again until at last, he drifted into a deep, dreamless sleep.

As the wind mingled through the trees with the coming of the dawn, it brought with it the promise of a gloriously warm spring day. The sun broke through the mists of rising dew, shrouding the forest in a sparkling veil. A lone sunbeam caught in the crook of a tree, sending a spear of light that fell directly into Ian's half-opened eyes. He blinked back the assault, then turned onto his back and yawned. He stretched his arms above his head and winced at the stiffness in his shoulders. As he swam up out of the depths of his sleep, he slowly began to remember where he was. He opened his eyes fully and sat up startled, realizing it was fully dawn.

"Bloody hell!" He looked around the camp for his companions, furious for allowing himself to sleep through the night without taking his turn to watch. Anger turned to panic when he heard the contented snoring on the opposite side of the corpse of the campfire and realized

Ephraim had also been sleeping, which meant the only one left to keep watch— "My God." He got to his feet and hurried to where Ephraim lay cradling his wine flask lovingly in his crossed arms. He nudged the vicar with his foot. "Ephraim! Wake up."

"Hmm? No, Josephine, it's too early—"

"Ephraim!" Ian shook the older man out of his stupor.

Ephraim swallowed a halted snore and turned a blank stare onto Ian, as he began to wake up. "Ian? Ah, good morning," he said, through a groggy yawn. He opened his eyes fully then looked up to Ian, and frowned. "What's wrong?"

"He's not here." Ian hauled Ephraim up by his shirt. The two stood, surveying the campsite. The only trace of William to be found was the chariot, which lay overturned where they had left him the previous evening, and drag marks in the earth leading away from it, ending abruptly four feet or so away from where Ian had spent the night sleeping. Ian knelt down, examining the tracks. He moved aside what he had first thought was a windswept pile of forest clutter, and dirt, then stopped, hand in mid swipe. The debris he had disturbed was red and sticky. Then he saw it. "My God."

"What is it?" Ephraim asked, craning over Ian's shoulder.

Ian slowly reached for the torn piece of bloodied leather and held it to his nose to be sure there was no mistake of what he'd found. He handed it slowly over his shoulder to Ephraim and stumbled into the forest to purge the contents of his stomach.

Chapter 4

March 1613
Lothlanne Castle, Lothian Scotland

S HE STOOD BEFORE the grand windows in Lord Ogham's throne room, surveying the landscape below. The sun sparkled off the Anlee as it meandered through the valley, carrying barges and smaller crafts from the seaport in Sutherland, to all points south. The traffic on the river seemed heavy today, and she smiled, thinking, *more trade routes than ever. And most no longer under Edward's thumb.* A long flat barge flying a flag bearing the two raptors of Sutherland pulled into a dock for inspection. She frowned at the sight. *Sutherland should be flying Ogham's colors by now. How Edward has managed to keep his fingers on that tenant for so long and after all this...*

She pulled the curtain closed and sulked away from the window toward a small wine cart that stood against the wall. Above the cart hung a portrait of a man with raven black hair and humorless green eyes. She poured herself some wine and tipped the glass toward the portrait, as if to raise a toast. *At least we prevented the little beast from actually ruling Sutherland as earl; did we not, my love? 'Twas a stroke of genius to bereft Edward of his chosen heir as you did. He has no choice now but to name our son successor to that title. After all, there's been no word nor trace to be found of her since we killed her wretched husband.* She took a sip, clutching the stem of the glass tightly between her fingers. *Still, I'm certain Edward must know where she is... I need to be certain—*

The door to the throne chamber swung open quietly. An elderly chamberlain spoke to her from the doorway, "My lady?"

"Yes, Chase? What is it?" she asked as she settled down with her drink into Ogham's gaudily opulent throne-like chair.

"The page you requested, my lady. He's ready for you." The chamberlain stepped aside to allow a young lad to enter the chamber. He carried a blank scroll, quill, and ink. He took several tentative steps toward her, then stopped.

"Come, come boy," she said, impatiently waving him toward the desk by the window. "I've want of your parchment. Chamberlain, leave us."

The chamberlain inclined his head politely, then stepped back through the doorway, closing it quietly. The page placed the parchment and quill onto the desk then looked up and asked in a timid voice, "Shall I scribe for you, m' lady?"

She looked up over the rim of the glass, and narrowed her eyes. "You think me incapable of writing, boy?"

His eyes grew wide, and the fear on his face pleased her, as he stammered, "N-nay, m' lady!"

She allowed a grin to hook one side of her mouth as she stood and walked toward the boy. She stopped close to him and looked down into his wide eyes and raised her brow. "Good," she said then sauntered to the desk and sat down.

The boy exhaled loudly then stood rigid when she looked up to him.

"Wait outside the door. Do not make me call you twice. Understand?"

"Aye!" The lad bowed briskly, then hurried to the door and opened it only enough to allow himself to slip through, closing it quickly behind him.

She chuckled under her breath, took another sip of her wine, then picked up the quill and dipped it into the inkwell. "Now then, how to write this..." She thought for a moment then set the quill in motion:

Dear Father, if I may be so bold as to address you as such after the grievous parting we endured. My heart has been heavy these six long years. I know I am partially to blame for the misunderstanding and do so wish to make amends. I know you do not approve of my marriage to my Lord Ogham and see him as your enemy, but I beg you please remember that I am, after all, your own flesh and blood. Perhaps it is too much to hope for, that you have mellowed in your anger toward me, but I pray you find a place in your heart to forgive me. I do so miss you and my dear sweet sister, Mehlyndia. It pains me deeply that I was not able to comfort her for her loss when William was taken in such a way. You must believe, by now, that it was Thomas and not I who brought such an unfortunate fate down upon the lad. You must see that my actions during his trial were not truly my own.

I am asking you allow me to visit Drumoak soon, Father, as I do not see how I can live with such grief as all this has burdened me with much longer. Perhaps you may even be ready to accept the son Thomas left me pregnant with, at his death, as your grandson, for he truly is. I've named him Edward in your honor. Please send a page with your reply.

Your loving daughter,

Bryndah.

She reread the words several times, then congratulated herself. "Nicely done." She sprinkled the ink with powder, rolled up the scroll and dribbled wax from the candle the pressed her signet ring on the seal.

"Page!" She called loudly. Then deliberately, before the lad could open the door, she called again. "Page, come!"

The boy skittered into the room and hurried to where she sat at the desk. "Yes, m' lady. Are you finished?"

"Of course I'm finished." She scowled at him, enjoying the discomfort in his eyes. "This is to be delivered by your own hand. Take it to Drumoak in Stonehaven. It is to be delivered to Lord Edward personally. Do not give it to a guard, a maid, a chamberlain, footman, or anyone other than the duke. Do you understand?"

The boy took the scroll with a shaking hand and tucked it into his tunic. "Aye, m' lady. To L-lord Edward at D-drumoak. No one else." He turned to leave, then stopped and looked at her quickly. "Is there anything more you wish of me?"

She stood and leaned over the desk. "Your skin if you fail me, boy; now go!"

She pointed toward the door. The lad wasted not another breath and raced from the chamber, leaving the door open as he left.

Bryndah picked up her glass and finished the last of the wine. "Good lad. Run. Run away, little one, run." She laughed out loud as the echoes of the page's footsteps faded away.

Castle Drumoak in Stonehaven

The streets of Stonehaven were a jumble of activity on this early spring morning. The winter had been forgiving this year and spring arrived early, bringing a boon of pre-summer flowers that young girls were selling from carts to the young men who had flocked to Stonehaven for the upcoming warrior games. The games would take place in another week and promised to be especially interesting this year. Several of the young men that would be competing for positions in Lord Edward's guard had grown up in Stonehaven and had at last reached the age of competition; among them, young Duncan Wilbrun.

Duncan grew up at Drumoak with his mother, Agnes. Duncan's father, Arthur Wilbrun, once the groomsman for the fine stables that were Lord Edward's pride, succumbed to a fever when Duncan was only two. His older brother Sean, who was fourteen at the time, became the man of the family. Duncan idolized his brother and wanted nothing more than to follow Sean's footsteps and become one of Edward's personal guardsmen. He was devastated when Sean was killed and made a personal vow that one day, he would fill his brother's empty place in Edward's guard.

Because Duncan was quite tall for his age and possessed of polite and gentlemanly manners, he was often mistaken to be far older than his fourteen years. He also bore more than a passing resemblance to his older brother. In fact, the taller he got, the more often his mother would stand back and stare, telling him: "If not for your brown eyes, and if I was nae your mother and knew better, I'd swear ye be Sean come back to us." Duncan would protest but secretly was pleased by the comparison.

Duncan found it curious, for many years, that Lord Edward made a place of honor on the gallery wall in the great hall for Sean. Though no one actually explained to Duncan about Sean's parentage, he was not a dull lad and eventually worked it out on his own. Sean may have carried the name Wilbrun but he had, in truth, been sired by Lord Edward's close friend and ally, Lord Henry Fylbrigge and not by Arthur Wilbrun— whom his mother was betrothed to at the time of Sean's birth. When Sean was killed, Edward saw fit to honor him by acknowledging his noble blood by having Sean's sword mounted in a place of pride, crossed over the sword of the only *other* man Duncan had ever idolized; William of Drumoak, Earl of Sutherland. The two swords hung under a portrait of William with along with a small bronze plaque that read:

The sons of Henry Fylbrigge, Earl of Aberdoir
William of Drumoak, Earl of Sutherland, 1587— 1607
Sir Sean Douglas Wilbrun,
Captain to the House of Sutherland, 1585— 1607
Requiescat in Pace

Not long before Sean died, William made a promise to Duncan that he would accept him as a foster son, to be trained for a place in his own guard at Sutherland. It was a promise that would never come to pass, as almost within the same breath that it was made, William was arrested. Duncan believed full heartedly in William's innocence. As far as he knew, William's death was nothing less than a murder that took place during his trial, and he now rested eternally in the crypt beneath Drumoak.

Duncan's memories of that terrible September were traumatic and yet vague. He lost four of the most important people in his life within a single week: his brother Sean, his friend William, the grandmotherly Elinor who had been his mother's closest friend, and the lass who he cared most for and had always been the one who he could go to with childish fears or joys, the young house maid named Laurel.

He was never told what became of Laurel and Elinor, he only knew they were gone. Agnes was close-mouthed about the entire event, hushing Duncan whenever he dared ask about it. The tales he heard in town or from the other servants were so far at odds from each other, he simply drew his own conclusions, choosing to believe the two women had gone to live in a far off country. Though deep down, he knew they were more than likely as dead as the sons of Henry Fylbrigge.

The only souvenir he kept of that terrible time was a little wooden sword that William gave to him for Christmas the year before they were all taken away. He kept the sword, with its intricately carved dragon and twine-wrapped hilt, on the wall in his bedchamber, displayed as proudly as the two that adorned the gallery wall. The good thing that came from that infamous September evening was that it was the last time a death-fire was lit in Stonehaven. Lord Edward saw to it that Bishop Dunkirk no longer went unchecked in his accusations of witchcraft or sorcery in Stonehaven, with each trial presided over by an impartial justice. That is not to say there were no longer any convictions— but public burnings were no longer a favored form of execution or entertainment in Stonehaven.

Curiously, it was the end of the fires that gave rise to the malicious tales surrounding William, and his alleged demonic affiliations. But like all the other rumors, that one, too, had several variations, so there again, Duncan preferred to draw his own conclusions and anyone who dared refer to William as *The Demon of Stonehaven* in Duncan's presence was sure to be hotly challenged.

As Duncan made his way through the crowded streets to the booth to sign up for the games, he was nearly knocked to his feet by a young page who was not watching his own steps.

"Slow down there, lad, where are you headed?" Duncan asked, as the page turned a startled look on him.

"D-Drumoak," the boy answered, catching his breath. "I'm to deliver a letter to Lord Edward— personally. Could you tell me how to find Drumoak Castle?"

"Well it be the only castle in town now, isn't it? The only way to miss it is if ye be blind," Duncan answered, pointing to the massive stone gate, not more than a hundred paces away.

The page looked where Duncan pointed, his face turning slightly pink.

Duncan clapped the lad on the shoulder and gave him a crooked grin. "I'm sorry, I didn't mean to embarrass you. M' name's Duncan. I'm Lord Edward's *personal* page at the moment; though soon enough, I hope to take a place in his guard." He motioned with his head toward the booth. "I was just on my way to sign that roster. Can't join the guard without first besting some rogue in the games, ye know. If you don't mind waiting a bit while I sign, I'll take ye straight away to the castle when I'm done."

The page nodded, knotting his brow, looking on the gates of the castle as if he believed them to be the very gates of hell. He swallowed hard, fidgeted with his tunic, removing the letter. He glanced up to Duncan, then to the castle again. The lad was clearly dreading crossing the gate into Drumoak.

"I'll take it to him if ye like, lad," Duncan offered, holding out his hand.

The page shook his head, stuffing the letter back into his tunic. "Th-thank you, no! My instructions are to give this to Lord Edward with my own hand. Will it take ye long to sign in? I'd like to be back on the road before d-dark."

Duncan looked over his shoulder toward the booth, then back to the skittish face of this young page. "Well, I suppose I've plenty of time to sign the roster later. Come on then, I'll take you to the castle now." He made a summoning gesture with his hand and the two headed toward the gates of Drumoak.

"Thank you, Sir—"

"Duncan. Just Duncan. I'm not a knight yet."

"Duncan," the page said, shyly.

"Do you have a name?"

"Matthew."

"Pleased to meet you, Matthew." Duncan smiled and extended a hand as they walked.

Matthew accepted Duncan's hand timidly, shook it once and released it quickly.

Duncan shook his head and laughed. "I must say, if I were half as nervous as you, Lord Edward would never have engaged me as his page. How old are you?"

"Ten, Sir— Uh, Duncan," Matthew answered, then went on quickly, stumbling over his words. "But I'm n-not nearly as n-nervous as you think. I'm sure if you had to endure taking orders from Lady Br-Bryndah of Lothlanne—"

Duncan stopped in his tracks and turned the boy to face him. "Bryndah of Lothlanne? Is that where the letter is from?"

Matthew nodded, then looked over his shoulder as if he were afraid of being overheard. He leaned forward and put a hand to the side of his mouth. "She's a d-devil that one. She'll cut me hands off at the elbows if I don't deliver this."

Duncan smirked, then leaned forward and matched Matthew's tone. "I know. Met her when I was a lad." He made a comical shudder. "Och! She's an ugly one. 'Twas a glad day at Drumoak when Edward put her out." He turned and began walking toward the gate again.

Matthew had to double his steps to keep up. "Have you been here *that* long?" he asked, then turned a fearful looking eye toward the gate as they approached it.

"I've been here my whole life," Duncan told him with a proud grin.

Matthew's eyes grew wide. Just as they were about to reach the gate, he came to a halting stop and stood staring at the massive entry.

"What's wrong with you?" Duncan asked when he realized Matthew was suddenly not walking beside him any longer. "I thought you were eager to deliver that letter."

"Well, it's just..." Matthew swallowed hard, then skittered to catch up to Duncan. "Isn't this where *he* was from?"

"Who?" Duncan asked, clenching his jaw. He had a good suspicion what was coming.

"The demon!" Matthew whispered. "You know, the one what couldn't be killed on account of the devil in him."

Duncan took a deep breath, fighting down the familiar wave of anger that came to him. *He's a child, and probably doesn't know differently than what he was told by that old hag, Bryndah.* He placed a hand on Matthew's shoulder and leaned down to look the boy in the eye. "If you're referring to William of Drumoak, then yes, he came from here. But I would not let Lord Edward hear you refer to him as a 'demon'."

"Wasn't he?" Matthew asked.

Duncan could tell the boy did not intend to be impudent, and that he was earnest in his question. "Of course not," Duncan answered with a sigh, then motioned Matthew to follow him. "Are you coming or not?"

Matthew took a tentative step forward and followed Duncan through the gates, then through the big main doors into the castle. When they entered the great hall, Duncan led him to the gallery wall and pointed to the portrait of William.

"Does that look like the face of a demon to you?"

Matthew tilted his head and wrinkled his brow. "That's William of Drumoak?"

"Aye, see the plaque? There's his name."

"But, he looks so... ordinary."

"Of course he does. He was!" Duncan laughed. "See the swords? This one belonged to my own brother, Sean. Now, you don't think I'd be proud to show you this if I believed my brother shared a father with a demon?"

Matthew finally showed the ghost of a smile on his timid face. "I suppose not." He turned quickly, eyes wide. "Does that mean William was *your* brother, Duncan?"

"No, lad. Sean was really only my half-brother. We come from different fathers, ye see. My own father, Arthur Wilbrun, was the groomsman here years past." He leaned forward, whispering, "I'd be thankful for ye to be gentlemanly and not ask how me mum come to bear the son of a nobleman."

Matthew blushed and looked down to his hands, whispering, "I understand, Duncan. My own mum wasn't wed to my father either. I don't even know his name."

Duncan patted the lad on the shoulder and smiled. "Well then, I shan't mention it again."

Matthew looked up and pointed out the lute that William held in the portrait, changing the subject back to William. "I've heard tales of that, as well."

"I'm sure you have." Duncan made a sour face and shook his head. "But before you ask, the answer is *no*. He did not use music to cast evil spells, sing people to death, or conjure flying dragons that stole babies in the night."

Matthew tried but failed to stifle a giggle. "You've convinced me, Duncan."

Duncan was relieved that the boy seemed to finally relax, and he was pleased to have set yet another misguided soul straight about the imagined demon of Stonehaven.

"Come on then. Lord Edward is probably in his solarium. Let's get that important letter delivered. Then I'll have just enough time to sign the roster for the games." He led the way across the white marble floor, then up the grand stairs with Matthew close on his heels.

"Thank you," Edward said, as he took the scroll from the

page. He scowled when he saw the seal in the wax, and let out a heavy sigh before he broke it and opened the letter. He scanned to the signature at the bottom, groaned, then rolled it again.

"Are you required to carry an answer back with you, lad?" he asked Matthew, keeping his voice as pleasant as possible. The boy seemed absolutely terrified and Edward attributed it to the likely threat of bodily harm Bryndah had made should he fail her.

"I was told only to d-deliver it directly to you, sir."

"Well then, you've done your task well." Edward smiled kindly to the boy, and he seemed to relax. "I shall require a day or so to think about my answer. Then you may carry it back." He looked up to Duncan, who stood quietly by the door. "Do you mind sharing your quarters with this lad for an evening or two?"

"My pleasure, m' lord," Duncan answered with his usual good-natured smile.

Edward returned the smile then gave Duncan a concerned look. "Have you signed the roster yet? Here I've kept you and time is growing short."

"Not yet. Matthew's mission seemed to take precedence. But there is still plenty of time to sign in."

"Well, I won't keep you any longer." As it happened often lately, Edward found himself impressed with Duncan's burst into manhood. There was no trace left of the imp, who only a few short years ago, had terrorized the corridors of Drumoak with his wooden sword on his imaginary dragon hunts. Edward could see that Duncan was eager to get out to that booth and sign up for the games, yet he had taken the time to lend a guiding hand to this frightfully jittery page. He could not help but compare the way Duncan behaved with Matthew with the gentle way Sean had persuaded an equally skittish William to come out of the barn when he had first arrived at Drumoak. *Good stock in the lad. Yes, the time has come. He'll be ready to travel soon.*

"You may go. Thank you for your help with our young friend, here."

Duncan bowed politely and motioned for Matthew to follow him from the room.

Edward held up a hand, a thought occurring to him. "One moment. On your way by the gate, please tell Sir Ewan to come see me right away."

"Aye, sire."

"Good luck with the roster, lad," Edward called as Duncan and Matthew left together.

He stood quietly, staring at the closed door, thumping the letter against his palm. *I suppose I should have expected to hear from her eventually.* He glanced up at the portrait of his wife that hung above his mantle. He spoke to the painting, as was his habit, as though the woman on the canvas could actually hear him. "Anne, my darling, so it begins again," he said, with a sigh and dropped himself into the chair by the fire and opened the letter to read it. "My God, she's produced an heir to the Fylbrigge line." He crumpled the parchment and tossed it onto the table. "That does pose a complication. I may need to call Mehlyndia back here sooner than I had planned."

A quiet rap on the door interrupted Edward's thoughts. "Come."

"You asked to see me?" Sir Ewan stood in the doorway.

"Yes, please; close the door, Ewan. Come sit with me." He went to his wine cabinet and poured two goblets of port, then brought them to the table and handed one to Ewan.

"Is something wrong, m' lord?" Ewan asked, accepting the cup.

"There may be," Edward answered, then shrugged. "Or not." He sat down in his customary seat at the head of the table.

Ewan McDonough was the last of the *inner circle,* as Edward had come to regard them, of William's contemporaries who remained in Stonehaven. The young sentry was a good friend who had been expected to take a post in Sutherland. More importantly, he was one of the few to take part in the deception that had saved William after his trial. Other than Edward, Ewan was the only soul in Stonehaven who knew that William was not dead in the crypt, but alive and living in New France with Mehlyndia and their son.

Edward retrieved the crumpled letter and smoothed it out on the table, then handed it to Ewan. "Read this."

Ewan read, then reread, then handed the letter back to Edward. "You don't believe her contrition, do you?"

"As much as I believe mules and goats make unicorns," Edward scoffed, then folded the letter. "She's obviously more interested in learning Mehlyndia's whereabouts than in 'making amends' for old wounds."

"To what end?"

"To level the field, Ewan. She's produced a Fylbrigge heir. By the terms of Henry's trust that I agreed to— should none of his sons survive, his fortune was to pass to the eldest grandson, and frankly, I'm not sure which child that would be— Melly's Seany or this boy Bryndah so thoughtfully named after me."

"Surely, you have some say," Ewan argued, clearly disgusted with Bryndah's letter. "After all, the estate in Aberdoir reverted to you along with the rest of the Fylbrigge fortune when Thomas was killed. Regardless of which child is older, it's only right that it go to Will's son over Thomas's."

"Aberdoir is less an issue since Ogham claimed it upon their marriage—not that I rule out reclaiming it eventually. But, it's not just Aberdoir and the Fylbrigge coffer that Bryndah is after, Ewan," Edward sighed and tossed the letter indifferently across the table. "She is keenly aware of the fact that I am in need of an heir. As far as I know, Mehlyndia's pregnancy was not public knowledge— at least, I've never heard mention of it in any of the *legends*. So it's a fair assumption that Bryndah has no idea of Seany's existence and assumes her own son would be my logical choice for an heir. But she's not one to leave anything to chance. That's her interest in Mehlyndia. To be certain there are no others who may lay claim of a lineage."

"The dragon is hunting," Ewan muttered under his breath.

"Excuse me?" Edward asked.

"Forgive me," Ewan said, looking up. "It's what Will used to call her. *The dragon.*"

"Ah." Edward laughed under his breath. "He did indeed." He took a drink of the port and sat back in the chair, staring silently for several moments.

"What news is there from New France?" Ewan asked, breaking the silence.

"The ships are slow, Ewan; I get news only twice in a year. In the spring and fall," Edward answered, still staring. "The letters I received this past week are dated months ago." He stood and went to his desk. He opened the small drawer under the writing surface and withdrew a thick bundle of parchment. He brought it to the table and sat down again.

"They have finally built a proper house, I hear. Seany is growing strong and well. Mehlyndia was expecting another when this was written in September. She must have birthed the new bairn by now," he said with a wistful smile, thinking about the grandchildren he had never seen. He shuffled through the letters, scanning another one. "Mehlyndia tells me pretty things of how lovely life is," he said with a chuckle. "She wouldn't tell me she was too hot if her dress was on fire, but Simon and Prissy seem equally happy, so I'm inclined to believe her if she says she is. Elinor, too, seems content in her new life, though she bemoans the loss of her favorite cooking kettle." He laughed and handed the letters to Ewan. "Remind me to include that kettle in the manifest for the next outbound ship."

"Aye," Ewan smiled, skimming through the letters. "They plan to sail within a fortnight. Expecting to arrive in New France by mid-May."

Edward nodded. "Good."

Ewan flipped through the letters, reading little bits here and there, then paused at Ian's latest update. A crease crossed his brow as he read the letter more thoroughly. "Will has been asking questions. He's beginning to remember?"

Edward took the letter from him and reread it himself, then laid it flat on the top of the stack. "It seems he has been having dreams, and flashes of memories. That was last September. God knows what he's recalled since then." Edward sighed. "From what Ian writes, even in his infirmity, William is still the same bold, stubborn, determined man he always was, and I'm certain once the pieces fall back into place for him, he'll want to come home. But how can I call him back safely? With all the tales of the 'demon that wouldn't die' still being bandied about, invalid or not, if word got out he was still alive, he'd be staked without trial the first instance he was recognized! The hysterics would be so fierce that I don't think I would be able to stop them." He shook his head. "I've done him no favors in allowing the rumors to perpetuate."

"Forgive me, m' lord," Ewan said, tentatively. "But I fail to see how you could possibly have stopped the tales from spreading. They took flight the minute the trial ended and nothing short of Gabriel's trumpet would stop them."

"You're right. But I must take blame somewhere." Edward gave Ewan a pat on the shoulder and a smile that faded as quickly as it had appeared. "Still, William is entitled to know the truth now, if he truly is beginning to remember." He flopped back in his chair and rubbed his weary eyes with his hand. "It seems I've no choice but to acknowledge little Seany as soon as possible, before Bryndah has a chance to cast her venom. They need to know what she's up to." He took a heavy breath and looked Ewan in the eye, "I've got to bring them home."

"How do you propose to do that?"

Edward turned his hands palms up, at a loss for an answer. "That's the question, Ewan."

~

"The roster is full, lad. You'll have to come back next year." The grizzled old soldier who was taking the names indifferently rolled up the scrolls and tucked them under his arm. He stood, gathering the quills and ink, and tucked them into a satchel, not giving another look to Duncan.

"But you knew I was planning to sign up," Duncan argued, tapping the man on the shoulder.

"I'm sorry, lad, it's first come, first served." The soldier shrugged as he continued to pack up his belongings. "I had to turn down others, ye not alone."

"But—" Duncan began to argue. The man gave him a look that told him that he had lost the battle; best retreat with his dignity intact. He threw his hands in the air in defeat.

"Look on the bright side," the soldier said. "You'll have a full year to be better prepared, and next year, you'll know to be first in line." He made an unsympathetic smirk, then walked away.

"Right," Duncan said under his breath, watching him go. "If I wasn't ready now, I would have had no business signing in in the first place; now, would I!" *Stubborn sot!*

"I'm sorry, Duncan, it's m-my fault."

Matthew had followed him out to the booth and now stood away, looking miserable. Duncan didn't know whether to laugh or feel sorry for the pathetic look on Matthew's face.

"No, it wasn't your fault," Duncan assured him, though he did place some of the blame on the boy. "I should have signed in before I took you to see Edward."

"But now you'll have to wait a whole year."

Duncan said nothing, not wanting to vent his frustrations

on Matthew. *A year. Another damned year. Sean bested the lot of them when he was fourteen.* He took a breath, then released it slowly and gestured for Matthew to follow him back to Drumoak.

"What are you going to do now?" Matthew asked, falling into step, taking extra wide strides to match Duncan's long legs.

Duncan shrugged. "Go home and prepare for next year." He tried to keep the angry edge from his voice, but Matthew shrunk away anyhow. He forced himself to smile. "And they'll be the worse for the extra training that I'll have. You wait and see."

Matthew smiled. "I'm sure of it. I bet you could win all the competitions this year!"

"You think so, do you?"

Duncan laughed, wondering what he had done to deserve Matthew's admiration, though he could not deny to himself that it pleased him. Matthew blushed, and grinned shyly. Duncan put a friendly hand on the boy's shoulder and hurried him along.

"Well, nothing more to be done about it. I'd better let Lord Edward know."

It was late in the afternoon, the following day, before Edward was satisfied with the answer he would send to Bryndah. He read, again, the response he and Ewan had labored over. The letter was short, and to the point:

Lady Lothlane, I see no need for you to present yourself at Drumoak. However, I am willing to consider acknowledging your son if you agree to send him to me immediately for fostering.

I have instructed the page who will deliver this letter to return within a day, and that he be accompanied only by your son. Should the page return alone, I will assume you have declined the offer and I shall not expect further correspondences from you.

He signed it formally, "Edward of Drumoak, Duke of Stonehaven," then folded it carefully and applied the wax and sealed it with the eagle crest, which was his designation.

"Do you think she will agree to send you her son for fostering?" Ewan asked.

"Oh, she'll agree. I've no doubt," Edward answered with a smug smile. "Her maternal instincts only go as far as her purse strings." He frowned looking down at the letter. "And I've a suspicion I'll be doing the lad a kindness to call him away from her."

A troubled look crossed Ewan's face.

"You don't agree?" Edward asked.

"Oh, yes of course... it would be a kindness. It's just... you're not seriously going to consider him as your heir, are you?"

Edward let out a heavy breath, then rested his chin in his hand. "No. But she doesn't need to know that. Better that she believes I'm considering her son. Perhaps then she'll lay to rest her search for Mehlyndia."

"We can only hope," Ewan replied, then stood and walked toward the door. "I've rounds to make, m' lord, if you have no further need of me, I'd like to take my leave now."

"By all means. Thank you, Ewan."

Ewan bowed briefly then turned to leave. As he opened the door, he was met by Duncan and Matthew. "Ah, your timing is perfect. I believe Lord Edward is ready for you. Good day to you." He bowed again to Edward then walked through the doorway.

Duncan smiled in greeting as Ewan walked past him, then turned his attention to Edward. "You sent for me, m' lord?"

"Ah, come in." Edward stood and waved Duncan to join him. "I've a task for you, Duncan."

"Aye, sir?" Duncan asked with an eagerness that pleased Edward.

"I'm sending you to Lothian," Edward answered, holding out the letter for Duncan to take.

"Lothian?" Duncan's eyes flared with a trace of excitement. It would be his first mission out of Edward's county. "When do I leave?" He took the scroll and tucked it into his tunic.

"It's a day's journey," Edward told him. "Leave at first light tomorrow, and you are to go alone. Stay on the main roads once you cross out of my territories. If you're harassed by any of Ogham's road warriors, show them the seal on this letter and tell them Lady Bryndah is expecting you. That should keep you safe."

"Understood," Duncan said with a mature, formal air, then looked up suddenly with a concerned crease in his brow.

"Is something wrong?"

"No, but... what of..." Duncan asked, giving a nod toward Matthew. "Shouldn't he come with me?"

Edward smiled and gestured to Matthew to step closer to him. The haunted look in the boy's eyes and his timidity had touched a tender place inside him that simply reminded him of William at that age. Edward still harbored a gnawing regret that he had not called William to Drumoak at an early age, rather than leave him with Bryndah until he was twelve. Though William had thrived once settled at Drumoak, he had been scarred— body, mind and spirit— from his years in Aberdoir. It was for this reason that Edward was moved to extend the offer to foster Bryndah's young son and to offer refuge, in the guise of employment, to this young page.

Matthew hesitantly took a step toward Edward.

"Do you have family in Lothian, lad?" Edward asked, in as friendly a tone as possible.

"M-my mother, m' lord," Matthew answered quietly. "She is in service as young Edward's nursemaid."

"I see," Edward stroked his chin in thought. *Surely the boy would want to return to his mother. Or perhaps...* "She's nursemaid to Lady Bryndah's son?" He smiled as inspiration hit him.

Matthew nodded.

"Duncan, hand me back that letter for a moment," Edward said, smiling at the thought that crossed his mind. Duncan handed Edward the scroll. He broke the seal and unrolled the letter, and reread it. He looked up at Matthew and winked, "Allow me a moment to rewrite this."

Edward retrieved a fresh piece of parchment and rewrote the letter verbatim with the exception of one added sentence:

... that he be accompanied only by your son and his nursemaid.

Satisfied with the revision, Edward read the letter aloud, then rolled and sealed it, and handed it back to Duncan. Matthew's eyes grew wide and Edward could see the light of understanding brighten the boy's face.

He placed a fatherly hand on Matthew's shoulder and said, "It would be my honor if you would consent to accept service at Drumoak, Matthew. You understand that Lady Bryndah may not consent to send your mother along with the child. The choice is yours, of course, if you wish to stay or return to Lothian, should your mother not return with Duncan."

Matthew stared up to Edward, a mixed look of disbelief and gratitude on his face. "Thank you, my lord," he said quietly. "It would be my honor to accept service here."

Duncan grinned and clapped Matthew on the back. "Congratulations, little mate."

Edward laughed and mussed the boy's hair. "Good then. You shall be a fine successor to Duncan as my page." He looked up at Duncan. "If that suits you, young man."

"Aye, it does," Duncan replied still grinning, then made a self-deprecating shrug and laughed. "If he doesn't mind waiting another year to take on the reins. Seems I've extended my tenure as your page at least that long, m' lord, by missing the games this year."

"You carry this to Lothian and back, and I've a hunch the wait will not be as long as you think," Edward said, with a sudden seriousness in his voice.

"My lord?" Duncan asked, with a guarded hopefulness in his eyes.

"Upon your return, we have much to discuss, lad," was all Edward would say, then he gestured to the door. "You two get some rest. Duncan, I expect you to be on the road with first light. Godspeed."

"Thank you, sir." Duncan bowed briskly before he and Matthew left the suite, closing the door behind them.

Chapter 5

DUNCAN AWOKE FAR earlier than he needed to begin his first mission away from Drumoak, as his excitement at the prospect of earning an early post in Edward's guard had robbed him of a full night's sleep. Being fully awake at two o'clock, he gave up trying to go back to sleep when he heard the chimes ring three. The first full moon of spring shone bright through the window, allowing Duncan to see Matthew sleeping peacefully on a little cot on the far side of the room. Matthew's breathing was light and steady, and Duncan was pleased to see him resting so well. His first night in Drumoak, Matthew had tossed and muttered in his sleep half the night, the next day awakening with circles under his eyes. Duncan attributed Matthew's now contented sleep to his relief at not being sent back to Lothlanne.

He slipped out of his bed and dressed himself quietly in the moonlight, being careful not to wake Matthew. Along with his anticipation for his first away mission came a certain sense of righteousness that he would be instrumental in helping this lad find a new life away from Lady Bryndah and Lord Ogham. Though his own memories were childish ones, he remembered enough about Bryndah to know she must be the most disagreeable woman on God's good Earth. Duncan clearly remembered watching from the kitchen as his brother and his mates, Simon and Ewan, carried her and her now deceased first husband, Thomas, bodily out of the castle on the day Lord Edward had banished them. The shrill sound of her shrieking and the fiery glare in her eyes, visited more than one bad dream to his sleep, though he would never admit that to anyone. He thought it only appropriate that, around Drumoak, she was commonly referred to by the name William gave her: 'the dragon'.

It seemed to Duncan that if Bryndah was trying to match the foulness of her first husband, she could not have chosen a more appropriate successor than Ogham. The man was generally reviled among the people of Stonehaven, but no more so than by the members of the household at Drumoak. After all, it was Ogham who put the events in motion that ultimately led to the loss of those Duncan held dear by sending an assassin after William on the very day he and Mehlyndia married. He could well imagine that the combination of Bryndah and Ogham would be enough to make the most stout-of-heart jittery, let alone this timid young boy.

"No more worries about her, little mate. I'll see to it your mum comes back with me, whether the dragon gives her blessing or not." He placed a fist to his chest in a gesture of promise to the sleeping Matthew.

Matthew stirred and rolled over, then blinked open his eyes. "Are you leaving all ready?" he asked through a yawn.

"I didn't mean to wake you, mate. I'm sorry," Duncan said quietly, as he pulled on his boots. "Go back to sleep."

"I want to see you off." Matthew pushed himself up to sit. Drawing his knees up, he wrapped his arms around his legs and rested his chin on his kneecaps. "You're leaving early, aren't you? It won't be light for hours."

"I'm not leaving yet. I'm just getting ready." He shrugged, then stood to find a match to light the lantern in his chamber. "I suppose I don't have to do it in the dark so long as we're both awake." He found the match in the holder on his night table and lit the lantern, filling the room with a soft yellow glow. He knelt and reached under the bed for the leather traveling pack he stashed under there, and tossed it onto his unmade bed. "I'll only be gone one night, two at most, so I won't need much more than a change of clothes."

"Just don't forget that letter," Matthew said with a sly smirk.

"Not likely," Duncan replied and laughed. He picked up the letter from his night table and held it out to show Matthew. "See? It's getting packed right here." He tucked it into his tunic and gave it a pat through the fabric.

Matthew nodded, keeping his eyes on Duncan's tunic. A deep furrow appeared between his brows. "It's a pity you'll have to bring *him* back as well as my mum," he said under his breath.

Duncan wondered if he had meant to say it aloud. "Who?"

Matthew looked up, and shook his head. "Oh, no one."

Duncan sat on the edge of Matthew's cot and looked the lad in the eye. "Is there something I should know about Edward's grandson?"

Matthew looked at him wide-eyed, then looked away.

Duncan tapped him on the knee to make him look back. "You've no fear to speak your mind here, little mate."

Matthew set his jaw. "He's a devil."

"The boy?" Duncan asked, startled by the fierce look in

Matthew's eye. "He can't be more than six. How bad can he be?"

"Bad." Matthew scowled, looking past Duncan. "My mother is responsible for him, and when he doesn't get his way, he does horrible things, then blames them on me! Lady Bryndah never believes my mum when she says the boy is lying, and it's always me who takes his punishments." Closing his eyes tight, he buried his face on his knees, hiding away from Duncan.

"Don't ye have a worry, now. Lord Edward will have none of that, here," Duncan reassured him, placing a gentle hand on the boy's back. "And he won't be apt to believe the whelp's lies either. He'll put it to right for you... and your mum, Matthew. Trust me."

Matthew nodded his head while keeping his face buried. Duncan could feel the boy shake, making him even more determined than he was before to bring the lad's mother back with him. He toyed with the notion of waking Edward to tell him what Matthew had said about the boy he was to retrieve, but decided to keep it to himself.

"Matthew, what is your mum's name? And what does she look like? I'd better be sure I bring the right woman back with me."

Matthew looked up and brushed his face with his hands. "Her name is Annlise and she's quite pretty."

"I'm sure she is. But what does she look like? It would be just like Bryndah to send me back with some other woman just to spite Edward's orders. I want to be absolutely positive."

Matthew's face turned red and the angry crease returned to his brow. "You're right, B-Bryndah is devil enough to do that." He took a breath and continued slowly. "My mother is small for a grown up lady. She's got long light ginger hair she always wears in braids wrapped up around her head. Her eyes are bright blue, and she has a small mole on her jaw, just below her left ear."

"Good, that will be helpful. Is there anything else? Anything special she wears or about the way she walks?"

Matthew thought for a moment, then looked up excited. "Around her neck, aye! She wears a little silver trinket in the shape of a knot. I've never seen her without it."

"That's perfect. Thank you. Now I'll be sure to know her." Duncan smiled broadly and gave Matthew a pat on the back. "I'll bring her back, little mate. With or without the whelp." He crossed his right fist over his chest again so Matthew could see it this time. "Knight's promise."

With the sun only moments from rising over the horizon, Duncan saddled Hawk, the stallion Sean once claimed as his favorite horse, and galloped away from of Stonehaven on the woodland road. Though Hawk was nine years old, he was still considered one the fastest and most prized of Edward's stable. Duncan would have liked to have ridden Cirrus, William's former mount, but the stallion had aged, and showed signs of going lame in the legs. He had been put out to stud, but it was apparent Cirrus would soon be put down. The groomsman suggested it gently to Edward only the week before, but Edward seemed reluctant and asked the groomsman to allow Cirrus to see one last springtime in the meadow. Duncan suspected Edward's reluctance to put the horse down had more to do with the fact he had been a gift to William, and all that Edward had left to remember his former heir by was the painting in the gallery and this horse. Duncan went over the route he would take to Lothlanne with Ewan, but made sure he had his map handy and ready, and obsessively checked the directions several times before he turned onto the road that would lead him away from Edward's territory. He was pleased with his progress and grateful for the warm traveling weather he'd been blessed with as he passed the morning portion of his journey.

At noon, he led Hawk to a small stream and dismounted, tossing the reins over a nearby sapling. He settled down on a large boulder, opened the traveling pack, and removed a hunk of cheese, some bread for himself, and an apple he had brought along for Hawk. He used the dirk he kept on his belt to cut the apple into two halves, then held it, flat palmed, to the horse. Hawk made a contented nicker and bobbed his head as if in gratitude as he chomped the apple. "You're more than welcome." Duncan chuckled and stroked the horse's neck.

He pulled Ewan's map from his tunic and traced the route with the tip of the dirk. "Now then, let's see just how much further this place is. We left Garioch Road here," he told the horse, as though it understood, then looked back toward the road. "We should be finding the markers for Lothian not more than a mile along this road. We'll be at Lothlanne hours before sundown." *And hopefully back on the road by then as well.* He realized that once out of Edward's territory, he would be away from his protectorates and as one of Edward's representatives, he was fair game for any of Ogham's soldiers. He subconsciously patted the letter in his tunic, remembering it bore Edward's seal and was addressed to Lady Bryndah, and how the duke had promised it would serve as protection. "I hope he's right." He frowned at the dirk in his hand, wishing he had had the forethought to 'borrow' his brother's sword from the wall, before he had set out.

Hawk snorted as if to agree with Duncan's musings and impatiently rattled the reins. Duncan laughed and got back to his feet. "Aye, Hawk, we're going. I've no wish to dally in Lothian County longer than 'tis necessary." He slid the dirk back into his belt, folded the flap on his pack and hung it on the saddle, then mounted and turned Hawk back toward the road. Minutes later, he galloped past the granite marker indicating he had just left Edward's territory for the first time in his life.

"Sit, Bryndah. You'll wear a path in the carpet."

Bryndah stopped her pacing and turned a rueful eye on her husband, who sat slouching in the cushioned chair of her private chambers, a half-empty wine bottle dangling from his fingers and a glazed cast in his half-open eyes. She gave him a disgusted sneer. *He's not half the man Thomas was,* she thought, as for the thousandth time she drew a mental comparison of her husbands. *Who would have imagined, the almighty, malevolent, Lord Ogham of Lothlanne, in reality is nothing more than a flaccid, feeble-minded, lecherous old sot with no more backbone than a tree slug.* "I'll pace if I choose," she said with a slight hiss, then went to the big window and threw aside the curtain, flooding the chamber with sunlight.

Ogham groaned and shaded his eyes with his empty hand. "Mus' you do that?" He took a long drink from the bottle, then dropped it to the floor next to the chair, the remainder of wine flowed out like blood onto the carpet. His eye's blinked once before the snoring began.

Bryndah stormed across the room. "Wake up, wretch!" She grabbed him by the chin and shook his face.

Ogham opened his eyes, and growled, seizing her wrist with his huge right hand. "You dare speak to me such, woman? I should remind you who your lord is."

Even in this drunken state he displayed an impressive amount of strength in the way he squeezed her wrist. Bryndah was well aware he was capable of snapping her arm like a twig if he chose. She also knew he dared not think of it.

"Break it if you wish, *my lord*," she said with a threatening grin. "But be prepared to learn what it means to cross me."

They locked eyes, challenging one another to be the first to look away, until Ogham's scowl slowly transformed into a salacious, almost hungry, smirk. He tightened his grip on her wrist and got to his feet so quickly she was almost knocked off her own. Without taking his eyes from her, he drew her hand to his mouth and kissed her palm before releasing it. She recognized the signs. His mood was amorous not confrontational though, she mused, it would be difficult for an unwitting observer to know the difference. *This is well then. He'll be far easier to control this way.* He reached for her but she deftly avoided his embrace by twirling on her heel and slinking off behind him.

"Are you to refuse me?" he asked, still maintaining his sickening grin.

"Only for as long as you behave as a tosspot, my lord." She laughed. "I would prefer you be aware of who you are abed with when I come to you. In your current state, you would not recognize your wife over the stable boy."

His face turned scarlet and the grin melted into a frown. "Perhaps that is so because there is little to compare between you and the stable boy."

"Enough," she said, dismissing the conversation as she returned to the window and looked out. Ogham made a disinterested snort in her direction and returned to his chair.

"What are you waiting for, anyway?"

"It's been four days since I sent the page to Drumoak," she answered, without looking at him. "I know my father well enough that he would not allow so much time to pass without an answer." She looked over her shoulder and grinned smugly. "I should think you'd be pleased to know at least *one* of us is taking an interest in expanding your fortunes."

"And you think fawning for your father's forgiveness is the way to expand my fortunes?" He laughed with an incredulous snort. "He'll sooner burn Stonehaven to the ground than take you back to Drumoak."

"'Tis true enough, what you say. But you forget, Ogham, he is in need of an heir, and my son— *our son*— is the only male from his blood who lives. Surely he will take some interest in that fact."

"Since when does a line of blood interest Edward in his choice of an heir?" Ogham scoffed. "The demon he chose before was not of his blood."

"He was married to my sister," she reminded him. "And my father possessed a soft spot in his heart for William that I still fail to understand."

"The softness is in his head, not his heart," Ogham answered with a laugh.

"Agreed." She joined in with a mirthless laugh of her own. "I suspect that soft spot still exists in him. Particularly where Mehlyndia is concerned. Should she suddenly emerge from the mists she is hiding in, Edward will not hesitate to name whatever progeny she produces as his heir. Regardless of whom she may choose to mate with."

"Are you so certain Edward will even consider our little Ned as an heir?"

"No," she admitted and turned back to look out the window. "But it is a way to begin. Stonehaven, Sutherland, Aberdoir, and the rest of the Fylbrigge fortune, which should have rightfully gone to Thomas, shall come to be mine— ours— through *our* son. I will not rest until I find Mehlyndia and make certain she poses no threat."

"*Your* son, Bryndah," Ogham corrected her. "No Fylbrigge spawn came from my loins."

She shot a furious glare at him. "You know as well as I, he is your son. It was only a ruse that I pled belly after I was accused of attempting to murder William. You were more than willing to accommodate me in my deception as I recall. But a woman remembers conception, Ogham, especially when it takes place in a prison tower! Why must you insist that Ned is Thomas's son?"

"All I need do is look at him!" Ogham bellowed and was on his feet, crossing the room to her. "He's got those damned green eyes I've only ever seen on a Fylbrigge."

"If it be his green eyes you're sure make him a Fylbrigge, perhaps you should look closer into mine!" she countered, opening her eyes as wide as possible. Though her eyes were not nearly as green as her son's or Thomas's for that matter, they were still a brownish sort of green; enough to cast that shred of doubt of her son's true parentage. But it was Ned's green eyes that she was sure would convince Edward that he truly was Thomas's son and therefore, the only rightful heir to the Fylbrigge's family fortune, which Edward held in trust. "You should be pleased and reassured that at least you know you're *capable* of producing progeny. I'm sure you'd produce more if you would choose my bed over that of a pretty stable boy more often." She laughed, knowing he would not challenge her on that accusation.

"You're too old to bear again anyway," was all he said, then returned to his chair, thus ending the argument.

"Is that the worst you can say?" She cackled and returned to her vigil by the window. She narrowed her eyes against the glare of the sun when she saw movement on the road that led to the castle. She quickly retrieved a spyglass she kept on the table near the window and peered out toward the lone rider. He was wearing the accouterments of a page and the colors were unmistakably those of her father's house. "An answer," she said, hopefully. "He's sent a page." She gave only a passing thought to the fact it wasn't the same page she had sent away, the one she could never remember his name but enjoyed terrifying all the same.

Ogham joined her at the window and took the spyglass from her and looked out for himself. He looked over the glass as if to double check what he was seeing, then again through the spyglass. "It can't possibly be who it looks—"

"Who?" Bryndah asked, confused, snatching the glass away.

"Sean Wilbrun!" Ogham said, watching the page draw closer to the castle gates. "I thought him long dead."

Bryndah examined the rider closely. "Look again, Ogham. Sean was a sentry. That is merely a young page. Although I admit, he does bear a striking resemblance— of course, it's the younger brother. His name is Durvin, or Duffland, or Dimwit or such," she said with a muffled laugh as she realized who was approaching. "My, my, how the child has grown." *The last time I saw him, he called me an ugly old lady. I wonder if remembers that... or if he is aware that I remember.*

"Well, if he be a Wilbrun, then he surely be from Drumoak as you expected. You know Edward better than I gave you credit. Let's see what he has to say, shall we?"

Ogham extended his arm and the two left the room together.

The sentry at the gate of Lothlanne held up his sword in a threatening posture as Duncan approached him. "What colors be you wearing, boy?"

Duncan swallowed hard before he answered, fully expecting this sort of greeting. He reached into his tunic and withdrew the letter bearing Edward's seal, and mustering up the most confident sounding voice he owned, he replied, "I've been sent from Stonehaven. Lady Bryndah is expecting this message from Lord Edward." He held up the scroll to show the sentry.

The sentry gave Duncan a wary look and motioned with his sword for him to dismount. Duncan obliged, dismounting slowly, keeping as casual an air as he could about him.

"Give it here, I'll take it." The sentry held out a hand for the scroll.

"I'm to deliver it personally to Lady Bryndah," Duncan informed him, coolly.

The man raised a brow and took a threatening step forward. "Do not defy me, boy. I decide who it is who enters through these gates. And no puppet of Edward of Stonehaven shall—"

"Stand down, Sir Angus."

The sentry spun on his heel. An elderly man, dressed formally in the vestments of a chamberlain, had come from inside the castle and was approaching with a mixed look of irritation and purpose on his face. Sir Angus spared a disapproving sneer at Duncan, then lowered his sword and nodded to the older man.

The chamberlain approached Duncan with a far less confrontational demeanor than the sentry had used. He bowed his head briefly for a moment before speaking. "You have been sent from Drumoak?"

"Aye, sir. I bear a letter from Lord Edward," Duncan answered, matching the chamberlain's formal tone.

"You've been expected," the chamberlain said. "What is your name?"

"Duncan Wilbrun," he bowed politely. "I am Lord Edward's personal page."

The chamberlain glanced to Hawk and then looked at the sentry, made a motion with his head toward the horse. "Sir Angus, please summon the groomsman to see to this horse. See that he is watered. It is a long journey from Stonehaven; I'm sure he requires rest."

"Aye." Angus muttered, then reached for Hawk's bridle.

Duncan instinctually closed his hand tightly around the reins.

Angus raised his brow and tilted his head with an impatient scowl. "I've not all day, boy. D' ye wish ye horse tended or would ye prefer he be left to wander off into the forest?"

Feeling slightly foolish for his paranoia, yet still not completely comfortable in relinquishing control of his horse to this ill-tempered sentry, Duncan reluctantly released his grip. "Thank you," he said, tightlipped, hoping the heat he felt rising to his cheeks did not show. "I expect I'll be leaving promptly once I've made this delivery. Where shall I find Hawk when I'm ready to go?"

"Chamberlain will send the groomsman to bring him around for you," Angus answered with a disinterested air as he led Hawk through the gate.

Duncan looked in the direction they walked, making a note of the location of the stable yard he could see just beyond the wall of the castle.

"Follow me." The chamberlain said, then turned and began a brisk walk toward the castle.

Duncan followed, matching the quick stride of the elderly man, somewhat astonished at the pace the man set. *He's in a bit of a hurry, isn't he!* Once inside the big doors, the chamberlain led Duncan to a small alcove off the foyer that was set apart by a thick velvet drapery. He motioned to a chair set next to a small table bearing a silver pitcher and goblet.

"Please sit here. There is water in the pitcher, please help yourself if you wish."

"Thank you," Duncan said, but did not reach for the water as he'd heard too many retellings of how Lady Bryndah had nearly killed William by dropping poison in his drinking water, and though he thought it unlikely this water was similarly *enhanced*, he thought it best to refuse the offer.

The formal, authoritative manner the chamberlain had possessed by the gate seemed to dissolve slightly, now that they were within the walls of the castle. In fact, to Duncan's eye, he seemed somewhat nervous, looking back over his shoulder, as though he expected someone to be listening. Duncan jumped slightly when the chamberlain turned abruptly and yanked the draperies, poking his head through and glancing side to side before closing them completely. He spun on his heel and leaned close.

"Where is Matthew?" the chamberlain asked, in a hushed voice that Duncan had to strain to hear.

For a moment, Duncan did not want to answer, but the look of concern in the man's eyes could not be mistaken for anything but true worry. "He's safe, at Drumoak," Duncan said, as quietly as the chamberlain had spoken.

The man placed a hand on his chest, crossed himself, and exhaled loudly. "Thank God." He shook his head, then turned a surprisingly warm smile on Duncan. "Thank you. His poor mother has been beside herself with worry since he's been gone longer than expected. I shall be pleased to tell her he is well. He'll be home soon then?"

"Sir, he is not planning to return, he's been offered a post at Drumoak."

The chamberlain's eyes opened wide. "What?" He said, in an astonished whisper, as a look of distress crossed his eyes.

"But this is his... his mother will be devastated if..."

Duncan spoke quickly to reassure the man, "She needn't fear, sir. I've orders to bring her back with me. Lord Edward has requested the child, young Edward, be sent to him for fostering immediately and that he be accompanied by his nurse."

The chamberlain smiled hesitantly, then looked away. "They'll never allow it. Ogham would not send a pig to be fostered at Drumoak, let alone his son."

Ogham's son? So she is playing games. Duncan set his jaw in determination. "I made a promise to Matthew that I intend to keep. With or without the child, I shall take her with me." The gratitude in the chamberlain's eyes was all Duncan needed for encouragement and to feel safe with the man. "Will you help me?"

"Tell me again." The man took Duncan's hand in both of his and looked him in the eye. "You swear it is so? Matthew is well?"

"I swear it... sir, how may I address you?"

"My name is Quentin Chase. I'm Matthew's grandfather. My daughter Annlise is his mother, and I shall gladly offer my last breath to have the both of them safely away from this place, and those—" He gave Duncan's hand a squeeze. "I've no reason to trust you, lad, but I feel as though I do."

Duncan stood and patted the man on the upper arm. "Thank you. I feel the same." He released Quentin's arm and withdrew the letter from his tunic again. "My purpose is to deliver this, and be on my way *with* Annlise before nightfall. I've a fear my exit will need to be in haste. She'll have to be ready and with me, and my horse must be saddled and waiting." He creased his brow for a moment as it occurred to him that Annlise would also require transport. "Can you provide a second horse?"

"I'll see what I can do without raising suspicion," Quentin nodded resolutely. "Now, I'll bring you to the drawing chamber and announce to Lady Bryndah your arrival. Follow my lead, agreed?"

"Agreed."

Quentin made a wry smile and leaned forward. "I may even consider defecting with you."

Duncan grinned, pleased and relieved to have found an ally at Lothlanne. "You'll be more than welcome to do so, sir."

"Please, call me Quentin. I've a feeling we're going to be fast friends."

"Quentin, then." Duncan shook Quentin's hand firmly.

Quentin opened the curtains slowly, again making his side-to-side survey of the foyer before opening them fully. He reassumed his formal countenance, walking stiff-backed and silent as he led Duncan to the drawing chamber. "Please, wait here," he said, stodgily.

"Thank you, chamberlain," Duncan bowed.

Quentin backed out of the door, closing it as he left.

Duncan took a long breath and looked about the ornately decorated chamber. On the hearth wall, made of river stones that rose to the vaulted ceiling, an enormous sculpture of an eagle, wings spread and talons flayed, its beak open in a silent scream, seemed to be diving off the wall ready to tear the flesh from whatever unfortunate prey lay in its path. Around the room, hanging from wrought iron pikes, the banners of Ogham's territories adorned the walls. Duncan frowned at the presence of the banner of Aberdoir, a tenant that, until recently, had been under Edward's rule. Beneath the banner of Aberdoir hung a portrait of the last earl of that estate, a dour-faced man who Duncan recognized instantly as Thomas Fylbrigge, the man whose treachery had nearly brought Edward's dukedom to its knees, destroying William of Drumoak— Thomas's own brother— in the process. The sight of Thomas's face in the portrait sent a wave of anger over Duncan. He didn't know for sure, but had always harbored a suspicion that Thomas Fylbrigge had been directly responsible for Sean's death as well. *Bastard. He killed both his brothers.*

He turned his back on the wall with the portraits and surveyed the rest of the room. A large chair, perhaps a throne, dominated a raised landing before an impressively large set of windows that were half concealed behind a heavy, black, velvet drapery. A fire roared on the grate, making it uncomfortably warm. The room seemed oppressively dark with the draperies half-drawn, and the darkness only seemed to enhance the heat thrown by the fire, conjuring a sudden image of Hell in Duncan's mind. *Don't let your imagination steal your courage, now.* He swallowed and found his mouth had gone dry. Wishing now that he had accepted Quentin's offer of the water, he looked about to see if perhaps there was any in this room. There was a table laden with several wine bottles, some empty, some full, and a few goblets, but no water.

Quentin opened the doors quietly, then stepped aside while the couple, Duncan assumed were the Lord and Lady of Lothlanne entered the chamber. The chamberlain lit the candles in the wall sconces to lighten the room. Duncan thought opening the curtains would have been more effective. Quentin risked a quick wink to Duncan before he backed out of the room, quietly closing the door.

Lord Ogham strode, tall and proud, past Duncan without so much as a side glance. He grabbed one of the goblets and a full bottle of wine from the table, then settled himself down onto his throne. He haphazardly filled the goblet, and swallowed the contents with one gulp. As he was tipping the bottle a second time, he looked up, and as though he had just noticed Duncan, he paused and slowly lowered the bottle. He set an unsteady gaze on Duncan's clothing, as his mouth twisted into a mirthless grin. "Bryndah, you're right, he wears the colors of the house of Stonehaven."

"So he does," Lady Bryndah, answered, one brow raised.

Duncan turned to face her as she approached. She did not seem nearly as tall as he remembered, and oddly to his mind, not quite so ugly. In fact, if he was not keenly aware of her history, he may even regard her has beautiful. Her hair and gown were decorated in gold netting and ornate jeweled beads that caught the firelight, giving her an almost ethereal glow as she crossed the darkened chamber toward him.

"You've something for me, I believe," she said, fixing an unblinking glare on Duncan.

Duncan reached into his tunic and withdrew the scroll bearing Edward's seal. "Aye, m' lady," he said, then placed the scroll in her outstretched hand. She clasped her fingers around it quickly, and Duncan withdrew, startled that her fingernails had scratched the back of his hand as she took the scroll from him.

She broke through the seal with the exceptionally long nail of her right index finger. *Talons,* Duncan thought. *William was right, she truly is a dragon.* He watched her face carefully as she read the letter. She revealed nothing of her thoughts as she scanned the page, her eyes traveling from one side of the parchment to the other, then again from top to bottom. She looked up over the scroll, the reflection of the candles caught in her eyes, giving them an eerie flicker that Duncan found unnerving. It was the same flicker that he had seen in her eyes years before, that had fed his childish nightmares. He forced the uneasy feelings aside. *Childish dreams have no truth to them.*

"Do you stare at me, boy?" she asked, looking at him from under her raised brow.

"Forgive me," Duncan muttered and quickly averted his gaze.

She chuckled. "You're not half as insolent as your brother was. He would have kept staring. There may be hope for you." She gave him a scrutinizing look, then grinned. "Yes, I know who you are, Wilbrun. No need to look surprised. For your sake, I hope you have better sense of where you set your loyalties than Sean did. It may help you live longer."

Duncan looked at her, feeling the unbidden scarlet come to his face. "What would you know of my brother?" he blurted angrily before he could stop himself, and regretted it immediately, as her faced lightened into a hideously satisfied grin.

"I know he was an arrogant fool who chose to align himself with a demon."

She's baiting me. Duncan locked his teeth, resisting the urge to retort. The heat in his face did not lessen and the redness only seemed to amuse her. Behind him, he heard a drunken chortle come from Ogham, and she glanced in that direction and laughed smugly under her breath, then put her attention back down to the scroll. Duncan stood, tensing his muscles against the angry tremble that was building inside him. He wanted nothing more at that moment than to reach out and strike the sneer from her face, but had the sense to know that would be a foolhardy move.

After a moment, she exhaled, a disgusted grimace on her face. "I should have expected as much."

"What is it?" Ogham asked, wiping his mouth with his sleeve.

"Read for yourself." She stormed toward Ogham and thrust the scroll toward him, then went to the table with the wine and poured a goblet for herself. "What do you think?" she asked, her back to her husband.

Ogham read the paper, holding it at arm's length, he blinked hard a couple of times as if to clear his vision. When he had finished reading, he crumpled the paper in one huge fist, and looked up. "No."

Bryndah spun on her heel to face him. "It could be the only means we have—"

"No!" Ogham yelled, pounding his fist on the arm of the throne. "I will have no member of this house fostered at Drumoak. I would sooner send the boy to Ireland than to be reared by that fool in Stonehaven."

"That *fool* is my father, Ogham—"

"Would you have him turn your son to the dark as he did William?" Ogham was on his feet, his voice bellowing throughout the chamber. "You've seen what he's done in that tenant, allowing the heathen peasants free reign with their demonic chants and charms. There's been not one brought for trial since the demon! Would you have your son taught to use the dark forces that are prevalent in Edward's house?"

"You don't really believe all those fairy stories do you?" She laughed and gulped down the wine.

"Do not mock me, woman." Ogham set a dangerous glare on Bryndah and took a step toward her.

She turned her back defiantly and refilled her cup. "I do not mock you Ogham. I pity you for allowing your superstitions to cloud your judgment. Though I am not eager to be parted from my son, I see the advantage in sending him to Stonehaven. I'm surprised you do not." She turned and grinned at her husband. "Unless you regard the Fylbrigge fortune as inconsequential."

Ogham stopped in his tracks and raised an interested brow. "Hardly," he said, then returned to his throne.

"Good. It is Ned's birthright, after all," she said, sauntering toward her husband. "He is the only one left of Henry's blood and the fortune is rightfully his. I see no other means for him to claim it than to send him to Drumoak now, as Edward requests."

Ogham scowled, resting his chin in his hand, thinking.

Bryndah traced her nails across his shoulder as she walked behind the throne, speaking in a cooing persuasive voice, "Thomas went to great lengths to ensure..." She shot that smug glance up to Duncan again. "... there were no others that could lay claim to Henry's lineage. I won't have that effort go for naught."

Duncan stood stiff, listening to the exchange, while the bile in his stomach churned as his anger grew. If he understood what Bryndah had just said correctly, his suspicions had just been confirmed. Somehow, Thomas had known of Sean's parentage and had arranged for him to be killed, and the vile dragon-woman had likely been party to the plotting.

"And what better means would there be," she went on, stroking Ogham's face as she spoke, "of keeping tabs on the doings in Stonehaven, than to have..." she leaned close and whispered something into his ear that Duncan could not hear completely, though he thought he heard the words 'Annlise' and 'spy'.

Ogham shook his head, "You're daft, woman. She'd bolt the instant she crossed the border."

Bryndah leaned down again, and continued in her cooing whisper. Again, Duncan could not clearly hear everything she was saying, but he heard 'Quentin will ensure... ' She glanced over her shoulder, looking Duncan in the eye for a moment, then turned back to Ogham, cupping her hands around his ear. Ogham's eyes grew wide, and his face split into a grin and he nodded as if in agreement.

"Aye. Do it," Ogham said, a glazed gleam coming to his eye as he seized her hand and kissed her palm. She raked her nails along his chin, not scratching, but enough to leave red trails on his flesh.

"As you wish." She winked and walked toward Duncan. "Stay here, Wilbrun. Entertain my lord until I return." She grinned to her husband, then left the room.

Duncan watched the door close. The small sense of relief he felt at her leaving was quickly extinguished by the heavy breathing coming from the throne. *They're plotting.* He reasoned that they would find a way to use the boy as a means to undo Edward, and that somehow, Annlise and Quentin were key to their plan. He wondered for a moment if he was wrong to place his trust in the elderly chamberlain. Perhaps he and Annlise were just as vile as Bryndah and Ogham. *No, that's ridiculous, Duncan. They are Matthew's family. Surely you don't suspect Matthew of being a spy.* He pushed the foolish notion aside. Quentin's concern for Matthew had been too genuine, and Ogham seemed convinced that Annlise would not willingly play spy for him, unless... *they're planning to threaten Quentin to gain her cooperation. I can't let that happen. I won't let that happen.* He also concluded that he would not, under any circumstance, return to Drumoak with the dragon's progeny in tow, and he was willing to face whatever repercussions from Lord Edward there would be for that decision.

"Wilbrun."

Duncan turned, to face Ogham. "Aye?" he answered, keeping the confident air in his voice as much as possible.

"Relax," Ogham chuckled under his breath. "She's gone."

"Sir?"

Ogham upended the wine bottle and drained the last of the contents into his goblet, then drank it down in one gulp. "I said relax." He stood on unsteady feet and attempted to pour more wine from the empty bottle. He closed one eye and peered down the neck as if to be certain it was truly empty, then turned the lone open eye on Duncan. "D' ye drink boy?"

"Uh, no, sir."

Ogham grunted an unintelligible response, then dropped

the empty bottle onto the throne. He staggered around behind it to the window and took hold of the drapery, drawing the curtain to a complete close. Duncan's right hand instinctually traveled to the handle of the dirk in his belt as the last bit of what little sunlight had been allowed into the room was banished. He stood with his back to the table where the bottles and goblets were, mentally tracing the route to the door, but in the dim light the distance between where he stood and the exit was difficult to judge.

Ogham staggered his way to the edge of the landing in front of his throne. He was a huge man, his height enhanced by the shadows cast by the candles and the hearth fire. He stood, leering at Duncan with an expression he could not read, but made him tighten his grip on the dirk.

"Hand me that bottle, boy," Ogham said raising an unsteady hand, pointing to the table.

It was then Duncan made the mistake of turning his back to Ogham to retrieve the bottle and, in what seemed to be no more than half a heartbeat, his mission took a very unexpected turn.

"My God! I've killed the bastard!" Duncan dropped the remnants of the shattered bottle and raced to the door, nearly tripping over a chair in the process. He flung the door wide, it banged the wall on its hinge as he ran through into the corridor. *Which way?* He stood for a moment, looking left, then right, completely confused of which way led back to the foyer. He cursed himself for not paying closer attention when Quentin had led him to the throne room. A trace of sunlight, cast through a transom caught his eye ran toward the door below it. In a moment, he had his hand on the handle but it wouldn't turn.

"Damn!" He struggled with the door handle for another moment until he heard the shrill shriek coming from the direction of the throne room.

"Guard!"

The corridors were suddenly a chaos of running feet and jumbled voices as guards and house servants seemed to materialize out of nowhere. Duncan recognized Bryndah's voice rising above the melee.

"He can't have gone far! Find him!"

"Aye, lady!"

Duncan struggled with the door handle one more time when he realized he was at the wrong end of the corridor. There was no curtained alcove next to this door, and no place to go except back the way he had come. He heard the sound of armor-booted feet dispersing hurriedly in several directions. At the far end of the corridor he saw the door that led out. He would have to run past two adjoining corridors and several rooms to get there, all while avoiding the guards.

No time to panic, just run. Keeping close to the wall, he ran, but did not get more than ten paces when he felt a hand come from behind, covering his mouth as he was yanked off his feet and pulled through an opening in the paneled wall. The panel closed quickly, sealing off the light from the transom. Duncan struggled away from the hand that clasped his mouth, and spun around.

"Who are—" he began to yell, but the hand found its way back over his mouth, silencing him.

"Shh! Duncan, you must be quiet!" a familiar voice said in

an urgent whisper. He heard the sound of flint against stone, and soon the glow of a candle flame illuminated Quentin's face. Duncan finally loosed his breath.

"We can't stay here, follow me." Quentin held the candle aloft and led Duncan through a narrow passage.

The walls transformed from rough-hewn wood to carved stone, and finally to rammed earth as Quentin led the way through the seemingly endless tunnel. After several minutes the passage widened and they entered what seemed to Duncan to be a station of sorts. It was a chamber, perhaps twenty paces square, with the entrances to several other tunnels along its walls. A light emerged from one of the tunnels and Quentin signaled Duncan to follow him in that direction.

"Father?" a woman's voice whispered from within the lit tunnel.

"Yes, my dear," Quentin answered in a reassuring voice.

A young woman, with ginger hair braided and twisted up around her head walked into the light cast by Quentin's candle. She peered over Quentin's shoulder with the widest blue eyes Duncan had ever seen. She wore a silver trinket of a tied knot on a chain around her neck, and Duncan assumed he had, at last, met Annlise Chase.

"Is this the young man from Drumoak?" she asked her father, not taking her eyes off of Duncan.

"He is," Quentin answered then turned to face Duncan. "This is my daughter, Annlise. Matthew's mother."

Annlise studied Duncan's face for a moment, an odd look of fascination in her eyes. She lifted the candle as if to see Duncan's face better then timidly reached up and traced the side of his cheek with a gentle hand then smiled and broke her gaze on him. "Forgive me. It's... you remind me of someone." She extended a hand and Duncan took it gently, and bowed politely over it.

"I'm pleased to meet you. I am Duncan Wilbrun. I was sent—"

"Wilbrun?" Annlise asked, a surprised look on her face.

"Aye." Duncan replied, taken aback by the way she was staring at him.

Quentin interrupted the introductions. "My dear, we do not have the luxury of time we thought we would. There has been a complication. It seems our young friend here has taken Lord Ogham to task."

Suddenly the reality of his situation came flooding back, as Duncan's panic crept back to him. *I killed him! I know I did. There was so much blood and...*

"What happened?" Annlise was asking.

"I'm not sure, but the call has gone out to the guards," Quentin answered her then turned to Duncan. "Lady Bryndah will have sent the whole of Ogham's guard out by now to hunt you down, lad, we'll have to wait until nightfall before we leave the protection of these tunnels. Have no fear, Ogham is blissfully unaware of the existence of these passages."

"I killed him Quentin! I didn't mean... it was an accident" Duncan grabbed Quentin's collar and frantically tried to explain himself, unintentionally shaking the elderly man as he spoke. "You have to believe me, I had no plan to do it... he surprised me, ye see... and he... and I just didn't have time to think and... the bottle was there..." Duncan lost his breath and sank to one knee, clutching his stomach as it threatened to purge itself in his panic.

Quentin crouched beside him and placed a fatherly hand on his shoulder. "Calm down, lad. You didn't kill him. He was on his feet moments after you fled the room. I was passing the throne room when I heard him call to Bryndah. He's angry to be certain, but he's very much alive."

Duncan took several long staggered breaths before his stomach settled. "I wanted to kill him," he said resting his head in his hand, balancing his elbow on his knee. "But I didn't mean to hit him." He looked up and took hold of Quentin's collar again, and looked intently into the elderly man's eyes. "They killed my brother, Quentin. And my friend. And when Ogham came close to me... I can't be sure what he intended but... I just wanted to kill him."

Quentin took Duncan's hand from his shoulder and helped him to his feet. "I'm sure I know what he intended. I'm sorry, lad, I should have warned you." Quentin made a disgusted sigh. "Ogham's perverseness is, unfortunately, one of his many methods of gaining control of his subordinates. You will not find any among the guard who will admit to any first-hand knowledge of Lord Ogham's preference for young men, yet none will deny that they've heard the rumors." He gave Duncan a reassuring pat on the back. "Though none would be half as brave as you were in clouting the bastard with his own wine bottle."

Duncan stared at Quentin in disbelief for a moment then shook his head. "Brave? Cowardly is more to the mark. I nearly swallowed my heart in fright! I assure you I acted purely out of an instinct to run as fast and far away as I could."

"Your instincts are wise. And brave I said and brave I meant." Quentin's eyes twinkled in the candle light. He shook his finger, good naturedly winking, and said, "No more arguments. Ye hear?"

"Aye." Duncan finally allowed himself to relax and survey his surroundings. "What is this place?"

Annlise stepped into the circle of light. "We call it *The Heather Path*," she explained. "These tunnels extend from the castle, under the village, the abbey, even the prison, out to the walls that border Lothlanne village. Many have passed through here, fleeing Ogham and his hunters, for the safety of Stonehaven."

"This is how we will leave here, Duncan." Quentin continued. "We've many allies among the village and the countryside who will see us safe passage back to the borders of your own territory."

Duncan looked around, amazed at what he had been told. "And Ogham knows nothing of these tunnels?"

"Nothing," Quentin replied. "It would be the end of it all if he did."

"You say you have allies?"

"Many," Quentin nodded, a proud smile coming to him.

"When night falls, we'll leave through this passage." Annlise held her candle indicating the tunnel exactly opposite the one he had just come from. "It will take us to the wall outside the castle, near the river."

"The groomsman is one of our number, Duncan." Quentin went on, "I've arranged with him to have your stallion and two others ready and waiting for us." He stopped, a worried knot coming to his brow. "I hope this complication hasn't delayed him. They will surely be scrutinizing the stables. That may, indeed, be troublesome."

Duncan suddenly remembered that Hawk had been led to Ogham's stable and realized Quentin's concern. They knew which horse was his, and it was a real possibility that it would not be Hawk who was saddled and ready for his flight back to Stonehaven. "Let's hope the groomsman was able to get Hawk away before the call went out."

"I understand your desire for your own mount, but we must be willing to accept what is available." Quentin said.

Duncan thought about Hawk being left in Ogham's stable and the thought was just completely unacceptable to him. Hawk was Sean's horse, and Duncan was absolutely not willing to leave the stallion behind. "You don't understand, Quentin. I *must* have my own horse. He belonged to— there has to be a way."

Quentin and Annlise exchanged glances then she said, "They'll do what they can, Duncan. But if you truly wish to be free o' this place, ye mus' be willin' to flee by whatever means possible."

Duncan reluctantly agreed but made a personal vow that, come what may, eventually he and Hawk would be a team again. "You're right, miss, forgive me." He looked into Annlise's blue eyes, suddenly aware of her resemblance to her son. "You must be eager to see Matthew again."

Her eyes widened, and a ghost of a tear filled the brims. "He's truly safe?"

"He is," Duncan assured her. "Lord Edward has offered him employment as his page."

"Thank the Blessed Mother." She blinked back her tears

and smiled. "Matthew knows nothing of The Heather Path, or the work Father and I have done helping people through. He probably arrived at Drumoak believing the horrible tales of 'the Demon of Stonehaven'. But 'twas for his own sake we did not tell him the truth."

"He did believe the demon tales." Duncan laughed lightly. "But I put him straight on that." He looked quickly from Quentin to Annlise, a thought occurring to him. "So you know the truth? That William was truly no demon?"

Annlise shook her head and laughed. Quentin chuckled softly under his breath as he explained, "*The Demon* is the founder of this little piece earth we are sitting in."

"What?" Duncan asked amazed, looking all around him again at the maze of tunnels. "William started this?"

"'Tis his legacy," Annlise answered. "'Twas his courage that inspired us, and the others who do the work, to build it. There be many 'long the way who he had a direct hand in rescuing from the death-fires. There've been none afore him, nor hence, with even half the courage he had to stand against the king's witch hunters. And during his travels through this county, he made many a friend among the country folk who are still faithful to the Old Ones of our faith." She cast her eyes down and shook her head. "'Tis our great shame that we could not find the same courage within ourselves to stand up for him when they took him. That was a black time, indeed. We were certain then that the death-fires would always be there. But when Lord Edward finally took a stand against the bishop and put an end to the fires in Stonehaven, in the wake of those ashes, our hope was born. Was then the Heather Path was born— in honor of Phoenix."

"Phoenix?" Duncan asked.

She smiled apologetically. "'Tis the name we call Lord William by. Phoenix, ye see. 'Tis our way of knowin' who is among our number." She fumbled in the pocked of her apron for a moment then removed a small sprig of heather, tied neatly with a length of rough twine. "When we greet, we say, 'I've been to Phoenix Grove' then we present the heather. If the person be our friend, he will ask if Còlan was in the grove as well. 'Tis how we know each other."

"Who is Còlan?" Duncan asked, amazed by what he was hearing.

She smiled at Duncan, the look of fascination returned to her eyes as she studied his face, "'Tis not only William of Drumoak we hold in our hearts, Duncan, but the companion who was always aside him as well. A man called Wilbrun."

"Sean?" Duncan said, his eyes widening.

"Aye, Sir Sean Wilbrun. William's captain. We call him by 'Còlan'; the companion." Quentin confirmed then grinned. "He was kin to you, aye?"

"He was my brother," Duncan said quietly.

Annlise nodded, still studying Duncan's face. "Aye, 'tis plain to see. 'Tis only the color of ye eyes that be different. His were green as spring grass."

"He got them from his father," Duncan said. "He was a Fylbrigge by blood. It was never acknowledged publicly while he was alive, but anyone who enters Drumoak now can read the plaque Edward placed in his honor."

Quentin grinned. "I always suspected as much! The two of them, William and Sean, were the very spirit of Henry Fylbrigge reborn, I swear."

"You knew Henry Fylbrigge?" Duncan asked, surprised.

"Indeed, I did. I was his chamberlain years and years ago, when he was Earl of Aberdoir," Quentin said, with a wistful grin. "He was a good man. Full of charm and wit. It was always a curious thing to me that his eldest son turned out to be such a lout."

"Thomas," Duncan said with a sour grimace on his face. "Too well do I remember him."

"I do too, unfortunately." Quentin mimicked Duncan's grimace. "When Henry passed, Thomas retained me as his chamberlain, but he was a far less pleasant master. I remember how beastly he treated young William and how the servants, on many an occasion, would risk his wrath, and Bryndah's as well, to hide the lad out of harm's way." His eyes clouded for a moment and his voice grew soft. "My dear daughter Rebecca, God bless her, paid dearly for her love of the child."

Annlise gave her father an affectionate squeeze on the arm.

Quentin patted her hand, and brightened his expression. "But the boy had it in him to rise above his brother, and well he did. He and Sean, together, riding the countryside, rescuing dozens from the death-fires with little more than his eloquence and passion for justice. 'Tis said that our Phoenix never once drew blood with the blade he carried. Yet I'm told, he could best the keenest swordsmen among Ogham's hunters. And Còlan, ah, now *there* was a fine fighter. When he swung his blade, it was as if he had called lighting into his hand to wield it. No one could take him down."

Duncan forced a smile, fighting the wave of emotion

that was threatening his already frayed composure. He had a fair suspicion that most of Quentin's account of William and Sean had been embellished by legend, but if the man wished to consider the two of them heroes of near-mythical proportions then who was he to dissuade him. *So be it,* he thought, allowing himself the pride that was building inside for being kin to *Còlan*. But the pride was not enough to banish the flush he knew was coming to his face, nor the lump that was forming in his throat. There had been at least one swordsman who had been able to take down his brother; the anonymous hunter who had ridden out of the dark and taken him by surprise, striking from horseback then galloping off into the shadows. But if the heroic legends of William and Sean had truly inspired this *Heather Path*, as Annlise had called it, and people were being helped to escape the false charges of witchcraft and the death-fires that followed then he would not protest or correct Quentin's perceptions.

"So how is it you came to be in service for Ogham?"

Quentin sighed loudly and shrugged his shoulders. "Not long after Thomas's passing, Ogham married Bryndah and took control of Aberdoir. Annlise and I, and a good number of the rest of the staff, were trundled off to this God-forsaken place."

"Why do you stay?"

Quentin chuckled and gave Duncan another pat on the back. "We're servants, lad. We don't have a great deal of choice of where we go."

Duncan looked around at the tunnel, a slow grin spread across his face. "Until now."

"Aye. Until now," Annlise said, matching Duncan's grin.

"We've made the best of our time here by our work with The Heather Path. And now, it's our turn to use it to quit this place."

"It is, indeed," Quentin agreed, chuckling, squeezing his daughter's hand. "My dear, I believe we have just become fugitives."

Duncan sat, quietly taking it all in. What had started out a harrowing experience had the promise of becoming an exciting adventure. One, he thought proudly, that was worthy of Phoenix and Còlan, and he mused that wherever they were, if they could see him, they would be pleased that he had taken up the reins of their crusade.

"Keep looking! They could not have vanished into the mists." Bryndah stood in the doorway to Ogham's bedchamber one hand on the doorframe, one on the door, as she spat her orders to the sentry. "Do not return to me empty-handed. Bring him back, alive or otherwise, I care little which, but find him. If Edward sees fit to send a would-be assassin in the guise of a page then he shall be shown that we do not take his treachery lightly."

"Aye, m'lady." Angus bowed briskly then turned to leave.

"Angus."

He snapped around on his heel, "Aye?"

"The chamberlain and one of my serving women, Annlise, seem to have also taken flight. It is my suspicion they knew of the plot against Lord Ogham. Find them as well."

Angus stood still for a moment as if waiting for further instruction.

"Go!" Bryndah waved her arm impatiently at the guard.

Without another breath, he spun and hurried away.

Bryndah slammed the chamber door. She turned a furious eye to her husband, who lay, moaning in his half-stupor, on the bed. *Fool!* "Ogham," she called to him as she approached the bed. He muttered something under his breath and turned his face. She retrieved a damp cloth from a basin that had been set on the side table, wrung it, and placed it on his head. "Ogham, wake up. There is much to discuss." He turned his head toward her and opened a groggy eye. He yawned, and the breath that came from him was fouler than the heap behind the stable. She sat back, disgusted. *The sot probably doesn't even remember what happened.* She grinned to herself, *in fact I'm sure he doesn't remember. Which means it shall be easy to plant the seeds in his well-fertilized brain.*

"Ogham, you've been attacked, my darling." She spoke in a singsong voice, feigning concern as she mopped his brow with the cloth.

"Hmm?" He looked at her curiously, one eye focused north, the other south.

"We've been deceived. Edward had no thought to consider our son. Instead, he sought to have you killed. He sent the boy to do his foul deed."

"The boy?" Ogham opened his eyes wide and set his gaze now on Bryndah.

"Yes! The page, young Wilbrun, you remember? He attacked you."

Ogham sat himself up, dangling his legs over the side of the bed. He reached to his head, and gingerly felt the spot that had been introduced to the bottle. A bandage had been wrapped around, and a trace of blood had moistened the edges. Ogham looked up, toward the mirror, confirming the presence of the bandage. "The wretch, must have come at me from behind. I never saw it coming."

"My poor darling," Bryndah cooed as she helped him to his feet.

He leaned on her and belched. She hid the grimace she felt on her face, maintaining her concerned air as she helped him to his chair by the window.

"I take it the boy has been captured, drawn and quartered by now?" Ogham said, as he lowered his ample backside into the chair. "Be sure to send his head back to Edward on a pike bearing my standard."

"I fear he was wily enough to elude the guards."

"What?" Ogham growled, turning a furious scowl to Bryndah.

"He took flight immediately, it seems."

"Call the chamberlain, he must have seen... what is it?"

Bryndah sighed in mock distress. "It seems Chase and Annlise have vanished along with Wilbrun, m' lord."

Ogham slowly got to his feet, fixing a dangerous threatening look on her. "Where is the child?" He said, taking two steps toward her.

Bryndah backed away until she was against the wall and could go no further. "He's in his chamber, Ogham, they left him behind."

Ogham stopped in his tracks, still keeping his scowl on her.

She kept her eyes on his. "It would seem Edward is not truly interested in claiming an heir, or Wilbrun would have had accomplices to help him take Ned to Drumoak. That tells me only one thing."

Ogham retreated to his chair. "What does it tell you?"

Bryndah raised a brow and shook her head, amazed at how dull-witted the almighty Ogham could be. "It tells me, my suspicions were not unfounded after all. There must be another heir someplace else, but where?" She tapped her chin with her longest nail and walked away from her husband, frowning. "It has always worried me that Mehlyndia would remarry and produce an heir to my father's seat, but frankly, it had never occurred to me she even had time..." She spun around, wide eyed at the thought. "Yes, that must have been the case. I'm a fool for not realizing it sooner! She was already pregnant when she fled!"

Ogham leaned forward in the chair, his eyes becoming more alert by the moment, as Bryndah rambled. "Go on."

"If she bore a son— a *Fylbrigge* son— I've no doubt my father would not hesitate to turn the remainder of Henry's holdings over to him. He always did favor Mehlyndia and... *the demon*... above me and Thomas, and would naturally favor William's spawn likewise over my son."

"That much is clear to me as well."

Bryndah ignored him, pacing back and forth as she spoke. "I'm sure my father knows exactly where Mehlyndia has been sequestered all this time." She marched to the window and threw open the curtain, and pointed toward the open countryside. "She's out there... somewhere, and I swear I will find her if I have to search to the far end of the sea! And I know just how to begin."

"Do you?"

"Oh, yes," she grinned. "It's time to call in your markers, Ogham. You've kept your part of the bargain all these years.

I'm sure Dunkirk has enjoyed the boon of your *charity* for his part in bringing William to trial. Surely it's time you reap the interest of the investment you have made in him."

"Bryndah, that *charity*, as you call it, is what bought you your freedom from Stonehaven tower," Ogham countered, with a disgusted humorless laugh. "If it was an investment bearing interest, I should have cut my losses long ago and stopped the payments." He narrowed his eyes, laughing as she turned away, insulted.

"Laugh if you will, Ogham but Dunkirk has his usefulness. I'm sure he's champing at the bit to resume the witch hunts in Stonehaven. From the rumors I've heard, the place has become a haven for heathens. My father has not allowed a single burning since that scrub girl took the one William should have owned." She laughed to herself at the irony, then scowled. "My own son Richard claimed that flame as well, the fool. He could have had the world at his feet. He had William's title and would likely have been named Edward's heir, but instead he chose self-immolation for the sake of some misplaced loyalty to the demon and his apprentice." Her jaw tightened as she set her eye on the portrait on the far wall. *Pity Richard didn't throw himself on the pyre before he cut Thomas in half. It would have saved me years of grief with this lumbering sot.*

Ogham scoffed, shaking his head as he went to the liquor decanter, and poured himself a glass of scotch. "So, Dunkirk misses the witch trials. That's his problem. There are other abbeys he can go to if he so despises Stonehaven. The payments I give him are owed to him for his cooperation in helping me reclaim my trade routes and for putting Fylbrigge down. There is no marker for me to call in. You'll have to find someone else to hunt down your sister."

"Hunt?" Bryndah turned to him, an inspiration coming to her. "Adrian."

"Tearlach?" he asked, disinterested as he drank his scotch down and reached for the bottle to refill the glass.

She impatiently took the glass and the bottle from him and filled the glass. She gulped down the scotch at once then refilled it and handed it to her husband. "Now there is a man who is clever in his resources, but more importantly... he can be bought."

Ogham took the glass, and grinned, apparently not too besotted to understand the plot she was spinning. "Indeed he can."

"I knew you would agree. Send for him, Ogham; offer him whatever he wishes to find my sister. He'll sniff her out and any progeny she may have in tow. Once we find her, I'll make certain she poses no threat in producing an heir to inherit my father's seat and that no other Fylbrigge exists to inherit the fortune that should rightfully go to my— *our* son."

Ogham poured another glass of scotch and handed it to Bryndah, then another for himself, and raised it. "To the hunt."

"To the hunt."

They clinked their glasses then drank. Ogham's face twisted as he threw his head back to swallow. He placed his hand on the bloody bandage around his head and grabbed the decanter with the other, scowling. "First, your sister. Then Tearlach will find Wilbrun and cut him down where he stands with the same blade used on his brother before him."

Chapter 6

SEVERAL HOURS OF waiting in the dark tunnels of the Heather Path had sapped the courage Duncan had struggled to maintain. He chided himself silently for his fears. After all, Matthew had made the journey from Lothlanne alone and he was far younger than Duncan and far more skittish. Sitting there shaking in his boots was certainly no way to live up to Sean's legacy and he was determined to keep his nervousness to himself. His first mission away from Stonehaven was certainly more eventful than he had anticipated and while he, Annlise, and Quentin sat waiting for the time to leave the tunnel, he had time— perhaps too much time— to think about all that had led him to where he was.

"D' ye drink, boy?" was what Ogham had asked him. Duncan locked his jaw, grateful for the concealing darkness that hid the childish tears he felt staining his cheeks. No matter how hard he tried, he could not push the memory of the slurring sound of big man's words or the leer that the Lord of Lothlanne had in his eye as he approached. Duncan lied when he told Quentin he had no idea what Ogham intended. In the brief moment Duncan had turned his back, there was no question of what Ogham intended when he came from behind, throwing his huge arms around Duncan's shoulders, one massive hand covering his mouth, the other groping at his loins. Duncan shuddered, remembering the

smell and touch of the man, and the overpowering rage that led him to react in the only manner that seemed appropriate. The bottle he was able to grab and swing over his shoulder met Ogham squarely on the forehead.

Surely, he could not be blamed for defending himself in such a way but he was also not keen on repeating the circumstances of the attack to anyone. Quentin seemed to know without Duncan being specific of what occurred, so there was no need to explain it to him. But what of the rest of the world? The guards had been called and word had gone out that Ogham had been attacked. He would have to defend himself eventually and he worried, *who will believe me?* He was in the heart of Lothian and, Heather Path or none, if he were captured, there would be no suitable defense for attempting to kill the Duke of Lothian in his own throne room. And he was certain that was how Bryndah and Ogham had painted him— as an assassin.

And what of Edward's order that he return to Drumoak with Bryndah's son? He had decided well before being left with Ogham that he would not bring the boy back with him if he could avoid it, but that had been before his need to flee and he half-doubted he would have truly defied Edward's order had Bryndah agreed to send the boy with him. But now, after too much time to think, he began to truly fear that Edward would be displeased with him. *More than displeased, he'll be out right furious. Especially if word reaches him that I'm wanted for attacking the sot!* He sank down against the wall and dropped his head into his hands. *There'll be no choice then. I'll have to tell him everything. He'll either believe me and allow me to enter his guard... or think me a lying coward and that will be the end of that.*

He sat quietly, drawing his knees up to his chin, then dropped his head on his arms and closed his eyes. There was still more than an hour before they would be leaving the tunnel and, with nothing else to do but mull it all over and over, he allowed himself to drift into a restless sleep.

"Now, what's all this?"

Hmm? Duncan looked up, then over his left, then right shoulder, seeking the source of the voice he heard, that came from an odd place behind his ear.

"Right in front of you," the voice said.

Duncan turned quickly to the front. For a moment he had the impression that a looking glass had been placed on the wall and that he was looking at his own image. On closer examination, he realized the image he was seeing was not a reflection, but a man sitting in roughly the same position exactly across from him in the tunnel. There were no candles burning, yet he could see the man clearly, as if the light was coming from him. The man held a concerned yet somehow understanding expression on his face. Duncan dropped his head back to his arms. *Go away, Sean,* he said mentally, as he always spoke in his dreams.

"Go away? Is that how you greet me?" Sean answered, his voice still detached from his mouth.

I can't face you right now. Please, just let me work this one out by myself.

"Duncan, look at me."

Duncan lifted his head and looked into the face of the one person who he least wished to know of the fear, shame and guilt he was feeling. He attempted to dress his face in a nonchalant expression, hiding the truth behind a mask of false calmness.

"Why are you hiding from me? I'm not here to judge you, brother. You've done nothing to be ashamed of."

Duncan looked into Sean's face and felt his resolve crumbling. *I failed, Sean. A simple mission, to bring the boy back, and I failed.*

Sean shook his head. "What are you talking about? You haven't failed." His mouth did not move with his words.

I was supposed to bring the boy back.

"You were supposed to bring *her* back."

Duncan glanced in the direction where he remembered Annlise and Quentin had been sitting. The strange light that illuminated Sean, now shown around her as well. She lay resting her head in Quentin's lap, eyes closed, breathing lightly. *Well, yes, Edward wanted her to return with me as well. She's the nursemaid to...*

"She's Matthew's mother."

Yes, I know... you know about Matthew?

"Of course I do." Sean smiled and seemed to laugh. "You promised him you'd bring her back." He placed his right fist over his heart, in the same gesture of promise Duncan had made to Matthew before he left. "You haven't failed. In fact, you've done quite well so far."

Duncan allowed a ghost of a smile to cross his face. *You're keeping tabs on me again.*

Sean nodded. "That's my job."

Then I suppose you know it all, don't you? The smile faded and he dropped his head back to his arms.

"I do. You hit him good and proper. He had it coming. I

don't think I would have handled it any differently."

You wouldn't have run away, scared out of your mind.

Sean shook his head. "Were you to stand there and wait for the guards? What would that get you? An early grave. Then you would be no good to anyone. You did exactly as I would have done; high-tailed it out of there without looking back. You're allowed to feel fear, Duncan."

But, Duncan looked up again, and began to explain himself in his mental voice, rambling, *It's complicated everything. They'll make it seem I was sent as an assassin! What happens if they retaliate? And what of Edward? He's getting older and won't be around forever, and he has no heir, Sean, and if Ogham sends an assassin and he's successful and there's no heir... I was supposed to bring him his heir!*

"Duncan, look at me." Sean's voice left the spot behind Duncan's ear.

When Duncan looked up, Sean was no longer sitting across from him, but had moved beside him. When he spoke, it was as anyone speaks; with his mouth.

"I was supposed to bring back Edward's heir," Duncan, said quietly.

"You will." Sean placed a brotherly arm around Duncan's shoulder. "But Edward's heir is not here. You haven't failed. You've not even started on that journey yet."

"I haven't?" Duncan asked, confused.

Sean shook his head. "No."

Duncan took a deep breath. "But, if the heir isn't young Edward, then who—"

Sean raised his hand, palm up, signaling Duncan's silence. "Trust me," he said, then got to his feet, taking his mysterious light with him, leaving Duncan in the dark. He walked quietly over to where Annlise lay, and knelt down to one knee next to her. He traced his hand down her cheek, then looked over his shoulder back to Duncan. "Keep your promise, brother, and bring her to her son. Follow the heather, just as they do, and you'll be back at Drumoak by the dawn." He turned back to the sleeping woman, bent, and lightly placed a kiss on her forehead. Then, with no further discussion, he stood, turned his back to Duncan, and took a single step, vanishing into nothing. The light that surrounded Annlise, vanished with him, leaving complete darkness in the tunnel.

"It's time to go." Quentin gave Duncan a light shake on the shoulder.

Duncan opened his eyes, startled by Quentin's sudden appearance. The elderly man stood over him, lit candle in hand. Annlise, standing not far beyond him, also held a lit candle.

"It's time to go," Quentin said again.

When Duncan had finally shaken the sleep from his head, he got to his feet. Quentin handed him a candle and lit from the flame of his own, then motioned for him to follow. Without conversation, Duncan fell in step with Quentin's pace, Annlise close behind.

The moon had already risen high in the night sky by the time Duncan, Annlise and Quentin reached the river. The air that met Duncan's face seemed the sweetest he had ever felt after the oppressively musty air of the tunnel. Quentin looked up to the moon— half-full and waxing— then frowned.

"What's wrong?" Duncan asked, keeping his voice as low

as possible.

"The clouds are covering the moon for now, but it's a thin veil," Quentin answered, still looking up. "I'm afraid She'll betray us this night if we do not guard our steps."

Annlise followed Quentin's gaze. She closed her eyes and spoke quietly, prayer-like, "Mother grant we make it to the forest before the clouds move away."

"Come," Quentin said, making a beckoning motion with his hand. "If the groomsman was able to rally mounts for us before the guards were called, they should be just beyond the edge of the wall there. Stay close, now." Without waiting for an answer, Quentin crouched and scurried cat-like along the edge of the wall. Duncan could not suppress a grin of amusement and admiration at the agility the old man possessed.

Giving a quick glance to the shaded moon, Duncan shared Annlise's sentiment, offering a small prayer of his own that the clouds would stay as they were. They moved quickly along a narrow strip of land that lined the riverbank next to the wall. Annlise nimbly avoided the brambles that grew in twisted jumbles along the path. Duncan did his best to place his feet in her footsteps, but met with near disaster twice when the muddy earth gave way under his heavier weight. By the time they reached the edge of the wall, he had sunken into the mud twice and his legs were plastered to his knees with muck.

Quentin held up a hand, signaling a halt as he cautiously peered around the corner of the wall. He put his fingers in his mouth and made a strange whistle that sounded like the call of a night bird. A moment later, his call was answered by a similar sound and he motioned for them to follow.

Annlise reached for Duncan's hand and gave it a squeeze. "It's safe," she said, with a relieved sigh.

When they passed the edge of the wall, Duncan almost cried in joy and relief to see that three horses, Hawk among them, were saddled and ready to go, complete with water skins and blankets fastened to each. Quentin was speaking quietly to a man Duncan assumed was the groomsman. The man patted Quentin's shoulder, then they shook hands, grasping each other's elbows in a gesture of farewell.

When he rejoined Duncan and Annlise, Quentin explained quietly, "We'll have to ride through the night, I'm afraid, and stay off Garioch Road. The guards will be thick there. We'll stay along the river until we reach the forest. Stay close by me and follow my lead. It may seem that I'm leading you into impossible terrain, but you must follow me exactly. We'll rejoin the Heather Path on the far side of Drunbalk's forest."

"Aye, Father." Annlise said, then mounted one of the horses with no questions.

Quentin looked up at Duncan with a reassuring smile. "Trust me, lad. If we follow the heather, we'll be to Drumoak by the dawn."

Duncan stared, half stunned as Quentin echoed almost the exact words that Sean had spoken to him in his dream. It had not been the first time Sean had visited Duncan's dreams but that's all Duncan had ever considered the visits to be— dreams. And dreams were never real. *Were they?* Until that moment he had been sure they were not, but the memory of his brother and the sensation of his arm on his shoulder, the clarity of the light he cast and the sound of his words, did not fade away on his waking as most dreams do. Sean had kissed Annlise, and for a half-moment, Duncan considered asking her if she had felt it but decided against it.

"I trust you," he said to Quentin, then mounted Hawk with a renewed sense of confidence. *And I trust you too, Sean.*

Quentin mounted quickly, then without further discussion kicked into a gallop, Annlise and Duncan close behind. They made it to the forest's edge just as the last wispy cloud passed away from the moon.

Through the night they moved, stopping only long enough to rest the horses, then pushing on. Drunbalk's forest, with its thick pine and spruce, provided ample camouflage. The underbrush was sparse enough for easy travel, yet thick enough to conceal the footfalls and the tracks left behind by the horses. Twice, Quentin had abruptly changed direction, almost doubling back in one case, when they encountered other horsemen in the woods. He led them into a shallow cave, and the three watched breathless as a small entourage of Ogham's scouts emerged out of the shadows barely twenty paces ahead of them. Duncan looked to Annlise, to warn her, but found her sitting, eyes closed, face to the moon, her right hand flat palmed just below her throat and resting on the silver knot necklace she wore. Her mouth moved in a silent prayer, or chant. She opened her eyes, and Duncan could see her lip curl into a smug smile in the moonlight as the guards inexplicably switched paths and galloped away.

When they reached the far side of the forest, the moon was low in the western sky. Dawn was still several hours away, and many miles between them and Edward's borders still to travel. Duncan's heart sank at the sight of the open meadow they would have to cross. Ogham's scouts had been on their heels most of the ride, though through a miracle Duncan could not begin to understand, they had yet to be seen. However it would be difficult for even a rabbit to stay concealed in this wide-open meadow.

Quentin motioned them to a large bolder near the edge of the forest. "We'll rest here until the moon is completely set."

"How much farther is it?" Duncan asked. He had completely lost his bearings hours ago, trusting Quentin's directions. He had a vague sense they were headed east, as the moon was setting behind them, but he had no idea where they were.

Quentin pointed across the vast field. "Past this meadow, we will cross into Edward's territory. Then it will be safe to join the road again. You're almost home, Duncan." He smiled, his eyes catching the moonlight.

"Thank God," Duncan said, then returned Quentin's smile. "How is it you know your way through this wilderness? And in the dark! I'd be hopelessly lost in the daylight with a good map. You must have traveled these woods thousands of times to know—"

"I've never been here in my life." Quentin said with an unconcerned laugh in his voice.

"But how do you know the way—"

Quentin nodded toward Annlise. Duncan turned to see that as she had done before, she was sitting silent, hand on her necklace, her face upturned toward the moon. Duncan shook his head, confused. "I don't understand."

"I don't either fully, but I trust it. We're being led, lad."

"But I thought we were following *you*, Quentin. Who are you following?"

Quentin made an ambiguous smile and shrugged his shoulders. "It's a matter of faith," was all he said.

"There, Father." Annlise pointed toward the middle of the meadow. Duncan followed her hand and saw the briefest and faintest of glows, as though a convention of lightning bugs had gathered together for an instant, lighting up a dip in the landscape.

Quentin nodded, "I see it." He dismounted quietly and motioned to the others to do the same. "It will be safer if we stay low."

Behind them, in the woods, they heard the sound of muffled voices and hoofs on leaves. "Scouts. We need to hurry," Annlise whispered and assumed the lead, heading toward the place she had indicated.

"But the moon... they'll see us." Duncan protested, but she held up her hand to quiet him.

"We've no choice. Come." She led her horse away from the protective covering of the forest into the open meadow, Quentin close behind. Duncan followed affording a last look over his shoulder.

It was then he saw the glint of steel as half a dozen of Ogham's hunters became clear in the moonlight. "Hurry!" he cried in the loudest whisper he could manage.

Annlise looked back. Her eyes widened and Duncan knew she had also seen the scouts. A shrill whistle broke the silence of the night, which was answered with a whooping cry and a man's voice called, "There!"

"Mount!" Quentin ordered.

Without wasting another breath, Duncan and Annlise were on their horses and kicked into full gallop, charging across the open meadow. Duncan could hear the scouts gaining on them, his heart was racing faster than the horse he rode. He looked forward, expecting that Annlise would abandon her plan of heading to the middle of the meadow and take them to the far edge, where Edward's border was. But she did not waver from her path and led them instead into the unprotected wide space of the meadow.

"What are you doing?" Duncan called as she raced on.

"Trust me!"

The arrows started to fly. Duncan risked a look back and saw the distance had lessened between himself and the scouts, and they were now within arrow range. He kicked Hawk harder than he had ever kicked and the stallion responded with a speed Duncan had never experienced. He turned forward, keeping his eyes squarely on Annlise and Quentin. *This is madness! They're leading me to the wide open!*

"Trust me!" she called back, as if to answer Duncan's unspoken concern.

The closer they came to the dip in the meadow, the closer the scouts were on their heels. Duncan felt the air move and heard the whoosh of an arrow as it passed only inches from his ear. The dip in the grass was only paces away now, he watched amazed as Annlise, then Quentin, disappeared into the dark place in the grass. He pushed Hawk in the same direction. Just as he entered the dark spot, he felt an explosion of stars in his left shoulder, followed by a dull thud as he made impact with the grass. He lay quiet, listening to the random sounds around him.

Confused sounding voices were saying, "This is impossible! They came this way, I'm sure of it."

"It must have been deer."

"No! I'm sure they came this way!"

"Well they are not here now!"

Duncan lay completely still, watching the hooves of the six horses that surrounded him turn, then gallop back toward the woods they had just fled from.

He closed his eyes and exhaled, then drifted into a merciful blackness that took with it the pain of the arrow that was lodged in his shoulder.

"Duncan. Wake up, lad."

Duncan opened his eyes slowly, blinking back the light that came through the window onto his face. As his vision cleared, he glanced around at his surroundings. The transom above the window was tilted half in and the tree that grew outside it was, as always, blocking the view of the village. *Stonehaven?* Confused, he looked up into the face of the person who had called him. "Mum?" He went to sit up, then lay back down quickly, wincing at the pain in his shoulder.

"Lay still, lamb." Agnes, his mother, sat on the edge of the bed, cloth in hand, looking down with the ever-worried crease in her brow. "Give yourself a chance to mend."

"How did I get home?" Duncan asked, then despite the pain in his shoulder and Agnes's protests, he pushed himself up to sit, closing his eyes against the vertigo blotches that assaulted him. When the sensation cleared he looked around the room again. Matthew sat on the edge of his cot, wide-eyed, a mixed look of concern and hope in his eyes. It was then Duncan remembered where he had been. "Annlise? Quentin? Where are they?" he asked, sitting up quickly and turning his head from his mother to Matthew. The motion made him dizzy and he covered his eyes with his hands.

"Lay down," Agnes, ordered, pushing him back down on the bed. "They are with the duke."

Duncan pushed her hands away, and sat up again. "Mum, please. I need to see Edward. He'll want to know what happened."

"Duncan Arthur Wilbrun, lay down or I will strap you to your bed!" she snapped, motherly concern turned fierce.

Duncan looked at her surprised by her tone, then smiled as her face softened, as it always did. He relented, and lay back down against the pillow. "I'm down," he said, then looked over to where Matthew sat quietly watching the scene. "Some sentry I'll be; aye, little mate? Surrendering so easily to me mum as I do?" He winked and then grimaced at the pain in his shoulder.

"There, you see?" Agnes, chided. "It would not hurt so much if you just lay still. You're fortunate that the arrow came clean through. It was easy enough to treat. We simply cut the head off and pulled it back out. You'll mend, son, but ye need to rest a bit." The crease returned to her brow. "You're determined to send me to an early grave with worry, I swear it." She shook her head, then gave him the relieved smile he had seen on her face countless times after she had patched up skinned knees or elbows, and all other manner of childhood injuries. She bent, kissed his head, then picked up her basin and cloth and set a stern eye on Matthew. "Now dinnae you keep him awake and chatting. He needs his rest."

Matthew nodded obediently. The moment Agnes was out of the room, he got up and stood next to Duncan's bed. "Does it hurt?"

Duncan glanced at his shoulder, then back to Matthew. "No, it's going to be fine." He looked toward the door to be sure there was no sign of Agnes before he sat up in the bed again.

"She said you're to rest." Matthew said, hands on hips.

Duncan could not resist a smile at the maternal expression on his young friend's face. "No worry, Matthew. Relax."

The young lad smiled, sat on the edge of the bed, and began talking quickly, rambling. "You did it, Duncan, you did it! I couldn't believe it when I saw you coming. I thought I was imagining things!"

"I don't even remember coming back." Duncan said truthfully, trying to remember how he came to be where he was. "The last thing I remember was hitting the ground."

"Well you were out cold across your saddle when you got here. We thought you were dead!" he said wide-eyed, then reached for Duncan's hand. "Don't ever scare me like that again."

Duncan shook Matthew's hand. "I'll keep it in mind. It wasn't my *intention* to catch an arrow with my shoulder, you know."

"No, I suppose not. You're right lucky my mum knows her healing. She knew what to do for you. But I must say, it took you long enough to wake up."

"How long?" Duncan asked, surprised. The sun was not

quite to noon, and he assumed it was no more than nine or ten in the morning.

"Two days," Matthew answered.

"Two days?" Duncan yelled, shocked, startling Matthew and sending him sliding off the edge of the bed. "Sorry, little mate."

"Aye, two days," the child said, then stood, brushing himself off. "Mum made a potion from some mushrooms that were in the cave you were hiding in and it made you sleep. She said it would help with the healing."

"Cave? I thought it was just a hole in the meadow."

"I don't know the details, you'll have to ask her. But that's what I heard her tell your mum."

Before Duncan could ask any further, the door quietly swung open and Edward peered in. "Ah, my boy, I see you're up. Good. We've got much to discuss. Are you feeling up to it?"

"Aye, sir." Duncan answered, then smirked. "Just don't let mum catch you keeping me up."

"Indeed, that is wise advice. There is no warlord as fierce as a mother with an injured son." Edward chuckled as he pulled up a wooden chair and set it next to the bed. "Matthew, would you excuse us for a bit. I'd like to speak to Duncan privately."

"Aye, sire. Mum is wantin' me to go with her to the market anyway. She used all her healing herbs up on your shoulder, mate."

"She did?" Duncan asked, examining the bandage at his shoulder. "She must be good at what she does."

"She is." Matthew said, then headed for the door, bowing

politely to Edward as he walked past.

"Oh, Matthew," Edward leaned back in his chair, calling over his shoulder, "a moment."

Matthew stopped, turning to Edward. "Aye, m' lord?"

"If you are going to the market, ask Agnes or perhaps your mum, to look for a nice bolt of blue silk for me." He reached into the pouch on his belt and withdrew four gold coins, and held them out to Matthew. "This should more than cover the cost."

"Silk, sir?" Matthew asked, marveling at the gleaming coins.

"A gift for my daughter. I'm hoping she'll be coming for a visit and I'd like her to have a new gown." Edward chuckled when Matthew's brow creased suddenly. "Mehlyndia, lad. Not Bryndah."

"Oh, of course, sir." Matthew smiled, in obvious relief as he carefully dropped the coins into his pouch. He smiled nervously, bowed again, then headed back to the door, pausing long enough to give Duncan another grateful smile. "Thanks, mate. For bringin' my mum back."

Edward watched the boy go, then turned to look at Duncan with a cheerful gleam in his eye. "I'd say it's a fair assumption to believe you've earned a friend for life in that boy."

"Perhaps so." Duncan shrugged modestly, but allowed himself a proud half smile.

Edward's smile faded and he took a breath. Duncan could see the subject was about to move away from Matthew and he braced himself, expecting a rebuke for failing to return young Edward to Drumoak. His heart began to race as his mind reeled through the possible explanations he could offer the duke, without coming right out and telling him the *real* reason he had attacked Ogham.

"Sir, about your heir, I'm sorry I failed—"

Edward held a hand to stall Duncan's protests. "I did not send you to Lothlanne to retrieve my heir. I sent you to deliver a letter. You did that. There was no failure on your part. I never expected Bryndah to send her son with you."

Duncan stared, relieved, but unable to find words to reply. *To deliver a letter.* He suddenly felt completely foolish with himself for building his assignment into something far more grand in his own mind. He had made his own mission of retrieving Annlise for Matthew's sake paramount to Edward's purpose. The simple truth that he had been sent merely to deliver a letter had been completely lost from him.

"I can't tell you how proud I am of you." Edward said gently. "Quentin told me what happened, Duncan. Yet, you managed to keep your wits about you and keep your promise to your friend at the same time. Your brother would be proud of you."

What Edward said next, came as a complete surprise.

"Duncan, the time has come. To do this properly, you need to get out of that bed." Edward stood and extended a hand.

Duncan took Edward's hand and gingerly got to the edge of the bed, then stood, relieved to find his feet steady beneath him, though he felt fairly foolish standing before the duke clad only in his bed-shirt.

Edward grinned and took a step back. "I'd ask you to kneel but I really don't think it's necessary."

Duncan's eyes widened as Edward removed his sword

from his scabbard, then touched the blade lightly on his uninjured shoulder, then moved it to the other, bringing it close, but not touching.

"It is my privilege and my honor to name you Sir Duncan Wilbrun, sentry to the house of Stonehaven. Do you accept your post and all responsibilities that lie therein?"

Duncan caught his breath, still unable to find his voice. He had dreamed about the moment he would take the oath since he was a child and William had handed him the wooden sword in a mock knighting. He knew the response that was expected and had rehearsed it hundreds of times, and now the time had come to utter it but all he could do was stare dumbly at Edward.

Edward grinned and lowered the sword, sliding it silently back into the scabbard. "I'll take that as a yes."

Duncan took a breath, then assumed a formal air and in the most confident, voice he had ever used in his life he said, "I accept, my lord, and swear my fealty, as is my honor, to uphold and defend your tenants. Under pain of death do I break this oath."

Edward extended his hand, and they grasped in the formal wrist-to-elbow manner. When they broke, Edward reached into his pocket and pulled out a silver badge, emblazoned with the crest that signified his house; the soaring eagle. He winked, then pinned it carefully to the bandage on Duncan's shoulder. "There now, Sir Duncan. It's official."

"Thank you, sir," Duncan said, toying with the badge. A wave of vertigo found him as he looked up. Edward caught him and gently helped him to sit on bed. Duncan blushed. "I guess I'm not as steady as I thought just yet."

"It will pass," Edward said as he resumed his seat in the wooden chair. "Are you ready for your first call to duty, Sir Duncan?"

"Aye," Duncan answered, then yawned. He swallowed it quickly, as Edward laughed. "Forgive me. What is my first call to duty?"

"Well, not until your wing is healed and you're back on your feet, of course." Edward's face turned serious and he leaned forward in the chair. "As my page, I sent you to deliver a letter, and you were ready to risk life and limb to retrieve my heir."

"I understand the importance of lineage, sir, and the need—"

Edward held up his hand, "Allow me to finish."

Duncan closed his lips tight and listened.

"Lines of succession are indeed important, Duncan, and it's true that I have not formally named a new heir after William. That is why I'm sending you on a journey."

"A journey?" Duncan pushed himself up with his hands.

"You heard me tell Matthew that I was hoping for a visit from Mehlyndia."

"Oh! Yes!" Duncan replied, feeling foolish for not realizing before that it was rather odd that Mehlyndia should be coming for a visit suddenly after being gone away so long. "Am I to escort the lady back to Stonehaven?"

"Yes, but more importantly, you are to retrieve my heir," Edward answered, setting unblinking eyes on him. "The rightful heir to my seat here and to the houses of Sutherland." He paused and leaned forward. "And Aberdoir."

Duncan's eye widened, "Another Fylbrigge?"

"No, Duncan. Not another. The Fylbriggen I named in the first place."

Duncan sat back, stunned, gaping at Edward. "William?"

Edward allowed a slow grin to spread across his face. "That's right, Duncan. It's time to bring him home."

Upon their arrival at Drumoak, after seeing Duncan safely to his quarters, Annlise and Quentin met with Edward in his chambers, telling him of Duncan's bravery and the details of their flight from Lothlanne. Quentin had not gone into full detail of the circumstances of how Duncan had come to strike Ogham with the bottle, but he told enough so that Edward understood. It was decided, for Duncan's sake, that unless Ogham was fool enough to send a retaliatory force into Stonehaven, the incident was best forgotten.

When Annlise hesitantly began to explain how they had eluded the scouts, by vanishing into one of the many grassy egresses in the meadow, she had been stunned when Edward had interrupted her to ask if Còlan had been in the meadow as well. He explained that Drumoak Castle was the last safe stop along the Heather Path to the sea. When he told them their Phoenix was alive, Annlise came close to swooning in her father's arms.

When Edward learned of Annlise's healing skills and her commitment to the path, he readily took her into his confidence and gone into detail of the deception he had been party to during William's trial; the potions Elinor prepared, the role Ian played in administering him an antidote in the guise of sacramental wine, and the how they carried William from the family crypt through the maze of catacombs to the sea wall far below the castle. The catacombs had since become the last leg of the Heather Path, and many a refugee had paused at the empty tomb—believing it truly occupied—to pay their respects and lay a stone on the ever-growing cairn before continuing on their way to the sea.

On the night Duncan was knighted, Edward called him, along with Annlise and Ewan, to his chambers to explain the details of their impending mission.

"And now the time has come to bring him home. Those of us here in this room are the only souls in Scotland who know the truth. Though admittedly, I don't know how I'll keep that secret once William is back on this shore. I suppose it would do no harm to tell your family, Annlise, as you'll be leaving them for a few months and I will certainly tell Agnes where it is I'm sending her son off to."

"I don't know what to say. It seems like a miracle." Annlise whispered, taking it all in. "He's truly alive and well?"

"He's alive," Edward nodded. "But, as for being well..." He took a heavy breath and walked to the window, idly looking out across the landscape. "There is much healing yet to be done."

He explained what he knew of William's current physical limitations, his shattered memories and of Ian's letters telling him how some of the memories had begun to trickle back. "I'll need him to be whole of mind when he returns. That is my biggest concern."

Annlise agreed at that point to accompany Duncan to New France. She could think of no greater honor than to be entrusted by Lord Edward with his confidence. If the Phoenix was truly alive, she would move heaven and earth to bring him home.

"I'm sending Ewan with you as well," Edward said, "I'm fully confident in your abilities, Duncan, but after all, you are still wet behind the ears. Remember it's not only William I need back here, but Mehlyndia and their son as well. Little Seany is next in line. With Bryndah spinning her webs again, I can't take any chances. I'll need *all* my heirs close by."

"You mean... he's alive?" Matthew stared, pie-eyed, as he sat cross-legged on Duncan's bed. The night was unseasonably warm again, and the window was thrown wide open.

"As alive as you and I," Duncan replied, affecting a wise-and-knowing countenance, designed to impress his young companion. "It's been a well-guarded secret with the duke ever since the trial. He's not told another living soul... until now. And *I've* been chosen to bring him home."

"Are you sure Lord Edward meant it was really and truly William—"

A strange scratching sound coming from outside the window took Duncan's attention. "Hold on," he held a hand to his mouth in a gesture of 'quiet', then carefully peered out the window. The moon was hidden behind a bank of clouds, making it difficult to see much passed the tree outside Duncan's window. He listened carefully for a moment and when the sound did not repeat, he lowered his voice and continued his conversation with Matthew.

"Yes, I'm sure it's him. Edward was very clear about it. He's been in the New World all this time. That's where we're heading."

The sound of a twig snapping, followed by a skitter of

scratching, came in through the widow. Duncan reached for the latch handle to swing the widow closed, fearful they may be overheard by one of the other house servants who was not privy to Edward's inner circle. Before he could pull it completely closed, however, he heard the plaintive meow and again the scratching. Relieved, he grinned at Matthew. "It's only a cat." He chuckled as he pulled the window shut.

A week later, Annlise stood on the beach outside the sea-wall caves below castle Drumoak saying goodbye to her father and son. It seemed heartbreaking to be separated from Matthew again, after all they had gone through to be together but she knew her greater duty was on the far side of the ocean. She embraced the lad tightly. "You behave now, learn your trade, and listen to Agnes. She's to be as ye mum until I return."

Matthew nodded but did not answer. Duncan and Agnes stood near the dinghy that would take them to the ship, similarly embracing. Matthew broke from his mother and went to Duncan, hand extended.

"Godspeed to ye, mate."

"And to you, as well," Duncan answered, accepting the lad's hand. Annlise's ministering of his injured shoulder had proven to be exceptional, and the wound was all but healed. Only a slight stiffness, that improved daily, remained. "Now don't be givin' m' mum trouble. She's fierce when she's angered." He grinned and winked over his shoulder at Agnes. "Oh, hold on, I've got something for you." He reached around to his back and withdrew the wooden sword William had given him. "I want you to have this. You know who made it, right?"

"Aye! Thank you, Duncan." Matthew accepted the sword with a wide-eyed smile.

"When he gave it to me," Duncan explained, "Lord William promised that it was a talisman against the fiercest dragons in the land." He traced the dragon carving with his finger. "He was right. The dragon can't touch you so long as you have it," he said in a gentle voice, then presented the sword in a proper knightly fashion, hilt first over his left arm.

"Thanks, mate," Matthew whispered, accepting the little sword reverently before he turned and wandered off toward the cave entrance, where a few crates and a large trunk had been placed in preparation for loading.

Annlise was impressed at Duncan's insight. Many a night had she comforted her son after he had been awakened, terrified once again of the dragon who had invaded his dreams. The same dragon, she suspected, who had haunted the dreams of another young man she had known when she and her sister Rebecca had lived in Aberdoir. The young man she was now setting off to heal if she could, and bring home. *She'll not be hurting them again. I'll see to it.*

"Are you certain you don't wish to come, Father?" Annlise asked, for the thousandth time. "They are still searching for you; you'll be safer away."

Quentin embraced her, rocking for a moment, then stood back, holding her at arm's length, his eyes bright with moisture. "I'm certain, my dear. It's as it must be. Besides, I'm far too old for adventures across the sea, and Edward is in need of a good chamberlain. And with Ewan going with you, someone has to be here to tend this end of the Heather Path."

Annlise brushed her eyes with her handkerchief and nodded. She knew he was right. "Please, be careful. I hate farewells."

Quentin smiled and kissed her cheek, "'Tis not farewell, child, you'll be back soon enough and I'll be right here to greet you... and our Phoenix." He gave her one more quick embrace before turning to head back to the caves. "Blessed travels, my dear."

She went to Agnes, and extended a hand to the older woman. "I can't thank you enough for looking after Matthew."

Agnes smiled sadly, then her eyes fell to the silver knot Annlise wore at her throat. "'Twas a gift from the lad's father?" she asked, bringing her hand to the necklace.

"Aye. How'd ye know?"

Agnes reached under the high collar she wore and withdrew a worn and tattered ribbon. Hanging from the end was a silver knot, identical to the one Annlise wore. "I would not turn away m' own grandson; now, would I?"

Annlise stood speechless. She had kept the sire of her son a well-guarded secret since his birth. Not only out of a slight sense of shame for having never married, but also for Matthew's own protection. Where Sean was revered among the people of the Heather Path, he had also earned his place among the demon legends as well. Ridiculous, as she knew it to be, she had feared that Matthew would have been considered demonic spawn by the closed-minded zealots of the king's church, and felt it best to keep the secret deep within her. But now, as Agnes embraced her, she felt nothing but relief and joy as, at long last, Matthew would learn the truth. "Will you tell him? Please, Agnes? When I'm to sea?"

"If ye wish, lass." Agnes assured her quietly, then spoke up, loud enough for the others to hear, "And I'll be askin' ye to care f'r Duncan as well. He's a handful, that one. Just like his brother, never knowin' how to keep his backside out of trouble. You will be careful? Won't you, son?"

"Absolutely." Duncan grinned at his mother. "I'm always careful."

Edward and Ewan approached carrying the trunk between them, then set it into the dinghy. "That is the last of it." Ewan said, wiping the perspiration from his brow. He squinted up to the sun and gave a satisfied nod. "We've been blessed with a clear sky and a gentle breeze. I'll take it as a good sign." He motioned to Duncan and Annlise. "Come on, time to row. We'll only have the tide in our favor for another hour."

Annlise turned to say one more good-bye to Agnes and Edward. She glanced around looking for Matthew and Quentin, then remembered they had gone back toward the caves. The sun was just setting over the ridge of the seawall high above and, for an instant, she thought she saw someone standing on the ridge, backlit by the setting sun. She shaded her eyes against glare, squinting to get a better look at the figure who stood on the cliff but it had already disappeared beyond the edge, and she dismissed the sighting from her mind.

From his vantage point, high above the shore, the lone horseman watched the group of sea-travelers say their farewells and load the longboat that would bring them to their ship. He could just make out the highest mast of the galleon that waited just beyond the horizon. He pulled his hood over his head and led the horse away toward the woods, smiling to himself, satisfied with the knowledge he had gained. He laughed ruefully, delighting in his own cleverness at how he had acquired a bit of priceless information, simply by following a young page about the Stonehaven marketplace, listening as the child muttered instructions to himself— *yarrow root, and barley, healing herbs*— following, staying hidden in the shadows— *what are you needing with silk, lad*— the merchant had asked, and it was the child's answer that had piqued the horseman's interest— *it's not f-for me. It's for Lady Mel*— the lad had caught himself, but his secret had been revealed to one who would know what to listen for.

He had stayed close, keeping out of sight, melting into the crowd and shadows around him, staying as close to the boy as possible. He chuckled to himself at how easy it had been to find the object of his quest, after only a few days of searching. A day dogging the boy and an evening spent lurking in the shadows beneath the open windows of the lad's quarters in Drumoak had given him all the information he needed, and even more than he could have dreamed, and he was eager to share what he had learned with his benefactor, as he was certain his news would double the compensation he would gain.

He made a shrill whistle between his teeth and a young page hurried up to his side. He took a scroll from his tunic, opened it, and reread what he had written:

My Dear Lord Ogham,

I have found your vein of gold, and the payload is twice what you expected. I shall have to renegotiate my fee. I shall arrive at

Lothlanne within the week for instructions.

   Tearlach.

He rolled the scroll and handed it to the page, sending the boy off with a sharp wave of his hand. He took a last look toward the ocean, a hungry, greedy grin growing on his lips. "So, he's alive after all. All the better for me." He laughed out loud, then kicked the horse into a gallop, riding into the shadows of the forest road that led away from town.

Ewan took up the oars as Duncan and Annlise settled in among the crates and, before the sun reached the horizon, they were climbing the ropes to the deck of the very same ship that had borne William and Mehlyndia to New France years earlier, the *Lady Anne*. The crew loaded the crates and the trunk, with a rope and winch, down into the hold. With the cargo loaded and the dinghy secured to the side of the ship, the captain gave the order to raise the sail. It billowed to life with the breath of a stout westerly wind as Duncan and Annlise stood at the aft watching Scotland disappear under the horizon.

Later, as she was settling into her cabin, Annlise looked through the porthole to the moon, closed her eyes, and offered a prayer to the Blessed Mother and Father to watch over Matthew while she was away. Though it had only been hours, she missed her son terribly already, but her loneliness would not last long when a soft knock on the cabin door broke her from her reverie.

"Come in."

Ewan entered silently and stood, hands on hips, shaking his head.

"What is it?" she asked.

He turned and made a beckoning motion to someone who stood out of her line of sight. "It seems we've a stowaway," he said, as a contrite looking Matthew stepped into her cabin. "I knew that trunk seemed heavier than I remembered it being."

"Matthew!" Annlise did not know if she was pleased or angry, but she held up her arms and the boy ran to her. "How in the world? Oh no, Father will be frantic!"

"No, mum." Matthew blushed and gave a wary look to Ewan. "Grandfather helped me get in the trunk. He said he'd explain it to Edward."

Ewan stood in the door, sighed, threw up his hand, then leaned against the wall. "Well it's too late to turn back. I guess we've got us an adventurer on our hands. Oh well, I suppose we can always use another set of hands and a cabin boy."

Matthew turned a grateful face to Ewan, then smiled. "So I can stay?"

"Well, unless ye think I'd toss ye to the whales, lad, of course ye be stayin'." Ewan laughed. "Just be willin' to pull ye' weight when it's called on ye."

"Aye, Sir!" Matthew said, saluting Ewan with a grin.

Chapter 7

"**Y**ou're certain?" Ogham paced the floor of his throne room, chin in hand; skeptical, yet willing to listen to what Adrian Tearlach had to tell him. He turned, narrowing his eyes. "Why should I believe such an absurd tale? The man is dead. I was there... *you* were there when he died. We *both* saw Edward carry his sorry corpse out of the meeting house. Edward may have power enough to keep Dunkirk in line and a near miraculous grasp on his holdings, but he certainly cannot raise a man from the dead. You're merely trying to extort a higher fee for your service."

"Perhaps I am." Adrian shrugged, then leaned back in Ogham's throne and crossed his left foot casually over his right knee. "But you must admit the fee I'm asking is still far less than what you stand to gain if I'm right. And I assure you, my lord... I *am* right. You've been had. But if you're not interested in hearing my proposal..." He turned his hands palms up, then moved to stand. "I shall beg my leave and waste no more of your time."

Ogham raised his hand. "Hold." Adrian cocked a brow, then sat back again. "What do you propose?"

Adrian leaned forward with a showman's gleam in his eye. "A sea voyage, my lord. Send me to New France to bring him back."

"Bring him back? Why not simply finish him? Finish the lot of them? Erase every heir to Stonehaven from the highlands to Hell! Then Edward will have no choice but to name my son—"

Adrian grinned, shaking his head. "No, that would not serve your purpose at all."

Ogham frowned. "It wouldn't?"

"It wouldn't." Adrian approached him, and placed a hand on his shoulder and looked him in the eye. "You need him alive."

"Explain to me, how Fylbrigge being alive is to my advantage? That only means Edward has plenty of heirs in which to squander his holdings."

"My lord, I should think it obvious. Should Edward's deception become known, his holdings may be seized, then there will be nothing for him to squander. Have you forgotten, my dear Lord Lothlanne, it is not only *you* who has been made to look the fool by his cleverness, but Bishop Dunkirk as well? And more importantly... one of the king's own magistrates—"

"Peter Garland! The trial judge." Ogham froze, understanding finally dawning on him. "Yes! Edward deceived the judge! If it could be proven that Edward knowingly put his holdings into the hands of a man who had pledged a demonic pact, purposely deceiving the magistrates— he'll be stripped of everything. The only reason he is able to hold onto it all is because Garland himself, believed Fylbrigge *died* in during his trial, something his pact would have prevented had it been real." He threw his hands in the air. "But he did not die! That proves he truly was— *is*— guilty and Edward knows it!"

"Exactly." Adrian grinned. "And quite possibly it is Peter

Garland who may hold sway with the king as to just *where* those holdings should go, and my guess is his logical choice would be to Edward's eldest daughter. Your wife, m' lord. However, there may be a hitch."

"What hitch?"

"You and I both know that Garland, God love him, is an insufferably *honest* man." Adrian grimaced at the word. "Even if he takes my word that Fylbrigge is alive, he may not see the benefit as we do in pursuing the case. After all, he will be the one made to look the biggest fool for falling for such an obvious trick. We shall have to make it worth his while."

"He may be honest, as you say, but he is also ambitious and for a price, any man can be bought." Ogham grinned smugly.

"How do you mean?" It was Adrian's turn to be intrigued.

"It's a known fact that Garland craves authority as much as the next man, and he's made no secret of his interest in *expanding* his horizons, so to speak."

Adrian nodded in agreement. "What do you have in mind?"

"It so happens, I've been given leave to stake a claim— in the king's name, of course— in the New World. James has wrested some territory from France recently and the word is, he has set his heart on colonizing that particular piece of ground where you are planning to sail."

"Interesting."

"And it also happens I'm in a position to send a governor. Someone... honest, of course. I think I know just the man for the job."

"But if Garland is there instead of here, how will he make

his recommendation as to where Edward's holdings will go."

Ogham shook his head. "My dear Adrian, it's quite simple really. Garland is a man who needs to see things for himself. When you find Fylbrigge there, Garland will sign the appropriate warrants, and you will bring him back to me. When you return— with a *living* dead man— we send the warrants off to His Majesty and that, my friend, will be that!"

"Brilliant!" Adrian laughed, then went to the liquor stand and poured each of them a drink. He handed one to Ogham, then raised his own. "To the New World. I can't wait to leave."

Ogham put his hand over Adrian's glass before he could drink. "One more thing."

"My lord?"

"You are to take a passenger with you."

Adrian lowered his glass and raised his brow. "My lord?"

"Lady Bryndah will accompany you."

Adrian glared at Ogham. "May I inquire why?"

Ogham turned his back and walked toward the window. He stood silent for a moment before turning back to Adrian. "Because I wish it."

"But—"

"These are my terms; your compensation will be doubled. Half now, half upon your return *with* Lady Sutherland and whatever progeny she may have in tow. I shall pay a boon of another twenty-thousand crowns to you should you actually deliver Fylbrigge to me alive, ten-thousand for his corpse, five-thousand if all you can offer me is irrefutable proof he lived at all in that settlement. Lady Bryndah will go with you for no better reason than I wish her gone! These terms are not negotiable. Accept them or leave no richer than when you entered."

Adrian drew his lips into a tight line and took a deep breath. After several moments he gulped down the drink and set the glass down hard on the table and slowly extended his hand. "I accept."

She crept out of the shadows of the alcove as Adrian stalked past on his way to the door, and placed a hand on his shoulder. He stopped, turned, and in a single motion, put an arm around her waist, sweeping her back into the alcove. He pulled the curtain closed and drew her close to him, staring into her eyes. Bryndah tangled her fingers into his hair and kissed him deep and hard.

He drew back, grinning. "I take it you were listening."

"Always."

"He made it easy for us. I did not even need to spin my own proposal for you to join me." He laughed under his breath and kissed her again. "It's absolutely perfect."

"We'll return quite wealthy, my love. And when I have my sister's fortune neatly tied up and have, once and for all, made sure there are no other Fylbrigges to lay claim to what should rightfully pass to me..." She traced her finger gently down his cheek, delighted with the desire showing in his golden eyes. "Then you and I will take care of the last obstacle in our way; then all of it— Aberdoir, Lothlanne, even Stonehaven— shall be ours."

He clasped her hand quickly, kissing her fingertips, never taking his eyes away from hers. "With luck, Ogham will have drunk himself into his grave before we even return."

"One can wish."

The two locked together in a passionate kiss, remaining in the alcove and reveling in the cleverness of their scheme. When the last rays of daylight faded from the transom above the grand doors, Adrian quietly slipped out into the shadows. She returned to her private quarters, happily mulling over the list of items she would need to pack for her journey.

Phoenix Flying

Freedom, sweet freedom.
Soaring, swooping, sailing
unfettered, unladen, unending.
Reborn in the glorious warmth
Touched by the caress of morning
The clouds below me, the sky above
I am my own again
I am free!

Chapter 8

Early June 1613
Port Edin, New France

"STILL NO SIGN, dear?"

"No." Mehlyndia sighed, not turning away from the attic window. She had gone up to search out the trunk she had brought with her from Scotland that held remnants of linen and silks, and such odds and ends that she thought would be useful in the next quilting project she was planning. When she got to the attic, however, her mission of the trunk was forgotten as she was distracted by the unobstructed view of the forest road from the window. She sat for what she reasoned was no more than a quarter of an hour looking out, hoping to see any trace of William, Ian, and Ephraim returning from their trip to the Mi'kmaq summer village.

"I'm sure they're on their way back by now." Elinor nudged Mehlyndia's elbow, persuading her to leave her vigil.

"I'm sure they are." Mehlyndia smiled, attempting to cover the worry she knew she wore on her face. Elinor's sympathetic eyes told her she had failed. "It's been more than a week, Elinor. Ian said they'd be gone only three or four days. What could possibly be keeping them?"

"Well, Akonni's people don't stay in one place, dear, you know that. Perhaps it just took them longer to find them than they had expected." Elinor took Mehlyndia's hand and led her back to the far end of the attic where her trunk was stored. "Remember last summer? Ian and Simon were two weeks gone, just looking for their hunting village."

"I suppose you're right, Elinor." Mehlyndia allowed herself to smile. Elinor was right, she reasoned, remembering how Ian and Simon had returned last year, dirty but pleased with themselves. She had a sudden image of William returning filthy and jubilant, sitting atop the wagon laden with furs. "He's probably having the time of his life."

Elinor smiled and gave her a motherly pat on the back. "I'm sure he is." She turned her attention to the trunk. "Do you have the key?"

"It's up here." Mehlyndia reached to a rafter and retrieved an old length of blue silk ribbon. A tarnished brass key dangled from the end of it. She slipped the key into the lock and gave it a hard twist. The lock had rusted over the years, but with a little force, it finally clicked as the lock sprang open.

"Melly? Elinor? Are you up here?"

"Over here, Prissy." Mehlyndia called. "I've found the trunk."

"Oh good," Prissy said cheerfully as she joined Elinor and Mehlyndia. "Do you have any silk?"

"Haven't opened it yet," Elinor answered as she and Mehlyndia struggled to open the lid. "It seems... to be... stuck."

"Well this won't do." Mehlyndia sat back, catching her breath. "We need something to pry it."

"There's a pry-bar over there," Prissy said, moving toward the window where Mehlyndia had been sitting. "I'll get it."

As she reached for the pry-bar, she glanced out the window. "Oh, here she comes," she said with a groan.

"Who?" Mehlyndia asked.

Prissy put on a comical haughty expression. "Her most holy, Josephine Ashcrofte, herself, on her way to grace our humble home with her regal countenance. I shall have to practice my curtsy."

"Prissy, you're terrible." Mehlyndia laughed. "Will you bring that bar here or not?"

"Coming, coming." Prissy picked up the bar and returned to the trunk. "How long has it been since you've opened this?"

Mehlyndia slipped the bar into a gap under the lid of the trunk and set her jaw. "Not... since..." She gave a mighty heave with all her weight. The lid flew open, sending a cloud of dust into the air. Mehlyndia thumped to the floor, landing squarely on her backside. "Scotland!" She sneezed, waving the dust away from her nose.

Elinor offered her hand, laughing out loud. "Well done, dear."

The ladies gathered around the trunk, still laughing when they heard the polite call from the foot of the stairs. "Hello? Melly, are you about?"

Prissy and Mehlyndia exchanged mischievous grins then Prissy put her finger to her mouth and made a shushing sound. "Maybe she'll think we're just bats in the attic—"

"Hello, Josephine." Mehlyndia gave Prissy a quick nudge to silence her as Josephine appeared on the stair. She swallowed the laughter she was holding in check and assumed a proper welcoming expression.

Prissy, her back still to the vicar's wife, crossed her eyes and wrinkled her nose before transforming her expression instantly into a polite smile before she turned around. "Well, hello Josephine, what a nice surprise."

Elinor's stomach shook with muffled laughter.

Josephine climbed the rest of the stairs, examining the puddles of dust that rested here and there about the attic. She tucked her hands into the pocket of her frock as if touching the dust was somehow a sinful thing to her. "I hope you don't mind, I let myself in. I was wondering if you'd heard from our traveling men."

"Not yet," Mehlyndia answered. "But I'm sure they'll be back today or soon after," she said, putting as much confidence in the statement as she could.

Josephine seemed contented with the answer as she approached the trio around the trunk. "What are you all about up here?"

"Oh, just getting some old scraps for this year's quilting," Elinor answered, turning her attention back to the trunk. "We're in need of a few more bits, and I remembered this old trunk was here and thought there might be something useful in it."

Josephine craned her neck and looked down her pointed nose into the trunk. "Looks like moths got to the linen."

"That's just the dust cover layer," Mehlyndia said, feeling a bit defensive. "The trunk hasn't been opened for years." She reached for the cover layer to push it back, then paused, a sudden uneasy feeling came over her. She looked from Prissy to Elinor then glanced back at Josephine. "I don't remember what is in here, to tell the truth."

Elinor seemed to understand Mehlyndia's discomfort and in her usual intuitive fashion, deftly averted Josephine's attention. "Josephine, would you be a dear and help me in the kitchen? I've got cakes baking and I thought we'd enjoy them with some brew. You always make such a lovely dandylion brew, perhaps you could show me the blend you use?"

Josephine smiled, obviously flattered, "Certainly, Elinor, I'd be glad to show you. It's all in the amounts and just how quickly you allow the diffusing..." She rambled as Elinor led her back down the stairs, nodding and smiling feigning interest in Josephine's prattle. She gave Mehlyndia a quick wink over her shoulder as she descended the stair.

When she heard the door at the foot of the stairs creak then close; Mehlyndia exhaled, not realizing she had been holding her breath. "Thank goodness," she said, then turned back to her trunk.

"Did you know she was coming?" Prissy asked, making herself comfortable on her knees next to Mehlyndia.

"Yes, unfortunately I'd forgotten about it," Mehlyndia sighed. "She cornered me in the square and asked me if she could drop by. What was I to tell her? No?"

"I would have," Prissy said, laughing.

"That's because you're wicked, Priscilla MacHenry." Mehlyndia laughed with her and then reached again for the cover layer in her trunk. She glanced at Prissy and took a deep breath. "Ready to see what we shall find?"

Prissy nodded, and they pulled the linen away together. The fibers had taken some damage from moths and some of it crumbled almost to dust in their hands, but most of it came away easily. Mehlyndia sighed loudly, when a large flat book-like leather case was uncovered. It was twice as long as it was wide, and about three inches thick. The top was tooled with a delicate ivy design.

"My drawings," Mehlyndia said, quietly. "I'd forgotten they were here." She eagerly lifted the case and set it down on the floor next to the trunk and opened it.

"Oh Melly, these are beautiful," Prissy said as Mehlyndia flipped though the images. "You did these?"

"Aye, I did. I had more idle time to do this sort of thing back in Stonehaven." She turned page after page of drawings done mostly in charcoal, some with color pigments, depicting the faces and places of Stonehaven. Even though the drawings were done quickly, her attention to detail was keen. A good many of the drawings were of William, sketched rapidly during their picnics to the sea. One drawing of him— poised on a rock on the shore, pebble in hand as if to throw— brought a sudden wave of grief on her, and she quickly turned the page over. She had drawn it the last afternoon she and William had spent together in Scotland. The following morning had been the day the hunters had come to arrest him.

Under the seaside drawings, she found several she had made of William sitting with his lute by the fire, or on the window seat. She had done these from memory during those terrible days he had spent in the prison tower, and had used them as models for the portrait her father had hung in the great hall. She turned them over quickly as well, scanning through several of the other faces in the stack. There was little Duncan, chubby cheeks resting on his fists as he sat on a stump outside the stables; Elinor laughing, wash bucket in hand as she spoke to Agnes, Sean's mother; Sean, casually leaning against a fence, cloth in hand and polishing the sword which was his pride and joy. And the drawing William had once said he liked the best; he and Sean on horseback, racing the woodland road.

"Who is this?" Prissy asked, holding up a drawing of a young woman with large round eyes and long hair and a shy but mischievous smile.

Mehlyndia smiled sadly and took the drawing from Prissy. "That's Laurel."

"The one who—" Prissy looked up quickly, not finishing her question.

"Aye, that's her," Mehlyndia confirmed. A wave of guilt flushed her face for a moment, as she thought of how unfair she had been in telling Prissy details about Laurel, and the role she played in William's trial, when she had never even told *him* of it.

"She was very pretty," Prissy said, matching Mehlyndia's quiet tone. "She looks so young."

"She was older than me by a year." Mehlyndia smiled, and placed the drawing carefully back in the case. "But yes, she did look like a child. My father used to call her 'little mouse' because she always seemed so timid and shy around him."

"Seems he misjudged her," Prissy said.

"We all did. She had a brave heart. I'll be forever grateful for what she did for William." Mehlyndia sat quiet for a moment, swallowing the lump she felt forming in her throat as she remembered her old friend. "If she hadn't convinced Ian to smuggle her into the prison, we would have never known what was happening. Father never believed William's stories of the tortures the bishop ordered on prisoners. You see, Father believed that Will's rank would protect him from all that, and he was content to just sit and wait. It took Laurel disguising herself as a boy acolyte to go with lan into the cell... to see with her own eyes, then tell my father what they had done. But she did it. She convinced him to do more than sit and wait. She was very brave to go into the gaol as she did."

"Aye, brave indeed," Prissy agreed with a sigh.

"She took it from him, Prissy."

"Took it?"

"The fire," Mehlyndia answered quietly then quickly closed the leather case.

Prissy nodded her understanding and did not ask further.

"Well then, let's see if there is anything useful in here." Mehlyndia took a breath, and returned to the trunk. "Here we are." She pushed aside another layer of linen, finding several neatly folded bundles of brightly colored silks. The remnants of many of the gowns she had once worn to the balls given by her father in Drumoak castle.

"Oh good!" Prissy helped Mehlyndia take the silks from the trunk. "These will do. Good colors, Melly, we can use this blue one for the edging." She smiled, and started to blush.

"What is it?" Mehlyndia asked, intrigued by Prissy's sudden change in expression.

Prissy's face turned even redder as her smile broadened. "Well it seems..." She glanced down at the blue silk, then placed a hand on her stomach and looked up, raising a brow.

"Oh Prissy!" Mehlyndia threw her arms around the girl's shoulders. "I'm thrilled for you!" The two hugged and giggled.

"Have you told Simon?"

"Aye, just this morning. I've suspected it for a while but I wanted to be certain. It's been a month, and the signs have started."

"Oh, Prissy!" Mehlyndia gave her a squeeze before releasing her. "The way he dotes on Seany, it easy to know that he'll be a wonderful father."

Prissy sat back, beaming. "I know he will. We've been married close to four years. We were beginning to think we'd never have a child. This little one should come in time for Christmas if I've guessed correctly."

"A wonderful gift." Mehlyndia smiled, and she sat back. Behind the trunk, now buried in discarded linen, the little cradle William had made rested gathering dust. Mehlyndia glanced in the direction, to be certain it was still there then reached around and uncovered it. She pulled it out to the open. "I think you should use this."

"Oh Melly, no, I couldn't."

"Please." Mehlyndia took her hand, silencing her protests. "It serves no purpose rotting in this attic. I want you to use it. And I'm sure William will insist that you take it as well."

Prissy gave Mehlyndia another hug and wiped a tear that had trailed down her cheek. "Thank you, Melly."

"Good then, that's settled. Let's gather up this silk and head on downstairs. I'm sure Elinor is in need of rescue from Josephine by now." Mehlyndia said, as she gathered the bundles in her apron.

Prissy went to close the lid of the trunk then paused. She moved the leather case aside and tugged on another length of cloth she had found. "What about this one?"

Mehlyndia looked at what Prissy had found and dropped the bundles she was holding. She reached into the trunk, hurriedly pushing the leather drawing case aside and pulled out the last thing in the trunk; the one and only gown she had brought from Scotland, a richly embroidered ball gown made of saffron-dyed silk. The sight of it brought full the tears that the drawings had begun.

"How beautiful!" Prissy said, brushing her hands over the train. She looked up at Melly and put an arm around her. "I'm sorry, Melly, these must be hard memories for you."

Mehlyndia nodded then brushed her eyes. She had worn this gown the night her father had formally bestowed William the earldom of Sutherland. She held the garment up at arm's length, staring at it as if she had never seen a dress before. Until that moment, she had not realized how badly she truly missed her old life nor how badly she wished to return to it. "Oh, if only," she sighed, and put the dress back into the trunk.

She picked up the case with the drawings again and flipped to the pictures of William on the beach. She remembered little of the conversation they had had that day, but something he had said while wistfully looking to the sea, came back to her; *Sometimes, I wish with all my heart we could sail away. Just you and I, and leave this all behind.*

Be careful what you wish, Mehlyndia, she scolded herself and closed the drawing case, burying it in the folds of the gown. She closed the lid on the trunk, gathered the silk scraps, turned a falsely cheerful smile to Prissy, then the two headed down to the kitchen.

"Oh, there they are." Elinor looked up quickly from her

cup, flashing an exaggerated grin that told Mehlyndia she was already tiring of Josephine's company. "Did you find the silks?"

"Yes, here they are." Mehlyndia emptied her apron onto the table. "Josephine, I'm sorry to have stayed upstairs so long. These were buried deeper than I thought."

"No trouble, dear." Josephine made a pinched little smile over her teacup. Her eyes widened, then narrowed to slits as she looked over the array of colorful silks. "Mehlyndia dear, these are exquisite, and so... rare. How did *you* come by them?" she asked, in the lofty English accent she put on as a reminder of her *superior* upbringing in London.

"Och, they be just scraps, Josephine." Mehlyndia said, deliberately enhancing her Scottish burr.

Prissy bit her lip against the gleeful giggle she was obviously trying to hide, but when Josephine looked at her, the expression transformed instantly to one of polite interest, then back to mischievous as soon as the vicar's wife turned away.

"They may be scraps, but the texture, and... look at the embroidery on this one. These must have come from fine bolts indeed." Josephine raised a brow and took a sip of her tea. "Expensive bolts."

Mehlyndia knew she was fishing for gossip. She felt the heat rising to her cheeks and locked her jaw to prevent herself from snapping at her. She had grown far too weary of Josephine's constant catty remarks, and a good part of her wanted desperately to put the old biddy in her place. Mehlyndia had done her best to keep her former life as Lady Fylbrigge, the Countess of Sutherland, a secret and to learn the domestic skills that were second nature to Elinor and Prissy, though she had yet to fully master the finer points of bread making and housekeeping. Josephine had given many a side-glance and smug sneer to Mehlyndia's linens, that hung a little less dazzling white on the lines than the Ashcrofte linens were, and she had made snide observatory comments about how Goody Philbrick seemed to possess only a nodding acquaintance with a butter churn or rug-beater. She had even called out Mehlyndia's ladylike manners as being a bit *overly proud* of what is proper for a simple woodwright's wife, even referring to William as *"lamed, broken and far too old for her."* Mehlyndia had suspected then that Josephine was itching to know how they had come to New France, and where they had come— or fled— from.

"Och! They were terribly expensive. The finest silks in the highlands, they are," Prissy chimed in, flashing an impish wink to Mehlyndia. "That's why we've only got *scraps.*"

"But, where did *you* get them? They are so intricate... they can't possibly be *Scottish*," Josephine said, rubbing a piece of amber silk between her finger and thumb.

Mehlyndia felt her face turn red.

"Of course, they're Scottish," Prissy answered with a completely serious expression. "You certainly don't get good silk like that from *England.*"

Josephine's lips pursed into a tight puckered scowl as she glared at Prissy. Mehlyndia caught the girl's eye and saw that she was pleased with herself. Elinor seemed about to bust, her face was turning red and her shoulders shook with stifled laughter.

Before Josephine could retort, Seany, his face alight with

excitement, burst into the kitchen from the porch door. "Mum! There be—"

"Child, you're interrupting," Josephine snapped. "Where are your manners?"

Seany stopped in his tracks, eyes wide and already beginning to puddle at her rebuke.

Enough is enough. "I'll thank you to not correct my son in my presence and in my own home!" Mehlyndia snarled then turned her back on Josephine's stunned, stupid-looking expression and crouched down to be eye level with her son. "Tell me what's got you so excited, darling."

Seany looked over his mother's shoulder to Josephine, then back to Mehlyndia. He cupped his pudgy hands around her ear and whispered. "Make her leave, Mum."

"It's not polite to whisper," Josephine said. "What a rude little boy you are."

Mehlyndia pursed her lips and turned to face Josephine. "Then *I* shall not whisper, lest you think *me* rude. Josephine, if you please, I'd like for you to leave now."

"The child will grow up with no manners, if you do not correct—"

"That's *my* worry, Goody Ashcrofte, not yours. He's obviously got something important he wishes to share with me, and I far prefer his company to yours. I should think you must have more important duties to tend to than nosing about my business and scolding my son."

Josephine gaped at Mehlyndia's outburst. Elinor stood, an equally stunned expression on her face, though hers also included a wry grin. Behind Josephine, Prissy was making pantomime punching motions, smiling from ear to ear.

"I will not stand here and be insulted," Josephine growled, but did not move from her spot.

"I don't blame you. It's far better to stand on the porch to be insulted," Prissy said, then scooped up Josephine's elbow and ushered her to the door.

"Loose my arm! I shall leave on my own accord." Josephine yanked her arm free of Prissy's grip then stormed out the door.

Mehlyndia cringed at the slamming of the door but allowed a satisfied grin to find her. "I'm sure we shall not hear the end of this."

"Oh, let the old scandalmonger stew. I'm proud of ye, Melly. It be about time someone stood up to her." Prissy turned her ever-cheerful smile onto Seany. "Now little man, what's the news? Ye were out with Simon at the pier fishin' last I knew. Did ye' catch us a fish for dinner?"

The lad's face brightened back into the joy he had worn moments before Josephine's rebuke. "No, I didn't catch a fish," he giggled. "But Simon let me look through his looking glass." He turned to face his mother, eyes wide. "Mum! There be a ship comin' and Simon says it's flyin' a blue flag with a white cross, and another flag with an eagle on it."

"A Scottish ship?" Mehlyndia grasped the boy's shoulders and then gave him an excited hug. "An eagle? You're sure?"

"Apple-slootly." Seany said, a serious expression on his face that made him look all the world like a miniature of his father trying to mimic William's favorite oath; absolutely.

"An eagle! It's the *Lady Anne!* News from Stonehaven." She picked up Seany and whirled him around, hugging him close, then set him down again.

Elinor had come around behind them and soon she and Prissy were caught up in Mehlyndia and Seany's giddiness.

"How far out is it? Did Simon tell you?"

Seany shook his head and raised his hands, palms up. "No, but he's on his way. He was just putting the fish *he* caught in the smoke house."

"Here he comes," Prissy said, looking through the little curtain on the kitchen door.

Simon hopped the steps going from ground to deck in one easy stride. He entered, shaking his head, a confused look on his face. "What bee has nested in Goody Ashcrofte's coif? She looks like she's swallowed a porcupine," he asked, laughing, then bent and gave Prissy a kiss on the cheek.

"Oh, never mind about her, tell us about the ship." Prissy took Simon's hand and led him to the table then busied herself getting a mug of ale for him.

Mehlyndia pulled up a chair opposite Simon. "Yes, is it *Lady Anne*? Seany said it was flying an eagle."

Simon took a swallow of ale then nodded, wiping his mouth. "Aye, if there be any flag I know, 'tis Edward's. 'Tis *The Lady Anne,* sure as I stand here. She be a half day out. If the wind holds as it be, she should anchor down afore sunset."

Mehlyndia could not resist jumping from her chair and leaning over to give Simon a kiss on the cheek. News from home had a magic about it for her and no matter how dreary her mood, a letter from Edward would always lift her spirits.

Simon blushed as Mehlyndia sat down. A crease knotted his brow for a moment and he looked out the window toward the wood road. "Have you heard at all from Will?"

Mehlyndia's lighthearted mood dimmed again. "Nothing,

Simon."

Prissy came around behind her, two teacups in her hands. She set one on the table for Mehlyndia, and then took the chair next to Simon with her own. "I'm sure they'll be back today, tomorrow at the latest, Melly."

"Thank you, Prissy. I'm sure you're right." She sipped her tea, and tried not to worry.

Ian pulled the horse to a halt just beyond the point in the forest road that would be visible from Port Edin, the final bend in the path that would take him and Ephraim home. The left front wheel wobbled lopsided on its axle, a side effect of the haphazard way they had used the horse to yank the wagon free of the mud, but it had managed to survive the trek back. It took them three days to find their way back to this road after roaming through the vast wilderness of the forest in a desperate search for their friend.

The first morning, after they had awoken to find William gone and after he had composed himself enough to think clearly, Ian practically ran the remainder of the way to the place he *thought* he would find Akonni's village. The only trace of the Mi'kmaq people to be found were the ruins of long dead cook fires, and faint worn spots where the wigwams had been raised the previous year. The nomadic natives had not yet set up their summer hunting camps.

Keeping the wagon within his sight and as his center of reference, Ephraim had searched the vicinity of their camp for any trace of William. It seemed impossible to the vicar that a man could simply disappear without a trace and it was obvious he hadn't just wandered off in his sleep. "Was a bear, I think," he told Ian, several times, but Ian would not be convinced without more proof. By the time Ian returned from his efforts to seek help from Akonni on the first day, the sun was low in the sky, and Ephraim had given up his search, instead spending his time digging the wagon wheel out of the mud.

"We should go back to Port Edin." Ephraim had said as they shared a meager dinner of dried meat and cheese from the provisions they had packed. "They'll want to know—"

"Not until we know for sure," Ian protested, closing the argument.

Ephraim retrieved his prayer book from the wagon and the box containing religious elements; candles, oil, holy water, and a fine white linen cloth. Ian, having been a monk for a good part of his adult life, recognized the preparations Ephraim was making.

"It's a bit premature to hold rites for the dead," Ian said, watching the older man prepare his make-shift altar in the woods.

Ephraim smoothed out the white cloth over a log, and set the elements reverently on it. "Is it?" he said quietly, not meeting Ian's eyes with his own.

"We don't know where he is, Ephraim. This is a huge forest. He could be anywhere," Ian argued, though he did not find the sound of his own voice convincing. "Perhaps he's found shelter in a cave..."

Ephraim finally looked up from his preparations. "Ian. He didn't *walk* away in the night. He's not off exploring on his own," he said gently. "It was an animal... a bear, or wolf... ."

He turned away, shaking his head, turning his attention back to his altar.

"He would have screamed, Ephraim. We would have heard... something." Ian sunk down, back against a tree and dropped his head into his hands, cursing himself. He knew the truth of that argument was that he had been far too drunk to hear anything. Ephraim had even more to drink and would not have known if God, Himself, had tried to wake him. "If it was an animal, why then was it just Will who was attacked? The two of us would have been easy prey as well in our drunkenness."

"I... I don't know." Ephraim opened the prayer book and placed it on the cloth. "Perhaps it was simply God's will, Ian. Please, come here and help—"

"God's will?" Ian looked up, yelling at the vicar through clenched teeth. "Why would God allow him to survive all he'd been through only to lead him to the woods to be eaten by wild animals? I don't believe that Ephraim, not for a moment." He got to his feet and turned his back on the vicar. "And I don't believe he's dead. I won't believe it until I see his corpse."

Ephraim made a heavy sigh. "Son, please. Come here with me for the rite."

Ian spun on his heel and set a fierce glare onto Ephraim. "He's not dead, damn it. Ephraim, I will not partake in a funeral rite! At first light, the two of us are going to set out to find him. We are going to search every tree, every rock, and every inch of this forest until we do. Do you hear me?"

Ephraim looked up to Ian, then closed the prayer book. "As you wish," he said, whispering as though to force himself to remain calm. "Brother Ian, and yes I call you that out of respect as I don't fully believe you abandoned your faith when you left your calling... wherever William is, he is not here, and at the very least, I'd like to offer a prayer of some sort."

It had been years since anyone had called him 'Brother', and the word stung him. Ephraim had been right. He hadn't abandoned his faith; though he had found himself, on more than one occasion, furious with the paths God had chosen for him. It was not his lack of faith that had led him away from the robe, but his disdain for the ungodly practices he had seen rampant throughout the clergy, particularly in Aberdoir and Stonehaven. It had been the bishop in Stonehaven, Gregory de Dunkirk, who had ordered William arrested and tortured for the imaginary crime of spell-casting, and it had been Joseph, the abbot from Aberdoir, who had carried it out. *In the name of God*, Joseph had sliced the tendons on William's ankles in an effort to elicit a false confession. No, there was nothing Godly in the actions of the clerics and Ian had known then, when everything Joseph had done was documented during William's trial, that he could not remain constrained within the hypocrisy of the clergy. But his faith was a different matter and Ephraim was dead right that he had not abandoned it. A prayer was most definitely in order.

"Forgive my anger, Ephraim. You're right. There is little more we can do this night, but pray." Ian went to the make-shift altar and lowered himself to his knees. Ephraim did the same on the opposite side of the log.

Their second evening in the woods, the vicar and former monk had spent the time in prayers of hope that they would find their friend the next day. The third night was much the same and the fourth. By the sixth, however, hope had turned to despair.

Six days of searching had turned up no evidence that William was alive, though Ian maintained to the last that other than the bloody piece of leather, there was no real evidence of his death either. He had hoped that they would have stumbled onto the native village in their wanderings, and find that William had somehow managed to be there, but it was as though Akonni's people never existed. When it became apparent their search was leading them in circles, the decision was made to head back to Port Edin. On the sixth evening, Ian relented. Grudgingly and tearfully, he participated in the rites reserved for the dead.

Three days later Ian stared at the path widening before them, as he sat motionless. He turned and looked over the contents of the wagon, most of it just as it had been packed the day they had left. The provisions, enough for three people for four days, had been enough to sustain two people for seven. When the provisions had been exhausted, they had subsided on wild berries and small game, but neither man seemed to have a complete appetite anyway. The litter William had finagled together occupied the back-most portion of wagon, the wooden box with the unfinished animal figures he had been carving for Seany lay on top of it, and to the side, the chariot. The sight of the empty chair brought on the wave of grief and shame Ian had been holding at bay for most of their journey home. His vision blurred behind tears as he stared at the thing. "I don't know how to tell her, Ephraim."

"It's never easy, my friend." The vicar gave Ian a gentle pat on the shoulder. "But prolonging the delivery will make the message no gentler."

Ian shook the reins, making a clicking sound with his tongue. A quarter hour later, just as the sun was beginning to set, the wagon entered unnoticed into Port Edin settlement. The square was oddly absent of life and a look toward the pier told Ian why. A large sailing vessel, flying the familiar blue and white flag of his homeland and the yellow and red eagle of the man who had entrusted him with the wellbeing of his heir, had set anchor off shore. A sight he had always welcomed joyfully before now only enhanced the heavy mantle of grief he wore. *I suppose then, it's time to go home.*

A ship landing, whether it be from France or Scotland, was always an exciting event in the settlement. Especially the first landing after a long, hard winter. It meant the arrival of new supplies; fabrics, tools, letters from loved ones, and most appreciated by the men, a new supply of good Scottish Whisky, and the hops and barley necessary to brew ale. It was an extra treat if the ships carried family members or old friends from home, such as this one did.

An hour before sundown, when it was apparent the ship would indeed make landfall during the daylight, Mehlyndia hurried her family to the docks. While the ship was still too far to see clearly the faces of the people on the deck, Mehlyndia waved from the dock and was able to tell the folks on the ship were waving back. Simon looked through his telescope and when they were close enough to see, he burst into joyful laughter. "It be Ewan! My old mate has come this trip!"

Mehlyndia and Elinor shared excited hugs at that news. "Who else is there, Simon; do you see?"

"There be a lass!" Simon said, as he lowered the glass and gave Mehlyndia a sly smile. "Ye don't s'pose ole Ewan finally landed himself a wife d' ye?" He laughed and not waiting for an answer, he put the glass back to his eye. "There be a young lad... could be a new playmate f'r ye, Seany." He mussed the boy's hair, then looked back to the ship. "And another man... no wait... I don't believe it, will ye look at the size... och! I dinna believe m' eyes."

"What is it?" Mehlyndia asked, tugging Simon's arm.

He handed her the glass and pointed over her shoulder, "Look fer ye'self and tell me who ye think the young sentry aside Ewan be."

Mehlyndia looked carefully through the glass. When she saw Duncan, she caught her breath, "My God, is that—"

"Duncan Wilbrun," Simon answered before she could finish her question. "Looks like he's earned his eagle. Have we really been here that long?" Simon asked wistfully, taking the glass back from Mehlyndia.

"Let me have a look." Elinor grabbed the glass from Simon and peered through the hole. An expression of recognition, then astonishment passed her face. "Blessed Mother! It could be Sean standing there. I always knew they resembled each other but last I saw Duncan, he was a wee thing, not much bigger than Seany. But just look..."

"Why do you suppose Duncan has come?" Mehlyndia asked to no one in particular.

"We'll know soon enough," Simon answered.

Within a half an hour, the ship had drawn close enough that the looking glass was no longer needed to see the people on the ship, and another quarter hour after that the anchor was noisily lowered into the water, its iron chain making a grand splash. The gang plank was lowered to the pier and soon the young woman was the first to descend to the dock. A young boy, looking a bit green but otherwise cheerful, followed close behind. She stood at the bottom of the plank and waited for Ewan and Duncan to join her before the four of them walked up the dock together.

"Ewan! Old sot, 'tis grand to see ye!" Simon clasped Ewan in a wrist to forearm embrace, slapping him on the upper arm with his free hand.

"And you as well, old friend." Ewan greeted Simon with an enthusiastic smile. He bowed politely to Prissy. She broke into giggles and threw her arms around his neck for a hug. "'Tis good to see you as well, lass. I see you've managed to keep this old rogue on a tight tether."

Prissy stood back smiling, "Ye can be sure of that, Ewan. 'Course it's easy to keep his eye from roving in a place such as this, since there be no tavern dancers to turn his head."

Ewan let out a hearty guffaw at that. "True enough, lass." He grinned, then turned his attention to Mehlyndia. He held out his hand formally to her and bowed his head. "M' lady, ye still be a lovely sight."

Mehlyndia pulled him close and gave him the same sort of hug Prissy had. "No formality here, Ewan. I'm simply Goody Philbrick," she said in his ear, not wishing the other curious settlers who had wandered down to the dock to hear. Josephine Ashcrofte was standing separate, a waspish brow raised, scrutinizing the entire reunion. "I'd be pleased for you to just call me Melly as everyone else does." She gave him an affectionate squeeze before standing back.

"Melly it is," he said, a warm smile in his eyes. "And who is this giant who be standing with you?" He said, giving an impressed look to Seany.

"I'm Seany Philbrick, sir," Seany answered politely, bowing to Ewan.

Mehlyndia could not resist a smug glance toward Josephine at how polite Seany's manners could be, when he chose. But the vicar's wife had wandered back up the path.

"I'm pleased to meet you, sir." Ewan bowed formally, mimicking Seany's seriousness, then grinned at Elinor. "Hello, love. You look younger than the day ye sailed."

"Hello, dear." Elinor gave Ewan a hug in greeting. "I may not be younger, but I certainly appreciate your compliment."

Duncan, the woman, and young lad had been standing back during Ewan's greetings. When he had finished, it was Simon who nodded to Duncan. "And could that really be who I think it is?"

Duncan came forward and extended his hand. "Hello, Simon."

"Duncan Wilbrun, as I live and breathe, I cannot believe my eyes," Simon said, shaking Duncan's hand heartily, then pointed to the badge on Duncan's shoulder. "I see you've stepped into your brother's place at last."

Duncan smiled proudly. "Aye. Lord Edward bestowed it just before we sailed."

"Well it suits you." Mehlyndia said, extending her hand. "You are every inch a Wilbrun. I'd swear it were Sean standing here."

"Thank you m' lady—"

"Please, I'm simply Melly."

"Melly." Duncan smiled, then turned and motioned the woman and lad to come forward. "I'd like you to meet some friends. This is Annlise Chase and her young son Matthew."

Mehlyndia held her hand out in greeting as the woman approached, "I'm pleased... Annlise?" An odd feeling she had known this woman crossed her mind. "Have we met?"

Annlise smiled, a kind twinkle in her bright blue eyes. "Aye, we have, years ago. I was in service at Aberdoir when you came to visit as a young lass."

"You seem more familiar than... I know you from Stonehaven..."

Annlise's eyes widened slightly as she gave a quick, but unmistakable nod toward Duncan. "No, m' lady. I'm sure it be Aberdoir you recall."

Mehlyndia glanced at Duncan as she suddenly recalled how she met Annlise. It was at Drumoak, and she'd arrived sharing Sean's saddle, supposedly after he'd 'rescued' her from an abduction. Of course she had never been abducted, but the look she was giving Melly was the universal pleading all women seemed to understand as 'please don't tell'. "Well it is good to see you again, Annlise."

"You, as well." Annlise nodded the motioned for Matthew to step forward. "This be my son, Matthew."

Matthew blushed and shook Mehlyndia's hand politely, then stepped back.

"Pleased to meet you."

"He was a last minute addition to our trip." Annlise explained, turning a mockingly reproachful grin on the boy. "I'm afraid he takes after his father in his want of mischief."

"I know well how that can be," Mehlyndia giggled.

"Seany has given me many a heart tremor on that count as well. He's got his father's bold streak running through him true and sure."

Annlise looked at Seany and her eyes grew wide. Matthew tugged on her arm, the look on his face matching his mother's as he too, seemed to be amazed with Seany. "Mum... that's Ned—"

"No, son," Annlise patted Matthew's shoulder, keeping her amazed eyes on Seany. "But he certainly looks like him." She shook her head, blushing apologetically to Mehlyndia. "Forgive me, m' lady, it's just the resemblance is remarkable."

"Aye, he does favor his father," Mehlyndia agreed, though she was not sure it was William who Annlise was referring to.

"Of course." Annlise smiled, then stepped to Seany and crouched down to his level. "Ye be ye father all over again. You've got the same light in ye eyes," she said quietly then placed her palm at the base of her throat and said something quietly that Mehlyndia almost didn't hear. "Aye, perhaps the child be of Fylbrigge blood... after all."

"Did you think otherwise, Annlise?" Mehlyndia asked, taken aback by the woman's wonder with her son.

"Oh," Annlise looked up quickly, again blushing through a smile. "No, m' lady. Please forgive me again. My manners must seem atrocious. It's the resemblance to his father I find amazing."

Mehlyndia smiled and accepted this explanation, but felt there was something else Annlise was not telling her, that somehow made her feel uneasy. She instinctually pulled her son closer to her, tightening the grip she had on Seany's hand, and made a mental note to ask Annlise the truth, if she found a moment to speak to her alone.

Seany looked into Annlise's eyes with a childish curiosity. "Do you know my papa, miss?"

"I did, lad." Annlise set a genuinely warm smile onto Seany that relieved some of Mehlyndia's apprehension about the woman. "When he was not bigger than you are right now."

"That was a long, long time ago," Seany said, wide-eyed. "Even before I was born!"

Annlise laughed. "Aye, 'twas at least that long!"

"So where is Will?" Ewan said when all the greetings had finished, then looking at the steep dirt incline that led to the pier, he shook his head. "Ah, I suppose he doesn't come down to the dock?"

"No, that's not it. He's been away for a few days with Ian," Mehlyndia answered, taking Seany's hand, as she ushered the group up the dock toward the path. "I expect them back any—" Mehlyndia stopped mid-sentence as she gained the top of the incline and glanced into the square. The wagon was parked in front of the communal barn. That is where Josephine had wandered to. Ephraim was speaking to her, one hand on her shoulder. She drew her hand to her mouth then turned quickly, looking at Mehlyndia with a strange wide-eyed gape.

"Papa's home!" Seany, broke free from Mehlyndia's hand and raced toward the wagon. She stood frozen, unable to stop him. Ian sat on the driver's bench of the wagon, stone-faced, staring directly at her, there was no one sitting on the bench beside him. For a brief moment, she reasoned that William must be lying down in the back of the wagon, perhaps exhausted from the trip, but the look in Ian eyes and the expressions on Ephraim's and Josephine's faces told her the truth. Her husband had not come back from the woods.

Chapter 9

ABOUT THE SAME time Ian was making his discovery of the torn and bloodied scrap of leather, William opened his eyes to find himself half-sitting beneath a shroud of balsam boughs, his back against a moss covered log, the quilt askew over his shoulder. Filtered sunlight made star-burst patterns in the spaces between the branches. Dazed, he raised his hand to his eyes to rub away the haze but stopped at the shard of pain that shot through his shoulder. He looked down to find his shirt in blood-stained shreds, plastered to his chest. He gingerly pulled a piece of fabric away to find his flesh striped by three long parallel gashes that looked as though they'd been made by a scourge or more likely, a claw— *an eagle's talon? Was Ephraim was right? Was I flailed?* he thought as he poked at the wound with his right hand.

"Ian?" he called out, then began to cough at the dryness in his throat, bringing with it a dull throbbing headache. He closed his eyes and rested back against the log, trying to clear his thoughts, trying to remember how he came to be in the place he now found himself. Wherever this place was.

I was with Ian, and Ephraim. That much I remember. He remembered the wagon falling into the mud, the construction of the litter, the brief nap he had taken, and the conversation he had awoken to. *Dead and buried? They think I'm dead and buried. The demon that wouldn't die is dead and buried. That's rather charming.* He laughed ironically then stopped as the coughing began again. He groaned and held his breath until the sensation passed. *Think, Fylbrigge! Where the hell are you?* He looked through the veil of boughs to see nothing but wild forest beyond. *Forest. Trees... Ian and Ephraim... wind. Moaning, black thing, the dragon is readying her fire. Dragon? No, that was a dream.*

He opened his eyes fully upon remembering the sensation of the hulking black presence that had loomed over him as he was reaching for Ian. He laid his hand on the wound on his chest, matching his finger tips to the gashes. *The dragon? No, that's ridiculous, it was a bear. It had to be.* He glanced in the direction of his leg and saw another gash, and a missing piece of his trousers. *Sean said it would heal. Sean was here? That was a dream. He's not here...*

He brushed away the forest debris that had gathered on his leg. The wound looked ghastly against his pale flesh. A cool morning breeze rustled through the arbor of balsam. Instinctually he pulled the edge of the quilt around himself, then stared at it, *this was on the litter. I couldn't reach the litter. How?* He shivered violently and pulled it close, remembering it had been Sean who had retrieved the quilt for him. *That's impossible. All of this is impossible. Back to sleep. Let it pass, it's still a dream. All a dream...* He closed his eyes, and allowed the blackness of sleep drift over him.

He lay there sleeping, not more than ten feet away from where Ephraim walked the forest calling for him. At dusk, it was Ian who searched that section of forest. Had either of them taken a look to the left, they would have seen William's boots sticking out from beneath the sheltering boughs.

Time passed unaccounted in his sleep. He was vaguely aware of the pain in his shoulder. Somewhere above him, the sound of wings taking flight, then the ear splitting sound of the scream of an eagle. *Give the eagle to my son. I know that. I promised to do that, so he can stand against the dragon.*

Images of Seany paraded through his mind. The sunny little face, all smiles, proudly displaying two scrap boards he had managed to nail together with his father's hammer. *That's my son. I need to give him the eagle.* From some clandestine perch, he watched his son tag along behind Simon with a fishing pole in his hand. Then he watched as Mehlyndia bathed him and readied him for bed. They were simple scenes of his home. Scenes he had watched in person innumerable times, but was now seeing from this odd place he could only call 'away'. In this place, he walked through his home, passing from room to room not through the doors, but through the walls and through the ceilings to the bedrooms on the second level. Prissy and Simon were talking quietly in the room they shared, she was smiling and placing a hand on her stomach. Simon scooped her up in his big arms and whirled her around before setting her gently down onto the bed. The scene made him smile, but he moved along through the floor to the kitchen where Elinor and Mehlyndia were sharing gossip and rifling through bits of colored cloth.

Somewhere outside the house, he could hear what sounded like music. He followed the sound, passing through the side of the house and out to his kitchen yard. It was louder here and he recognized it as a flute. *Ian? Is that you, friend?* The music came from beyond the yard and the square. *It's in the woods.* He followed the sound over the buildings to the edge of the forest. The music grew louder and was most definitely a flute, but it was sounding less like any music that Ian ever played. Deep into the depths of the woods, he followed the sound, seeing the trees from the top instead from the ground, until the sound was right in front of him.

He felt a nudge in his ribs and opened his eyes, startled. "Stop that," he groaned, and the music came to a sudden stop. Someone, or something, jumped away from him as he forced his eyes open. A small figure crouched near the trunk of the balsam, holding a long stick. It jabbed at him, a little more gently this time. "Please, stop that," he said again, then tried to grab the end of the thing that poked him. The figure skittered backwards then dropped the stick, sitting cat-like, staring at him.

"Muin?" It asked, in a childlike voice, shyly pointing toward his shoulder.

William glanced at the wound then back to this little visitor. "I don't understand you."

It crept cautiously closer and he could see clearly now that it was a child, perhaps eight years old, dressed in the garb of the Mi'kmaq. He relaxed a bit, drawing a deep breath that brought about a coughing jag. The child skittered back again. William raised a hand palm up and spoke as calmly as he could, "Please. Don't be afraid. I could use a little help."

The child crept back, closer this time, and now he could see it was a girl-child.

"Muin?" she asked, again motioning to the wound.

He shook his head and shrugged, attempting to communicate that he didn't understand what she was saying.

"Muin." She held her hands up, claw-like, and growled,

hunkering down. "Muin."

"Moo-ween?" He tried to imitate her word as close to the way he had heard it, finally understanding her pantomime. "Bear?" he said, then made a similar claw gesture with his hand. "Bear, yes, muin."

"Ba-eer," she repeated his word, then smiled, nodding. "Muin, ba-eer." Keeping a wary eye to him, she reached for his shirt, and pulled away the fabric, revealing the wound. A sad, concerned look crossed her face. She said something rapidly in her own language, nodding and tapping his face as if to reassure him. She stood, then held out her hands, in an offer to help him to his feet.

"I can't, little one," he said, knowing she didn't understand what he was saying. "Thank you, anyway." He shook his head, pointed down to his legs, and shrugged again.

She made a sad face, pointing to the wound on his leg.

"Well, that's not why, but if it helps you understand..." He nodded an affirmation.

She hunkered down on her haunches, resting her chin in her hand in a posture of thought. William noticed the skin she wore on her hip and wondered if perhaps she was carrying any water with her. He didn't know how long he'd been there, but he knew he was desperately thirsty. He pointed to the skin, "Is that water?"

She tilted her head in question.

He pointed again. "Water?" He made a drinking gesture, then pointed again. "To drink. Water."

"Sam'qwan. E'e," she nodded, enthusiastically, then repeated his own word, even managing to intone a bit of his burr in her interpretation. "Waa-terr." She held up the skin.

"Sam'qwan, waa-terr."

"Sam-kwaaan." He nodded, hoping he was correct. "Could I have some? Please?" He pointed again, then made a beckoning motion with his hand.

"E'e! Sam'qwan." She held out the skin to him and nodded, seemingly happy to accommodate.

He took a sip, then relieved that it actually was water he was drinking, took a good long swallow. The water went down easy and was followed by a growl from his middle.

"Misjisi'k?" She giggled, pointing to his stomach.

"If that means, am I hungry? Then yes, I suppose I am. Mizz-jiss... whatever it was." He forced a smile and shrugged again.

"Misjisi'k," she said, resolutely, then reached around to her back, where she carried another small skin pouch. She opened it, and pulled out what looked like a square of yellowish bread. She broke it in half and handed part to William then took a bite from her own, showing him it was food.

"Thank you." He took what she offered and bit off a small piece. He smiled at her in thanks as he chewed. He recognized the morsel as a treat Akonni's people had once shared that was very much like the bannock Elinor baked they called luskinikn.

He thought about Elinor, Melly, and Seany, home waiting for him to come back. How long had he been in the woods? *Sweet Mother, they are probably frantic. Ian must have gone back for help by now... I hope.*

His little companion nudged him, drawing him away from his worry for the moment. She spoke rapidly again in her own language, but he half understood she was telling him she was going to get something or someone and bring it back to him. At least that was what he hoped she was saying. She stood, brushed the crumbs from her hand, and went to leave him, and he suddenly did not wish to be left alone again.

"Wait."

She turned to look, "E'e?"

"Please, don't leave, just yet. Sit. Tell me your name." He knew it was hopeless, but he kept talking anyway. He patted the ground next to him, then motioned to her. "Sit. Please."

She looked over her shoulder to the forest, then back to where he sat. Making a decision, she came to sit next to him.

"Thank you." He said, then placed his hand on his chest. "I'm William."

She shook her head and shrugged.

"William," he said, again pointing to himself.

"W'yiam." She smiled pointing to him. "W'yiam, E'e." She mimicked his motion, placing her hand on her own chest. "C'ara," she said, smiling. "C'ara."

"Cara." He sighed, hoping he was right, that was her name. "I'm pleased to know you, Cara."

She smiled shyly. "W'yiam."

"I don't suppose you know Akonni?" he asked.

"Akonni! E'e!" She was on her feet, suddenly excited, clapping her hands. She spoke rapidly again, pointing to the forest. "Akonni!" She turned and ran into the woods, disappearing into the shadows.

I hope that means she's gone to get him. He looked to his side and smiled, grateful she had left her water skin with him. *Thank you, Blessed Mother.* He took a drink, then allowed himself to drift back to sleep, hopeful that C'ara would return with Akonni by the time he woke again.

Another dawn found him where he had been the day before. Under the tree, staring at the forest. C'ara's water-skin had been nearly full when she had first given it to him, but now it was nearly empty, with only three or four mouthfuls left. He would save it as long as he could, hoping the little girl came back, or even better, that Ian would show up. In his gut, without knowing why, he knew that Ian would not come for him.

Sleep came in fits, and the wound on his leg turned an evil greenish color that leaked and smelled foul. He was half-grateful he couldn't feel it but he was feeling the fever it brought on, and he knew that meant the wound had festered. The gashes on his shoulder ached, but seemed to be less of an immediate problem as they had already started to close on their own. *Ian would know what to do... or Elinor.* He took a swallow of the water, and rested back against the moss and the dreams came...

"Now, now, Will dear, let Laurel answer on her own. She knows the right thing to do, don't you?" It was Elinor speaking, standing in the herb-house behind Drumoak, a large leather bound book opened before her. William was ready to answer the question, but bit his lip while the girl standing next to him screwed up her face in thought.

"Come on, child, you know what to do for that sort of wound," Elinor said, with an encouraging smile.

"Use the moist side of the oak moss to clean it out... to draw out the evil," Laurel answered, pleased with herself.

"Very good." Elinor smiled.

"See, Will. I know it as well as you do now."

"So how do you hold the moss on the wound, smarty?" William asked, a monkeyish grin on his face.

Laurel crossed her arms across her chest and sat back on a bench with a defeated sigh. "I forgot the proper way." She turned a mischievous grin on him. "But I can think of a charm that would make it stick—"

"Laurel!" Elinor gave her a stern look, placing her hands on her hips. "You know better. Charms are not to be used willy-nilly. Remember, the Blessed Mother and Father demand their price for every charm you place."

"She's right, Laurel." William shook his finger, mocking Elinor's stern expression. "You cannae be casting your charms willy—must you call it that, Elinor?"

Elinor and Laurel burst into giggles, and soon he laughed with them until the image swirled into a blur of colors. The laughter echoed in his head, melting into something less gleeful; his own voice, older, urgent and panicked. The swirling ended and the blur became clear. It was that night... the last night he had spent in Drumoak, when his life had begun to fall apart...

"Yarrow! He needs yarrow! Make a paste and put it under the bandage, here let me... ." He frantically tore away the garment from the wound on his brother's chest as he lay on the table in the kitchen of Drumoak, and applied the paste he had made while Agnes stood aside. "Blessed Mother, please..." He closed his eyes, pressing on the wound with his hand, reciting his chant, silently calling on every fiber of his being to heal... chanting... praying... he wasn't strong enough, he drew his hands away wet and bloodied, he knew he had failed. He turned, whirling, dizzy, the scene changing until he stood before his wife on the beach... .

"... charms and chants and folk magic... we've gone from a matter of faith to casting spells?" Melly's voice was soft, the fear that came to her eyes when she looked at him hurt him so deeply he could barely meet her gaze. He reached for her and she withdrew, and suddenly they were no longer at the shore, but in the bedchamber they shared in the castle. She was holding his journal, the same simple leather bound book he'd written in almost every night. She held it away from herself as though it were something vile that she didn't wish to touch. "You charmed this? Why?"

"Everything I've learned from Elinor is in this book, and things I've found on my own. My chants, powders, potions, charms, songs....I charmed it to keep it private. To anyone else who reads it, this book would seem like a simple collection of verse and songs... at least I hope so. I'm not especially good at charms and I've never had cause to test this one"

"William, you're frightening me."

"I'm not a sorcerer. Please don't be frightened of me."

She turned away from him, rushing to the fire, as though to throw the book into the flames.

"No!" He cried out, reaching his hand to her, but unable to reach, finding himself trapped in his own bed because he couldn't move his legs. It was no longer a book she held, but a simple log in which to stoke up the fire in their bedroom in Port Edin...

The fire on the hearth was already blazing, it didn't need the new log, but it wanted it... he saw it, in the flame... its long tail making lazy cat-like sweeps from side to side, its fire-born eyes staring at him... the dragon.

He opened his eyes with a start, perspiration trickled down his forehead, stinging his eyes. He caught his breath, waiting for the panic brought on by the dream to subside. The images stayed with him, as clearly as he could see his hand before him, he could see them. *It wasn't a dream... it was more than that.* Even the dragon was terribly familiar to him, and her eyes— *her eyes*— seemed tangible. *The dragon is readying her fire...*

He pushed her image away, pulling back the memory of Laurel, and Elinor... *Elinor! She knows everything! She taught all of it, to me. It's in the journal... I remember that. I remember what I could do, what I was...*

He stretched his left arm out to the log and grabbed a fistful of the moist thick moss that was growing there. He had lain against it for how many days? Was it oak moss? Did that matter? It was all he could put his hands on. He covered the wound on his leg with a thick layer and pressed down, forcing the moisture from the moss into the gash until a sticky, brown and green liquid oozed from it. His stomach wretched from the musky smell of the moss as it mingled with the sickening sweet odor that came from the infection. When he pulled it away, the wound lay open, muddied and wet, but the greenish-yellow trickle that had flagged the infection had been washed away, and the puffy swelling around the edges had already subsided.

He turned his face skyward under the mantle of green, allowing what sunlight filtered through the branches to fall on his face. "Thank you, Blessed Mother and Father."

As if in answer, a gentle breeze wafted through the branches, as soft as a kiss on his face, as the fever began to leave him. He stayed that way for a long time, drinking in the wind, as one by one long lost pieces of himself returned to him. The flood gates had, at last, been pushed aside and the river of memories had finally begun to flow. He had been trained in the ancient crafts by Elinor. The crafts of the herbs and the charms. She had taught him her faith, revering both God and Goddess, The Blessed Mother and Father, the Old Ones, and he had embraced it. He had learned to use the Gods-given gifts of the Earth. Folk magic. Melly knew and he now understood why she had kept it from him, and why Elinor had reacted so strangely when he remembered the recipe for the feverfew tea; not because they reviled it or feared it, but simply because in their homeland, under the ever watchful and superstitious eye of king and clergy, these talents he had learned and the faith he had kept hidden would have been given a name. A name that was misunderstood and unjustly used against him. He would have been called— a witch.

William's newly recovered insight not only put to rest some of the nagging questions that had been eluding him for years, but it gave him something valuable to address a more fundamental need; something to eat. He'd been sitting there for days, with nothing more in his belly than that one piece of luskinikn C'ara had given him. It had crossed his mind more than once that even if he survived the infection, if someone didn't find him soon, he was likely to starve. But as the memories of his talents with the herbs and plants came to him, so then he became more aware of his immediate surroundings. He had stared at the little sprouts that grew near the base of the tree for a couple of days not realizing what they were. *Fronds.* The first of the spring ferns had pushed through the soil and were still curled into tight green spirals. They would serve as a meal for that day. Behind him, large funnel-shaped leaves of a ground lily had captured the dew from the morning, trapping it in the well of the greens. If he was careful enough, he could drain it into the skin, and there would be at least a little bit water for another day.

With the wound now cleaned, the fever broken, and something in his stomach, he settled back against the log, taking a mental accounting of all he had remembered. There were still more holes in his memories. He still didn't remember any trial or the tortures Ephraim had alleged he'd endured. But what he did remember was that Laurel had learned the craft alongside him, which meant that she would also have been in danger of being accused. Ian had not seemed eager to speak of Laurel; was it because he knew what she was? Or was it that he knew what had really become of her? Had she stood trial with him?

He dozed, dwelling on the thought, forcing himself to imagine a courthouse. A few times, he came perilously close to pulling a clear picture into his mind. He saw two long tables. To his right, the man he called 'father', Lord Edward, sitting somber-eyed next to a young man dressed as Sean had, in kilt and brat, wearing a crest of the dual raptors on his shoulder. He could not bring the man's name to mind, but he looked familiar. In fact he looked almost like himself, with the same green eyes and black hair. *Was that my other brother?* In front of Edward, seated on a plain bench, he recognized Ian dressed in the garb of a cleric, sitting next to a young acolyte. *Ian's assistant? No, that's a girl... Laurel? No, that can't be right.* He tried to concentrate on the face of the acolyte, but the image would be lost, dissolving into a haze.

The only other image of his trial that came to him, he dismissed immediately as a product of his near delirium. After all, it was ridiculous to think that a four-headed dragon was actually in attendance at his trial. Twice he forced himself to discard the image of the monster, crouched on the table where the witnesses for the prosecution had gathered. But it came back, clearer each time, a hideous four-headed dragon that seemed eager to devour him where he sat. One head looked like a dragon with fiery eyes and long jagged teeth. Next to the first, the head of a jet-black snake with beady green eyes. Next to the snake, the head of a wild boar, nostrils flaring. The last head, seemed to be a human skull staring at him from compassionless, eyeless sockets, a tall mitered hat resting over its brow. *There was no dragon in the courtroom.*

The dragon is readying her fire. What did that mean? Sean? Are you still with me? Is that the dragon my son will face? I don't understand, please come back...

He would have slept the remainder of that day, had he not been awakened again by the flute. *Ian? It's about time...*

"Kwe'?" A man's voice was speaking. It wasn't Ian. The flute music continued, coming from somewhere behind the speaker. "Kwe'? W'yiam? Hello?"

At the familiar word, William opened his eyes, shaking his head to clear it. A man dressed in deerskin trousers and shirt was crouching near the tree. "Akonni?" He almost cried with relief at seeing the familiar face of the Mi'kmaq Shaman.

"W'yiam? Is that you, my friend?" Akonni's accent was thick, but he had learned English well in his dealings with the settlers. He held aside the lowest balsam bough, allowing the sunlight to fully illuminate William's face. "C'ara." He turned to the little girl, who was sitting on a rock just beyond the tree, playing a little wooden flute, and motioned for her to join him. She smiled and skittered up next to him. He spoke softly, in a gentle voice, giving the child a hug as he did then turned back to William. "She got confused in her mind of where you sat. That is why it has taken me two sunsets to find you."

"I'm just very glad to see you now," William said, then gestured to his leg. He had plastered another layer of moss onto the wound before he had fallen asleep the last time. "I've a bit of trouble here, I'm afraid." He pushed the moss away, displaying the wound.

Akonni examined the gash, then looked over his shoulder and gave C'ara rapid instructions in his own language. The little girl listened closely, then repeated what he said before she got to her feet and raced away into the forest. "She goes for more water and fire wood. This will need to be cured."

"Firewood? Akonni, I've been here for days, I don't want to camp anymore, I'd like to go home. Could you help me go home please?"

"In time. The wound is foul, my friend. It will not wait." The Shaman pulled a small skin from his pouch and poured a clear liquid from it onto William's leg. It smelled of spirits— distilled spirits. *Whiskey?* When it hit the wound, it reacted to something on his skin and bubbled up around the edges.

Akonni frowned, then put the skin back to his belt.

"It has festered, yes. It was worse, but I drew it out with the moss," William explained, as he re-examined the wound himself. The edges had begun to turn again. "Can you dress it for me, then take me home?"

Akonni seemed to ignore William as he closely scrutinized the gash, then turned his attention to the parallel cuts on William's shoulder. "You are fortunate Muini'skw has protected you."

"Who?"

"Muini'skw. The Bear Woman," Akonni told him matter-of-factly, as he went about opening a pack he carried. "Muini'skw protects Her own, Her children. She is the Sacred Mother, the Provider. She has provided for you," he said, gesturing toward the patch of fronds and the sheltering boughs above him. "And She has protected you."

"Blessed Mother," William said quietly. "Yes, She has provided."

Akonni withdrew a small hide blanket from his pack and laid it on the ground, then reverently arranged an assortment of dried leaves, powders, small stones and porcupine quills onto it. He sang something in his own language under his breath, picking up each item and holding it aloft in offering before he placed it back onto the skin.

Though the words the man spoke were foreign to him, William recognized that he was praying, calling the power and wisdom of his Gods into his elements of healing. A ritual not unlike one he may have performed in his former life when he practiced his craft. He half-smiled at the irony of how it was not unlike the way the Christian clerics held their elements of communion to God for blessing. *Father in Heaven, Blessed Mother, God Creator, Provider, Muini'skw... many names for the same being.*

"Akonni?" C'ara had returned, her arms laden with dried wood and twigs. She dropped her burden in a pile just beyond the bough.

"Wela'like, C'ara, thank you." Akonni smiled to the child, then motioned for her to sit down. "She's brought the fire wood. I will make use of the bones of your campfire to light it." He backed out from under the boughs.

"What campfire?" William asked. "I've had no fire the entire time I've been here."

Akonni stopped short and stared, a genuinely confused look on his face. He held up the branch high and pointed to a ring of stones surrounding the ashen remains of several small logs within the circle. "The winds have yet to scatter these to the woods. They cannot be more than four or five sunsets." He reached into the ash, and withdrew a blackened mass of *something* that had been skewered to the end of stick. He held it out to show to William, then set it aside and reached back to the ashes. He shifted them around, sifting them through is fingers until he retrieved a fistful of small bones. "Was this not your meal of rabbit meat?"

William was thunderstruck at Akonni's discovery. *The rabbits. They were real. Sean made me eat..." You really should eat something. It may be a long time before you have the chance again."*

"W'yiam?"

William saw Akonni rushing toward him as he felt himself listing to the side as everything went black.

When he opened his eyes again, he found himself lying prone on a skin blanket looking at a lattice work of birch logs, and bark, the pungent aroma of smoldering wood stung his nose and eyes. A flaxen dressing covered the wound on his shoulder, and a poultice made from oak moss was fastened to his thigh with a course twine. He managed to get his elbows under himself enough to push up and lean on them and was startled to find that he was naked, and he had been cleaned of mud and grime. "Oh my." He looked around his surrounding, not sure whether he were awake or dreaming. He was alone in the lodge, though he could hear muffled voices just outside. "Akonni?"

The murmurs quieted. The animal hide that served as a door was pushed aside, allowing William a glimpse of the sun, just now setting beyond the ridge. *Another day lost.* A young woman, perhaps twenty, entered the lodge carrying a large wooden bowl. William reached for the edge of the skin he was lying on, and self-consciously pulled it over himself, even though he reasoned that this woman may have been the one who had washed him. Akonni entered the lodge behind her.

"You have awakened. This is well for you, my friend." Akonni spoke, calmly in easy candor. He laid his hand on William's forehead briefly, then frowned, but said nothing. William was aware of the disorientation that comes from a fever.

Akonni was dressed in a more elaborate costume than the one William had first seen him in. The shirt was made from a single piece of hide, a moose perhaps, that had been dyed white and lavishly embroidered with symbols of animals, and birds. Beads made from shells and bones, sewn in painstakingly minute patterns along an elaborate breast plate sparkled in the light. He wore a head covering that resembled the head of a bear, and a cape, also made of hide, that was adorned with an intricate quill pattern and more beads. He carried a rolled skin in his right hand and in his left, a long staff decorated with the fur of a fox, some rabbit, and a few large feathers. He nodded to the woman and, speaking quietly in his own language, seemed to be giving her instructions. She listened closely, then placed the bowl down next to the cot, before leaving the two men.

"Food, W'yiam. Please, eat until your belly is content."

William reached to the bowl with his right arm, while trying to balance on his left. He was hungry, to be sure, but eating while lying down was proving to be awkward. He never liked to ask for help from anyone outside his family and was reluctant to ask Akonni to help him sit up, but one glance down to the skin that covered him and he had to laugh at himself. *What's left of my dignity to guard?* He held a hand to the Shaman, and swallowed his pride. "If you please, I need to sit up."

Nonplused, Akonni set his pack down and grasped William's arm, elbow to wrist, and helped him up. His vision blurred into blotches from the fever as he sat, but he closed his eyes for a moment and the sensation passed. The cot rose only about a foot above the floor and he found he needed to arrange his legs to cross at the ankles to keep his balance. He did this the only way he could, by lifting one foot and then the other, putting them where he needed them. He hid his embarrassment with a smile and a quip, as he did with

Mehlyndia each morning. "I've been intending to get these repaired. I just haven't found the time."

Akonni smiled in return, then lowered himself to a thatched mat and sat cross-legged facing William. "It was not my purpose to cause you to fear. Please—" He gestured to the bowl. "—eat. Muini'skw has provided."

"I'm not frightened."

"Your eyes tell a different tale." Akonni's expression softened. "But I tell you, you are among friends."

"Why am I here?" William asked, pulling the skin around his lap. "And why..." He looked down at himself. "It's not that I'm ungrateful for your help... but..."

"The need to bring you here was shown to me," Akonni said. "I could not do as Niskam told me I must, there under the tree."

"Niskam?"

"The Creator. The Spirit."

"God?"

Akonni nodded and motioned to the food. "W'yiam, I can count the bones under your flesh, do you never eat?"

"Of course," William smiled apologetically, then ate a small piece of luskinikn and some dried berries, from the bowl. "I did not mean to offend... I am grateful for your help, but if you please, I'd very much like to go home to my wife and son. I'm sure they must be worried—"

"Eat," Akonni interrupted. "The sun is beyond the hills. When it has returned, I will bring you to your family. But for this time, you must eat."

William didn't argue and ate more of the berries and several pieces of dried and salted meat. The woman entered the lodge again, this time bearing a large pot of a steaming liquid. Akonni dipped a wooden cup into the brew, then handed it to William.

"It is pitewey."

"Thank you." William accepted the cup and blew into the hot liquid. The aroma was pungent, acrid, and nothing at all familiar to him. He sipped slowly, then finding the taste to be far more pleasant than the aroma, he drank all that was provided, and admitted that it was the most satisfying meal he'd experienced in a long time. He was disappointed to lose another night away from home, but could not argue with the logic in waiting for the daylight.

As William ate, Akonni spread out the skin, as he had under the tree. He arranged the bundles of leaves, and powders as he had before, reverently chanting under his breath with each element he placed. *Just as a priest blesses the Eucharist...*

"Akonni? Did Ian come to your village?"

Akonni looked up, a half-surprised look on his face. "He did not. The village has moved, as it does each turning of the season. I was on my way to seek him in Port Edin. I did not think he would know to come here."

"The village moved?" William felt an unexpected wave of anger rise up. Ian had not been nearly as prepared for this trek as he had let on. He had taken him into the woods without knowing where he was headed then had fallen asleep, drunk. William had assumed that Ian must have gone to look for him or, at the very least, he had sought out Akonni to help in the search. But given the haphazard way Ian planned the trip, the sickening realization came to William that his friend— his best friend— had more than likely given him up for lost and returned to Port Edin, not to recruit help but to inform them of his loss. "I have to go home. Now. Akonni, I can't wait until morning."

"It is not wise. The forest belongs to the four-legged in the night."

"But they may think I'm dead," William argued, his voice taking on an edge of panic. "My wife... my son, I have to go home! I have to give the eagle to my son!" The days spent in the woods had more of an effect on him than he had originally thought and he suddenly discovered he could no longer keep control of his own emotions. In near panic, he tried to explain to the Shaman what he did not even understand himself. "Sean told me, I have to give the eagle to my son. Don't you understand? He'll need it to face the dragon." He reached forward toward Akonni. The world was suddenly a swirling blur again.

Akonni was able to catch him before he fell off the edge of the cot. "The shade is clouding you. It is as I was shown." He took William's shoulders in his hands and guided him to lie down again. "Niskam will guide me. It must be done this night. The shade wishes to be heard."

William took a breath to steady his nerves, he was finding it more difficult by the moment to keep his eyes focused on Akonni. "Shade?"

"The one who led me." Akonni kept his hands on William's shoulders until he finally relaxed and lay still. "All will be told you. The power you possess has been shown to me. The shade has told me it is time for you to do as you must, but first, we must banish the darkness that you carry. The purification must be done this night."

William shook his head, now even more confused, and though Akonni's expression was one of reassurance, his words were alarming. His head was swimming more and more, and he was beginning to wonder if the pitewey was responsible. "Purification?"

The Shaman nodded, an enigmatic expression on his face. He turned and returned to the cloth and continued his preparations.

A purification? He's preparing for a ritual that much is clear. A healing? How bad can that be? It's just a prayer. That's all it is, they mean to help me. William's self-assurances turned to panic when, even through his less than perfect vision, he recognized one of the objects Akonni was holding aloft; William's own wood carving knife that he always carried in his belt.

Akonni's voice took on a monotone drone. "There is death around you. It must be cut away," he said, as he placed the knife onto the cloth.

William's eyes widened. "What?"

Akonni ignored him, continuing his drone, "It must be done. It is as Niskam has shown."

It became obvious to William, at that point, there was more than a prayer session planned for him, and he had no say in his own participation. The half-comfort he had taken in the similarities of Akonni's faith to what he remembered of his own quickly drained away as Akonni's preparations became more foreign and he realized he had really no understanding of the Shaman's faith at all. He had never believed the rumors he had heard muttered about the settlement of the native religion and how they were believed by some to partake in ritualistic blood-letting. It had all sounded far too fantastic to him, but— *there is death around you, it must be cut away—* did not sound the least bit reassuring.

He tried to voice his protest, but found he was unable to form the words. *The pitewey! Stay awake, Will. Stay awake. I'm not going to allow it. Stay awake. Stay with the living...* His arms became impossible to move and his eyelids far too heavy to remain open. His eyes betrayed him and closed briefly. He forced them opened again. *Stay awake!*

The woman who had brought the food returned and stood over him, a palm-sized bowl in her left hand, a stick tipped with a piece of fur in the other. She dipped the stick into the bowl and withdrew it, wet with a pasty red substance, and drew a line from his left cheek to his right, over the bridge of his nose, then made three dabs on his forehead, chanting the whole time. She removed the flax from the wound on his shoulder and painted zigzag patterns onto his chest and stomach.

His eyes closed briefly and when he looked again, she was gone. Akonni, bear hood drawn down over his eyes, stood at his head, chanting in a near musical drone, his staff raised skyward in supplication. A drummer, hidden from his sight, began a rhythmic accompaniment to the Shaman's song. Six people approached out of the shadows and stood around the cot, their hands also raised, antiphonally answering Akonni's chant. At his feet, an elderly woman, small and shriveled, yet with eyes that shown bright with life, assumed the lead in Akonni's chant, and the others now answered her.

Akonni laid down the staff and walked to where he had

lain his elements. The others moved away from the cot, enlarging their circle to the edges of the lodge, encircling Akonni, William, and the fire ring. The Shaman picked up a bundle of leaves from his cloth and held them aloft before crumbling them into a large seashell. He chanted; the others answered. The elderly woman stepped forward, and using another shell, plucked a few burning embers from the fire and added them to Akonni's leaves. Smoke rose from the shell. He held it to the east and droned his musical call. He turned to the south, then the west and north seriatim, blessing the four corners of the lodge and each of the assembled people with the smoke. He dipped his finger in the ash left in the shell and drew black lines across William's face and chest, matching the pattern the young woman had made with the paint.

The elderly woman crouched to the skin and retrieved a handful of the powder and handed it to Akonni. He raised his face and made a less musical sound, deep in his throat. He spoke rapidly in his own language then tossed the powder into the fire, sending a flash of orange sparks spiraling up through a hole in the roof of the lodge. A thick orange cloud of smoke billowed up with the embers, sending wispy tendrils up into the night sky.

William watched, mesmerized by the flame, his fear momentarily quieted in his fascination as he watched Akonni's eyes flutter and roll back. The Shaman stood rigid, arms raised, until it seemed he would leave the floor in flight. He stayed that way for several minutes before he lowered his arms, and turned to William. "It is time," he said. "You have a power within you, but the dark spirit you carry has kept it from you. The death must be cut away in order for the light to guide you."

William tried to answer, but could only watch, feeling trapped within his own skin, his arms still heavy at his sides. All that he could move were his eyes and he was struggling to keep them open. *Why can't I move?* He could see and hear all that was taking place around him, but the smoke and the shadows cast by the fire clouded his thinking. He struggled to move even an inch, concentrating desperately on merely lifting his hand or twitching a finger. *I can't move! Blessed Mother, help me!* He watched, helpless to respond while Akonni moved dance-like in the glow of the fire. The drumming and chanting grew faster and louder as Akonni's dance became more intense, the fringe of his cape flayed in a feather-like blur as he dipped and whirled. Beyond the Shaman, the spectators' faces melted and transfigured before him into the shapes of the demon-like beings he had seen beyond the doors of Drumoak in his nightmares, melding in and out of the smoke. William stared, afraid to blink, deafened by the beating of his own heart as it seemed to echo the sound of the drum. He caught his breath and held it. At the same instant, the drummer ended his beating with one tremendous strike and the chanting suddenly silenced. Akonni knelt and picked up the knife and reverently placed it into the embers of the fire.

The blade can burn as well as cut. William was overcome with an overwhelming urge to scream as he stared, immobile and helpless, at the glowing blade, but even his voice was not within his control. One by one, the distorted faces of the people faded from his vision, swallowed into the smoke, until all he could see was Akonni, the fire, and the knife. The Shaman withdrew the blade from the embers and held it aloft. William watched, horrified, as now Akonni, as the people around him had done, began a hideous metamorphosis into a monstrously huge man-beast with massive hands. The bear-hooded cape shifted into the brown woolen robes of a cleric, the bear face transfiguring into a hideous boar with golden eyes and blood staining its piggish snout and teeth.

Around him, the birch bark walls of the lodge dissolved revealing rough stone blocks in their place. In a rush of vertigo, William was overcome with the sensation that he had been lifted from the cot, though he could neither see, nor feel who—or what—was lifting him. He felt his arms being raised and held taught over his head as he was lifted vertically from his prone position. The beast in the robes turned to face him, the eyes flashing menacingly in the fire light, as it gazed at the hot blade it held. He stared transfixed and terrified as his own carving knife, as familiar to him as his own hand, now glowed and writhed like a red tongue of molten steel, elongating itself then solidifying into a flat double-edged dagger.

"I made no pact!" William screamed out, though his voice seemed lost in his throat. His eyes were wide, though he distrusted what they were showing him. The dagger came closer, seemingly floating in front of the mysterious cleric who wielded it.

"Close your eyes, Will." A calm and blessedly familiar voice spoke to him from behind his ear. "This isn't what you think."

Sean? William almost wept in relief, but could not take his eyes away from the glowing blade.

"Right behind you," the voice assured him. "Don't look at it, it will make it easier."

No! I won't allow it. Not again!

"It's not what you think, they are here to help you."

What are they doing? Sean, I've been here before. I won't allow it again.

"Look into the fire instead!" Sean's voice held no room for argument. William forced his eyes from the blade to fire. What he saw there seemed even more terrifying than the monster with the knife.

It's here, Sean. She's back. The dragon is in the flame.

"Look over it. Look at the Shaman."

I can't see him. It's not Akonni anymore, it's... God Sean, it's him. The boar. I see the fire in his eyes. The dragon is telling him what to do. It's happening again! I won't allow it...

"No, Will, they're not real! It's time to let them go. You have to let them go, or you'll never be able to give the eagle to your son."

The dagger moved even closer, and seemed to be hovering only inches from his face. William forced himself to look past it, to the fire. *Tell me what to do! Sean, what do I do? I can't move again.*

"Look at me!" Sean's voice left the place behind his ear, coming instead from within the fire. William forced his attention there.

As the smoke swirled up, illuminated by the flame, it began to take the shape of a man. *I can see you.* The fire itself had also begun to transform, and soon the terrible and familiar neck and tail were plainly visible. *She's in the fire, Sean. I see her.* He was aware of the dagger in front of him, but kept his eyes on the fire.

"Tell me when to do it," Sean said, as the smoke figure raised its arms, displaying a long broadsword.

When? To do what?

The dagger moved down, away from his face, but he could feel the heat close to his chest, then near his stomach, then hip, moving slowly along his torso. He set his eyes unblinking at the dragon. It stared back through fiery orange eyes, revealing sharp needle-like teeth in a ravenous grin. *She's readying her fire!*

"Tell me when to strike!" The smoky sword was lifted higher, held in pre-strike.

William's body began to convulse as he stared, and he could smell the searing of his own flesh, and knew the molten dagger had made contact with his skin. The dragon released a banshee-like screech of laughter then sprung from its haunches, leaping from the ring of the stones, leathery wings beating against the ground.

Now, brother! Do it now!

In an elegant arc, before the dragon could fully take to flight, Sean brought his ethereal sword down on its sinewy neck, severing the head and sending it hurling back down into the fire. He let out an earsplitting whoop of victory as the rest of the creature disintegrated into sparks and drifted benignly into the night sky, carried away by his smoke. When the last of the sparks had vanished, the smoke image of Sean lowered his sword and turned his head toward William. For an instant, his eyes shown clear and green, and his form seemed solid.

Thank you, my brother.

Sean nodded and half-smiled before his eyes began to turn gold, and the features of his face and cheeks began to transform. As tendrils of smoke swirled up around him, he spread his arm and they became glorious eagle-like wings which effortlessly lifted him with the heat of the fire through the hole in the roof and away into the night sky.

Come back, Sean... don't leave again. "No!" The sound of his own scream brought William back to himself. To his relief, he found he was still lying prone on the cot, his arms resting beside him, and not bound above him. The stone walls dissolved back into the birch bark they actually were, and once again it was Akonni, and not the cleric he remembered from the prison, who now stood above him.

He caught his breath and looked down to the source of the pain that had made him cry out. Akonni, had cauterized the gash on his leg with the knife, cutting away the edges of the infected wound as he did so. The burn was excruciating and his first impulse was to lash out at the Shaman as the blade was withdrawn. But instead, he lay grinding his teeth against the pain. His entire body was drenched in perspiration and his head pounded. He closed his eyes, drawing his breaths carefully as he slowly began to relax. *It's over.*

Akonni began another chant, which was answered by the people. Then slowly, they turned and filed out of the lodge one by one until only Akonni was left.

When they were alone, William opened his eyes, forcing his breathing to be steady. He distrusted the messages he was receiving from his own mind and body, but after a few moments, he came to realize there was no mistaking what he was feeling. He swallowed hard and at last was able to find his voice. "Akonni, my leg hurts."

Akonni turned and casually removed the bear hood he had been wearing, and shed the painted cape as well, laying both hood and cape reverently on the ritual skin. He approached William and leaned over him. Tears trailed down the man's face. "You have done well, my friend. The dark spirit that has long held you has been cut away."

"He killed the dragon," William said, allowing tears to find him as well. Though his were a mixture of joy, and agony from the pain in his leg.

"I saw," Akonni said. "You are stronger than the dragon and the other that has haunted you. I saw the animal spirits around you. Those that came to do harm; the boar and the fire snake. Those that came to uphold you; the eagle and the field mouse. They are with you still. Your strength will come from knowing this. The spirit of eagle and mouse are your guides."

"I saw the eagle, but..." William looked toward the hole in the ceiling, then to back to the ring of stones that contained the waning fire, "I saw no mouse. I don't understand."

"Mouse is a shy spirit and stays hidden. But she is fierce of heart and protective of her own. She stays close, though you may not yet see her."

William listened only half understanding. He had seen only the dragon and the image of the man who had always been at her beck and call, the one who always took the shape of a boar in his nightmares. He knew now, the boar was the same man who had wielded the dagger that had put him off his feet. It was Joseph, the Abbot of Aberdoir. And he knew the dragon as well. It was the woman who had been his foster-mother for twelve long years, Melly's sister; Bryndah, the Countess of Aberdoir. *The fire snake and the boar.*

Like the random colored stones in a mosaic, one by one, the pieces were joining together to make a clear picture. The image was not all together pleasant to see, but he relished the sight of it anyway because it meant his life was returning to him, just as the excruciating pain in his leg meant that life was returning to his limbs.

Akonni stayed with William for a few hours into the night. He mixed a potent brew from pungent bark and mushrooms that he assured William would help dull the pain and allow him a comfortable night's sleep. The Shaman resumed his spot on the thatched mat in front of him. William sat on the edge of the cot with the skin blanket drawn around his shoulders, sipping the brew in small doses. His mind reeled from all that had happened and he really was not eager to go to sleep just yet. The pain of the burn had lessened, thanks to a poultice of aloe and dandelion milk. Akonni had taken care to dress it loosely, preventing the injury from sticking to the dressing. For the moment, the most obvious sensation he could feel in his limbs was the pain from the burn. Subtle touches, like the weight of the blanket on his lap or the touch of a breeze were not quite apparent to him, though he was keenly aware of the prickly numbness that was making its way from his thighs down to his knees. The sort of numbness that comes from sitting too long. It wasn't much, but it was worlds more than he had felt in years.

The elderly woman and the younger woman who had

delivered the pitewey had come back to the lodge after the ritual with clear water and cloths. William offered no protest as they washed him of the ceremonial paint and ashes. Once he was clean, they brought him a pair of trousers and a shirt both made of the soft buckskin the Mi'kmaq favored for their clothing. Akonni explained that his own clothing had been fouled with the infection and had been burned. His boots, however, were returned to him.

"Thank you... I'm sorry, I don't know your name," William said shyly, as the younger woman gathered up her bowls and cloths. She looked at him, blushing with a girlish giggle. William judged her age to be close to his own. "I suppose you don't understand what I'm saying, do you?" he asked kindly, more to himself than to her.

Akonni chuckled. "This is my daughter, Ah'Reehl."

She smiled, peeking up through her dark bangs.

"Ahhh-reeeaal... *Ariel*," William said the name as he had heard it, trying to match the way Akonni had pronounced it. "I'm pleased to know you, Ariel."

"Teluisikl, W'yiam?" she said, tilting her head.

William looked to Akonni.

"Ah'Reehl, asks if she may call you W'yiam."

"Oh, William. Yes." He nodded to her with a smile.

The tea was beginning to take effect by the time the woman had wrangled him into his new clothing. When he was dressed, Ah'Reehl stood back with an amused look in her eye. She whispered something to Akonni with a shy giggle. Akonni laughed in response.

"Am I allowed to ask?" William said, amused at the woman's laughter.

"My daughter says the clothing makes you look L'nu'k. As one of our people."

"Kusapun," she said, pointing to William, and then running her hand through her hair, "maqtewe'k, tepkik."

William smiled politely, then shrugged.

Akonni, patted her hand, and said to her, "Speak in his tongue, Ah'Reehl. Do not be afraid."

She nodded, then tilted her head, choosing her words, before she said, "Your hair. It is like L'nu'k."

"Oh. Yes, I suppose it is," William laughed quietly. "It used to be *all* quite black. I'm afraid the white streaks make me look rather like a skunk." He grinned, hoping his little joke would help the girl relax a bit.

She gave him a puzzled look and shook her head. She looked at Akonni and the two shared a shrug. "What white do you speak of?" Akonni asked. "Your hair is black as Raven's son."

"Well these..." William raked his hands through his hair where he knew the streaks to be. He had let it grow quite long— past his shoulder— and was able to hold it out far enough to easily see the white that framed his face, but what he was raking through his fingers now seemed completely black. "I dinnae understand. It's all black again!"

Akonni let out a hearty laugh. "You will find there are many changes within and around you." He leaned forward and tapped William's right knee lightly.

The touch sent a faint wave of prickles down William's leg. The sensation brought a wince followed by a grin to his face. "It's already more than it was an hour ago." He closed his eyes and gave his knee a thump then laughed loudly at feeling the impact of his hand on his leg. "I suppose it's too much to dream that I'll be able to walk. Right now, I'm just grateful for this much."

Akonni reached for the ankle on William's uninjured leg, supporting it under the calf, he straightening the knee. "Close your eyes. Tell me what this feels like." The Shaman ran his thumb along William's sole from heel to toe.

"Go ahead," William said. He opened his eyes to see Akonni frowning. "I didn't feel a thing."

"Close your eyes again, and tell me where it stops."

William closed his eyes and was easily able to tell where Akonni was touching his leg at the knee, behind the calf, the shin, the crease behind his knee. But then— nothing. William opened his eyes. Akonni was holding his foot, but the sensation was lost below the scars on his ankles. The Shaman gently lowered his leg and they repeated the exercise with the other. It was the same. The life was returning to his legs, but his feet were still as foreign as if they were part of someone else's legs rather than his own.

"I suspected as much," William sighed, and drank the remainder of his tea, swallowing his hope with the brew. "I was deliberately hobbled by a knife cut on my ankles," he explained quietly, staring past Akonni. "I didn't know that until tonight. It all came back during the ritual. I had hoped that part was only a dream, but now I know it was real. I felt the cut when he did it and at that moment, I knew... the damage that was done. The cut should not have stolen the use of my legs, but something else... I don't remember clearly just yet... something else happened later. Something must have been done to my back."

"You have carried anger in your heart and it has served to feed the dark spirit that had lived there." Akonni matched William's quiet tones. "When the dark spirit was sent away, the healing could begin."

"My ankles will never heal," William said flatly. "But my back... I think something may be working there again. At least a little."

Akonni chuckled under his breath. "You do not fully believe it was Niskam and Muini'skw who touched you this night, do you?"

William only made a halfhearted grin, and averted his eyes. "I've seen too much in my life to discount anything completely. I'd like to believe it... but..."

"Backs and muscles heal best when the body is fully relaxed," Akonni offered, in a logical, scientific manner. "Perhaps, it was merely the pitewey and days under a tree with nothing better to do but sleep that eased the injury to your back."

William gave Akonni a wary look, suspecting the man was humoring him. "I spent five months asleep after it happened, Akonni. Rest alone did not cure this. There has to be something more to..." He stopped and caught the gleam in Akonni's eye. "I've just proven your argument, haven't I? That the healing came from..." He gestured with his hand toward the sky.

"The answers are not all mine to share. My purpose tonight was to drive the death-infection from the wound on your leg. That is all I hoped to achieve. That is all I set out to do. The rest is as much a mystery to me as it is to you."

William nodded, then yawned. The tea was taking its

course. "Whatever it was, I'm grateful beyond words."

Akonni smiled and got up from where he was sitting. "Sleep, my friend. And we will pray, each to the Spirit of our own choosing, that the morning brings you further healing." He assisted William to lie down, then drew a covering, that turned out to be Melly's quilt, up over him. William smiled, seeing that the quilt had been spared the fate his clothes had met, and that someone had taken the time to wash it clean for him.

"Thank you." He closed his eyes and before Akonni had even left the lodge, he had fallen asleep.

His dreams that night were full of mixed memories, some pleasant, some terrifying. He watched the drama of his life unfold in vivid clarity, from Aberdoir to Drumoak. From Drumoak to Port Edin, each image etching itself indelibly into his mind.

He dreamed of Aberdoir, where he had spent his childhood. He saw himself terrified, hiding behind the skirt of a young woman who was protecting him. Bryndah had followed him to the kitchen and the woman, Rebecca, had slapped her to keep her from hurting him. He saw Rebecca later, bound to the stake and crying for him to run away.

He dreamed of his wedding and the invader who brought the celebration to an abrupt ending with an arrow. The arrow that was meant for himself had found another victim instead, and he watched as Isaac died in his arms.

He dreamed of Sean and the childhood adventures of pirates and dragons they had played in the caves under Drumoak. He saw them older, swords drawn facing down a squadron of hunters in a crowded meetinghouse then racing away unscathed after the encounter. He saw Sean angrily holding him against a wall, telling him to stay where he was, it was too dangerous to go out with him that night. And he saw Ian performing the death rites over Sean's dying body.

He dreamed of Laurel, sweet and small with her wide brown eyes and mischievous smile, always there with a kind word and a helping hand. He saw himself teaching her to read and write, and, astonishingly, how to read Latin. She learned quickly and William was so proud of her, though they had kept the secret of her learning well-guarded between them. He saw her in the trial chambers using that knowledge in a dangerous gamble to save him from the death-fire. She stood, hands bound behind her held by two hunters, her eyes afire, intoning a blessing in Latin in a dramatic voice that had convinced the judge that it was she, and not he, who was the witch. He saw her led from the chamber on her way to the scaffold and stake that had been meant for him.

Though his dreams were painful, his sleep was sound, and even the tears he shed did not wake him. He dreamed of rain falling lightly on the roof of the lodge, sending random drips through the bark. A gentle nurturing rain that fell on him, washing away the pain, but leaving the memories intact.

The thunder came at dawn, rolling endlessly through the mountains, softly at first and then louder, until a particularly loud clap startled him awake. His face was still wet, though the rain had not really come, and the morning sky was clear and cloudless. Yet the thunder continued. He was about to discount the rumbling as a dream when he heard it again, echoing through the valley.

Chapter 10

I AN STOOD WHEN Elinor entered the parlor and crossed the distance from his chair by the fire to her quickly. "How is she?"

"She's finally asleep," Elinor said, wiping her face with her apron. "Poor thing. She took a strong powder and cried herself to sleep."

Ian took Elinor's hand and led her to her favorite chair by the fire. It had been a long emotional evening for everyone. With the arrival of Ewan and Duncan earlier that day, the evening should have been spent in laughter and the reminiscing between old friends, but instead it had turned into a wake. And he felt responsible. Of course it was his fault. He was the one who brought William out there to the woods on a fool's quest for a nomadic tribe who never stayed in the same place more than a few months. For what purpose? He couldn't even remember. And then what had he done? Gotten them deliberately stranded just to stop Ephraim from telling William about his own life. *His own life! He had every right to know what had happened to him! What right did I have keeping it from him? Would it have really made a difference?*

He pushed his own self-pity aside to give his attention to Elinor. Her face was blotched and swollen around her eyes. He knew she had done her best to be strong and stoic for Mehlyndia's sake, but he could see that she could well use a dose of her own sleeping powder.

"Elinor, you've not taken a rest in hours. Sit. I'll get you something to drink if you like."

"I'm fine, dear, really," she assured him, lowering herself slowly into the chair. "You've done enough, Ian." Though her tone was kind, her words were like an arrow to his heart.

She's right to blame me. "I'll... just look in on Seany then."

"Seany is asleep with his mother."

He nodded silently, then turned to leave.

Elinor reached for his hand and turned him back to her. "Ian."

"Aye?" he answered softly, forcing himself to look her in the eye.

"Ye did nae set out to hurt him. I know that." She stood and faced him, taking both his hands in her own. "You loved him as we all did. And I know you did everything you could—"

"Did I?" Ian tore his hands away from her and turned his back. "What have I done for him? Tell me. For years, I've done nothing but lie to him. I kept the man from knowing his own mind and his own faith, Elinor." He dropped himself heavily into the chair by the fire. "I convinced myself that it was for his own good that he believe himself to be a *proper* God-fearing Christian man and to just accept his fate as it was given him. I was wrong!"

Elinor crouched next to Ian's chair, placing her hands on the sides of his face. "How can that be wrong? You kept him safe—"

"Safe?" Ian sniffed and brushed her hands aside. "I kept him down. Can't you see that?"

"I don't understand what you mean."

"You didn't notice? Each time that a piece of his memory came back to him, he gained back a bit more of his physical strength. Before he put the bough to the peak last September, he could barely hold his carving knife. While he was up there, something jarred his memory. Probably the damned pulley and rope, I don't know for sure, but something brought back the memory of his ordeal. I'm sure of it because I saw the look in his eye, and it was terror. He remembered, but then it was gone again. But after, within a few days, he was carving again."

"How can memories bring back strength?"

"I don't know!" He raked his hands through his hair as he spoke rapidly. "But look at the strides he started making then. Four years of not being able to even get out of his own bed and within a month, he had devised a way to get in and out of his chair, and had gained enough strength to push it along the wall." William's psaltery still occupied the place next to the hearth. Ian picked it up and lightly brushed the strings. "The night Melly gave him this and told him about his lute, he remembered the music, and within no time he was moving his fingers on these strings in ways he had not been able to move them in five years! He was getting stronger, Elinor. Every memory brought him back. But did I encourage it? No, I did my best to help keep it all buried."

Resting his elbow on the arm of the chair, he dropped his forehead into his hand. "Now, of all times, he should be here celebrating. Ewan has come all this way to bring him home... had they arrived last week..." His voice caught and he covered his eyes, desperate not to sob like a child in front of Elinor.

"Yes, the timing is difficult." Elinor brushed Ian's face and pulled his head to her bosom, and spoke in the gentle maternal way that was her nature. "But it is what it is."

Ian surrendered to her motherly embrace without protest and purged his grief on her shoulder, grateful that she was even willing to be in the room with him. When he had explained his story to the others, Melly had lunged at him with such pain and hatred in her eyes, he felt his soul had been torn from him. Simon and Prissy had pulled her away, kicking and screaming. *"You promised me Ian! You told me it was safe! How could you let this happen?!"* The echoes of her accusations resonated in his head against the walls of his own hall of guilt. *She has every right to hate me.*

Prissy, though less hysterical, had also looked on him with the same anger in her face, and had said nothing to him as she ushered Melly to her bed chamber. Simon had scooped up a terrified Seany as he raced after the women, crying.

Oh Seany. Sweet child, what have I done to you? The look of joy that had melted into confusion on the boy's face when Ephraim had stopped him from running to the wagon and then the tears that came at the disappointment of not seeing his papa, would haunt him forever. Ian had always marveled at the easy affection William had freely displayed to his son and no son was so much in awe of his father than Seany of William. He told Seany as gently as he could his papa wasn't coming home but it was naturally a difficult thing for the child to hear and understand. He had run to the barn crying calling Ian a liar. Amazingly, it was Duncan and the lad who had tagged along, Matthew, who had managed to calm Seany down and coax him back to the house. Matthew had even given the tyke a present; a small, carved wooden sword in the hope of cheering him but to no avail. Later, Elinor persuaded the lad to drink a bit of her *special* possett, and he was now curled up with Mehlyndia.

When Ian finally finished his release, Elinor stood and held out her hand to him. "Come on, I think you need to get some sleep yourself. Your room is all made and ready. You've not slept between sheets for a long time."

"Thank you, dear lady. But I'm sure they would prefer me to absent myself from the house. It's best I go back to my own cabin where I can cause no more grief."

Elinor put her hands on her hips. "Ian Proctor, you are not going anywhere. Now, I understand your pain and you must surely understand Melly's. But believe me, she would not wish you separated from the family. Not now, of all times."

"Family?" Ian said, shaking his head. "I'm hardly family. She hates me, Elinor. And rightfully so. Look what I've done to her."

"There was a time she hated me as well." Elinor smiled sadly and spoke in her quiet reassuring way. "Do you recall how the whole journey to this New World began?"

Ian shook his head, unsure what she was referring to. "Melly hated you for bringing her here?"

"She hated me because for a long time she blamed me for Will being arrested in the first place, which led to our exile. And I felt she was justified in her feelings. After all, had I stayed home the night the hunters were searching, she and William could have left Drumoak through the caverns safely without worrying about the likes of me. But he would not leave unless he knew I was safe. And by then, it was too late..."

"I remember now." Ian nodded. "I had overheard the bishop plotting to use you to bait him. I went to warn him and practically begged him to flee in the night. His worry for your safety, and his own foolish pride, kept him from running."

"That's right, you did come to warn us. We should have listened to you then and fled, pride be damned. But I had promised a friend whose wife had passed that day that I would help him prepare her for burial, so hunters or not, fool that I was, I left the castle anyway. That mistake cost Sean his life that very night and led to everything William endured after. Many a night since then when I close my eyes, over and over I see him lay his sword down and surrender himself to spare me from the hunter's blade." She spoke quietly, steadily, her voice not betraying the tears that filled her eyes. "So you see Ian, I know what a ponderous weight guilt and regret can be. Thankfully, I also know Mehlyndia and how forgiving she truly is. You are family. You've been William's best friend and confidant since he woke up on the *Lady Anne*, and you know how grateful she's been for all you've done for this family. She won't throw all that away in her anger."

Ian accepted her hand and allowed her to lead him to the guest room. She left him briefly, then returned with a steaming cup of her sleeping brew, and set it on the night-stand with strict instructions that he drink it while it was hot.

Ian would leave the brew untouched where Elinor had set it down. Left alone with only the small circle of light cast by his meager candle, he gathered what belongings he had in the room that had come to be regarded as 'Ian's room'; a change of clothes, fresh boots, his flute, a stout leather cape he wore in foul weather, and his shaving supplies, tying them all together in a bundle. His room was on the side of the house that overhung the lower level with the trapdoor opening in the floor. He moved the rag rug that concealed the hinged door and lifted the handle. He dropped the bundle to the ground before lowering himself, allowing the trapdoor to fall shut after his exit.

~

Elinor entered the kitchen quietly, nodding a greeting to Prissy and Annlise. She took her place at the table silently, not wishing to interrupt the discussion that was taking place between Ewan and Simon. Duncan was sitting half-listening in a chair by the stove while Matthew dozed at the table next to his mother.

"There is no point in staying any longer than it takes to load the hold and set sail, Simon. I say we launch with the first outbound tide," Ewan said, rolling a mug of ale between his palms. "If the winds are kind, we can be back to Stonehaven by July and they can put this all behind them."

"But surely ye can understand that Melly will want time to adjust and explain it all properly to Seany," Simon argued. "This has been home for nigh onto six years and 'tis the only home the little lad has ever known."

"Surely she can explain it while we sail."

"I'm sure she could, but Ewan, have a heart..." Simon lowered his voice. "There are others in Port Edin besides us who cared for Will... they'll want..." His face flushed as he looked toward Elinor with a silent plea for help in his argument.

"We need time for a funeral service," Elinor finished for Simon.

Ewan opened his mouth as if to argue then closed it again. "Of course, you're right. Forgive me. I must seem like a cold-hearted brute."

Annlise was sitting to his left. She placed her hand on his arm. "You are merely thinking as a knight who has a mission to fulfill. It's understandable."

Ewan half smiled and patted Annlise's hand. "I admit, that's where my mind was. I promised Lord Edward I would return with his heir as quickly as God would allow. When Ian told us about Will... I simply changed the focus of my mission to Seany."

"I don't fault ye for it." Simon finished his ale, and set the mug down lightly. "But I've not had to think as a knight for a few years and I can't seem to do it now. I've known Seany since his birth and been like an uncle to him that whole time. He's never been told what his father was before we came here, or that the day may come when he may be expected to go back to Scotland. Do you think that's something we can explain with one simple good-night story to a five year old boy who's just lost his father?"

Ewan sat back, rubbing weary looking eyes between his thumb and forefinger. "You're right that it will be a hard transition for him and believe me, I fully understand Mehlyndia's grief and don't wish to add to her pain, but there is something you need to know... it may be nothing... but it's troubled me since before we landed."

"You saw them too?" Duncan had a renewed expression of interest on his face as he moved his chair closer to the table. "I had meant to ask you about it."

"Saw what?" Simon asked.

"Ships, half a dozen," Ewan answered staring into the empty mug in his hand. "To the southwest, perhaps no more than two, maybe three days out. They were not at full sail and too far out for me to see clearly what flag they be flying... are you expecting ships from the south?"

A deep crease knotted Simon's brow. "Not from the south. A supply ship from France is expected by early June and there are always the odd trading vessels from Denmark or Spain, but they come from the open sea, not up from the south."

"Who would be coming from there, then?" Duncan asked, leaning in toward Simon.

Ewan and Simon exchanged silent glances. Each man nodded as if coming to the same conclusion and the expressions on their faces sent a shudder of dread through Elinor. She caught Prissy's eye at that moment and saw that the young woman shared her fear.

"Virginia?" Elinor asked, quietly.

Ewan nodded, an angry grimace came to his face. "We've heard rumors that King James does nae wish to share this New World with the likes of France or Spain. It's likely he's sent his fleet up from Virginia to lay claim to this shore."

Simon slammed his hand to the table then stood up. The sound made Matthew start, and sit up quickly.

Annlise put a comforting arm around her son. "Could they just be trading ships?" she asked with a hopeful but skeptical look in her eye.

Duncan answered carefully, "They were galleons. Heavily armed."

"Are you certain? Four masts?" Simon asked, leaning over the table.

"Yes, sir!" Duncan answered. "I know a galleon when I see one."

Prissy stood and took hold of Simon's arm. "Why is that important? Simon, what's happening?"

Simon softened his expression and took a long breath. "Well, as Ewan said, it could be nothing to worry about, but... if the English *are* sending galleons up from Virginia..." He glanced around the room, making eye contact with each of them. "You can be certain it isn't for the purpose of trading furs."

Ewan nodded his agreement then stood, leaning on his hand. "Do you understand now? Why we must sail as quickly as possible?"

"Aye," Simon said quietly, then turned abruptly and grabbed his cloak from a hook on the kitchen wall.

"Where are you going?" Prissy asked, following behind him.

Simon threw the cloak on his shoulder and reached for the door handle; he paused and took her hand. "The rest of Port Edin has a right to know what may be comin'. I'm going to see Charles Blackwood." He turned to face Ewan. "We don't have much in the way of an army or militia here. We're fur traders and homesteaders mainly. But the few trained men we do have need to be on the ready."

"I'll go with you," Prissy said, reaching for her own cloak.

Simon stopped her. "It's not necessary. Nothing will happen tonight and I won't be gone long." He pulled her close for a quick embrace. "Stay here and take care of my son." He smiled and kissed her forehead, then turned toward the rest. "It may be a long night. And Ewan is right, we'll need to sail as soon as the hold is loaded. So gather up whatever you wish to take and have it ready."

"Good," Ewan said. "We'll sail tomorrow with the outbound tide then."

Simon nodded briskly then opened the door. He was halfway off the porch when Elinor stood suddenly, causing her chair to tip over behind her. "Simon, wait!"

Simon turned with an impatient glare. "What is it?"

"She'll want a funeral. Simon, you know that. Will there be time, perhaps, while the crew is loading? Please?"

Simon sighed loudly and his eyes softened. "After I see Charles, I'll wake Ephraim and tell him to ring the church bell at first light. I'll see to that."

Elinor embraced the big man affectionately. "Thank you. Now go. Do what ye must."

Simon turned and hurried away into the dark toward Charles Blackwood's home.

Elinor felt a soft hand on her arm. Prissy had joined her on the porch. "It looks like we're going home."

Prissy gently led Elinor back to the kitchen. "So it seems."

Annlise and Matthew sat quietly together at the table. Elinor felt suddenly awkward for them. When she stepped off the ship, Elinor wondered why she had been sent. But Ian had brought the news about William immediately, and Elinor had not given the young woman another thought. But here she sat in a room full of mourning strangers and the poor lass seemed like a lost lamb in the forest. "My dear, I'm afraid I've neglected you this whole evening."

"Please, sit. Don't worry about me." Annlise smiled kindly,

then stood and headed toward the kettle. "Let me freshen up your cup."

"Thank you, dear." Elinor offered no protest, and set herself down heavy in her chair. "I'm afraid my manners have a lot to be desired. I never asked what brings you to New France. Had you planned to settle here?"

Annlise brought a fresh cup of steaming brew to Elinor and set it on the table in front of her. "No..." She began hesitantly. "Lord Edward sent me as part of the mission. He wished his heir to come home... healed. That was to be my task."

"Heal him?" Prissy said skeptically. "Does Lord Edward think Ian and Elinor have not tried? Forgive me, miss, but I don't think you would have been able..."

Elinor quieted Prissy with a pat on the hand. "It doesn't matter dear, he's not here to heal." She smiled politely at Annlise. "Though I would like to know why Lord Edward thought you might be able to. You must have impressed the duke somehow."

"She did," Duncan interrupted. "She saved my life, Elinor." He told his tale of the flight from Lothlanne and how Annlise had seemed to *magically* keep the scouts from finding them. He told of the chase through the meadow and the arrow that had sent him to the ground. "I took the whole of the shaft through here." He pointed to the place on his shoulder. "I should have bled to death right there."

Elinor took a sip from her cup. Though she was impressed with Annlise's courage and her ability to keep a cool head in a crisis, she did not find the mere fact that she treated an arrow wound as miraculous enough to convince Edward that she had a ghost of a chance to heal William. "You merely removed the arrow?" she asked, trying not to sound too unimpressed.

"No it's not just that," Duncan resumed his oration. "The arrow went clear in. It tore me up pretty badly... but Elinor, look..." He blushed slightly then pushed his tunic aside, revealing the place where the arrow had purportedly pierced his shoulder. The skin was as smooth and unmarked as a newborn. No sign of any wound, front or back, was evident on Duncan's shoulder. He flexed the arm up and down quickly to demonstrate that he had been absolutely cured of the injury. "It's stronger than it ever was."

Prissy and Elinor both examined Duncan's shoulder twice. Prissy insisted he show her his other shoulder just to be sure he wasn't mistaken of which side he had taken the hit. In her determination to find a trace of that wound somewhere, she had practically torn the tunic off the young man. Elinor had to pull her away when she saw Duncan's eyes widen and his face turn scarlet.

Prissy also blushed and sat herself down. "I'm sorry, lad... I forgot myself."

Duncan smiled shyly and straightened his garments. Matthew snickered beside him but held his tongue.

Elinor set her cup down. "I must admit. I would swear to the Blessed Mother, Herself, there was never an arrow in that shoulder. I can see why Edward was impressed with your talent, lass."

"She impressed me for certain," Ewan chimed in with a sly grin.

Annlise blushed and looked down at her hands. "It was

nothing, really. The Gods were kind that night and led me to do what I needed to do. Duncan is young and strong, and the wound was not grave. I must confess, however, I hold my own doubts as to whether I could have truly helped our Phoenix to be whole again."

"Phoenix?" Elinor asked, confused.

"William," Annlise said, quietly. "'tis how he is remembered." She stood and retrieved the kettle from the stove and refilled each cup. Then she sat and told them of the Heather Path.

"*Our* Will?" Prissy wiped her eyes and stared at Annlise as the tale was told. "He would be so honored to know all this."

"It was my hope to be the one honored to tell him. I, as most, believed he had died at the end of his trial. You can imagine the joy I felt in learning the truth, that the Phoenix truly did live, and what it meant to me to come here, to try... to heal..." Her voice trailed off. She took a breath and forced a smile. "Ah, but who am I to think I could have truly healed the man."

"There would have been no harm in trying," Prissy answered quietly. "Phoenix. 'Tis a fitting tribute. I'm glad to know he's remembered as a hero back home."

"Well, there is a dark side to his legend, I'm afraid," Ewan sighed, scowling.

"Unfortunately yes," Duncan said. "Most people call him something quite different."

Elinor matched Ewan's scowl. "Dare I ask?"

Ewan shook his head, and grudgingly told the story of the 'Demon of Stonehaven'.

"But that's a lot of rubbish!" Prissy snorted. "Will was no demon! He was one of the most decent people I've ever known... Aye, Elinor?" Her face began to turn scarlet and her eyes filled.

"Yes, dear, calm down—"

"All they had to do was watch the way he was with Seany and with Melly... and how heartbroken he was about the baby... no *demon* ever had such a heart!" Prissy burst into the tears. Elinor put her arms around the girl and rocked her gently against herself.

"Forgive me for upsetting you, lass," Ewan said, quietly.

"I'm sorry, Ewan. It wasn't your fault." Prissy blew her nose on her handkerchief and wiped her eyes. "Poor Melly, she won't take that well at all."

"She won't take it for long," Elinor said, giving Prissy a reassuring pat. "If I know her as well as I think I do, she will move Heaven and Earth to put his memory to right. You mark my words."

Prissy smiled through her tears. "That's for sure. Just look at the way she put Josephine Ashcrofte in her place."

Elinor laughed lightly. "Exactly."

Matthew stifled a loud yawn, then looked up, red faced. "I'm sorry."

Ewan yawned as well. "I think we could all do with some rest."

"The rooms are made up," Elinor said, as she stood and picked up a kerosene lamp and led the way out of the kitchen. "We can all take a few hours' sleep, at least."

Elinor saw to it that Ewan and Duncan were comfortable in the room across from Prissy and Simon. Annlise and Matthew would occupy the room across from Ian.

When she was sure all her guests were comfortably settled

and they knew where to find the candles and extra blankets, she paused outside Ian's door. In all the years she had known him, she had never seen him fall apart as he had earlier that night. It was understandable to her, of course, that he would be upset at the loss of his friend, but the way he had assumed the full burden of blame troubled her greatly. A nagging unnamable fear chewed away at her while she stood outside his door, foolishly trying to convince herself that it was proper and expected of her to enter the man's bedchamber in the dark of night— just to check on him. Tentatively, she placed her hand on the doorknob and turned it. After a half-turn, the knob resisted any further motion. *He's locked the door. He's never...* "Ian?" she tapped lightly, calling in a half whisper, listening carefully. After a moment of silence, she convinced herself that he was simply sleeping soundly from the possett she had prepared and that he wished his privacy. Reluctantly, she turned away from the door, making her way to her own bedchamber.

I'll be up first and I'll be sure to wake him soon after. Poor man, just wished his privacy. He'll be fine in the morning. She muttered her reassurances as she dressed herself for bed. *Yes, first light, I'll be sure to wake them all. Ian will want to be there for the service...*

"Charles?" Simon wrapped on the thick wooden door of Charles Blackwood's tiny cottage. "It's Simon MacHenry. Charles, are ye awake?"

"Simon?" A groggy, tussled Charles opened his door, squinting over the lantern light that Simon held. "What's the trouble?" He led Simon to the meager space that served as his kitchen.

"Ye saw the ship that landed today?" Simon asked, placing the lantern on the middle of the table as he sat down.

Charles drew up a chair across from Simon and thumped himself down. "Yes, I saw it. One of yours, isn't it? Bringing supplies to the Philbricks, I suppose? I seen ye greetin' them at the dock."

"It is from Scotland, yes. I've got some news ye need to know." Simon drew a long breath, finding all he needed to say to the man coming heavy to him. "There's a fleet of galleons coming up from the south."

"Galleons?" Charles eyes opened wide, the grogginess disappeared instantly. "How many?"

"Six."

Charles gaped. "Six? We've no fire power to stand against six galleons."

"I know. There's no way to fight back. Ewan guesses they are still two or three days away. That gives us just enough time to move the women and children to safety. We can put them on the ship and send them to Mount Desert Island until it's safe."

Charles shook his head. "That ship isn't nearly big enough for everyone. Some will have to stay behind or go overland to the north shore." He threw his hand up in a gesture of frustration. "These people are not soldiers! They're families! We can't possibly get them all together and organize this in time."

"There'll be no choice, Charles. If we stay, it will be a slaughter. You said yourself, we've not the fire power to fight. We lost too many of our men this past winter. I'm the only one left with any battle training and that's with a sword. A blade is no defense against the cannons on an English galleon."

Charles stood and paced the floor scowling. "Bloody crime, we must run with our tails between our legs without a fight. But I see your point. That hellish fever. Look what it left us with to defend ourselves. A blacksmith, a few inept fur hunters, a drunkard vicar, an apothecary, and a crippled wood-wright. A fine army we make!"

"We don't even have that much anymore," Simon said, quietly.

Charles turned slowly to look at Simon. "I heard a rumor today. I didn't want to believe it. Is it true?"

Simon nodded and made a sarcastic half-smirk. "Our army is less one crippled wood-wright, as you called him."

"Oh no. Simon, I'm... sorry." Charles lowered his eyes to his hands. "I didn't mean to be disrespectful... you know I liked Will. I had a lot of admiration for the man."

"Thank you" Simon said, drawing a long breath.

Charles went to a small wooden cupboard and pulled out a dusty bottle, three-quarters empty, of good Scottish whisky. He wasn't a heavy drinking man, and Simon suspected that one bottle had lasted since before the fevers had come and taken his son Kevin from him. Charles had shared a drink with Simon at that time as well. It seemed to be his way of mourning.

Charles took two glasses from the cupboard and placed them on the table, filling each with whisky. He sat down, passed a glass to Simon then lifted his own. "God love him, I hope he's found his peace at last."

"Amen to that." Simon clinked his glass with Charles's. Both men drained their drinks in a single swallow.

"So, how are we going to get everyone organized?" Charles asked, breaking an uneasy silence that had come after the toast.

"We have our good friend to thank for that." Simon turned the little glass in his hands. "When I leave here, I'm going to wake Ephraim and tell him to ring the bell at first light to call everyone to chapel for the service. We'll honor our friend and use the gathering to tell everyone what needs to be done."

"You're assuming they'll all show up to chapel," Charles snorted skeptically. "Ephraim hasn't exactly inspired his congregation. There be more empty seats than filled on Sundays of late."

Simon creased his brow and nodded. "True enough. But this is not a Sunday meeting. It's a funeral for someone who was well liked in this settlement." He sighed. "But to be safe, would you consider visiting the houses tonight? Just to give them fair warning?"

"I'll get m' coat." Charles stood and headed for the door, grabbing his cloak and another lantern. "Go on to Ephraim's and I'll make rounds to the houses."

Simon gave him a clap on the back, picked up the lantern, and the two left the cabin together.

Charles headed to the nearest neighbor while Simon walked the narrow alley on his way to the little cottage behind the chapel where Ephraim and Josephine lived. The moon offered no guidance on this particular night and Simon found that the lantern barely lit his path. He cursed himself irritably for not filling the kerosene well before he left. As he passed the last cottage in the alley, the light sputtered and died, leaving him in near total darkness. "Damn," he muttered, rattling the handle, as though it would bring the little flame back to life. He stepped beyond the corner of the building, when he noticed the slightest bit of light coming from the window of the old cottage. The cottage that had been the first Philbrick dwelling and was now Ian's, when he wasn't staying at the garrison.

Simon looked curiously at the half-opened door. Last he knew, Ian was back at the garrison, and no one else would have reason to be here. He tapped lightly on the door and cautiously peered in. Silhouetted by the single candle that burned in the center of the table, Simon could clearly see the form of a man sitting with his back to the door.

"Ian?"

The man sat stone-still and silent. Simon pushed the door fully open and stepped quietly into the cottage. "Ian? Is that you?" He spoke louder and lightly placed his hand on the man's shoulder, hoping he would not startle him. But it was Simon who was startled when he finally saw the face that shown in the candlelight. Ian's face, calm and unlined, but not wearing any expression Simon had ever seen on his friend before. The pale blue eyes, which always held a sparkle of mischief, stared flat and glassy, blindly fixed on the dancing flame. The light reflected star-like on the wet streaks on Ian's cheeks. He sat with his hands resting on the table, concealed under the voluminous sleeves of the brown cleric's robe that Simon had not seen him wear for nearly six years.

Simon gripped Ian's shoulder and shook lightly. The

expressionless pale-blue eyes turned vaguely in his direction, then back to the flame. Simon dropped the lantern and reached for Ian's hand, instead squeezing a fistful of wet and sticky sleeve. "My God!"

In the dim candlelight, he had not been able to see the stains seeping into the dark colored cloth, but the stain left on his hand was unmistakable. Fighting a sudden wave of panic, he shoved the sleeves up past Ian's wrists. "No, Ian. What have you done?" he moaned at the sight of Ian's hands resting in bloody puddles under the sleeves, both wrists flayed open with a single swift cut. Ian's shaving blade rested in the open palm of his left hand.

Without hesitation, Simon grabbed the razor and sliced two strips of cloth from the overcoat he wore, and tied them as tightly as he could around Ian's wrists. Ian offered only mild protest to Simon's frantic ministering, creasing his brow and whimpering, an unintelligible lament.

When he had bound the wounds to his satisfaction, Simon grabbed Ian's face at the chin. "Ian, talk to me, lad. What are you doing?"

Ian turned a glassy eye to Simon, but would not speak. His face dissolved into a pitiful mask of despair and he dropped his chin to his chest.

"Ian! Speak!" Simon shook his friend, taking his face between his hands, forcing the apothecary to look him in the eye. "Why, my friend?"

Ian's eyes seemed to soften and focus on Simon. He shook his head slightly and spoke in a strangely calm whisper. "It was necessary, you see? I took vows. It's the law... *qui percusserit hominem volens occidere morte moriatur.*"

"What law? I don't know your Latin, Ian."

"He that smiteth a man, so that he die, shall be surely put to death." A sad, terrible smile, spread across his face before he dropped his head again. "It is my fate, you see? God leads us to our fate..."

Simon spoke gently, holding his friend. "And what smiting have you done?"

"You know what I've done. I killed him, Simon."

"Drew a sword and cut him where he sat, did ye?"

Ian looked up, confused and startled. "No... of course not."

Slightly encouraged by the ghost of defensiveness in Ian's gaze, Simon asked, "Ye put a musket to him then? Or did ye simply strangle him with ye own hands?"

"No, how can you accuse—" Ian stopped, sniffing, he turned his head. "I see what you're doing. But you're wrong. It *was* my fault. I took a life... I owe an equal debt."

"Do ye?" Simon said, gently lifting one of Ian's bloodied wrists. "Is this how you planned to make good on that debt? Do you think this is what Will would have demanded as payment from you?"

Ian pulled his hand away. Simon had bound the wounds tightly to halt the flow of blood, and his hands were turning dark and puffy. He started to remove the strapping on his left hand, Simon placed his own on top.

"Leave it!"

"It's none of your business!" Ian spat back, with a sudden fierceness. "The debt is mine!"

Simon released Ian's hand, planting his own on the table as he leaned over, placing his face close to Ian's. "Then pay it if you must! But not while I'm here with you!"

"What?"

"Pay your debt," Simon said, taking on a more complacent tone of voice. "Let yourself die where ye sit, drowning in your own blood drawn of self-pity. I just ask ye wait 'til I've gone before ye do." He pulled up a chair by the back, and sat down on it backwards, resting his chin on his folded arms across the back of the chair. "And by the way... I'm not going anywhere."

"It isn't self-pity! It's... what I owe him... go and let me do what I... must do." Ian glared, though Simon noted he had stopped attempting to open the bandaging.

"No," Simon said, simply.

"Leave me alone!" Ian yelled then stood suddenly. He tottered on his feet for a moment. Simon stood quickly and caught him before he fell.

"No. I won't leave ye alone, Ian." Simon said, helping the man sit. He looked around, irritated by the darkness. "Where are ye oil lamps?"

"In the cupboard," Ian answered wearily, resting his head in his palms. "Bring down the whisky as well, while you're there. It looks to be a long night."

"The last thing you need is whisky," Simon muttered as he found two small oil lamps and set them on the table, lighting them from the candle. "That's better." The room was soon brightened in the warm yellow glow of the lamps. In the light, it was easy to see the ghastly red stains soaking into Ian's sleeves. The table itself looked as though it had been used for the slaughter of a sacrificial lamb. He realized, then, that his own hands and clothes were covered in gore.

Ian's own eyes widened when the macabre stains were revealed. "You can't go home that way," was all he said.

Simon looked at his hands, then half-heartedly laughed, "No, I can't. I don't suppose you have a clean shirt I could borrow." He pointed to the robes Ian wore. "And something more appropriate for yourself."

Ian looked down at his own clothing. "How ridiculous this all must seem." He took a long breath and stood, slowly this time, keeping his feet under him. "There are shirts in the chest by my bed. Help yourself."

Simon reached for one of the oil lamps and began to head to the bedroom. He stopped, turned to his friend, and made a beckoning motion. "Come on."

"Go on, Simon. I'm fine. I promise I won't do anything foolish."

"Humor me," Simon insisted.

"Very well," Ian sighed and plodded his way across the room on unsteady legs.

He's lost more blood than I thought, Simon noted. A slight shudder found him, which he concealed from his friend. *Had I been only another moment later...* He shook his head, banishing the unpleasant thought.

Ian lowered himself to sit on the edge of his bed. "Over there," he said pointing to the chest. "Take what you wish."

Simon stripped off his stained shirt, tossed it dismissively into a corner then pulled a fresh shirt from the drawer. "That's why I've always liked you, Ian. I can borrow your clothes and they fit so nice," he quipped, keeping half an eye on his friend. When he had dressed, he pulled more clothes out and brought them to Ian. "Your turn. Get dressed. We've got a lot to do."

Ian took the clothes slowly. "*We?* What are you talking about?" He looked up suddenly, a hint of his old self coming back to his eyes. "How did you know where I was?"

Simon chuckled, "I didn't. I wasn't out looking for you at all. I thought you were sound asleep in the garrison." He made a wry smile. "I guess God led me to forestall your fate."

Ian stared back for a moment with a look that told Simon the crisis had passed. "Thank you, my friend."

Simon smiled. "Any time. Get dressed, I need your help."

"Help?" Ian asked as he freed himself from the monk's robe. "Why *were* you out?"

Simon explained the situation with the galleons and the fears of an imminent raid. When he explained how he planned to rally everyone at a funeral, Ian laughed unexpectedly.

"What's so funny?" Simon asked.

"'Tis a far better tribute to Will to use his funeral to launch an adventure than what I had in mind."

Simon laughed as well now. "You're right, he'd find it poetic. The Will I knew back in Scotland was always the first one ready for a wild adventure, caution be damned. He and Sean... they were quite the pair."

"I wish I had known him then." Ian stood, seeming far steadier than he had only moments ago. "I love your stories of those days."

Simon led them back to the kitchen and retrieved the whisky, and filled two small glasses. "I suppose a wee sip won't hurt ye." For the second time that night, he shared a toast in his friend's honor. "To the days of Willie Fylbrigge and his famous trained monkeys."

Ian smiled, a hint of the old sparkle coming back. "To Willie Fylbrigge."

They drank and then, leaving the glasses on the table, left the cottage together on their way to wake Ephraim.

Chapter 11

"**M**' LADY, IT would honor me... that is... I would be..."

Mehlyndia blushed, hiding a giggle behind her hand. The young man before her stumbled nervously over his words as he lowered himself awkwardly down onto one knee.

"What do you wish to ask me, William? We're expected in the great hall."

"Oh, aye... uh, they're waiting. Well... this can wait... I suppose." His face flushed through a sheepish smile as he moved to stand up.

"They'll wait." She placed a hand on his shoulder, preventing him from standing. "What do you wish to ask" She smiled coyly, knowing full well what he was intending to ask but taking great delight in his shy stammering.

He took her hand and with great seriousness looked up into her eyes. "M' lady Mehlyndia... Father... that is... Lord Edward has given me his blessing... ."

She felt a tremble in his hand and burst into gleeful giggles at the solemn expression on his scarlet face.

"What's so amusing?"

"You are trying too hard, my love," she said gently, then astonished her suitor by getting down on her own knees before him.

"What are you—"

"Shh." She placed her finger on his lips, then smiled. "Father has given you his blessing?" she asked, without taking her hand from his mouth. William nodded. "And are you feeling nervous about what you're about to ask me?"

William nodded again, a grin spreading under the finger she held on his lips.

"Then, allow me." She removed her finger and took both his hands in hers as she leaned forward until her forehead was resting on his. "William Mastin Fylbrigge, would you do me the honor of making me your bride?"

Foreheads still together, they both began to laugh, and he kissed her softly, then he leaned back feigning surprise. "My lady! This is so unexpected. A lad needs time to consider such an offer."

They dissolved into laughter as he stood and helped her to her feet. He picked her up at the waist and whirled her in the air twice, then slowly brought her feet back to the floor and kissed her. Then, placing one hand on her cheek, the other finding the ring he had tucked in his pocket, he formally asked, "My Lady Mehlyndia of Drumoak, would you do me the honor of becoming my wife?"

A little hand brushed Mehlyndia's cheek lightly. "Mum?"

"Hmm?" Mehlyndia buried her face into her pillow, clinging to the waning memory of the dream she had been having. "Yes, I'll marry—"

"Mum?"

"Seany?" Mehlyndia rubbed the haze from her eyes. The early morning half-light cast little more than dull shadows in the room and all she could see was the vague silhouette of her son next to her bed. "Do you want to sleep with us, little one?" She hitched herself over to make room for the tyke, half-expecting to come up against the warmth of her husband's sleeping form, instead finding a cold, empty place in the sheets. The reality delivered a phantom-like blow to the pit of her stomach as Ian's voice invaded her memory. "We *searched for days... I'm sorry... so sorry...*" She closed her eyes and shrunk into the bedding, longing to reach back into her dream and stay there.

Seany shook her lightly. "Mum? Elinor says we have to get up."

She threw her arm around her son quickly and pulled him to her, thoroughly enfolding him within the blankets. "Stay with Mum for a minute or two, then we'll get up." She buried her face in the little one's neck for a moment, thankful that the darkness would hide the distress she knew she was wearing. Seany squeezed her, his little hands giving reassuring pats on her back. They stayed together that way for only a few moments before the door swung open quietly and Elinor padded in balancing a light breakfast of bread and dried berries on a tray in one hand, and an oil lamp in the other. She set the tray on the table beside the bed and placed the lamp in a bracket on the wall above it.

"Dear? Are you awake?"

"We're awake," Seany answered, pushing away from his mother.

Mehlyndia reluctantly pushed herself up to sit, shielding her eyes with her hand from the intrusion of the oil lamp. "Elinor, please move that. I can't bear the light right now."

Elinor obliged by placing the lamp further away from the bed.

"It's barely dawn, why must I face anything so early?"

"There's a lot to do." Elinor helped Mehlyndia situate herself comfortably and then placed the tray on her lap. Seany sidled up beside her and hugged onto her, pressing his cheek against her arm.

"Little one, would you like to help me in the kitchen?" Elinor asked.

Seany shook his head, his little lower lip tightened above a wrinkled chin.

Elinor brushed a shock of black hair from his face, tucking it behind his ear. "Well, ye stay with yer mum, then. We've still an hour or so until it's time to go to chapel."

"Chapel?" Mehlyndia asked, idly picking at the bread. "Today? So early? For Heaven's sake, why?"

"For the service—" Elinor gave a glance to Seany, then bit her lip. "Dear, there's a lot I need to tell you. Ye best eat up and get dressed, I'll explain it all when ye come down." She stood and headed for the door.

"Elinor? What's wrong?" Mehlyndia asked, extricating her arm from her son. She tossed aside the blankets and placed the tray on a nearby nightstand.

Elinor stopped and turned, one hand on the doorknob. "Little ears," she said, with an apologetic half-smile.

Understanding, Mehlyndia gave her son a quick embrace and said to him, "Be a good lad, and let Mum and Elinor talk alone for a moment, would you?"

"No... Mum, I don't want to leave," he cried, clinging fiercely to his mother. "It's still dark."

Heartbroken for his tears, Mehlyndia gave Elinor a pleading look. "Just tell me. Nothing can be more difficult for him to hear than what we had to tell him yesterday."

"Very well." Elinor took a long breath, then returned to the bed, and sat down on the edge. "We must be sailing today, dear. We're to leave with the outbound tide."

"What?" Mehlyndia's eyes grew wide. "Today? Why the hurry?"

Elinor explained as carefully as possible about what Ewan had seen on the southern horizon, and why he felt it prudent to be gone from this shore swiftly. "I knew you would wish a proper funeral service before we left, so I begged them to give us at least that."

Mehlyndia listened quietly, hugging her son tighter with each detail Elinor told about the galleons to the south. She already accepted the fact she would be leaving Port Edin, and had told Seany as much, but assumed they would be given time, perhaps as long as a month or two to prepare for the voyage. She offered no protest in leaving, admitting to herself and everyone else that without William, she had no desire to stay in the primitive little settlement. But she had also not wished to tear Seany from the only home he had known so quickly on the heels of losing his papa. "It's not fair." She cried quietly, clutching her son.

"Nothing is." Elinor sighed. "But it is as it is." She stood and headed back to the door. "I've got to wake the rest of the guests. The church bell will be sounding soon after sunrise, and that's when we must go." She cast her eyes down for a moment, fidgeting with the strings of her apron. "I took the liberty of preparing a proper mourning gown, dear. I'll bring it in for you."

"I'm sorry you took the trouble with the dress, Elinor, but

I shan't be wearing it." Mehlyndia threw the bedclothes aside and quickly got out of bed, Seany scrambling up behind her. She grabbed the oil lamp and headed for the door. "If we must shake the dust of this place from ourselves so quickly that I am not given the *time* to mourn properly, than I shall not dress as if I am."

"What's all the commotion?" Prissy met Elinor and Melly at the door, yawning, a sleepy confusion in her eyes.

"Prissy, come with me, I'll need your help," Mehlyndia said, not looking at the girl as she swept past.

"Of course... what are you... Melly?" Prissy called, confused as she and Elinor followed Mehlyndia's quick stride.

"Melly Philbrick! Where are you—" Elinor began.

Mehlyndia stopped short before the attic door and spun on her heel, "Fylbrigge! My name is Mehlyndia Fylbrigge! I am the Countess of Sutherland."

Elinor and Prissy froze in their steps, both wearing the same stunned expression. Seany peered from behind their two skirts wide-eyed, his little mouth pursed looking at his mother in confusion. Mehlyndia turned from them quickly, flinging the attic door wide, she stormed up the stairs to the dusty trunk in the corner. She set the lamp down, and threw open the lid. The first rays of dawn were beginning to crest the horizon and the slightest bit of that early sunshine shed its light onto the elegant fabric at the top of the trunk. Tearfully, reverently, she traced her hands across the saffron colored silk and lifted the gown by the shoulders before slowly turning to face the two startled women and the frightened child on the stairs.

She took a breath and held the gown in front of her.

Affecting the regal countenance due her true rank, she spoke calmly, "William hated the name Philbrick. The only piece of his former life he was ever truly certain about was his name. And we took it from him. And though we never allowed him to learn the truth of why he was forced to abandon it, he trusted us... and he accepted the burden of the deception." Her eyes filled as she spoke, but her voice remained steady. "But you see... it is no longer necessary to shield him. I shall not send him to his rest with a false name. I shall not allow him to be forgotten again."

A slow smile of understanding spread on Prissy's face as she approached Mehlyndia, tears staining her cheeks. "Allow me to help you dress, Lady Sutherland."

Ian and Simon crossed the square back to the garrison before the sun crested over the horizon. Simon took command of the night quite effectively, in Ian's opinion, and a new-found admiration and respect was born in him for the man. The compassion Simon had shown him had taken him completely unprepared and had touched him greatly. After all, Ian still believed Simon was more than within his right to shun him for his part in William's disappearance. And wasn't Simon's mission of organizing the settlers in the face of imminent invasion far more important than rescuing him from his pitiful attempt at self-atonement? Ian felt more than a twinge of guilt at seeing the weary dark circles growing under the big man's eyes and knew he owned some of the credit for putting them there. He chided himself silently for his own foolishness in believing that no one would miss him or that no one would *care* enough to stop him from what he was attempting to do.

Simon agreed to keep Ian's unfinished act a guarded secret between them, much to Ian's gratitude, and it was decided that Simon would help him enter the garrison the same way he had exited—through the trap door in his room. That way, no one need ever learn that Ian had not been there all night.

With a helpful boost, Ian climbed through the open hatch, back into the guest bedroom. He lay on his stomach, as Simon handed him the bundle he had wrapped before he had left the night before—*minus* the shaving supplies. He tossed the bundle haphazardly behind him and reached back through the hole, extending his hand. "Thank you, Simon."

Simon shook Ian's hand, a weary smile on his face. "My honor, my friend." Before walking away, toward the proper entrance of the house, he placed his fist on his chest in the knightly gesture of promise. "It dies with me."

Ian trusted without question that Simon would keep his word. And as long as he kept his wrists concealed until the wounds healed, no one would ever know what he had been about during the last night of peace in Port Edin.

Simon let himself in through the kitchen, noting that Elinor, ever reliable, had already started the stove fire and set a large kettle of water to boil. Taking a cup from the shelf, he filled it with hot water and dropped a handful of herbs into the infuser. While he waited for it to steep properly, he settled himself down at the table with a grand yawn, the evening's activities finally catching up with him.

"Simon?"

A gentle hand brushed his face. He opened his eyes,

startled, to find he had fallen asleep at the kitchen table. He must have been there longer than he thought, the tea had gone cold in the cup. Annlise sat down quietly across from him, pouring a fresh cup.

"Thank ye, lass." He yawned again, scrubbing his eyes with the heels of his hand to wipe away the sleep.

"Ye were gone all night. Is all well?" she asked, stifling a yawn of her own. Simon suspected that she had not had more than a few moments of sleep herself.

He took a sip of the tea, considering how to answer such a simple question. "Is all well?" he repeated, shaking his head with a sarcastic laugh. He softened his face immediately at the sudden hurt expression on her face. "I'm sorry lass, I was nae laughin' at ye." He took a long breath and another sip of tea. "Truth is, no, all is not well. The ship is not big enough to carry all the families safely to another island, and even if it was, I don't think we'll be able to convince them to leave. I've just left the rectory, after spending the better part of the night tryin' to convince the vicar to ring the bell at first light to call everyone together— not just for Will's funeral, ye understand, but to get them all together so we can warn them— but I'll be surprised if he even remembers I was there come daybreak." He sat back, disgusted with the whole situation.

"How would he forget?"

"Because it took his wife dousing him with a bucket of water to even wake the sot up!" Simon slapped the tabletop with his palms, startling Annlise. She sat back wide-eyed, staring fearfully at Simon. "Oh, lass, I've scared ye again," Simon moaned, apologetically.

She relaxed, her eyes becoming sympathetic. "Did ye manage to explain it well enough to the vicar at all?"

Simon shrugged. "We'll know soon enough. He should be ringing the bell soon." He stood and stretched, then walked to the kitchen window, looking to the east to judge the remaining time before sunrise. "Charles Blackwell is coming," he told her, pushing the curtain aside, watching the man approach.

Charles walked briskly, as though he had news he was eager to share. Simon opened the door before Charles had gained the porch stairs.

"I've told as many as I could rouse," Charles said, as he entered the kitchen. "But, most of the men are off trapping, Simon, and the bloody daft women are reluctant to leave without—" He stopped talking when he noticed Annlise in the room. "Forgive me."

"No worries, sir," she told him. "Please tell what ye must."

Charles removed his hat and bowed slightly to Annlise, before turning back to Simon. "The women... the wives, Simon, they won't leave without their men."

"Damn!" Simon raked his hand through his hair in frustration. "Do they not understand? It won't be safe!"

"What's all the noise?" Ewan asked as he entered the kitchen. "Simon? What's wrong?"

"Damned stubborn—" Simon threw his hands in the air, turning to Ewan. "The village women! They won't leave without their husbands! They be out trapping now and usually be gone weeks on end. We cannae possibly wait for them to get back." He pointed furiously out the door toward the square, yelling at no one in particular, but aiming his anger toward Charles. "Don't they see what's happening?"

Charles shook his head and shrugged, mimicking Simon's frustration. "I told them! They don't wish to go. We've never been threatened before and, frankly, I think they just don't believe us."

"But they don't understand!" Simon shouted.

"Then we must leave them!" Ewan grabbed Simon's shoulders, halting his outburst.

Simon stared, stunned in disbelief. "Leave them?"

"Aye, we have no choice," Ewan said, in a calming quiet voice.

"But... the galleons... the children... I can't leave them." Simon grasped Ewan's forearms. "We have to do *something*."

Ewan shook his head. "We can't force them to come if they don't wish it. And even if they did there simply is not enough room on the ship for them all. I don't mean to sound heartless, but I've an obligation to fulfill. Edward is waiting for his daughter and his heir, and I am sworn my oath to him to bring them home safely."

"You once swore an oath to Will. To defend him and his tenants or die trying." Simon released Ewan's arms angrily, and turned away from him.

"Simon, please, stand down," Ewan said, a wearily. "Aye, I swore an oath— the same one you did— to William of Drumoak all those years ago. But Will isn't here now."

"But these are his people! Do you think he would be so eager to leave them all to ruin if he *were* here?"

"No, he wouldn't. He would want to stay and put himself in the middle of the madness, as always, and go down fighting with his fellows, with you and I right beside him until the last blow... but—" Ewan placed his hand back on Simon's shoulder, forestalling another angry protest. "—he would not want Seany and Mehlyndia to be part of that battle."

Simon opened his mouth to argue and closed it again, admitting to himself that Ewan was right. William would gladly risk his own life if it were called upon him, but not if it meant putting his family in peril. If he had been there to speak for himself, Simon reasoned, William would most assuredly see his wife and son safely away from this place, regardless of who chose to go or stay. His thoughts turned suddenly to Prissy and the news she had shared with him only days before that he was to become a father himself, knowing that he, too, would sooner see his wife and child safe than to take up arms defending a group of ungrateful, disbelieving villagers.

"And what of you, Charles? How think you?" Simon asked.

"I'm of two minds, Simon," Charles said, quietly, then looked to Ewan, extending a hand. "Name's Charles Blackwood, I don't think we've met properly."

Ewan grasped Charles's hand and shook it firmly. "Ewan McDonough." He gestured toward Annlise. "The lass is Annlise Chase."

Annlise inclined her head, Charles answered with a polite nod.

"Two minds?" Simon asked.

"Yes," Charles answered, twisting his hat in his hands. "On the one hand, I've a good mind to pack it all in here and sail away with you. Now that Rachel and Kevin are gone, there is really nothing to hold me to this God-forsaken little island. And I've no desire to stand here and be slaughtered by the

English to be sure... but on the other... " He shook his head and turned toward the door, looking out toward the square. "There are the others who won't leave— even though I think they be fools not to take the opportunity when it's in front of them— they will need a strong arm with them, someone to stay to help them fight." He turned back to Simon, and grasped his forearm. "But you need not stay, Simon. Honor Will in the best way possible, and take his family someplace safe, and take your own pretty wife and go while you're able."

Simon looked from Charles to Ewan, then Annlise. Their expressions telling him they were all in agreement. Reluctantly, he admitted to himself they were right. He would take his family— Will's family— away from the danger. And though Charles's argument convinced him that it was right for him to leave, the demons in his conscience where telling him he was leaving his fellow settlers to certain slaughter. "You're the better man for stayin', Charles."

Charles stepped out onto the porch, and then stopped and turned, extending his hand to Simon, "God grant you a safe journey, my friend."

The tinny clank of the chapel bell tolled its doleful call, one strike at a time; twenty-six strikes commemorating the life-span of the deceased. Somberly, the population of Port Edin filed into the little chapel, taking their places on the benches that served as pews, reserving the front for the members of the Philbrick household. The women, dressed respectfully in black gowns, were seated on the left of the pulpit while the few men who were not off trapping sat on the right. They spoke in hushed voices, some women dabbing the corners of their eyes with handkerchiefs, exchanging the proper platitudes usually spoken at such services.

A corpulent woman with a ruddy complexion leaned forward and spoke to Josephine Ashcrofte, sniffling into her handkerchief. "Such a pity, the poor man. I'm certain he's in a far better place."

"Yes, Ester," Josephine answered with a pinched up little smile of faux sympathy. "I'm sure he is."

"Perhaps it was a blessing," Ester continued, with a deep sigh. "After so many years, to finally be relieved of his infirmities."

Josephine's eyes narrowed slightly, a ghost of a grin curling the corner of her mouth. "Not as many years as you might think."

Another woman, who had been seated behind Ester, craned forward, an interested lift to her brow. "What do you mean, Josephine?"

"How old do you think he was, Isabelle?" Josephine asked.

Ephraim placed his hand on Josephine's shoulder and glared down at his wife. "This is not the place for gossip! Have respect, woman!"

Josephine opened her mouth to rebuke, but he placed his hand over it.

"Not now!"

She pursed her lips and turned in her seat to face forward, but not after giving Ester and Isabelle a quick look that told them she would have more to tell— later.

Ephraim took his place behind the pulpit and looked out into the congregation. A few more people filed in quietly, filling in the few remaining empty places. The newcomers who had arrived on the ship bearing the Scottish flag the day before— two men, a young woman, and a lad— all stood to the back. After Simon's visit in the night, he reasoned the men were the sentries that had been sent from Drumoak to retrieve William. He clenched his jaw and busied himself by preparing his prayer-book, marking the pages he required, all the while scolding himself for what he knew was the most foolish mistake he had made in his life; getting drunk the night before and telling Josephine what he had learned about William from Ian.

He glanced up when the doors at the back of the chapel opened again. Simon MacHenry and his young wife walked slowly down the aisle, Elinor behind them. They filed into the empty pew at the front, then stood and turned facing the door. The rest of the congregation rose when Mehlyndia appeared at the door, Ian at her side, Seany holding hands between them.

A susurration of surprised mutters wormed through the congregation when she entered in her elegant saffron gown, her hair piled high on her head, draped with a richly embroidered silken veil. She walked with the grace of a princess, eyes dry and fixed ahead, not meeting any of the astonished gapes she was receiving. The early morning sunlight that shown through the east windows caught on the myriad beads on the gown, casting a wraithlike halo, illuminating her against the sea of black gowns. Ian led her past the thunderstruck congregation, to the front pew. She took her place aside Elinor and sat quietly, opening her prayer book. She looked up to Ephraim with a calm, composed half-smile. "You may begin now, Vicar, if you please."

Ephraim forced the foolish gape he knew he was wearing from his face and stammered his greeting. "Uh... Please, be seated." The congregation slowly settled into their seats, some necks stretching to catch another glimpse of the glowing widow in the front pew. To his dismay, Josephine stared at Mehlyndia with malicious gleam in her eye, resembling a cat preparing to pounce on an unsuspecting mouse. Ephraim glanced under the pulpit longingly at the flask of sacramental wine he had tucked there, wishing for an opportunity to steal a sip to calm his rattled nerves. "Ahem... Dearly beloved, we are gathered here today to pay our final respects to William Philbrick—"

"Fylbrigge," Mehlyndia corrected him, not angrily, but loud enough for her voice to carry easily through the chapel.

Ephraim stared at her, shocked. "I beg your pardon, Goody Philbrick?"

Mehlyndia stood slowly, not taking her eyes from Ephraim, and stated simply, "His name was Fylbrigge. Not Philbrick. He was an Earl. William Mastin Fylbrigge. William of Drumoak, Lord Sutherland. I wish him to be remembered as such."

Shocked murmurs and gasps echoed through the chapel for several moments while Ephraim tried to quiet them. "Please, people, settle down... please..."

"Earl? He was an Earl?"

"I had no idea! What was he doing here of all places?"

"It's impossible. She's lost her mind in her grief."

Ester leaned to Isabelle. "But wasn't William of Drumoak, the one—"

"He couldn't have been *that* William of Drumoak, he died

years ago," Isabelle exclaimed, wide-eyed, then both woman leaned forward, tapping Goody Ashcrofte on the shoulder.

Josephine turned slowly, a knowing look on her face. "Yes, ladies. *That* William of Drumoak."

The two women exchanged shocked expressions, clutching their handkerchiefs to their mouths.

Mehlyndia stood stoically amid the clamor of the congregation, squeezing Seany's hand, the little lad clinging to his mother, burying his face in her skirt.

Ian tensed his jaw, giving side glances to the people around him, until finally looking Ephraim in the eye. "Go on, Vicar."

"Please! People!" The vicar pounded the pulpit with his hand in a vain attempt to settle them. "For the love of God, please, be quiet!" He picked up the huge prayer book and slammed it onto the pulpit. The congregation silenced instantly. "That's better. Goody Philbrick— Fylbrigge," he corrected himself, casting a wary eye across the stunned faces of the congregation. "Please, take your seat."

"Lady Sutherland," Mehlyndia said, in the same calm manner, though the shaking of the prayer book she held belied her confidence. She turned to face Josephine. "That is how I wish to be addressed."

"Lady Sutherland, is it?" Josephine scoffed with a waspish little cackle. "If you expect me to bend my knee before you, you are sadly mistaken, *m' lady.*"

"Josephine!" Ephraim snapped. "This is a funeral for God's sake! Conduct yourself appropriately or remove your presence from here."

"'Tis not *I* who be inappropriate," she spat back,

approaching the pulpit. "I have not arrived for my husband's funeral dressed as I would for a garden luncheon with the queen. Look at her! She does not even shed a tear for her loss. And why should she?" She turned, pointing to Mehlyndia. "She's been consort to the Demon of Stonehaven!"

Prissy was on her feet instantly, sending her prayer book tumbling to the floor. "He was not a demon!" She lunged forward, hands outstretched, fingers splayed, ready to pounce on the vicar's wife. Simon deftly jumped in front of her, catching her around the middle before she could sink her nails into Josephine's neck. "Let go, Simon! She doesn't know what she's talking about."

"No, Prissy!" Mehlyndia cried to her friend, her calm façade shattered by the outburst.

Prissy struggled against Simon, red faced and furious, glowering at Josephine. "Don't let her get away with saying that, Melly, tell her! Tell her she's wrong! Tell them all!"

"Prissy, please!" Mehlyndia pleaded, the tears now showing, she threw her arms around the girl, and they cried together before the confounded congregation. "I care little what they think."

Josephine stood back, smug, and satisfied. "You see? She does not deny. I've suspected for months the Philbricks are not what they claim to be— and wasn't he the first and only one to survive the devil's fever without the apothecary's brew—"

"Josephine!" Ephraim hollered. "Silence yourself this instant!"

"How many of you have been awakened this past night and told you must flee this place?" Josephine spoke above

Ephraim's hollers. Heads began to nod, and looks exchanged among the parishioners. "They say we must abandon our homes to flee into the heathen forest, that there is danger if we don't— but look who it be who brings us this warning." She pointed to the four people standing in the back, "The minions of the demon himself, come fresh from the sea, who wish nothing more than to steal our souls—"

"Enough woman!" Ian jumped to his feet, slamming his prayer book to the floor. "The danger is real! Is your petty jealousy toward this good lady so fierce, you would condemn the entire village and defile the memory of a kind and decent man only to discredit her?"

"Look at her!" Josephine screamed back. "She's learned the demon's dark craft of deception! Be she a witch as well?"

"She's not! And my papa was not a demon!" Seany ran forward so quickly, none could stop him. He kicked Josephine square in the shin, sending her to her knees. "You're the witch, you ugly old cow!"

"Devil spawn!" Josephine shrieked clawing at the child, scratching his face with her nails. He kicked her again, then ran down the middle aisle, nimbly dodging those who tried to catch him. He raced out the chapel doors, the lad from the ship and the younger of the two sentries running after him.

Ephraim stole the opportunity of the diversion to grab his flask and slip unnoticed out the back door of the chapel.

What happened next, happened fast. The congregation was on their feet, mulling into the aisle, blocking Mehlyndia from chasing after her son. Ewan and Annlise pushed themselves through the throng to the front, trying to reach Mehlyndia.

People swarmed everywhere in the little chapel, creating a human log jam in the middle aisle that prevented any from moving very quickly.

"Seany!" Mehlyndia cried, desperately trying to swim through the crowd to the door.

"Duncan and Matthew have gone after him!" Annlise's voice rose about the tumult.

Mehlyndia climbed onto one of the pews and looked over the crowd until she saw the wide-eyed face of Annlise amid the chaos.

"M' lady! Go to the side... the side." She was pointing toward the east wall, her small arm rising above the heads of the people around her.

Mehlyndia looked were she was pointing and saw Ewan and Simon, navigating the crowd toward the back door of the chapel. She hopped the backs of the pews until she was almost even with Annlise. They were separated by Ester and Isabelle. "Annlise! Give me your hand!" She reached over the Isabelle's head.

"Don't touch me!" Isabelle turned and railed at Mehlyndia, a wild panicked look in her eye, she thrust herself forward, sending her companion and Annlise crashing to the floor amid the rushing crowd.

"Annlise!" Mehlyndia screamed when she lost site of the young woman. "Someone help her!"

"Go to the side!" Annlise's voice called up, but Mehlyndia could not see from where. "Go with Ewan!"

"Where are you?"

Before she heard Annlise answer, she felt herself being lifted off her feet from behind and whisked back over the tops of the pews toward the back door. She struggled against the arms that bore her until she recognized her rescuer as Ian, as he held her fast in a firm but protective embrace. "We've got to get you out of here."

"Someone help Annlise! She'll be trampled," Mehlyndia told him, breathless, as he trundled her through the back door to the churchyard beyond.

"Ewan went for her! I've got to get Elinor!" Without waiting for her response, he raced back into the chapel, emerging a moment later with a terrified Elinor in tow.

"Where is Seany?" Elinor asked, looking all around.

"I don't know," Mehlyndia cried. "Annlise said Duncan and Matthew— there!" She ran toward the barn where she saw Seany, hunkering near a haystack. Duncan was on one knee, embracing the lad. "Seany!"

Seany looked up, wiping his eyes with a pudgy hand. Duncan stepped aside, allowing the boy to run to his mother. She scooped him up, clutching him to herself, crying onto him.

"Are you all right, little one?"

"Why did she say those things, Mum? Why did she say papa was a demon?" He cried on her shoulder, squeezing her around the neck.

"She's just a mean-spirited old biddy, Seany, don't you worry about anything she says." She sank to her knees in the barn doorway, still embracing her son, then looked up at Duncan and Matthew. "Thank you for finding him for me."

"It wasn't difficult to figure where he would go," Duncan said, mussing Seany's hair. "He has a fondness for hiding in this barn, don't ye, lad?"

Seany nodded, though he did not look up to Duncan.

"Just like his papa," Mehlyndia whispered.

"Mum!" Matthew shouted suddenly, then took to running.

Mehlyndia suddenly remembered Annlise, falling into the throng in the chapel. Panicked, she turned to see where Matthew was running and let out a grand breath of relief to see Annlise, supported on Ewan's arm, approaching the barn. Relief turned to concern when she saw the bruises on the young woman's arms and face, and the difficulty she was having keeping her footing.

"She's hurt!" Duncan said, running to meet them. When he reached them, he slipped his arm under hers opposite Ewan, and the two together carried her to the barn, helping her gently to a hay bale.

"I'm well, please, no fuss," she said, catching her breath, rubbing her ankle. "Nothing broken... only bruised a bit."

"Thank goodness." Mehlyndia reached out and embraced the young woman carefully. "You didn't need to take that risk to get to me... but I thank you."

The crowd had begun to spill out of the chapel and were mulling about in confused little clusters. The woman who had screamed at Mehlyndia, Isabelle, leaned on Ester, staggering on her left leg. Mehlyndia found it hard to feel sympathetic when she saw Josephine Ashcrofte also limping about, bent and grasping her knee. *I hope it's broken! Old harpy.*

Mehlyndia searched the crowd for the rest of her adopted family and her heart fell when she saw Simon rushing toward the barn, carrying Prissy in his arms. He set her down carefully in the hay next to Annlise, she moaned, clutching at her middle. Simon knelt above, a helpless panicked look on his face.

"Prissy?" Mehlyndia took her hand. "What happened?"

"She's hurt... pushed down in the crowd," Simon said, brushing the hair from Prissy's face. A mean looking purple blotch stained her cheek. "She's going to lose the bairn."

Annlise lowered herself next to Prissy, examining the woman carefully. "Matty, quickly, run to the house, get my box of simples and herbs, go!"

Matthew raced back through the door, nearly colliding with Elinor and Ian as they entered the barn.

"What's happened?" Elinor rushed to where the others were huddled.

"Please, everyone, give her room," Annlise told them, taking control of the situation.

"But Elinor knows what to—" Mehlyndia began, then stopped when she felt the hand on her shoulder.

"Let her do what she must," Elinor told her gently. "She knows far more than I."

Mehlyndia reluctantly backed away, standing with Elinor and Ian. Duncan and Ewan stood back as well, while Simon and Annlise knelt on either side of Prissy. Matthew scrambled back into the barn, bearing the box Annlise had sent him for.

The noise from the crowd rose, and to her horror, Mehlyndia heard Josephine above the din, yelling, "They've run to the barn! There!"

Without hesitation, Duncan and Ewan pulled the heavy barn doors closed, throwing the beam across.

"This is madness!" Ian said as the pounding on the door began.

Seany clung desperately to Mehlyndia, shaking from all the noise. She patted his back, doing her best to sound reassuring, though she didn't know which was the more urgent of crises at the moment; Prissy or the mob of former 'friends' trying to burst through the barn door.

"We've got to get to the ship," Ewan said through his teeth, moving a heavy barrel of grain against the door. "Before those idiots out there decide to set the barn afire!"

"Would they do that?" Duncan asked, grabbing a crate to add to the barrel.

"I'm afraid so," Ian hissed. "Foolish superstitious lot we've settled with. And Josephine has managed to stir the wasps nest quite nicely!"

"It's my fault!" Mehlyndia cried. "My damned pride! I only wanted William to be remembered for who he truly was. What is all this madness about demons?"

"You couldn't have known, dear, you mustn't blame yourself," Elinor said, huddling with Mehlyndia and Seany.

"I can't believe the damned demon stories have traveled even this far!" Duncan growled, as he and Ewan hoisted a large wooden log onto their pile. "It's ludicrous!"

The banging became fierce as one of the panels on the door began to give. "They're using a ram!" Ewan yelled.

"There is no ram in this village!" Ian said, grabbing another barrel of grain. "It can't be more than a wagon."

"Whatever it is, it will be in here in minutes if they keep it up!" Ewan yelled over his shoulder, hoisting a sack of feed onto the barricade.

Seany wiggled away from Mehlyndia's arms, suddenly scrambling over the hay bale to the back side of barn.

"Seany! Stay with me," Mehlyndia called.

"I'll get him," Matthew said, running after the tyke.

"I need water!" Annlise shouted over her shoulder, bringing Mehlyndia's attention back to Prissy. "Quickly!"

Mehlyndia hurried to the rain barrel in the corner, and took the silver dipper from a hook above it. She hurried, careful as possible not to spill much, and handed the dipper to Annlise.

Annlise dropped a fistful of musky smelling leaves into a little wooden bowl, then ground them to a powder with a pestle. She took three pinches of the powder and placed them into the dipper, mixing it gently with her finger. "Help her sit up, now."

Simon gently held on to his wife, cradling her in his big arms, while Annlise brought the dipper to her mouth. "There, sweeting, drink it all."

Prissy choked down the entire contents of the dipper, then fell back limply against Simon. He looked at Annlise, startled, "What did you do?"

"Fear not, it is as it should be," she assured him.

The banging became louder and more fierce. A box on the top of the barricade tumbled to the floor with a crash. Ian and Ewan hoisted it back onto the pile, while he and Duncan together tossed a large wooden yoke onto the growing barricade, a ram from the other side sending it sliding halfway down again.

"This won't hold much longer!" Ewan shouted.

Mehlyndia looked away from the men, forcing her attention to Prissy. Simon had lain her flat in the hay and had moved aside as Annlise had instructed him. She watched, astounded at what happened next.

Annlise kneeled astride Prissy and placed her right hand, flat palmed, on top of the silver charm she wore at her throat, and her left hand she placed on Prissy's stomach. Face to the rafters, she closed her eyes and began to chant, rocking on her knees. Her words were foreign to Mehlyndia but her voice was clear and sweet as the chant became melodic. She sang, and the song became a prayer, her voice growing louder until Mehlyndia barely noticed the sound of the crowd trying to break the door. She glanced to the men and they too, had stopped their frantic efforts to block the door, caught up in the song Annlise offered to the sky.

When Annlise ceased her song, she froze, sitting stone like. No one dared move until she did, all watching, enraptured, as a pale blue glow formed around the two women.

"Blessed Mother!" Elinor whispered, dropping to her knees in the straw. "She *is* mage."

Mehlyndia stared, dumbstruck as the glow flared and ebbed, then vanished completely with a flash. Annlise crumbled sideways, into the hay.

"Simon?" Prissy opened her eyes slowly and blinked up at her husband, brushing at the wet streaks on his face with her hand. "Are you hurt, my love?" she asked, then sat up and embraced him.

Simon held her to him close, then pushed back, examining the places where the bruises had been. There were none. "The bairn?"

She placed her hand on her stomach, and smiled. "All is well."

"Annlise?" Mehlyndia reached for the young woman and

shook her gently until she opened her eyes. "Are you all right?"

Annlise sat up slowly, looking around through glazed eyes. Elinor rushed to her, bearing a dipper of water. Annlise sipped slowing, the color returning to her cheeks. She discarded the dipper into the hay, returning to Prissy's side. "It is truly well?"

Prissy embraced her, smiling. "Aye... thank you—"

"They're still in there! Keep pounding!" A voice from outside broke the trance they had fallen into. The men resumed their building again, as if Annlise's magical song had never occurred.

"Ewan!" Matthew shouted from the other side of the barn suddenly. "Someone is coming in over here!"

Ewan crossed the barn in a flash, his sword in hand. He stood at the ready above a panel. Mehlyndia caught her breath and grabbed hold of Elinor at the sound of wood splintering and nails giving way.

Ewan raised his sword and was beginning his down strike. He quickly stopped himself short, nearly toppling to his knees. "Charles!"

A moment later, Charles Blackwood stood in the hay at the back of the barn. "I thought you'd need some help." He smiled at them. "No one is interested in this side of the barn, they're all damned idiots. If you come through, a couple at a time, you can all be on your ship and out to sea before they get through the door."

"God bless you, Charles Blackwood!" Mehlyndia threw her arms around the big man and kissed him on the face.

He blushed and stood back. "Now, now no time, for that.

Take ye lad and get on that boat. I'll cover ye."

"Seany! Come." Mehlyndia held her hand to her son.

"I can't catch Dragon," he cried, skittering around on his knees, sifting through the hay with the toy sword Matthew had given him.

"There's no time for the cat, Seany, come!"

"But—"

"Now!" Mehlyndia's call was punctuated by a particularly hard bang on the door that sent some of the barricade tumbling. Seany abandoned his quest for the cat and ran to his mother, dropping the sword in the hay. He went to grab it, but was scooped up by Ewan and passed, quickly to Charles.

"My sword!" he cried. "Papa made—"

"There's no time, darling," Mehlyndia told him as she squeezed through the opening, following Charles who was waiting just beyond the barn wall. "Run! I'm right behind you!"

Charles held Seany close in his big arms, quickly leading the way from the barn, down the embankment to a concealing crop of balsams growing wild between the rocks. He made a trilling bird-like whistle, then waited for a moment until a similar sound came to them from the direction of the ship. "The captain is ready, I've told him what's happening, but they won't stay anchored long. They know to wait for you and ye son, then to sail as quickly as possible."

Mehlyndia grabbed Charles's arm. "What about the others? You don't expect me to leave them, do you?"

He shook his head, catching his breath. "No, no. But ye can't all be running at once, it may draw attention. Go. Get on board, I'll get them one at a time."

Satisfied, Mehlyndia held Seany's hand tight, and the two ran to the dock, and onto the ship. Moments later, Elinor boarded, and behind her, Matthew scrambled up the gangplank, breathless, but looking pleased at his accomplishment.

"I didn't stop even once! Fastest one from the barn to the boat," he boasted, then handed a squirming burlap sack to Seany. "Look what I brung for ye, little mate."

"Dragon!" Seany cried happily. "Did you get my sword too, the one ye said my papa made? I dropped it."

Matthew frowned and knelt in front of Seany. "I'm sorry, Seany. I didn't see ye drop it."

"Thank you, Matty, at least he has his cat." Mehlyndia, smiled wearily.

It was another five minutes before Simon boarded, carrying Prissy.

Mehlyndia tearfully embraced her friend. "We're going home," she said. "All of us."

Their embrace was interrupted by the earsplitting grind of the anchor chain as it was spooled up from the ocean floor.

"We're not all here!" Simon called up to the captain. "There are four left to come!"

"Sorry, sir, we can't stay!" the captain answered, then pointed to the top of the highest mast, where another man was perched in the crow's nest, looking glass to his eye. "They've crested the horizon! Six galleons. We've not the fire power to engage them. McDonough gave orders to sail at first sighting."

"No!" Mehlyndia cried. "We can't leave them! Ian! Hurry...

you can make it!"

Simon grabbed her and pulled her close. "There's no choice, Melly, we have to be away from here before they fire on us."

"No!" She buried her face in the big man's chest and wept bitterly, as she felt the sway of the waves begin to carry the boat away from the dock, away from Port Edin, and away the home she had shared with her husband. When she finally looked up, they were already far from the shore.

Prissy and Elinor stood on the stern looking back toward the land. Between them, standing stoic and still, Matthew watched silently as the shore faded away into the horizon. "Good bye, Mum," he whispered to the wind.

From somewhere far to the south, through a crystalline sky, the echoes of the malevolent thunder of the cannons, reverberated off the water. Mehlyndia held her son close to her and turned away from her last view of New France. *Good bye, my love.*

Chapter 12

AS THE BANGING on the barn door continued, Ewan and Annlise crouched by the hole in the back wall of the barn, waiting for Charles to tell them it was safe to make their flight to the ship. When it seemed far too much time had passed since Charles had come for Matthew, Ewan stepped through to risk a look toward the dock.

"They've sailed," he said simply.

"What?" Annlise looked out to see the ship drifting steadily away from shore. "Matty! Wait! Why?" she cried.

Ewan pulled her back into the barn. "They had orders—" He was interrupted by a sudden explosion and a shower of wood splinters raining down from the rafters.

Ian scrambled up the wooden ladder to the hay loft and risked a look from the small window above the door. "The galleons! They're here. They've started to attack!"

"Bloody hell!" Ewan growled through his teeth as he hurried up the ladder to where Ian was looking out.

"I thought you said they were at least two days out!"

"I was wrong, hang me later!"

"The fools are just standing there!" Ian cried, looking out onto the square. A moment later, the stunned settlers scattered in every direction, when a barrage of cannon balls rained down onto the wooden chapel, demolishing it completely into heap of shattered splinters.

Families separated in their panic, some heading for their

homes, others diving for shelter within the nearest building as another hail of cannon fire pummeled the settlement.

"We can't stay in here!" Ewan pulled Ian away from the loft window just as the barn wall was struck with a cannon ball, sending him tumbling from the loft into the hay bin below, Ian falling after him.

"Ewan!" Annlise cried, crawling over the hay to where he had fallen.

"I'm all right! Move!" Ewan was on his feet, extending a hand to Ian, who had also landed safely. "Where's Duncan?" He asked looking wildly around, as the rafters began to groan under another assault.

"I'm here! Quickly! This way!" Duncan called from the back wall, motioning everyone to the escape hole.

The four of them hurried through the hole and ran down the embankment away from the communal barn, away from the maelstrom of cannon fire and the panic stricken mob of villagers. They ran toward the pier without looking back, Ewan in the lead, Ian and Annlise close behind, and Duncan following up.

"Get down!" a voice called from in front of them, and they dove into the soft embankment, barely escaping a blast that sent chards of wood that had once been the dock, showering down around them.

Ewan landed protectively over Annlise. He lay on his stomach on top of her, his hands laced over and behind his head. After a moment, he raised his head, surveying his immediate surroundings. Ian and Duncan lay in a similar posture not far away. "Is everyone all right?"

Ian looked up and gave Ewan an 'all's well' signal making a

circle with his thumb and forefinger, then turned to Duncan who was warily lifting his head as well.

Annlise moaned below Ewan and he rolled off her. "Are you all right?"

"Aye... I've only lost my breath... oh!" She looked up the path toward the direction the warning voice had come from and pulled her fist to her mouth.

Just beyond the protective balsams, Charles lay sprawled on his stomach, impaled by a spear-like length of dock debris.

Ian groaned and hurried to where the man lay. "No! Charles!" He haphazardly threw broken pieces of wood aside until he could kneel next his fallen friend. "Please... Dear God... no... ." When it was apparent that the man was dead, Ian brought his hands to his face and wept silently.

Ewan approached slowly and placed a hand on his shoulder. "I'm sorry, Ian. But we can't stay here. We've bigger problems to deal with."

Ian looked up, his eyes red-rimmed and glassy. "What more?"

Ewan pointed toward the place where the dock once stood. "They've sailed on without us."

Ian spun his head to see for himself. An ironic smile crossed his face and he got to his feet. "Melly and Seany made it. That was the whole purpose of your mission, was it not? To safely send Edward his heirs?"

Ewan nodded, patting Ian's back. "Aye, 'twas that. They made it. God willing, they should be out of view of the galleons if they stay between the islands. She has a good captain. He knows the water better than anyone."

Annlise stood stone-faced, staring to the open sea,

Duncan at her side. "Lady, grant them safe passage." She turned to Duncan and threw her arms around his neck, burying her face on his shoulder. He embraced her, allowing her to cry on him.

"So mote it be," he whispered to her.

Another explosion from within the village ended the moment and the four scrambled back to the embankment to the shelter of the balsams.

Ian shielded his eyes against the glare of the sun on the water, squinting toward the galleons. "They've launched their longboats. They mean to occupy."

"Occupy?" Ewan spit. "That's not their way."

"What do you mean?" Ian asked.

"They'll simply pillage the place, then leave, taking whatever plunder they wish if they find value in it, destroying the rest." Ewan scowled at the longboats as they drew closer to the shore. "They've done it to the other settlements. They strike, destroy, and abandon! They don't like it that the French have laid claim to this island, and they'll sooner destroy it than share it."

"But the people..." Annlise whispered. "The children..."

"They don't care about the people!" Ewan snapped at her, than shook his head apologetically. "Ian, is there any place for them to go that we can we lead them?"

Ian shook his head. "They would not follow us if we offered. Some may flee on their own into the forest to the native village. The Mi'kmaq have no love for the English so they may find shelter with them. But the rest... it will be..." He trailed off, not finishing his thought.

Ewan nodded his understanding. "Aye. I've seen enough

English battles to know ye right, Ian."

"What?" Annlise asked, her eyes growing wide and terrified.

Duncan squeezed her shoulder. "They'll round them up. Kill any who resist or become a hindrance, take the rest as prisoners."

"Aye," Ewan agreed, "it's their way."

"I may have done Will a favor after all." Ian muttered to himself, staring passed his companions.

Ewan heard, and turned a curious eye to Ian. "How d' ye mean?"

Ian sniffed, and half-laughed at the irony, and turned a rueful eye to Ewan. "He'd be among the first of the *hindrances* the rogues would have shed."

"That be the terrible truth," Ewan agreed, then leaned close to Ian. "You know this land and the people best, Ian. I'm going to count on you to tell me where we should go and how to get there."

"I *thought* I knew *them*." Ian turned an angry sneer back toward the settlement. "I would have never imagined these folk would turn into an angry mob as this. They're no better than the population of Stonehaven." His face flushed for a moment and he turned away from Ewan. "Forgive me. Stonehaven is your clan... I meant no offence."

"None taken," Ewan assured him quietly. "Sadly, I have to agree with you. I remember how they all turned on Will, claiming him as hero one day, cheering for his execution the next."

"But these people... they *know* him. They're friends, neighbors. Half of them owe him their lives after he concocted a remedy for the fevers this past winter. He was well loved, Ewan. By everyone, or so I thought." Ian closed his eyes for a moment, struggling to keep what was left of his composure. "I wish to heaven I had stayed with my gut and never told Ephraim about Will's past."

"Why did you?" Ewan asked.

"Will started to remember things. Small things... events, people. Ephraim recognized what the scars on his wrists were and started to comment on them. Anyway, it seemed like it was time to talk about the scars. I had no idea Will had become a *legend* and that the good people of this *happy little village* would be so daft as to believe such rubbish." Ian stared toward the village, a disgusted grimace on his face.

"Is there anyone left here who we can trust?" Ewan asked.

"A day ago, I would have said Ephraim Ashcrofte, but I can't say that now." Ian shook his head slowly, staring past Ewan. "The only other would be Charles Blackwood. The dead man on the bank..." He choked on his words, absently crossing himself at the mention of Charles's name, then dropped his head into his hand. After a moment, he drew a long breath and looked at Ewan. "Perhaps Akonni, the native Shaman I was seeking out on my misguided trek through the woods. But it could take months to find him."

"Will the natives be eager to assist us? I should think they'd be more concerned with safeguarding their own."

"I'd trust the Mi'kmaq sooner than the mob over there." He took another deep breath and assumed a no-nonsense demeanor. "But before I lead *another* expedition into the wilds of New France, we'll need supplies and weapons. The only place I know to get them is on the other side of the stockade fence. We'll need to get to the garrison house." He made an ironic grin. "You see, we were advised by the French governors to fortify the house against attack from the natives when we were building, and that all we needed to scare away the ignorant *heathens*, as the *civilized* King of France calls them, were short range arrows and perhaps some flash powder. Will knew better. The threat from the Mi'kmaq is remote to non-existent at best. But he stocked the house all right, with weapons more appropriate for fighting *our own kind*."

"Muskets?" Ewan asked, feeling more hopeful.

"And ammunition."

"But... I was in that house. I saw no signs of—" Duncan began.

"You forget who built it. It's there," Ian assured him. "Hidden within the walls."

A slow grin spread across Ewan's face. "God bless Will, he always was three paces ahead of the rest of us."

"Oh, aye. That, he was," Ian agreed, then climbed up the embankment on his hands and knees. Craning his neck, looking from left to right, he frowned. "Damn." He beckoned Ewan to join him.

Ewan clamored up the muddy embankment, then looked where Ian was pointing. The garrison house, being the tallest of the structures in the village, was plainly visible over the top of the stockade fence. The roof at the west end of the house stood open to the sky, a gaping hole revealing the upper floor. The east end was still intact, but a smoldering black smoke was beginning to rise above it.

"Can we still get to it?" Ewan asked, keeping his voice low.

"Ewan! Ian!" Duncan called from the bottom of the embankment. "Longboats!"

"That answers that," Ewan grumbled as he looked toward the shore at the swarm of English longboats gaining the beach, each carrying a dozen men or more, all armed with muskets and side blades.

"The woods." Ian pointed away from the village. "We can cut behind the stockade this way and into the forest."

"How long can we last without weapons?" Duncan asked, helping Annlise to climb the muddy slope.

"Longer than we'll last sitting on this pile of mud." Ewan grabbed Duncan's wrist and hoisted him the remainder of the way up.

They skirted the perimeter of the fence to the north end, the forest gate of the village. The large gates had been closed, barring reentry to any who had left the settlement, and sealing those who had not within. Ewan shook his head, disgusted at the lack of preparedness and military expertise. He hoped the majority of the people had had the sense to leave for the relative safety of the woods, as those who had sealed themselves in would be easy fodder for the raiders. *Shooting deer in a stall! God grant they had the sense to flee.* From within the fence, he heard the chaotic panicked sounds of the people, as if to mock his prayer, and by the sound of it, few had left.

The noise intensified suddenly, punctuated by musket blasts, and high pitched screams. The great gates began to pulse, as though a hundred souls were pushing on them.

"They're panicking!" Ian ran toward the gate, then pounded furiously with his fists against the wood, "Push up the bar! People! Push up the bar!" he shouted to the people on the other side, but his cries were lost within the tumult and gunfire. "They're going to crush each other against this gate!"

"Dear Mother!" Annlise cried, as the sounds grew louder. "Can we help them?"

Duncan joined Ian's frantic pounding and calling through the gate, "People! Push up the bar! Push up the bar!" But his voice was equally unheard above the noise.

"It's no use." Ian cried. "They cannae hear us and if they can, they nae be listening! There isn't an ounce of sense within them!"

Ewan crouched next to Ian. "These are the same people who were trying to hang Melly and the rest of us on the word of that one shrew. Do you think they'll gladly listen to us now? There's nothing we can do."

Ian glared at Ewan for a moment, then turned his streaked and disheartened face to the gate. Duncan and Annlise flanked him, each attempting to help him up off the ground. He pushed them both back furiously. "They were my friends, don't you understand? There are children in there!" Ian pounded again and again, until his fists were bruised. "Please, Ephraim! Please, push up the bar..."

From within the gates, came the horrific war cries of the raiders as they scaled the stockade fence on the far side of the village, and the terrified screams of the people trapped within. Ewan and Duncan hauled Ian to his feet and ran to the forest, Annlise leading the way. "There!" She pointed a large jumble of granite boulders that formed a sheltering cave, just large enough for the four to squeeze in.

From the shelter of the cave, they listened and waited for the battle to end. The destruction of Port Edin came surprisingly fast and just before dusk, an eerie silence fell around them.

It was Ian who left the cave first, carefully staying low in the shadows until he could see the gate clearly. It remained intact, though light shown through several cannonball sized holes. Beyond it, nothing but a complete and unnerving silence. Duncan joined him and the two cautiously peered through a hole in the gate.

"Not a one is left standing." Ian whispered. "They're all... they're all dead."

Duncan placed his hand on the apothecary's shoulder. "Surely *some* made it out."

Ian looked toward the barn, and nodded slowly. "Someone got the door open... perhaps they did find their way out through the back as we did."

The raid had been quick and efficient and, just as Ewan had feared, served no other purpose than the destruction and ransacking of a peaceful settlement. Annlise and Ewan stepped up behind them, each taking a cautious look through the gate. Nothing moved. Even the raiders had retreated to their longboats, leaving the dead— mostly women, one or two men, a half-dozen children— where they had fallen. Several of the cottages were aflame, and others smoldered. The thatched-roofed cottages burned quickly and soon, more than half of the buildings were reduced to rubble. Of those left standing, only the barn seemed untouched by fire. The garrison had not completely caught fire, though the second floor and the roof were riddled with holes.

"We can't leave them like that," Ian said, to no one in particular, staring through the fence.

"Aye," Duncan replied.

Without discussion, the four headed back into the ruins of Port Edin to take care of the dead. The gate opened easily, disintegrating on its burned out hinges. As night fell, a different sort of fire lit the square of Port Edin. They stood silently together until the pyre was nothing more than smoldering ash. Duncan suggested one of them go into the garrison to retrieve the weapons from the walls. But, with the roof still sending occasional billows of smoke, Ewan decreed the risk of an explosion from the gunpowder stored there to be too great. Instead, they gathered a few blankets and cooking supplies from the ruins— what they could easily carry— then left the village on foot as even the horse who had hauled Ian's ill-fated wagon had fallen victim to the raid.

"Where will we go then?" Annlise asked as they headed into the woods.

"Away," Ian said, then led them into forest.

Chapter 13

THERE ARE NO clouds, there is no rain. It isn't thunder. *Wake up. You have to give the eagle to your son. It isn't thunder. Wake up, brother, it's time...*

"Sean?"

Wake up!

William awoke slowly at first, clinging to the dreams that had flooded his mind like a river of forgotten elements of his life. He lay still for a few moments listening to the sounds of the morning; the rustle of the breeze in the balsams, the call of a mourning dove, and the echoes of a distant roll of thunder rumbling across the forest. *It's going to rain,* he thought idly, yawning. His mind waded out of the murky depths of his deep sleep and forced open his heavy eyelids, his vision gradually becoming clear. He looked around, confused at first by the unfamiliar surroundings before he remembered he was in a birch lodge in Akonni's traveling village.

He brought his hands to his face, wiping away the wetness around his eyes, rubbing his palms against his cheeks, then again to be certain of what he was feeling against his hands. As part of Akonni's ritual the night before, he remember the young woman— *was her name Ariel?*— had cleaned his body, and shaved his face, removing the few days-worth of the stubble that had grown during his days beneath the balsam tree. His beard never grew as quickly as most mens his age, and he could go days between shaves before it was noticeable. *How long have I been here?* He rubbed his stubble on his cheek with the back of his fingers and a knot of realization twisted in his stomach— he had been there longer than one night.

He closed his eyes, trying to account for the time he assumed had passed since Akonni had brought him to the village. *One night! It should be only one night. This is impossible, it takes days for my beard to grow this much. How could I have slept...* Still lying on his back on the cot, he looked around for clues until he saw the wooden cup on a fir mat. *The pitewey. They must have given me more.*

Furious that he had lost more time away from his family, he flung the quilt aside and before he realized how he had done it, he rolled easily onto his side and sat up on the edge of the cot. His limbs reacted violently to the sudden and unaccustomed motion, sending painful waves of fiery wasp stings coursing through his thighs and calves. Instinctually, he drew his knees to his chest, wrapping his arms around his legs, and rolled onto the matted floor, waiting for the sensation to pass.

The pain ebbed after a few moments giving him a chance to catch his breath. He relaxed the grip he held around his legs, allowing his knees to straighten slightly. He lay on his side, forcing his breathing to come in slow breaths, acclimating himself to the sensation of life returning to his legs. Soon the wasp attacks lessened to pins and needles until all that remained was a dull ache. He relaxed completely then, lying knees together and bent, on his side on the mat. He stared at his right knee, resting atop the left, and gingerly poked it with his finger. The dull memory of the pins radiated from the touch and reflexively the muscles tensed as he drew his leg up slightly.

I moved it! He stared, disbelieving, at the sight of his own right knee as slowly it inched away from the left. The left leg, as if it had obtained a mind of its own, straightened and withdrew from beneath the other. "I moved them!" he said in an astonished whisper.

"W'yiam?" Akonni was standing by the door flap.

"I moved my legs!" William shouted, forgetting his anger with the Shaman for the moment. "Akonni! Watch! I think I can bring it around and sit up on my own." He steeled his jaw and concentrated on bringing his right knee up closer to his hip, successfully moving it a few inches before his muscles rebelled with another attack of wasps. He groaned through his teeth and collapsed flat to his back, holding his breath again until the worst of the pains passed. He rolled back to his left side and planted his right hand flat to the floor and pushed himself up, balancing on his left elbow. The waves began and he bit his lip, determined not to let the pain stop him from finishing the simple task of sitting up without the aid of a railing. "Just... a little... more," he said, and drew his left leg up only slightly before the wave overcame him and he abandoned the attempt.

Akonni knelt next to him, offering his hand in assistance. William pushed the Shaman's hand aside impatiently. "I can do it!" he snarled, then planted his palms on the mat again. Jaw clenched and aching, his face twisted into a grimace as he growled and summoned every ounce of strength he possessed. With a shriek of painful victory, he brought himself to his hands and knees.

He pushed against the mat and straightened his back, kneeling, sitting on his ankles as he waited for his breath to return. He cried freely for a moment, both for the joy of his accomplishment and in agony for the pain. When the firestorm in his muscles subsided, he laughed unabashed, kneeling before Akonni.

Akonni knelt silently, facing William with a warm smile of shared joy on his face. His eyelids sparkled as he reached out his hands and grasped William's. "The Spirits have smiled on you, my friend. The pain is part of the passage, but will not remain a part of you forever."

William nodded, finding his voice lost in his throat. He squeezed Akonni's hands in response.

"When you are ready, I shall bring you to your home. Your people surely must grieve for your absence."

A sudden flush of anger rushed over William. "Akonni... why—" he began but was silenced by a spasm in his thighs.

Akonni leaned forward, placing his hands on William's shoulders. "You are angry you have been kept here longer than you have expected."

"Yes." William looked up, his anger waning at the compassion in Akonni's voice and the look in his eye. "Why?"

"As bad as it seems, W'yiam, you must believe me that the pain you feel now has lessened greatly since the first morning."

"Lessened? How could you know that?"

"You screamed in your sleep even though the pitewey was strong. We gave you more and your mind entered the dream world unaware of the pain of your body. It seemed a kindness for you to sleep. When your cries ended, you were given no more pitewey and were left to awaken in your own time."

William mulled Akonni's words. *A kindness. Was it a kindness to Melly to keep me away?* "Has anyone gone to my family? Do they know I'm here?"

"Three men set out three days past. They have yet to return." A crease crossed the Shaman's brow and he turned away. "They left the morning of the thunder."

"The thunder?" A vague memory of a passing storm flashed his mind, along with the last trace of the dream he had been having just as he had awoken.*There are no clouds, there is no rain. It isn't thunder.* "Akonni, has something happened?"

"I do not know, W'yiam." Akonni shook his head, then got to his feet and extended a hand, to help William to his feet. "Shall we see what healing has occurred, and perhaps what more can be expected?"

William tentatively accepted the hand, looking up to Akonni. Skeptical yet hopeful, he grabbed tightly, and pulled himself up. "It still hurts quite a lot," he said through his teeth as he raised himself from sitting on his feet to fully kneeling. Akonni supported him until he was certain his upper legs would hold him, as though *standing* on his knees. William grinned through in pain, as Akonni let go of his hands and he successfully remained upright on his knees. "This is so much more than I've done in years," he said before the spasms told him it was enough for the first attempt. He allowed himself to fall forward to his hands, taking the burden of his weight off his knees.

Akonni crouched before him, matching his grin. "And less than you will do tomorrow."

William nodded his agreement and without protest,

allowed Akonni to lift him, as Simon and Ian had been doing for years, and carry him to the cot. "I'll be glad to take it slowly. Akonni... thank you."

"The pain is still powerful?"

"Yes."

Akonni went to the door flap and called out something in his own language. A moment later, Ah'Reehl entered the lodge with a pot of steaming liquid.

"Please... no more pitewey. I'll deal with the pain," William protested when he recognized the aroma coming from the pot. "I don't want to sleep. I want to go home."

"It will not put you to sleep," Akonni assured him. "This does not contain the crushed seeds from the blossoms of the morning flower as the other did. It will allow you to keep your mind clear."

Ah'Reehl retrieved the wooden mug and poured some of the liquid into it. She held it out for William, with an encouraging smile. "Take. It will help."

William looked at the cup, still skeptical. The last thing he wished was to lose more time away from home, but the wasp stings were gaining again and the pain was becoming more than he could stand. Reluctantly, he accepted the cup and held it between his palms.

She nudged his elbow. "Drink."

With little choice and great trepidation, William drank the tea that was offered, shuddering as he swallowed the bitter blend. His mouth involuntarily twisted at the aftertaste. He handed the cup back to Ah'Reehl, forcing his face into an appreciative smile. "Thank you, Ariel."

She smiled shyly taking the cup from him, then bowed

her head respectfully to the Shaman and left the lodge.

It took only moments for the burning in his legs to calm as William sat on the edge of the cot. Tentatively, he shifted his right knee slightly to the right. Only a faint sensation warmed his muscles. Encouraged, he moved the left, meeting with the same success.

Akonni knelt on the mat. "Now, we can judge how much you have regained."

"The movement in my legs is coming back," William said, drawing his left leg to side. "But my feet... it's still as if they don't belong. See?" As he moved his leg, the foot merely dragged the floor, flopping at the ankle. "I can't even feel that."

Akonni lifted the leg at the thigh. "Can you raise the lower part of your leg?"

"I think so." William clenched his teeth and held his breath while focusing on the portion of his left leg below the knee. With effort, he was able to lift it half-way and hold it out for a few seconds, though his foot still hung lifeless.

Akonni placed his palm on the sole of William's foot and pushed it up. "Hold it." He released the foot, and it immediately fell back, flaccid again. Akonni gently lowered the leg.

"It's no good," William sighed. "I told you, I was hobbled. The best I can hope for is to get around on my knees I suppose." He drew his knee to his chest, the motion becoming easier by the moment. "Still, it's far more than I've been able to do for a very long time. It will make life that much easier that I won't have to rely on anyone else to get in and out of bed." He looked up suddenly and smiled as another benefit occurred to him. "I may even be able to ride a horse again."

"This is well, W'yiam. And perhaps, given more time, Niskam will smile upon you again and you shall gain your feet as well."

"That's more than I could hope, I fear," he replied quietly, tensing and relaxing the muscles in his leg. "But I'm beyond grateful for this much."

"Akonni! Come! The men have returned... hurry." Ah'Reehl called from outside the lodge. Her voice sounded strained and urgent. Akonni and William exchanged concerned glances and then the Shaman left the lodge.

It wasn't thunder.

The encampment was suddenly filled with the sounds of running feet and excited voices, some speaking Mi'kmaq, some in English. The dogs the natives used for hauling and hunting yelped noisily, barking and scratching at the ground of their pen.

"What's happening?" William called, still sitting on the cot in the far end of the lodge. He wasn't surprised to receive no answer. *Time to move my own arse to the door.*

He massaged his thighs for a moment, relieved that no stinging pains replied to his hands. *Good, it's working.* He glanced at the door flap, judging the distance to be not more than twelve feet. *Not too far. You can get that far. Just to the door.* Grabbing hold of the edge of the cot, he eased himself forward, gently lowering his knees in front of him as he did so, grateful that the cot was so low to the ground. After a moment, he had managed to plant his knees to the mat. *There. That wasn't so hard.* He looked to the door again. *Twelve feet. That's not far.* He bent forward, landing on his palms.

At first, it seemed logical to walk his knees, one at a time, just as Seany used to do when he was a babe and had yet to learn to walk. He pulled his left knee forward and soon discovered the error in that thinking, as his single leg could not bear his weight enough to allow him to pull the other knee forward. He sank to his stomach on the mat. *I can't get there prone. I know that much.* He held his breath and managed to get back to his hands and knees. His shoulders were beginning to protest, just as they had the night he had attempted to drag himself across the camp. *Come on, Fylbrigge, just do it. Only another eleven feet. Both knees together.* Balancing his weight on his arms this time, he drew both knees together and brought them up under his chest, and relaxed. *Good! That was two feet. Good. I can do this.* He placed his palms further out in front of himself, then repeated the maneuver. *Eight feet left... six... almost... four...* He rocked back on his knees, breathing heavily, allowing his arms to rest.

To his dismay, it became apparent that whatever strength had been given back to his legs, none of his newfound healing had seemed to find his shoulders and arms. The muscles that had been torn years ago and the joints that had been mangled protested fiercely that they should be required to bear his weight now, after so many years, and the spasms that had undone him at the camp, threatened to do the same now. But there was only four more feet. *That's all it was last time. A miserable four feet! I can go that far, damn it!* Palms to the mat, eyes to the door, jaw clenched, he covered the final distance to the open door flap, then at last yielded to the spasms and rocked back on his knees, satisfied and exhausted.

His self-congratulations ended abruptly when he saw what had caused the excitement in the village. Two of Akonni's tribesmen were crouched on the ground tending a third native man, who lay sprawled, unconscious before them with a ghastly purple bruise on his forehead. Beyond them, two more men stood flanking three terrified looking women; one small framed and one quite rotund, the third, William recognized them at once as Josephine Ashcrofte and her two cronies, Ester and Isabelle. *What in God's name are they doing out here?*

"I didn't mean to hurt him!" Isabelle shouted, pleading to the native man who stood beside her. "Please, believe me, I thought he meant to attack... I thought he was one of the raiders!"

Raiders? William grabbed the skin flap tightly, pulling himself further out of the lodge. "What's happened?" he called, but was not heard over the frantic voices.

Akonni reached for the woman's shoulder, but she flinched back, as if repulsed by his touch.

"Don't hurt me!"

Josephine stood between Isabelle and Akonni, her eyes wide and panicked looking. "Leave her alone!" she screeched.

"I mean you no harm." Akonni spoke in a kind, but firm voice as he slowly lowered his hand. "You are safe here."

"Stand away!" Josephine glared wildly, her eyes darting between Akonni, and the two men who stood around her. "Devils! Don't touch us!" She blithered incoherently, while shielding the other women from Akonni.

"Josephine... Isabelle, please... settle down." Ester cried, pushing her way between her two frantic companions, "They are friends... please."

The voice of reason, William thought at first, though at a closer look saw that she too, wore a dazed and frenzied glaze in her eye, as she spoke. "Please, good sir, forgive my sisters, we've been wandering for days, you see. Days... in the woods... the men are gone, you see, and we were left to fight... alone, you see? The men are gone. All gone."

William's heart began to race as he listened and watched. *The men are gone? All gone?* "Akonni! What has happened?" he called in a near panic, trying to get the Shaman's attention.

Josephine glanced up, catching William's eye. She looked at him curiously, as though puzzled. For a moment, William thought she recognized him and he was about to call out her name, but he held his tongue when her eyes grew unnervingly wide and glassy. He saw her raise a shaky hand, pointing to him, before her arm went slack and she swooned into Ester's arms.

"Josephine! Isabelle, help me! Josephine? What have you done to her?" Ester sank to the ground, cradling the vicar's wife in her arms. Isabelle knelt beside them, burying her face in her hands, rocking on her knees as she cried and rambled.

"All gone... all gone."

Akonni tapped Ah'Reehl on the shoulder and leaned down, speaking to her in a soft voice, gesturing to the women. Ah'Reehl nodded and went to the women, and said something William could not hear. Isabelle looked at her with a sad, sweet, yet uncomprehending smile, and to William's astonishment, allowed the native girl to help her to her feet and embrace her. Ah'Reehl nodded to Akonni over her shoulder.

Akonni knelt before Josephine and gently lifted her in his arms. Ester made only mild protest, before accepting a hand from one of the native men. The Shaman led the group into a long lodge at the edge of the village. A moment later, he emerged and rejoined his injured tribesman.

The man on the ground began to moan and stir, then finally with Akonni's assistance, he sat up. Akonni spoke softly to his fellows, then turned and called for Ah'Reehl, who was out of the lodge and by his side almost instantly with her wooden bowl and cup already in her hand.

"Akonni," William called. "What has happened?"

Akonni spoke a few more words to the native men, then excused himself to join William. "My friend, I have grave news for you."

"Tell me!"

"These men are the ones I sent to tell your people where they may find you." He cast his eyes down for a moment, true grief on his brow.

"What happened?" William growled impatiently through his teeth. "Tell me!"

Akonni looked up sadly. "Your village... it is no more."

William stared, "What?"

"These women were discovered wandering in the forest. They had no food or shelter for three days when my men found them. The woman they call Isabelle mistook Sosep's intention for evil and struck him with a stone. He is well now and Ah'Reehl has taken your women to be fed and rested."

"My women? Why were they in the forest?"

"Driven to flee by the thunder of the cannons and the attack from the ships."

"Ships? Cannons?" William's stomach tightened as the panic rose in him. "Port Edin was attacked? Melly! Seany! My God, I have to find them! You have to help me!" He struggled to pull himself up, forgetting his non-responsive feet, he fell forward. Akonni caught him by the elbows before he toppled to the ground.

"Settle, W'yiam! I shall take you to find your kin," Akonni reassured him.

"Do you have a horse? I think I can ride now."

Akonni nodded and gently assisted William to sit by the side of the lodge. "We have two," he walked away briskly.

Moments later, Akonni returned leading two horses saddled only with woven mats and blankets, their reins of deer leather attached to bone bridles. Without protest, William allowed the Shaman to lift him level with one of the horses, and then under his own power, he swung his right leg across the animals back and took up the reins.

The ride was unsteady at first, but it did not take long before William discovered ways to compensate for his lack of foot control, using his knees to move the horse along. It had been six long years since he had ridden, an activity he always loved, but the elation of the accomplishment was drowned by the sense of dread that settled on him as he followed Akonni through the woods, back to the village... *his* village. The village that was no more.

Chapter 14

WILLIAM SAT ASTRIDE the horse just beyond the remains of the forest gate staring at the ruins of the village beyond that had once been his home. *This can't be real. It must be a dream. Please, dear God, let this be a dream.* The wooden remnants of the gate were charred black and the iron hinges twisted out of shape and ripped away from the rest of the fence. The bar that held it closed was split in two, each end still in its bracket. He sat silently surveying the blackened, skeletal remains of the buildings, some still sending stubborn tendrils of weary smoke skyward. He urged the horse forward slowly through the gate, warily looking about for any signs of life, but finding only more piles of charred debris strewn about the square. *Where are they?* The hoof falls of the horse scraping against the gravel that was once the village square echoed eerily against the stillness around him.

"Hello!" he called out, but the only response was his own voice, *"... ellooo... loo..."* echoing from the ruins.

"Is anyone here?"

"... eeone heeeere... ere..."

"There are none to answer you, W'yiam."

William turned, startled and nearly falling from the horse as Akonni rode up quietly next to him. "Where are they?"

Akonni frowned, then extended his hand slowly toward what appeared to be the remains of a large bonfire, occupying the place where the chapel once stood. Within the middle of the rubble and still smoldering slightly, something stark and white shone out against the blackened heap.

William moved the horse closer to the pile. The pungent stench of the burned wood hung thickly in the air, carrying with it another sickeningly familiar odor he had not known for many years but was unmistakable. The closer to the rubble he got, the more familiar the smell and the tighter the growing knot in his stomach twisted. Only paces away now, he could clearly see what the stark white object actually was that was sticking out of the ashes; the skeletal remains of a human hand, fingers flayed as if groping for him from the ruins of humanity, the third finger still adorned with a glittering band of ornately carved gold, resembling a chain. *Ephraim.*

"Oh God!" he groaned, leaning over the side of the horse. Akonni dismounted at once, and helped ease him down onto the ground and to his knees. He clutched at his stomach with one hand while supporting himself with the other and vomited onto the gravel.

After a few moments, he caught his breath but remained on his hands and knees trembling, while a cold sweat beaded on his brow. He forced himself to look at the pile before him, reasoning out its existence. "It's a death pyre," he told his companion in a near silent whisper. "Look how they are arranged. Neatly, arms crossed. These souls were already dead before the fire was lit." He turned away quickly, setting eyes on Akonni as a sudden realization occurred to him. "There must be survivors... other than those who wandered into your village! These people did not arrange *themselves* on this pyre and I don't think the bastards who attacked would have taken the care to do it. Where are the survivors?" He clutched at the Shaman's shoulders, catching sight of the structure at the far end of the square. Half of the upper floor was burned out and its windows looked out like a corpse against the crystalline blue sky.

"My house! The lower level is still there!" He turned on his knees, grabbing at the blanket and mat that had been strapped to his horse as a make-shift saddle. Lifting him by the waist, Akonni helped him gain his leverage and, with some effort, he threw his leg across the horse, ignoring the fire wasps that had begun to stir again within his muscles.

He reined in hard and kicked in with his knees, pushing the horse to as close a gallop as he could manage, charging directly toward the porch steps of his home.

"Melly! Seany!" he called, as he gained the steps, bringing the horse right up onto the porch deck. "Mehlyndia!" No answer met him, not even the teasing echo from the square.

He ducked his head and entered his home on horseback through the open kitchen doorway. The scene inside the kitchen was surreal with everything still in its proper place, shelves neatly arranged with crockery, the kettle in its customary position on the back of the stove top, Elinor's apron hanging on a hook next to the oven; yet each item was blackened with a thick layer of soot. William steeled his jaw and pulled the reins. The animal nickered a protest but moved as it was bidden from the kitchen and into the parlor beyond.

The parlor, just as the kitchen, was for the most part undisturbed save the heavy dusting of black soot that coated every inch of the room.

"Melly, please... answer me!"

The only reply to his call came from the widow, in the form of a gentle breeze wafting through the broken glass, raising a small whirlwind of soot across the floor, leaving a wispy path in its wake. He followed the path of the wind as it touched on the familiar objects of his home, now desecrated under a shroud of black; Mehlyndia's chair, the shawl she wore in the evenings still draped over the arm; the spinning wheel; Ian's books, mostly about herbs and gardening, stacked neatly on his writing desk. He could barely bring himself to look at the little rocking horse he had presented to his son just this past Christmas, or the object that rested next to his own soot-covered chair— the psaltery that had given him back his music.

"This is impossible..." *Melly... where are you?* He hung his head, closing his eyes against the sight, as unbidden imaginings of his family, screaming and terrified, fleeing from the invaders coursed through is head. *They're in the woods... Dear Mother please let them be in the woods... someone had to have set that pyre...* the pyre. "No, Blessed Mother, they can't be among..."

He sat still for several moments, listening to the silence of his home. The relentless breeze still danced across the soot ringing through the strings of the psaltery. From the yard beyond, untouched by the folly of the humans about them, the songbirds twittered their obscenely pleasant songs in the contemptuously happy sunshine. A slight movement in the corner caught his eye, a little mouse skittering along the wall, its smoky gray coat blending with the soot. *Best take care, little mouse, or Dragon will make a quick meal of you,* he thought, then realized that even his cat was not to be found.

He watched the little mouse for a moment, sniffing the floor, whiskers twitching, as it made its way to the edge of the door frame that led to his bedroom. He half expected it to stay close to the wall and disappear around the corner but was mildly surprised that it wandered to the middle of the open space, then turned and sat on its chubby haunches facing him. From beyond the doorway, sunlight streamed in through a jagged scar in the wall left behind by the fire. A shadow darkened the opening, large wings fluttering on a nearby limb, painting its image across the floor directly on top of the curious little mouse.

"If not Dragon, then that eagle will find you, little one."

As if in answer, the mouse stood on its hind legs and turned abruptly, running into the bedroom. William dismissed it, continuing his visual inventory of his parlor when to his amazement the little creature came back to the door way and again sat looking at him. "You're a brave little mouse, I must say—" *Brave little mouse... those that came to uphold you, the eagle and the field mouse. They are with you still. Your strength will come from knowing this. The spirit of Eagle and Mouse are your guides.* The little mouse turned from him and hopped into the bedroom, then back again. *It wants me to follow it.*

He nudged the horse carefully forward, the mouse did not move until he was nearly to the threshold of the bedroom, then it skittered across the floor, vanishing under the remains of his chest of drawers. The bedroom was in far more ruinous condition than the other rooms had been.

This side of the house had taken the brunt of the damage. He saw now that the hole that had allowed the sunlight through was vaguely rounded. He followed the imaginary path he assumed a cannon ball would have flown and got his confirmation. The iron sphere had lodged itself in the wall directly above the headboard of his bed.

Outside the gaping hole, perched regally on a cedar branch, the eagle rested preening his feathers, disinterested in the destruction around it. It glanced up at him, then bristled his head feathers, staring at him. Just below the hole— and in full few of the eagle— the little mouse perched on the dressing table.

There was not room enough to move the horse to that end of the bedroom, but William felt drawn— no, *led*— to get there. He sidled as close to the bed as possible, and carefully drew his leg over the horse and allowed himself to slide onto his bed, raising a choking cloud of soot as he landed. He managed to right himself, sitting again on his knees and, in the same doubled-kneed crawl he had used back in the lodge, he got himself to the far end of the bed, and sat on the edge within reach of the dresser where the little mouse was still sitting contentedly watching him.

"All right, I'm here."

With that, the mouse hopped to the front of the dresser and into the semi-opened top drawer.

William opened the drawer to find the mouse sitting on top of the wooden box that held his few pieces of jewelry; a signet ring he used to wear, but now could never hope to pass beyond the gnarled knuckle of the finger it once adorned; a couple of gold button clasps he wore rarely, and an object in a velvet pouch. He emptied the pouch into his hand, catching the silver eagle badge that had been given to him from Edward on the night Mehlyndia had accepted his proposal of marriage. He cradled the silver in the middle of his palm. *Laurel gave this to me in my dream... she told me to give it to my son. Sean said it...* "Give the eagle to my son. *This is the eagle!*"

The eagle in the tree screeched as in agreement, then took to flight, furiously beating his wings against the wind.

"Laurel, how am I to pass this to Seany now? I don't know where he is..." he cried, staring at the badge as he allowed the tears to fall unchecked from his face to his hand, drenching the eagle until the impatient scratching of the mouse stole back his attention. "What now?"

The mouse burrowed about in the drawer for a moment, then popped up again. William moved aside the folded clothing, sending another cloud of soot into the air until he found the journal that he had been keeping since he was about twelve years old. He had read and reread the entries countless times while trying to recover his memory and had many times chided himself for not being more specific in his details of the events of which he'd written. There was a passing mention to the night of his adventures in the tavern with Sean, but none of the meaty details Simon had shared with them on Christmas Eve. The book was filled with such half-memories prior to Port Edin and because of that, he had made an effort to write more often and with more detail, hoping to someday give the book to Seany as a keepsake. Other than Melly, Ian was the only living soul that William had ever let look into his journal as Ian himself had actually made several of the entries in it during the dark time aboard the *Lady Anne.* William turned to the first entry his friend had made, and read:

4 October 1607

... He does move his arms about in his sleep, not his legs. Mehlyndia has been told of the damage to his back, but remains optimistic that William will walk. I have not the heart to explain to her that the cuts to his heels will prevent him from ever walking. In time, she'll come to learn this on her own.

Elinor takes care to see the dressings changed often. Oddly, she is keen that he keep the little eagle on his shoulder. She has pinned it to his bed shirt...

Just as she had during my fever... she said it was for the silver... He held up the little eagle again, studying it, and reread the entry. *What is so special about this little eagle?* As if to answer the unspoken thought, from somewhere high above the forest, the scream of the eagle echoed back to him. He looked up through the hole in the wall in time to see it light on the tallest of the pines. The little mouse sat upon its haunches, also facing the direction of the regal bird. "Little mouse? Do you have the answer?" he asked, aloud, feeling slightly foolish for talking to the creature, though oddly certain she actually would have an answer. The mouse merely twittered her whiskers and scurried to the far end of the dresser, more interested in a dead fly that lay there. William dismissed his folly, turning his attention back to his journal.

He held the book on his lap for a moment, running his hands over the tooled leather cover, wondering if there was any reason now to continue to keep it. *It was for Seany... but he's not here to read it.*

He impatiently wiped the wetness from his face and took a breath. "I've no proof they're lost to me yet. Do I?" he asked the little mouse, who looked up from the fly and perked her ears when he spoke, the little oil-drop eyes fixing on him. "And until I do... they are not lost. Right?"

He glanced up into the looking glass above the dressing table and for a half-breath didn't recognize his own reflection. The white in his hair had vanished and the native clothing did make him look like one of Akonni's tribesmen. The black streaks he'd made across his eyes while wiping the tears with a sooty hand, only enhanced the effect.

"What shall you do now, *W'yiam*?" he asked the mirror, mimicking Akonni's name for him.

"Come back with me, my friend."

William turned to find Akonni standing in the doorway of the bedroom. He opened his mouth to answer, then closed it catching his reflection again in the mirror and his uncanny transformation.

"Perhaps we shall find others, as those who came to our village. Your kin may yet be among those in the woods."

Though he spoke gently, the assertion of Akonni's words did not match the look in his eye. A look that told William the Shaman held little faith that his hope would be realized.

William looked away for a moment, idly stroking the cover of his book. "I should like to take a few things with me if you don't mind helping me." He reached for the wooden box, placing it on top of the book, then reached into the drawer rooting around for a moment until he found what he sought— his quill and a small vial of ink and a well-warn, soft leather satchel, just big enough to hold his book and his box. He bundled the two together in the sack, tying it closed with a strap, then turned to the Shaman and held it out to him.

"Is this all you wish to take?" Akonni asked, as he took the bundle from him.

"Yes," he answered quietly and turned away for a moment, not willing to make another emotional display in front of his companion. Akonni seemed to understand and turned his back.

"I shall be near when you are ready, W'yiam. Call and I shall come for you."

"Thank you."

William turned his attention back to the dresser, opening the next lower drawer. Melly's night dresses and handkerchiefs still lay neatly folded. Yet even in the closed drawer, the soot had invaded. He pulled out a lacy embroidered handkerchief, the one she had carried on their wedding day and shook it a bit to loosen the soot, then tucked it into his shirt. "I should think that's all I need," he said, speaking again to the little mouse. "Except, perhaps a friend."

He reached his hand to the creature not knowing why exactly, but certain the little mouse would walk into his palm. He was nonetheless surprised when she actually did. He drew it close to him, allowing the mouse to crawl around on the back of his hand, then climb his sleeve. She got to his shoulder and nestled down on his collar and closed her eyes. William lightly brushed between her ears with his finger tip.

"Seany will be pleased with you..." He swallowed, steadied his breathing, and then called for Akonni to come take him away from Port Edin.

By mid-afternoon, William and Akonni had put many miles between them and the ruins of Port Edin. Once they had cleared the desecrated gate, William had not spared even half a glance behind him, instead setting his eyes only on the forest path before him. His legs had begun to vex him terribly as they had set out, and the waspish needling pains had grown steadily over the course of their trek. He did his best to ignore the inconvenience, not wishing to take any more of Akonni's potion for fear of fogging his mind. But as the day wore on, and no matter how slowly he led the horse, the spasms in his legs would no longer be ignored and reluctantly, he asked Akonni for a small dose.

He choked down the cold brew quickly, acknowledging his thanks with a silent nod and a low glottal grunt. Akonni took no offense at William's silence, allowing him his privacy of thought for which he was grateful. The last thing he was in the mood for was idle conversation, though he had never known Akonni to be much of a talker anyway. He half-smiled at the notion that had he been with Ian, rather than his native companion, he would have been regaled with endless tales of the former monk's exploits among the abbeys of Scotland. William never fully believed all of Ian's stories and at times had grown quite weary of them, but he always listened without protest to his friend's comical narratives. He'd give the world to hear one now.

His mind strayed to thoughts of his friends and family, wondering what had become of the ever-cheerful apothecary— his anger had long since left him where Ian was concerned. And what of Simon and Prissy? Were their bones among the ashes of the pyre he'd left behind in Port Edin?

He put the image out of his head, refusing to consider further that his family had met the very fate he had fled Scotland to avoid. *Death fires everywhere. Ye can't get away from what ye can't get away from... it's all the same.*

When the cold pitewey began to calm the spasms, they continued unhurried through the forest back toward Akonni's village. Twice he saw movement in the woods and had thought perhaps they had at last come across some of the displaced Port Edin settlers. But the first turned out to be a moose, moseying about in the pines, the other merely a wind devil whipping around the under duff.

They're all gone, Fylbrigge, can't you accept it? Just ride and look at the trees ... damned trees. Damned pains... "Akonni?"

The Shaman turned silently.

William pointed to the water skin Akonni wore. The one containing more of the potion.

Akonni shook his head, creasing his brow.

"I don't need much."

"Let what you have already swallowed work its way," Akonni said firmly, kicking his horse into a slightly faster pace.

"Fine," William grumbled, then kicked in with his knees, grimacing at the spasm that came from the motion.

Akonni slowed down, then finally came to a halt. "Is it truly that bad? Or is it the pain in your heart, and not your legs, that you wish to silence?"

William stopped his horse. "Does it matter?"

Akonni stared, unmoved, his expression kind and yet somehow disapproving.

William looked away, a foolish redness coming to his face. "Aye, my legs hurt. Is that what you want from me?"

"I want nothing of you, W'yiam." He removed the skin from his waist and tossed it to William. "Your legs are mending, the pitewey will help ease that journey. Though it may too calm the ache in your heart for a time, it will not cure it. Do not make that mistake, my friend."

"If I wanted to ease the pain in my heart, I'd have asked you for the whiskey you carry instead." He pulled the stopper and took a long hard swallow, shuddering as the cold pitewey made its way down his throat. He re-plugged the skin and tossed it back to Akonni. "Fear not, my serious friend. I am fully aware there is not enough pitewey nor whiskey in the new world, or old, that would take care of the pain in my heart. But why should I endure these leg spasms if I don't have to?"

Akonni reattached the skin to his belt, not taking his eyes away from William. "Eventually, you must give up—"

"Give up what?" William growled, suddenly fiercely angry. "Give up the pitewey? To let the wonderful-magical-miracle of healing tear me up? You're the one who decided I needed it for... how long? Three days? Four? Days I should have been with my family while the *kindness* of your pitewey kept me blissfully unaware. Do you think I give a damn now about... walking, when I should have been with them?"

"And if you had been?" Akonni asked, his voice matching William's anger. "What could you have done to make it different? Where do you think you'd be now—"

"With them!" William shouted, his voice echoing back from the woods. He took a long, steadying breath and could see Akonni doing the same. "With them," he said again, quietly. "Where ever they are, alive or... otherwise, that is where I would be."

Akonni tossed the skin back to William. "For your legs," he said, and urged his horse back into motion.

William pulled the stopper and raised the skin to his mouth but paused before taking a quick mouthful. He replaced the stopper and attached the skin to his belt, making a mental promise not to drink anymore— yet.

They traveled in silence after that. William kept his eyes on the path. Akonni took the lead, only occasionally making sure William was keeping up.

They stopped on the edge of a large clearing just before sunset, to make camp for the night. Akonni helped William dismount, easing him gently to the ground. William was pleased to note the fire wasps had given up for the time being, and so had most of the demons that had been haunting him for the better part of the afternoon. Akonni frowned when the empty skin slipped from William's belt. William smiled, half-apologetically, then shrugged while Akonni settled him down with the blanket he had taken from the horse.

"I will get some wood for a fire. Will you be all right for a little while?"

William turned a foggy gaze on the Shaman and allowed a sarcastic smirk to find him. "Dinnae worry. I'll nae run away." *I love to be in the woods alone. It's one of my favorite pastimes... just ask Ian.*

Akonni shook his head wearily and went into the woods

while William watched him methodically gather twigs and branches. Every minute or two, Akonni would look in his direction and William waved back *All's well. Muini'skw hasn't come back for me yet.* He watched wearily, allowing the pitewey-borne fog to slowly overtake him.

Isn't this about the time I start imagining spirits? Sean? Are you lurking in the trees tonight? Aren't you due to come tell me to stay with the living? What if I don't want to? Hmm? A motion on his shoulder stole his attention. "Little mouse? I'd forgotten you were with... where are you going?" Even this little mouse didn't seem interested in his company anymore as she turned from his palm and scurried away into the duff. William watched the little creature hide away under the leaves only to emerge again a few feet away, as she had done back in the house, stopping to look at him until she came to a rest, perching on a stump at the edge of the glade, directly opposite from where Akonni was gathering wood.

William stared dully amazed at the little creature, whose sole purpose in life it seemed was to confound him. As he watched the mouse, he caught the movement in the trees just beyond. His eyelids were getting quite heavy as he squinted through the trees to see what was moving this time. As the fog closed in on him, he smiled, watching two other people who were also gathering wood; a young man wearing a highland kilt and young woman with long hair tied in a braid at the back of her neck... *Hello Sean, I knew you'd be by eventually. Laurel, it's good to see you... .*

By the time Akonni returned with the firewood, his companion was fast asleep, and Duncan and Annlise had made their way back to their own camp on the far side of the clearing, neither party aware of the other.

Chapter 15

THE SUMMER PASSED slowly for Edward, each day much like the one before; hot, dry. The promise of a glorious harvest that was expected after an unusually mild winter and spring had not come to be. The steady spring rains that fell gentle and mild on the spring crops ceased to fall with the coming of June, and by July the crops in the fields began to turn from supple and green to crisp and brown. The fear of a lean winter prompted Edward to send orders to his tenants to prepare for rationing, and the topic of gossip among the town's people rarely strayed from the fears of the famine that had surely befallen them. The more superstitious and pious minded among Edward's shire were quick to point a finger of blame to the duke himself, claiming the lack of rain to be God's retribution for allowing the heathen peasants to flourish unchallenged in his realm.

Through the dry weeks of July, the whispers grew steadily louder. Edward did his best the quell the tremors by assuring the people that the previous year's boon would be sufficient to carry them through another winter, so long as they were prudent and followed his rationing advice. He had even gone so far as to placate his land barons with promises of monetary gain in return for enforcing the rations, but had rescinded the

offer almost immediately after receiving reports that some of
the barons were hoarding for their own households and not
for the subjects of their tenants. He had taken issue with one
Baron James Kirkstone, of the tenant of Bannenvale, who
Edward had fined heavily for having a peasant family beaten
for pillaging from the baron's silos. Kirkstone retaliated by
stirring up a hornet's nest, convincing the easily swayed that
if Edward would renounce his practice of protecting the
heathens, then God would send back the rains!

The baron had apparently been intrigued with the rumors
coming from Lothlanne of an attempted assassination and
had ingratiated himself into Ogham's graces by eliciting the
support of a fairly formidable *army* of narrow minded allies;
most notably, Gregory de Dunkirk, the Bishop of Stonehaven,
who readily seized the opportunity to call for a resumption
of the witch hunts, sighting the drought as an omen that
demonic forces were once again afoot in Stonehaven.

Fortunately for Edward, during the first week of August
and before the year's harvest was declared a complete
loss, the rains returned on their own accord. Kirkstone's
supporters fell away— though Dunkirk made it clear he
would be watching Edward closely— and a modicum of
peace returned to Stonehaven. By mid-August, to Edward's
profound relief, the doomsayers had grown tired of pointing
to him as the deliverer of destruction.

It was on a blessedly rainy afternoon that Quentin Chase
burst into Edward's salon. "My lord... Oh forgive me for not
knocking... but I bring news, my lord. *Wonderful* news!"

Edward looked up from the book he was reading into the
twinkling, smiling eyes of his new chamberlain, and could

not suppress his laughter at the almost childlike glee in the elderly man's eyes. "Have you? Tell me so I can share your happy mood."

"The *Lady Anne* is returning," Quentin beamed. "She's been spotted from the parapet."

Edward was on his feet instantly, grinning. "How far out are they?"

"They should make landfall by sunset, my lord. They're back!"

Edward clasped his hands together tightly, smiling at the old man. "Thank the heavens! And the timing could not be better."

"Och, I agree with ye there." Quentin laughed. "Had Lord Sutherland returned during the height of the drought..." He rolled his eyes dramatically. "I can't even bear to think about how Kirkwood's dimwits would have received him."

"To be sure, Quentin. I can imagine quite well that the drought would no doubt be blamed, not only on me but on the return of *the demon.*" He laughed for a moment, then grew more serious. "It will be difficult enough to explain his return to the living."

"Aye, it will," Quentin agreed. "But we need not worry on that just yet. You don't plan to parade him through the square, do you?"

"No." Edward chuckled. "William's homecoming will be a very private one. Only those within this house and on that ship out there need know... for now."

"Indeed."

Edward's grin returned and he motioned to the door extending his arm. "Join me on the parapet, will you? We'll watch from there."

"My pleasure, my lord." Quentin started toward the door, then stopped, snapping his fingers, "Agnes! I've yet to tell her. If you'll excuse me, I'll run and get her. Oh, she will be so pleased!"

"You do that, then we shall all watch together while our children come home."

Mehlyndia shielded her eyes with her hand, squinting toward the horizon. "There it is."

Seany stood on a crate next to the rail, on the starboard deck that had been placed especially for him by the captain to be used as his lookout. "That's Drumoak?" he asked, looking where his mother was pointing. "It looks small."

"Oh, it's quite grand, little one. It only looks small because we're still so far away." She forced a smile to her face and sat on the crate so that she would be eye level with her son.

"Is it even bigger than our barn? That was the biggest building in the world."

"Oh it's much bigger, and with an even bigger barn. And stables. So many stables, each filled with teams of the most beautiful horses in the highlands."

Seany looked at her wide-eyed. "Is Cirrus there?"

Mehlyndia looked at him curiously, taken aback by the question. "You know about Cirrus?"

"When Simon was being Father Christmas, he said that Cirrus was Papa's horse. Don't you remember?"

"Oh." Mehlyndia put her arm around her son, and gave him a quick squeeze. "That's right, he did. You have a good memory, little man. I'd forgotten all about that. I don't know if Cirrus is still there. He may be, but he'd be quite old for a horse by now."

"He's there, m' lady."

Mehlyndia turned, greeting Matthew with a smile. "Good morning, lad. Cirrus is still among the stable team?"

"Aye, but as you say, he is right old and not suitable for a saddle at all." Matthew came and leaned against the railing, looking toward the shore. "The groomsman wanted to put him down, but Lord Edward had no heart for it and has put him to pasture instead."

"Why does the groomsman want to put him down?" Seany asked, alarmed. "That's Papa's horse!"

Matthew opened his mouth to say something, looking at Mehlyndia as if for permission to answer. She understood Matthew's quandary and answered Seany for him in as gentle a way as possible.

"I think what Matthew is saying is that Cirrus has gone… lame?" She looked to the lad for confirmation, he nodded that she was right.

"What does that mean?" Seany asked.

"The horse doesn't walk so well anymore," Matthew answered. "So he's not as useful, and he's more than likely in some pain, so they would put him down as a kindness."

"They would put him down just for that?" Seany asked, looking suddenly older than his five years. "Just because he's lame?"

Mehlyndia brushed the hair from her son's eyes. "It's a hard thing, but that's what's usually done—"

"Papa didn't walk *at all*." Seany knotted his brow. "Did someone put him down for bein' lame?"

"Oh, Seany." Mehlyndia caught her breath and pulled the little boy close to her. "No, no. That's not the same at all."

"I'm sorry, m' lady, little mate... l didn't mean to upset ye. It's a horse we're speakin' of... not ye father... no one put ye papa..."

"Shh, both of you. Come here, Matty." She took both boys in her arms and gave them each a squeeze. "Now, we cannot be greeting ye grandfathers all a-muddle; now, can we?"

Matthew stood back, hurriedly wiping his face with his hand. Mehlyndia had grown quite fond of the lad during the crossing, though he had seemed terribly timid around her at first, and she wondered what she could have possibly done to intimidate him so. She had gone out of her way to be gentle with him but it wasn't until she abandoned the grand gown in which she had fled for her more customary linen frock that he seemed to come around, and then she understood; it was her resemblance to her sister in *her* fine gown that had put him off.

Matthew spent the first week of the crossing sulking below deck, spending long hours sitting on his bunk, not speaking to anyone. It was Seany who finally convinced him to come on deck to see a pod of whales that they had come across. Though at first, neither child had much to say to each other, they stayed together. Comfortable in their silence, eventually solidifying their friendship, each helping the other cope with their losses. It wasn't long before Matthew came to realize that though she may *look* like her sister, Mehlyndia was nothing like the dragon of Lothlanne.

"Matty, the others are below. Would you run and tell them we've spotted shore?"

"Aye, m' lady." Matthew smiled, taking a steadying breath. He held a hand toward Seany. "Come with me, little mate?"

Seany hopped off the crate, taking Matthew's hand. "All right, but I get to ring the bell!"

Matthew laughed. "You always get to ring the bell!"

Mehlyndia watched the two head toward the lower deck, then turned back to look at the shore. *Home. I'm almost home, my love. Father will be watching from the parapet, I'm sure. He'll be so glad to see me, and he's going to adore Seany, don't you think?* Silent tears fell as she watched Drumoak grow on the horizon.

The longboat made slow but steady progress toward the shore, Simon on the oars at the stern, Mehlyndia, Prissy, and Elinor seated near the bow, and Matthew and Seany in the middle. A wiggling Dragon wailed and hissed, protectively tied in a sack at Seany's feet. Simon had entrusted Seany with his looking glass, and the lad was given the job of lookout for this last leg of their sea journey.

"Look to the shore, Seany. See if you can see the people there," Mehlyndia told him, shielding her eyes against the glare on the water.

Seany screwed up half his face, pressing one eye to the glass as he aimed it skyward. "I don't see any people, Mum, but there's a lot of clouds. Best be gettin' us ashore before the wind turns afoul, Simon," he said in a serious voice, mimicking phrases he'd heard the sailors use during the long months of the crossing.

Simon chuckled between strokes. "Aye, aye, Cap'n Seany, I'll do m' best." He looked up to catch Mehlyndia's eye. "Looks like they know we're comin'."

"Aye." Mehlyndia said, looking back to the shore. "I see Father, and who is that with him?"

Matthew craned his neck, squinting passed Mehlyndia. "That's my grandfather!" He waved his arm swiftly, looking toward the shore. The old man waved back. "Ahoy, Grandfather!"

"Oh, yes. And Agnes is there as well." She sighed, then turned away. She found it difficult to look on the expectant faces of the three who stood waiting. She was keenly aware of the five empty seats on the longboat, as she sat brooding, not relishing the forthcoming task of informing this eager looking group that half of their party had been left behind to an uncertain fate. *And you, my loved... what to tell them of you?* She had spent the better part of the journey desperately trying not to worry what had had become of Ewan, Annlise, Duncan and Ian, hoping and praying they had made it safely out of the barn and into the woods before the raiders landed. She missed Ian and his lighthearted banter in particular. He could brighten the gloomiest of days with the flute music that William so loved to hear and play along with on his psaltery. She hoped he had his flute with him now and was playing for the others, keeping them cheered as well.

"Annlise must be heartbroken," Prissy said quietly for only Mehlyndia to hear. She placed her hand on her stomach, her pregnancy just now beginning to be apparent. "I've yet to hold this little one and the thought of being separated that way... oh, I do hope she's well."

Mehlyndia took hold of Prissy's hand and squeezed it. "Me too. I've been thinking, Prissy." She pulled the girl close to her and spoke softly, "It's still early in the year and ships have been known to sail west as late as November..."

"Aye, that's true," Prissy said, then grinned, a light of understanding shining on her face. "You're going to send the ship back for them?" She squeezed Mehlyndia's hand excitedly.

"Of course I'll have to ask my father; after all, it is *his* ship."

"It's a grand idea!" Elinor chimed in.

Mehlyndia blushed, then smiled. She had intended not to speak loud enough that Matthew would hear, not wanting the lad to have his hopes raised too much. She glanced over her shoulder to see Matthew looking expectantly to the shore. Motioning Elinor and Prissy close to her, they put their heads together.

"I've not had a single night's sleep free of worry for what's become of Ian and the others," Mehlyndia whispered.

Elinor clasped her hands over Mehlyndia's. "Nor I, dear. And I've been thinking about poor Agnes this whole time. She'll be shattered when she learns that Duncan was left behind. I remember how she took to her bed for days after Sean passed."

"Then it's only right that we send *Lady Anne* right back to Port Edin as quickly as she can be made ready," Prissy asserted in her no-nonsense way. "Annlise saved my life back there. I don't pretend to understand how, but I'm sure she did *something* miraculous and... I never got to thank her." She looked over her shoulder to Matthew. "He's heartbroken, you know. He puts up a brave front, mostly for Seany's sake, I think. But I know he misses his mother terribly."

"I'm sure you're right, Prissy." Mehlyndia squeezed Prissy's hand tightly, then huddled her close again. "But have either of you considered that... I mean, I can't bear to imagine it, but... what if—"

"They're not there?" Elinor finished.

Mehlyndia nodded slowly. "Aye, what if Josephine and her gaggle of harpies actually got to them?"

"I don't think Josephine gave them, or us, a second thought once the cannon fire began," Prissy said, quietly, her voice catching in her throat. "I worry more that they were taken by the raiders... or worse." She drew a long breath. "But I still believe there be hope and it's only right we send someone back for them, and until I know otherwise, I will believe they're all still alive well. After all, we've no proof to the contrary, have we?"

"No... we've no proof to believe *any* of them are dead." *Including you, my love.* Mehlyndia looked up to the shore to see how much farther they had to go. "We're almost there." She raised her arm, waving to the trio on the shore. They waved back.

"What are you three conspiring about?" Simon asked while he rowed. "Already plotting the homecoming feast?"

Prissy sat up straight and gave her husband a playful smile. "Feast? I think not, we've decided to take over Scotland and rule it on our own. Melly will make a lovely queen, don't you think?"

Simon laughed and assumed a lofty voice. "That she will, indeed."

"Oh stop, you two," Mehlyndia laughed, then could not resist giving Prissy a hug. "You are an absolute treasure to me, Prissy MacHenry, I don't know what I would ever do without you."

"What's all this?" Prissy asked, patting Mehlyndia on the back.

"I just wanted to say it." Mehlyndia took a breath and sat straight, and turned to Elinor, and gave her a hug as well. "And I don't know how I would have gotten through without you as well, Elinor. Please, don't ever let me forget to tell you how much you mean to me, and to Seany as well." She gave the older woman a squeeze allowing the tears she'd been holding back to finally come through.

"Thank you, dear." Elinor smiled, then the two laughed a bit and looked toward the shore.

"I guess I'm just feeling sentimental about coming home," Mehlyndia said, wiping her eyes. "I've missed Father terribly. I was certain I'd never set eyes on him or Drumoak again."

"I've missed him too." Elinor spoke quietly, her eyes fixed on the people waving from the shore. "More than I could tell you, child."

"Land ho!" Seany announced, as the bottom of the boat scraped on the sandy beach. "Ye can hoist the oars and lower the mains'l, Simon. We've run ashore!"

"Aye, aye, Cap'n," Simon laughed heartily at the little captain's commands. "Though there be no mains'l to lower on this here craft, Cap'n. But I'll be right pleased to quit rowin'." He lifted the oars into the locks, then stood up carefully in the stern. "Come on, Matty. Time to get ye feet wet."

Simon hopped over the side of the boat into the shallow water. Matthew did the same, taking up the tow rope while Simon pushed on the stern. Between the two, it took them only moments to bring the little craft safely to the shore, the bow resting on the dry sand of the beach next to the seawall beneath the shadow of Drumoak castle.

"Secure the rope with a rock now, Matty, then go greet ye grampa. He's looking eager to see ye, lad," Simon said, wading to the side of the craft, his arms held out to Seany. "Come on, Cap'n, the voyage is over, time to be a landlubber again. Don't f'get your squallin' cat." Seany gathered up Dragon's sack in his arms, then Simon carried both lad and cat to the dry sandy beach.

"Father!" Mehlyndia stood quickly, almost toppling out of the boat. Simon set Seany down quickly and was able to catch her before she fell, lifting her by the waist, up and out of the boat. "Thank you, Simon," she said absently, then ran to Edward, throwing her arms around him.

"Mehlyndia, my darling daughter! Thank God in Heaven you've made it back." Edward embraced her tightly, rocking back and forth for a moment before they broke, each taking a step back to look at each other. "You are still the most beautiful creature I've ever seen," he said, his smile nearly too big to fit on his face. "And who is this fine looking fellow?" he asked, bending down to Seany's level, extending a hand.

Seany looked up to Mehlyndia with wide eyes.

"It's safe, darling. This is your grandfather, Lord Edward of Stonehaven."

Seany put his hand to his mouth quickly and blushed. "Oh!" He cleared his throat, extended his hand and, in the serious voice he'd been practicing during the crossing, said, "I am Seany... uh Sean William Philbrick... uh *Fylbrigge*, and I'm pleased to meet you, Grandfather."

Edward accepted Seany's hand and bowed his head in

a serious manner. "I'm pleased to meet you, as well," he said, then laughed as a yowl of protest sounded from the squirming sack at Seany's feet. "And what manner of wild beast have you trapped in this sack, Sean William Fylbrigge?"

Seany's face lit into a dimply grin. "Oh that's just Dragon. My cat. She doesn't like it in there, but it kept her from jumping out of the boat."

"Dragon, is it? A curious name for a cat. She must be fierce indeed," Edward said with mock seriousness.

"Absolutely," Seany replied, completely serious.

Edward laughed and stood up, glancing expectantly toward the boat, Elinor and Prissy were walking toward him. "Elinor!" He met her half way, embracing her in a bear hug. "Oh my dear, you look as young as a maypole maid, I swear."

"And you are still a wondrous liar," she laughed squeezing him. "And you are a fine sight for these old eyes, m' lord—"

"Edward," he corrected her, "remember? We agreed before you sailed away."

"Aye. Edward." Elinor blushed and gave him another hug.

Matthew had run to his grandfather, and was now leading the man by the hand back to where Edward and the women were. Simon was retrieving satchels and traveling bags from the boat. When he set the last bag to the sand, he motioned to Edward to join him. Agnes followed Quentin, shading her eyes, looking back toward the ship, as though searching. Mehlyndia took a breath and went to greet her.

"Agnes, it's so good to see you again." She embraced Agnes for a moment then stepped back.

Agnes smiled, then looked back toward the ocean, then back again at Mehlyndia. The disappointment in the woman's eyes was almost more than Mehlyndia could stand, and she wondered how she would find the strength to tell her, when she was rescued, once again, by Prissy.

"There's been a delay," Prissy explained gently. "We couldn't all return on *this* trip."

Tears welled in Agnes's eyes. "Are they lost?" she asked, quietly.

"Duncan, Ewan, and Annlise were all alive and well, when we set sail," Prissy said slowly, looking back and forth from Agnes to Quentin, as though speaking to children, but it seemed to ease the fear on Agnes's face. "We need only send a ship back for them. Ian is with them as well, you see? There's nothing to fear."

Agnes nodded, a wary, sad smile coming to her. Quentin put a supportive arm around her, and she clung to him. "Thank you for telling us, lass," he said wearing the same skeptical, yet grateful expression Agnes wore.

"Yes... thank you." Agnes gave Prissy's hand a squeeze, then looked at her curiously for a moment, then looked toward the boat, then to each face around her. "William? Is he with them as well?"

Mehlyndia met Agnes's eyes only for a moment and dropped her chin to her chest, shaking her head, unable to find her voice. Edward placed a hand on Mehlyndia's shoulder and she turned, burying her face on his shoulder.

"Simon just told me," Edward said, quietly into her ear. "Oh my child, I'm so sorry..."

Mehlyndia allowed the tears to flow for a moment, allowing herself to take comfort in her father's arms as she had as a child.

All stood heads down for several moments, the only sound about them, the waves and the call of the sea birds above them. An impatient nickering from the horse attached to the waiting carriage broke the silence.

Mehlyndia lifted her face, took hold of Seany's hand, and said, "I think it's time to go home." With that, the somber homecoming celebration ended as the carriage was loaded and the driver shook the reins to take them home.

Chapter 16

"YOU LOSE AGAIN, W'yiam." Sosep grinned, kneeling over the wooden game bowl across from William, while scooping up the remainder of the counting sticks from William's woodpile, the tallying markers used in a game of waltes he had learned— or rather was *trying*— to learn. The game was played with six half-rounded bones, painted on the flat side with a symbol, smoothed on the other. The bones were placed in a shallow wooden bowl, then thumped against a straw mat. Depending on how many landed up and how many down, counting sticks were taken from a pile or an opponent's pile, the object being to gain the most sticks... or so he thought. One stick represented an old man, two others were marked as wives, and they carried a point system that confounded William, as during the course of the game the points changed depending on factors he had yet to fully comprehend, and he suspected Sosep was making them up as he went along.

"But... now, wait a minute," William scratched the back of his ear re-examining his last move. "I rolled all up... and then counted out five... I should have had four left... or no, that's not it..." He threw his hands up, laughing. "You win. I will never understand this game."

Sosep laughed heartily, rocking back on his knees. "That is because you were not born to it, white man."

"I guess so." William smiled, trying not to take Sosep's comment personally, though it was one of many half-slights he had made during the weeks William had spent in the Mi'kmaq village. "I should like to challenge you to a game of chess and see if you fare any better at one of *my* games."

"Chess?" Sosep snorted with a disinterested shake of his head. "I've seen it. Hours of thinking. No thrill of chance. Where is the challenge in a game you simply think your way through? I have no wish to learn."

William grinned. "You're right, it involves far too much thinking. You'd never be able to learn it properly."

Sosep's laughter ended and his face hardened, straining the tentative peace that had been shared between the two men. "You think me not as wise as you, white man? You who cannot even grasp a simple game that even our youngest children play with skill?"

William glared at Sosep for a moment, refusing to be baited into a war of words with the man. Sosep had made no secret of his disdain for all things *aklasie'w*— white man— but for all his hard words and distrustful side glances, Sosep never acted on his resentment. But he did seem to take great delight in goading William into arguments. *Let it pass, he's not worth it.*

Sosep's smug grin returned at William's silence. He gathered up the elements of the game and stood, looking down to where William remained kneeling on the mat. "Perhaps little C'ara would be a more suitable opponent for you," he chortled and turned away.

William bit his tongue, watching Sosep strut off. *Ass. He cheats. And he'd never be able to learn chess.*

"W'yiam?"

He turned to see Ah'Reehl approaching from the large lodge toward him, wearing a warm welcoming smile. She carried her wooden basket laden with summer berries. He smiled in return and waved. "Kwe' Ariel," he said the native greeting awkwardly, still pronouncing her name as best he could.

"Kwe'. I bring you breakfast." She knelt on the mat, placing the basket between them. "How are you feeling today?"

"Better, thank—"

"Ah'Reehl!" Sosep came up behind her, scowling. "Let *aklasie'w* retrieve his own breakfast, as the rest of us do."

Ah'Reehl's eyes flared and she was on her feet facing the man in an instant. "I brought *yours* to you," she pointed out.

Sosep raised his voice and said something in his own language, pointing toward William. He didn't understand the words, but the tone of the man's voice and the look on his face was unmistakable. Ah'Reehl set her hands on her hips, answering Sosep's arguments rapidly, also pointing to William. Sosep's tone became defensive. *She's winning,* William thought, looking back and forth between the two as they continued their verbal joust. Their arguments carrying loudly throughout the village until called to an abrupt halt by Akonni.

"Enough!"

The two silenced instantly, both turning quickly to face the Shaman. Ah'Reehl's face flushed contritely, the defiance and fire she had shown to Sosep replaced immediately with a submissive bow of her head.

"Go. The elders have need of you," Akonni told her sharply, pointing toward the main lodge.

She glanced toward William briefly and half-smiled, then bowed to Akonni before hurrying back toward the main lodge.

Sosep stood steely-eyed, glowering at Akonni, his jaw muscles flexing against his clenched teeth.

"What have you to say? Speak!" Akonni demanded.

"He is *aklasie'w*," Sosep answered, setting an unblinking stare onto the Shaman, "and has shown no contribution to the people. The moose have moved, we must follow. Yet two sunsets have passed and we do not." He turned his glare to William. "Because this *aklasie'w* cannot travel as we do."

"I'm not keeping anyone—" William began.

Akonni held up a hand to him. "It is not for you to question my judgment. Niskam has shown me what is inside this man. It is right we wait until I am told we must move."

"Has Niskam decreed we have no meat for the winter? Is it Niskam's plan that all L'nu'k must suffer for the sake of this one? Did I not see to the safe return of his women back to their own village? Could they not see to his... feeding?" Sosep took a threatening step forward, raising one hand as if to strike.

William flinched back defensively, surprised by the sudden show of aggression. Akonni raised his staff swiftly, blocking Sosep from completing his strike. The two locked eyes, frozen in place for several long moments, neither seeming to draw a breath until finally Sosep relaxed his muscles and lowered his arm. William released his own breath, unaware he had been holding it.

"Go!" Akonni pointed toward the forest. "Seek the answer from the Spirit on your own, if you so distrust my decision."

Sosep flared his nostrils and glared at William. "Enjoy your breakfast, *aklasie'w,* and pray it not be the last you eat." He spun abruptly on his heel and stalked away toward the edge of the forest.

Akonni stood motionless until Sosep was out of sight. "So much anger. My heart is heavy for him. He chooses to look only two steps ahead rather than to keep his eye on his destination. He would cut the tree at the trunk to reach the best fruit without thought, then mourn that the tree no longer grows."

William looked up, surprised to see the look on the Shaman's face had gone from dark anger to something more akin to despair. "He's young," William said, trying to keep his own anger out of his voice. "He'll learn. Rash and reckless actions may satisfy a need for the moment, but they do tend catch up with a man."

Akonni relaxed and looked to William, his face softening into the congenial gentleness William had come to know. "That is the lesson you have learned, is it not, my friend?"

"You could say that," he answered, then gestured to the empty space opposite him. "Join me for breakfast?"

"It is why I came," Akonni said, as he settled down on his knees. "But it is words I must share, not food."

William could see the turmoil on the man's face, as if he had bad news he did not know how to share, and he had a fair idea what it was. "Sosep is right, isn't he? I'm holding you all back."

Akonni drew a long breath and looked him in the eye, nodding. "It is true the moose have moved to the summer grounds and the time has come that the village move to follow. Sosep has stirred his grumbles among the rest of the people that you should be left behind. My people look to me for the answer, trusting that I will lead as Niskam has shown me. But they see, as Sosep has, that we do not follow the moose as we should and I have been unable to quiet those who do not understand why it is you have been allowed to stay. They see you only as..."

"A burden?" William finished his thought for him.

He nodded. "I am sorry."

"Don't be. They're right. I've been a burden to a lot of people. For a long time." An image of Mehlyndia, standing aside his bedside, hands outstretched and ready to lift him out of bed, crept to his mind. He pushed it aside, only to have it replaced with other like memories; Simon, pushing him through his living room in his chariot; Ian lifting him from the litter to visit the forest on their last evening together.

"I am to do as Niskam has shown me." Akonni spoke quietly, a look of true grief on his face. "Though reasons have not been revealed. It may seem harsh, but—"

"I'm to be left behind," William said, flatly.

Akonni nodded. "It is what I have seen. I cannot question what Niskam has told me. He has a reason that you be sent alone into the forest. Whether it be for the good of my people or for the greater plan, I cannot say, but I was led to guide you in the beginning, to make you stronger, and set you on a path of healing, which I have done. I must trust Niskam, now."

William sat silently as Akonni spoke, a surreal detachment to the conversation coming over him. He was to be left, that much he understood, and Akonni was not happy about it, but would demure to the pressures of his people, convincing himself that it was Niskam who had made the decision for him. *Wash the guilt from your hands, Akonni. Do it in God's name...*

"I will provide you a horse, enough food for many days, and blankets," Akonni was saying.

Food for many days... and a horse, how generous of you.

"Travel in the direction of the rising sun, it has been shown me. Trust, W'yiam. I do not send you off to die."

"Don't you?" William replied sharply.

Akonni averted his eyes. "It is as Niskam wishes—"

"It is as *Sosep* wishes," William countered angrily. "Him and the ones who follow his lead. Where I come from, that's just simple politics. But if it eases your conscience to believe it is your Niskam who tells you what to do, then so be it. You're absolved... bless you."

"Your anger is reasonable, but you are wrong," Akonni answered quietly, then stood, not looking to William. "If it were death that Niskam had planned for you, he would not have led me to the tree where I found you, but have hidden you away to die alone."

"It would have been better had I died there."

"Better?" Akonni turned to look at William, a bewildered and hurt expression on his face. "To be dead? When now, your legs are alive again and your memory is returning? Why do you say that, W'yiam?"

William tightened his lips, forcing control of his anger.

Akonni's expression told him the Shaman was truly astonished at his declaration. Perhaps the man truly did believe he was acting on the part of his god, and who was he to question the man's faith.

He swallowed hard, steadying his breath. "I admit, I am grateful to have back this little use of my legs but the price has been dear. You must understand why I do not share your trust in your Niskam as he has proven himself to me to be cruel in his kindness. He gives with one hand, then takes back two-fold with the other. Yes, he has returned to me some of my memories, but only those that bring me pain. The tower... the knife... ." He trailed off for a moment, closing his eyes and pushing the sudden images of Joseph aside as he continued, "... but I still cannot recall my wedding night; the times with my wife when I was still whole; the night my son was conceived. Your Niskam has seen fit to allow my legs to move, yes, but I still cannot stand and walk. Niskam wishes that I should continue to live and breathe, but I must do so without all those who I hold dearest to me. And I do not have a moment of peace that I am not haunted with grief and worry of what has become of my wife and my son." He turned his face a moment, catching his breath. "Had I died under that tree, you see, perhaps we would be all together now, in the next world."

The Shaman stood silent a moment, then turned to leave. He stopped outside the opening and spoke quietly, keeping his face turned. "Gather your belongings. I shall bring all I have promised. Trust, W'yiam. It must be as I have been shown." He silently walked away.

Trust? How many times have I heard that in my life? He

fought the shudder that raided his spine while he crossed the lodge to his cot. *Trust who? God? Akonni?* He remained on his knees beside the cot for a moment, anger descending rapidly into panic as he mulled over the situation, realizing full well there was no way to persuade the Shaman to change his mind. In little less than an hour, he would be cast out to the wilderness again, with only Akonni's admonition that he should simply *trust*. He folded his hands in front of himself, resting them on the quilt that was spread across the cot. *Time to pray in earnest, Will. Pray you're wrong and Akonni is right... trust. Blessed Mother, please give me the answer... please help me to trust... to find the confidence I need... confidence... banish my fears...*

He looked up sharply from his prayer. *Banish my fears! I know those words... I know them!* He groped under the bed for the leather satchel he had carried back from his garrison. *My journal. It's in here. It must be. Remove my doubts... banish...*

He removed Mehlyndia's quilt from the bed, musing how, not long ago, he had never regarded the circular pattern she had sewn into the patches as anything more than pretty. But he had come a far journey since he had last seen her and the pattern had gained a new meaning to him. He lay the quilt flat on the matted floor, then carefully folded it into quarters, leaving a square panel on top, revealing one complete circle. He smoothed it, reverently tracing the circle with the flat of his hand, then reached beneath the cot and retrieved the leather bound journal and placed it in the center of the circle.

"This is my book, Melly," he spoke to the space around him, quietly. "Remember the first time I showed it to you? It frightened you and you wanted to burn it." He frowned at the memory of the night he had given it to her to hide— the night before they had come for him. "But you trusted me and you kept it safe for me. I'm glad you did." He traced the image of the hawk that was tooled into the leather, then opened the cover slowly, turning the pages gingerly.

In his years in Port Edin, he had believed this book to be nothing more than a diary, filled with his fanciful whims of youth, a bit of poetry and the idle thoughts he'd had since he began writing in it at the age of twelve. He had spent innumerable hours poring over the entries, trying to glean traces of memories from what he had written, but learning little of his past from the scant words he'd left for himself to read, chiding himself over and over for his lack of details.

But that was before.

He opened the book to a page he had read hundreds of times dated, 15 September 1605 which read: *At long last, Elinor showed Laurel and I how to make a simple charm today. Just a little one that is supposed to make your footsteps quiet. Mine failed miserably, and Sean heard me coming from the other end of the castle. But Laurel's worked perfectly. It made her absolutely quiet as a mouse.* He had read the entry many times, scoffing it off to youthful fancy.

But that was before.

He flipped through the pages for a moment, none of them seeming any different than they had for the past five years, though he knew better now. At last, he found the entry he was seeking dated 6 April 1607, reading: *God help me, I used the chicory today, and it worked!*

This is the one. He placed his hands flat on the open page, and set his eyes on the quilt circle that surrounded it, staring until his vision dimmed to all but the quilt and the book. He closed his eyes, seeing the ghost of the circle still before him, concentrating only on it and the book alone... the circle... the book... *I charmed it Melly, to keep it private... anyone who reads it would see it as a simple book of verse... I charmed it... I used the chicory charm... for confidence, to banish... I charmed...*

He slowly opened his eyes and pulled his hands away from the book, then smiled as faintly, but surely, the words he had written shifted on the page before him until they revealed what he had been hoping to see:

~ For Confidence ~
Divine Mother, show me the way
Remove my doubts and banish my fear
God and Father, creator of days
Guide my words that they be clear

"There it is," he said quietly. "This is the one that brought me to where I am today, and it's this one that will bring me home again."

Within an hour, everything he owned in the world; his book, the wooden box with the silver trinket inside, Melly's handkerchief, the quilt, his carving knife, two changes of clothing and food and water skins provided by Akonni had been bundled up into skin sacks, and fastened onto a litter of his own fashioning. The poles for the litter were long, with a thick piece of hide serving as the platform. He harnessed the pulling ends to the back of the horse in a style he had suggested to Akonni weeks before, that had been scoffed at by Sosep and his mates as too unwieldy for the horse to maneuver.

The saddle too, was made at William's behest and by his

instruction soon after arriving in the village. The Mi'kmaq generally rode bareback or with only a blanket between them and the horse; a method William was quite comfortable with as a boy. However now, with the limited use of his legs, it was nearly impossible for him to stay on the horse and control it without some sort of support under his feet. Therefore, he had shown the native people a drawing in the sand of a saddle with stirrups and a proper harness to keep it on the horse.

He had grown particularly fond of a jet black mare with a long mane and a shock of white in her forelocks. *Kindred,* he had called her. Over the course of his days in the village, he had built a rapport with the mare, learning her rhythms and her moods, and she learning his. He was grateful that it was Kindred who Akonni brought to him for his journey into the woods.

Without conversation Akonni helped him load the litter, then silently handed him the reins.

"How am I to mount?" William grumbled, staring stupidly at the reins in his hands as he knelt on the ground aside the mare.

"Trust, W'yiam," Akonni answered, placing his hand on William's shoulder. "Your destination is to the east."

"Tru—" William closed his eyes, drawing his mouth in tight, halting himself from arguing as he knew it would do him no good. He let his breath out slowly, pushing the anger down as he asked, "Trust who? The horse? She knows east from west?"

Akonni looked unblinking into William's eyes. "Trust what is in your heart, my friend. The path seems impossible to you and you fear that you cannot follow it to the end. You see and hear only with your eyes and your ears, but it is from within that you must follow." He placed his palm on William's chest, above his heart. "Niskam has provided all you will require. Trust, W'yiam. You will not be alone." He turned his back and walked to the darkening path of the forest.

"Akonni, wait—"

The Shaman turned, raised his hand in a gesture of farewell, then to William's astonishment, he took a step backward, his hide cloak melding into the shadows about him, giving William the impression that the Shaman had simply vanished into thin air.

"Akonni?"

The horse shook the reins in his hand. He looked at it, then back to the forest. Branches and ferns lay undisturbed on the forest floor, marking no trace of the man who must have passed that way. He stared, unwilling to miss the slightest proof that Akonni had actually left him, suddenly hopeful that perhaps the Shaman was staying close by after all, watching. But the shadows cast by the trees were merely reflections of themselves, no human form joined with them, and his hope faded. *Akonni?* Kindred snorted, then inclined her head toward him, nuzzling against his neck. He stroked the velvety nose and patted her neck, still staring where Akonni had stood. "Well, Kindred, it looks like we're on our own."

She shook her head, nickering in response, then stepped forward, then back as if impatiently waiting to get moving. He looked up to the stirrup knowing it was going to be impossible to reach it. "Trust? Do you know how I'm to mount?"

Kindred whinnied quietly, bobbing her head, then she bent her front legs, then the rear, folding them under bringing her belly to the ground. She nuzzled him again. He smiled and stroked her neck appreciatively, then knee-walked to the side of her. She stayed still, patiently waiting while he wrangled himself onto her back, mounting from his knees and pulling himself belly-to, across the saddle. Once astride, he put his feet into the leather stirrups with his hands, then shook the reins. "Up, girl."

Kindred obliged him, gently standing to her feet. "Good girl." He looked to the sky, judging the direction of the sun, then turned her to the way he assumed was east. *Banish my fears....* "Let's go home... where ever that is."

Chapter 17

DUNCAN TROMPED AROUND the underbrush, grumbling, slashing at ferns with his sword and kicking at rotting moss covered stumps, as he was once again relegated to the loathsome task of collecting firewood for the evening's camp fire. *Is this what I have spent my whole life preparing for? Wood gathering in the never-ending forest? Why can't Ewan gather wood for a change? Or Ian? I may be the youngest but, blast it all, I am a sentry, same as the glorious Ewan McDonough his own self.* He snapped a dead branch from a fallen log, scaring up a cloud of sawdust where it broke. He sneezed as he breathed in the wood dust.

"Duncan? Have you got that wood?" Annlise called from the clearing they were planning to camp in for the night.

"Aye, aye," he answered, attempting but failing to keep the irritation from his voice.

"Duncan? Did you hear me, lad?" she called again. "Have you got—"

"Aye, I said!" he shouted, then stomped his way through a pile of muck to the clearing. He dropped an armload of kindling in a heap, then turned to walk back into the woods.

"Duncan."

The maternal tone she had been fond of taking with him began to grate on his nerves.

"Lad, we're all weary of this forest. Ye been a walking storm cloud the better part of the day. What's bedevilin' ye so?"

Duncan stopped and stood with his back to her, feeling the heat rise to his face. *She means well, let it go.* "Nothing. I'm fine," he answered, then began to walk away.

"If this be fine, I'd be sore afraid to see ye troubled."

He stopped short, took a breath, then turned to face her. "Annlise, if you don't mind, I'd like to be allowed to keep my thoughts to myself. Is that too much to ask?"

"Well then, take ye'self and ye thoughts back to the woods," she said, abandoning the motherly drawl. "We'll need far more wood than this tonight."

"Why can't Ewan get it? Or Ian?" he snapped at her. "I've gathered enough wood these last weeks to build us a damned ship to sail off this miserable island!" His face flushed and he looked away.

"They're off hunting for supper, you know that," she answered curtly. "They do their share, as do I, to keep the sorry lot of us from dyin' in this blasted forest!" She picked up a piece of the wood Duncan dropped and tossed it sharply onto the fire. "Do you think you're the only one unhappy out here? Well I'll be happy to tell ye that you are not!"

"Annlise, I'm—"

"I know you're angry that they treat ye like a boy. Always tellin' ye what to do and how to do it, and not takin' your ideas seriously."

"Exactly—"

"It's maddening for ye! Ye have ye talents and ye skills, and wish to Mother they'd realize..." She stopped abruptly, covering her eyes with one hand.

Duncan saw the scarlet come to her cheeks and he realized then she had been ranting about her own frustrations rather than his. "Annlise, I'm sorry," he said, letting his anger drain away.

She waved him off, showing him a false smile, then turned to busy herself in tending the camp fire.

"Annlise," he reached for her elbow, turning her to look at him. "I didn't mean to yell at you. You're right. I am frustrated. Not just with Ewan and Ian, God knows they are doing what they must, but it's the whole..." He gestured to the trees around him, searching for his words. "The whole situation that has me frustrated."

"I know what ye mean." She motioned to a large granite bolder nearby. "Sit yourself down here. The fire can wait."

They settled down together on the bolder.

Duncan scowled. "This isn't what it was supposed to be."

"I know."

"I bet they've already made it back to Stonehaven."

Her hand found its way to the base of her throat, laying it flat-palmed over the silver knot. A ritual, Duncan had come to realized, she performed whenever her thoughts strayed to Matthew. "Aye, I bet they have. Mother willin', it was a safe crossing."

"Aye," he agreed, then sat silent for a moment, staring into the woods at everything and nothing at the same time.

"If the furrow in ye brow were any deeper, lad, we could sow turnips in it."

He turned to see her smiling kindly at him. He could not resist a half grin back.

"That's better," she chuckled lightly. "What's on ye mind, Duncan?"

"Failure," he said quietly, feeling slightly embarrassed.

"Ye believe ye failed at something?"

"Well... yes. This was supposed to be my first mission. To come here, retrieve Will— Edward's *heir*, then sail home." He allowed a sarcastic grin to find him, then shook his head. "Simple, right?"

"Aye, simple enough. And ye couldn't even do that simple thing, aye? Ye right, ye are a miserable failure. 'Tis all ye fault the village be destroyed."

He looked up to her surprised, but could not resist laughing a bit at the teasing smile she was wearing. "Aye, 'twas. How silly of me to allow all those English galleons to attack while we were all enjoying a perfectly good riot. *What* was I thinking?"

"I can't tell ye, but I'm sure ye mus' have a grand excuse."

They laughed together for a moment, then grew serious again.

"Edward is going to be devastated when he finds out about William, you know," Duncan said, reaching for a long stick to poke at the fire. "After all this time, waiting for the day he could call him home again..." He shook his head. "Do you know what the first thought was to cross my mind when Edward told me Will was alive?"

"What?"

"I let myself hope that if Will was out here, hiding all these years while we all thought him dead, that perhaps... Sean was out here too." He looked away, feeling the flush come to his cheeks. "Glad as I was to hear about Will... it was Sean I was truly hoping to find out here, even though I know better. Mum was with him when he passed away, ye know... she wouldn't lie about such a thing... but still, I had that hope. Childish, isn't it? "

Annlise looked down to her hands, fumbling with her nails "No, 'tisn't childish." Her face turned red as if she was going to cry again, but she took a breath and the threat passed before she spoke again. "Truth be told I had the same thought, Duncan. And 'twas a grand dream I had... to be the one to bring them back home... Phoenix and Còlan, together again." She set a wistful gaze to the woods, "Och! To think of the joy it would bring to folks of the Heather Path to have them back again."

Duncan nodded, "Aye, you're right. Ah, well," he sighed, then stood up from the rock. "I should have known it was a fantasy. Neither one of them is real anymore, are they? I sometimes think they never were."

A rustle in the forest and the sound of voices announced the return of Ewan and Ian. The two emerged from a thicket, each bearing two rabbit carcasses hanging from snare lines.

"Supper," Ian said, swinging his rabbits by the string to show them. "And tonight the fare be a delicacy not served often enough on this fine shore. Pheasant, with new potatoes, sweet beets, and freshly baked bread." He drew a long breath of mock satisfaction, then thumped the rabbits onto the rock.

"You only got pheasant?" Ewan raised a comical brow. "I've a yearling buck, fully dressed and roasted in raisin gravy." He tossed his rabbits next to Ian's.

"Pity," Duncan sighed. "I was hoping for rabbit again."

Ewan clapped Duncan on the back with a chuckle. "I'm glad to see your mood is brighter, lad."

"Oh, it isn't," Duncan shrugged. "I'm still likely to draw

and run you through without provocation."

Ian and Annlise exchanged amused chuckles. It had become an almost daily ritual that Ewan or Duncan would call the other out in a mock duel. Ewan had been charged with Duncan's training, and whether they be in Stonehaven or lost in the wilds of the New World, he had taken that charge seriously, and Duncan had relished the sparring. Truth be told, Duncan was quite good with his sword, owing a good deal of his style to the play-training Sean had giving him as a youngster. When William had presented him with the little wooden sword, Sean was keen that his little brother learn to hold it appropriately. Toy or not, Sean had told him, if wielded properly, even a simple child's toy could cut down the fiercest of dragons. In their game, Sean had coached his stance and thrust, and taught him the importance of keeping his balance on center and his eyes on his adversary, not on his blade. The first time Ewan had worked with Duncan, he had been impressed with the lad's talent, even commenting that his style was *pure Wilbrun*, a high compliment to Duncan.

"Run me through, will you?" Ewan reached for the hilt of his sword setting a threatening eye on Duncan.

"Quicker than you could blink, old man." Duncan placed his hand on his sword.

"Old? I think not!" Ewan drew his blade. "Have at, you suckling bairn!"

With a wild grin, Duncan drew his blade deftly deflecting Ewan's first strike with a loud clash sending echoes through the forest.

"Best step away, m' lady." Ian pulled Annlise clear of the fray, the two laughing as the two displaced sentries battled over the soon-to-be camp fire.

Duncan swung, then blocked, spinning nimbly on his heel and striking toward Ewan's knees. Ewan whirled as well, arcing his sword just in time to deflect Duncan's strike.

"You're getting stodgy, old man, I nearly hobbled you!"

"Not today, little one!" In a near dance-like leap, Ewan cleared the wood pile, swinging his sword in a graceful arc that caught the tip of Duncan's blade and sent it flying from his grip. In his next motion, he spun on one foot catching the back of Duncan's knees with the other, effectively knocking him off his feet, laying him flat on his back. Ewan put his foot on Duncan's chest and pointed his sword to his throat. "Stodgy, did you say?"

"Did *I* say that?" Duncan asked, looking up the blade to Ewan's hand.

"I think you did," Ian called, helpfully from the sidelines. "Go ahead, Ewan. Run him through already so we can get supper started."

Ewan laughed out loud, then sheathed his sword and extended a hand to Duncan. "Well done, lad."

"Well done? You nearly skewered me."

"Aye, but only because I got you off guard. You were watching my blade and not my feet."

"Your blade seemed the more likely threat," Duncan argued, retrieving his sword from the ground and sliding it into his scabbard. He shook his head, the scowl returning. "Had you been a true adversary, I'd be a dead man. Perhaps it's a blessing after all there are none to fight out here but each other."

"Don't belittle your talent, lad. I've fought my share of

Ogham's guards, and fierce fighters they be, and I can tell you true, you could hold your own against most of them." A wry grin came to Ewan's face. "And didn't you lay Ogham himself out cold with nothing more than a wine bottle, eh?"

Duncan's face flushed. He wasn't sure how much detail of his encounter with the Duke of Lothian Ewan was aware of and was not keen on filling in any holes in the story. Instead, he turned a smug grin to the older man and bragged, waggling a finger in the air. "And don't you be forgetting it, Ewan McDonough."

Ewan nodded and gave Annlise a bit of a side glance that Duncan could not help but believe was a secret code of some sort. She responded with a slight widening of her eyes that she discarded when she looked at Duncan, confirming his suspicion. *She's told him the real story.* He looked toward Ian, making note of the way he too was exchanging a clandestine message with Ewan. *And he knows about it too. Well fine. Let them think me a coward for clocking the sot on the head and running away. What does Ian matter? The man's never swung a blade in his life... who is he to judge...*

"One more go?" Ewan placed his hand casually on his sword.

Duncan shook his head. "Not now," he said, then gestured toward the meager kindling he had collected. "If we're wanting to eat tonight, I best get more wood."

Ewan relaxed his stance and smiled. "Aye, you're right. Go on, we'll do the skinning."

Duncan pulled his dirk from his belt by the handle, then skillfully tossed it up end-over-end, catching it deftly by the flat of the blade, handle away from him. "You'll need this.

Your knife has gone quite dull." He tossed the dirk to Ewan, handle first.

Ewan caught it with a quick flick of his wrist, spinning it in his own hand like a showy street juggler. "You're giving up a weapon without a fight?" He teased. "Suppose you get attacked in the woods?"

"I've got my sword," Duncan informed him, turning his back to head back into the forest. He'd gotten no more than ten paces into the thicket when he felt something warm and heavy descend onto his shoulder, grabbing him across the chest. He reacted on pure instinct, seizing the arm tightly, hauling the vandal over his shoulder with a fierce growl. In the next breath, his blade was drawn and held to the throat of a genuinely astonished looking Ewan, who lay flat on his back at Duncan's feet.

"Whoa, lad! You have me!"

"Don't *ever* do that again!" Duncan growled, angrily sheathing his sword. He held a hand to Ewan, grasping his forearm tightly and hauling him up to his feet quickly.

"I was testing your reflexes, Dun—"

"Do you know how close I came just then to truly running you through?" Duncan flared, feeling the heat rise to his face.

Ewan held up a hand. "Peace, lad. Relax, now."

Duncan forced his breathing steady and allowed himself to calm down before he spoke again. "So? Did I pass ye test?"

Ewan smiled and nodded. "Aye, lad. And I'll be sure to never be attacking you from behind again. For a suckling bairn, you're a fierce one."

"And don't you ever forget it." Duncan thumped Ewan's shoulder, now fully in control of his reflexes. "Go on back and skin those bunnies, stodgy old man." He laughed and turned back to the woods. He took two paces, then spun around quickly, as if warding off another attack.

Ewan laughed, waved him off, then headed back to the campsite.

Duncan's smirk faded as he watched the older sentry join the others and exchange those *knowing* little nods and glances with his companions. *Attack me from behind again, old man, and I will run you through.* He scowled, then trudged back into the woods toward an old tree he had made note of earlier. *Enough wood for dinner, and the night. Let them fetch it tomorrow!*

"It's almost sunset, Kindred. I suppose we should find a good place to stop for the night." William pulled in on the reins, easing the horse to a halt. He arched his back, stretching his aching muscles. "I wonder how far we've gone." He looked toward the fading orange streaks of sunlight that filtered down through the trees. "That would be west, so we've been heading east all day... I wonder if it makes a difference? This whole forest looks the same anyway."

Kindred's ears turned back for a moment, as though she were listening. He patted her neck. "Well at least I'm not alone." She nickered her response with a shake of her mane. He looked to the sky again, then all around him, frowning. "I just wish this damned forest wasn't so much the same in every direction. I swear we've passed this log four times today."

East, he said. Trust, he said. He patted the horse's neck again, *well he was right about Kindred.* He looked again toward the sunset, cursing himself for not paying closer attention to the path when Akonni had led him from Port Edin the first time. "Perhaps I should have gone with Sosep when he escorted Josephine and her gaggle back to Port Edin. Aye, Kindred? There must be at least a couple of men back from their trapping by now. I bet they've already fled back to the forest to escape the old crone's never ending nagging." Kindred snorted loudly, rattling the reins. William allowed himself a chuckle. "You're probably right. I'm far better off here than there. It will be more pleasant to die in the woods than by having my last shred of sanity chewed to grizzle by the likes of her, I suppose." He stroked the horse, his smile leaving him. *Forgive me, Ephraim...*

He cleared his throat as though Kindred were actually understanding him. "You know, I'm not even sure that east is the proper way home. For all I know, Port Edin is somewhere far to the south, or to the north, or has fallen into a fairy hole someplace on the moon! And where are the rest of the people? Surely *someone* is wandering about in this part of the forest other than the two of us, Kindred. Josephine sure was not the one who made that pyre..."

A cold chill wormed down his back, as for the first time a new— and horribly disturbing— thought occurred to him. *What if the rest were all taken prisoner?* Unbidden, images of his family huddled in the belly of some dank ship, cold and terrified, being sailed off to God-only-knows where by one-eyed pirates, invaded his mind. *No, that can't be it... Blessed Mother, please not that...*

He forced the images away, closing his eyes, planting his face in his hands. *I should be with them!*

He stayed silent, not moving on Kindred's back for a long while until he finally brought his emotions and thoughts under control. *This is no way to be, Fylbrigge. Look at you. Shaking like a lad at lessons with a stern task master. You're not a child anymore. And you're not an invalid! You know how to find your courage again... .banish my fears... .*

"Down, Kindred."

Kindred obeyed, gently lowering herself to her belly.

"Well done." He released his feet from the stirrups one at a time, then in the only manner that seemed possible, he rolled himself off Kindred's back onto the ground, landing neatly on his knees. "There. See! I'm not so helpless," he told the horse. "If Ian were here, he'd faint dead away at the shock of it."

The thought of his old friend brought on a sudden wave of anger. "Idiot." He growled as he kneed his way toward Kindred's head. "Of all the nights to let himself get potted. Do you know why he did that?" He tossed her reins over a nearby sapling. "Because he didn't want to tell me the truth! He believes my mind to be as feeble as my body. Well, for a while... I suppose that was true, but not anymore."

Kindred nuzzled him as he spoke, then nipped at the moss that grew on the forest floor, spitting it out with an indignant snort.

"Yes, yes I've got something for you to eat and there's some ferns close by you'll find agreeable." He crawled to the back of the horse where the litter was secured to the poles,and retrieved one of the skin sacks. "Berries and nuts?" He made his way back to her front and held it out to her. "And my body isn't that feeble anymore either... see? It only took me five minutes to get this for you and it was a good eight feet away. As good as eight miles only weeks ago." He laughed at the irony of his situation. "If I could have accomplished this much on that night... you would not be eating this fine morsel now, my equine friend, because I would not be here to give it to you. I'd be with my family... wherever they are."

Kindred ate noisily, chomping her teeth together. When she had finished, she lowered her head, as a dog does when it is ready for sleep. William stroked her forehead. "A rare beauty you are, indeed. I've never known a horse who slept on her belly."

He made his way back to the litter and got some food for himself and a bit of water, then ate and drank his meager meal quietly, while the shadows of night slowly took over the landscape. He retrieved Melly's quilt, his journal, and the quill and ink bottle from his pack, then hunkered down against Kindred. He opened the book to the next blank page. He stared at it for a while, wondering what sense it made to keep writing in it, but it brought him a bit of comfort to imagine that maybe one day by some miracle, Seany would actually read it. He began to write while the shadows of the forest thickened around him, until he could no longer see the page. He pulled Melly's quilt around himself and lay down against the warmth of the mare, with an unnamable trust that she would not move until he was ready to leave in the morning. The last thoughts in his head before he fell into a fitful sleep, as they were each night, belonged to Melly and Seany. He muttered a silent prayer for their well-being. *Mother bless you... Father keep you well... .*

Why are you worried?

"Hmm?" He blinked his groggy eyes open, but saw nothing but the shadows of the forest and the tree limbs swaying lazily in a gentle breeze, backlit by the soft yellow glow of the full moon.

They've gone home, Will.

"What?" He sat up, looking around him, waiting for the apparition to appear. His wait was not long. Almost in the same heartbeat, just as he expected, the image of his brother stepped out of the darkness as though emerging from a curtained alcove to stand before him. William had grown accustomed to the dreams and no longer needed to question if he were sleeping or not. He knew he was. But these visits in his sleep had become somehow more than dreams to him. Even the light that seemed to emanate from within the figure who came to him no longer seemed odd nor unearthly, but a purely natural and logical occurrence. And for reasons he could not put into words, he believed beyond reason that his brother was genuinely with him in the only way that was possible to him; in a dream.

"They've gone home," Sean told him, as he casually sat down on a nearby rock.

"They're back in Port Edin?" William asked hopefully.

"Port Edin?" Sean laughed. "Didn't ye hear me? I said they've gone *home*."

William shook his head, confused. "Port Edin *is* home. That's where I'm headed." He pointed a thumb over his shoulder. "It's someplace east of here."

"Will, Port Edin is about forty leagues west and to the south."

"What? Then why did Akonni tell me to head east if—" He

stopped, mouth agape as he understood Sean's implication. "You mean they've gone home to *Stonehaven*?"

Sean grinned. "Well, that would be to the east; now, wouldn't it?"

"They've gone back to Scotland?" William tossed the quilt aside, and got to his feet— another benefit he'd come to relish about these dreams. "When? Are they safe? Truly?"

Sean stood and joined William, placing a brotherly arm across his shoulders. "Relax."

"Relax?" He brushed Sean's arm away. "How can I relax? They're gone back? Are they safe?"

"They're safe," Sean assured him, placing his fist over his chest in a gesture of promise.

"Thank God," William exhaled, giving Sean a grateful smile as he forced himself to relax, the rush of panic quelled for the moment. His smile melted quickly as he thought further on it and he turned away, hoping Sean didn't notice the flush coming to his face.

"What's wrong?"

"Why did they leave without me?" William asked, feeling suddenly childish.

Sean turned his hands palms up. "Why do you think?"

William knew the answer. He made a disgusted sigh, then dropped himself back down to where he had been sitting before. "They think I'm dead."

"Sorry to say, but yes." Sean resumed his former seat on the rock. "You seem to be making a habit out of that, you know."

William didn't share the humor, confounded by Sean's amusement. "Am I?"

"Uh huh." He laughed, but ignored the question, an annoying habit. "But don't worry about that, now. You have bigger problems."

"Bigger? You mean, besides my family thinking me dead and being abandoned in the woods an ocean away?"

"Aye, bigger," Sean said, his face suddenly serious. "You need to get home."

"Not likely to happen," William grumbled. "I can hardly ride Kindred all the way to Scotland. And I'm not much for swimming."

"You'll get there."

"How?"

"Same way ye got here, lunk. *Lady Anne* is on her way back for you."

"Why would Edward send a ship back for me if they all believe me dead? Are ye... sure?"

"Of course, I'm sure," Sean said indignantly, then stood. "Follow me."

"Now?"

He nodded, then took his customary step backwards, disappearing back into the veil of black.

"Follow you? Into there—"

From out of the dark place, the furious sound of beating wings taking flight preceded the appearance of the golden eagle as it whooshed passed him, screaming into the night sky.

"Sean?" William sat straight up, as the echoes of the scream faded away. He blinked hard, seeing only the moon lit shapes of the night forest. *Dreaming again.*

He was about to settle back down when another echo startled him. Only it wasn't the sound of an eagle's scream, but the unmistakable sound of steel on steel—*sword play?* Followed by human voices. *Is that laughter? No... it's shouting?*

He strained his eyes, staring toward the sound for a moment. Amid the clamoring of steel and laughter, the eagle screamed almost impatiently from the same direction. With little deliberation in his mind, as foolish as it seemed, he left the relative safety of Kindred's side, and set out on his knees into the woods, following the echoes.

Keeping the campfire within his direct line of sight, Duncan put as much distance between himself and his companions as he could without getting lost. He had to collect wood anyway, but it was the solitude he was truly hunting for in the shadows. *Training? What's the use of training? What duke or earl or lord of the manor is there to be in service to out here?*

He found a flat-topped boulder and sat himself down on it, staring back toward the campfire. He was still close enough to hear the sound of their conversation, but far enough that their words were muffled. He watched Ewan and Ian, busying themselves with the skinning of the rabbits, while Annlise tended the fire. Ian said something clever apparently, and the other two were laughing in response.

She told them, he brooded. *They know why I hit the sot with the bottle... Why else would Ewan test me without warning... well he won't do it again...*

He sat silently brooding over his thoughts for a long while before he reasoned they would become concerned and start calling for him. He hated that. No one ever worried for Ewan or Ian when they went off alone, calling to them every five minutes to check on their whereabouts. Ian often sought out the solitude of the woods, requesting time for meditation and was given all the time he required without Annlise putting on a maternal scowl if he was gone longer than he had expected. But let Duncan be gone two minutes and he could almost mark the time by the "Duncan, where are ye, lad..." or "don't go too far, you don't want to be wandering... mind the bears... ."

I'm not a child for pity sake! Edward saw fit to make me one of his guard, after all...

A flutter in a tree above him took his attention. He looked up to see a large bird preening on a branch. "Have they sent you to call me for supper?" He quipped sarcastically, then with a sigh, grudgingly got off the rock intending to head back to camp. "Fine, I'm go—"

He turned suddenly as he heard the faint crackle of the breaking twigs somewhere behind him. He held his breath for a moment, listening, and a moment later he heard it again, followed by the rustle of leaves. *Something is out there.* He instinctually placed his hand on the hilt of his sword, straining his eyes into the dark trying to see. The sound continued, a slow steady movement, low to the ground coming toward him. He relaxed his hand. *It's an animal. Probably just a deer,* he assured himself. He gave passing consideration to waiting behind the rock and slaying the beast with his sword, enticed by the prospect of a meal of roast venison, but decided it may be more prudent to head back to the campfire instead. *It would be just my bad fortune that it turn out to be a bear.*

He stood silent in his indecision, squinting into the woods. As the creature moved closer, he began to hear the heavy breathing it made. *It is a bear!* He took a step backwards, intending to turn, but caught his foot in a low growing vine and tripped, falling gracelessly in a heap on the forest floor. "Damn!" he yelled, unintentionally, as he twisted around to gain his feet, only further entangling himself in the vine. The creature came closer and he imagined he could even feel the hot breath of the bear as he struggled with the clinging growth. He groped for his sword intending to slash the blasted vine, but before he could draw, the beast was on him, the paw touching him lightly on the shoulder.

Before he gave it a chance to rip into his flesh, and with the fury that comes of panic, Duncan reached across his shoulder seizing his attacker with both hands. With a strength that astounded even himself, he hurled it over his shoulder to the ground in front of him.

"Wait!" it yelled as it sailed above him, silencing abruptly when it made impact with the ground.

Duncan stared dumbfounded at the bear who lay sprawled before him, realizing with a sudden wave of horror that it was not a bear after all, but a man. A man who now seemed lifeless on the ground. "Oh no, I've done it again!" He reached for the man's face, shaking it lightly.

"Mister? Wake up... are you....Oh God... Ewan!" He called. "Ian! Come quickly!"

He looked up to see Ewan and Ian react instantly, for once grateful for their vigilant watch over him. Ian seized a burning log, and held it aloft for a light, while Ewan bared his sword. The two raced toward Duncan, meeting him in what seemed less than a heartbeat.

"Duncan, what is... who is that?" Ewan dropped to one

knee next to the man on the ground, "Did you just trip over him?"

"He looks to be one of Akonni's tribesmen," Ian said, standing behind Ewan, holding the light. "They're generally peaceful people... he didn't hurt you, did he?"

"No... I thought he was attacking... God, he's not even wearing a weapon! He merely tapped me on the shoulder... and I..." Duncan rambled in near panic. "God... did I kill him?"

"Calm down, Duncan!" Ewan said. "He's not dead! Look, he's stirring."

Duncan looked for himself.

Ewan grinned. "Well, this fellow has learned the same lesson I have tonight to not be sneaking up on you from behind."

"Let's get him back to camp, he may yet be hurt," Ian said, taking the practical track. "Annlise may have something for his head."

"Aye, wise plan. If this fellow knows these woods, it may be our good fortune to have found him." Ewan hoisted the man onto his shoulder, carrying him sack-like to their campfire.

Annlise rushed forward. "What's all this? Duncan, are ye well, lad?"

"Aye, I'm fine, but this fellow... well, it was my mistake, I thought he was attacking... and..." He blushed and looked away.

"Well, are ye sure he wasn't?" she asked, giving half a glance to the native clothing he wore.

Duncan shook his head. "He's not even armed, Annlise."

"Well let's just see... he may have been more wily than ye think." Ewan paused, a curious furrow coming to his brow.

"What is it?" Ian asked, as he and Annlise spread a blanket for the man to lie on.

"Oh... nothing." Ewan brushed off his look. "For a moment, he looked familiar."

"How many Mi'kmaq have you met?" Ian chuckled. "Here, lay him down. Gently now... that's it—" Ian froze, an incredulous look on his face. "My God!"

"What?" Annlise asked, as she retrieved her kit from their gear.

Ian said nothing, as he tentatively held up one of the man's hands, turning it palm up, examining the digits, he rested it down, then examined the other in the same manner. A mixed look of confusion, joy, and astonishment crossed his eyes, as he reached up and brushed the man's hair from his face. "It is!" he whispered, then shouted, "Will! It's Will!"

"What?" Duncan shouted back, matching Ian's astonishment.

"It' can't be... are you sure?" Ewan dropped to his knees next to Ian, taking a closer look. "You said... this fellow has no white hair... and look... his knees are soiled, it can't be Will, Ian, this man's been crawling."

"It's Will! Look at his hands... and the scars," Ian insisted, then shook the man's face. "Will, wake up. Come on, lad, it's me, Ian... wake up. Annlise, get me some water on a cloth if we've got any."

"'Blessed Mother! 'Tis our Phoenix returned to us?" Annlise stared, frozen in her astonishment.

"Annlise!"

"Oh... aye," She jolted back into action, finding a water skin and a cloth. "It's him? Truly?"

Ian took the cloth and wiped the man's face. His eyes began to flutter open slowly until finally setting a blinking glazed look on the former monk. "Ian?"

"Yes! Will!" Ian grinned with giddy half-crazed sounding laughter.

"Ian?" William muttered, then opened his eyes wide, and to the astonishment of all who stood around, closed one hand into a fist and panted it onto Ian's jaw, sending him sprawling. "It's good to see you," William said, then closed his eyes and passed out.

Ian sat rubbing his jaw with the same half-crazed laughter behind his breathing. "I'm sure I earned that," he said, between breaths. "It's good to see you too, my friend."

Laying on his back, his hands folded neatly over his stomach as he struggled to pull himself up out of the murky fog of unconsciousness and back to the world of the living, William was aware of only three things: the customary aching in his arms and shoulders, a fierce throbbing in his skull, and the vague memory of following Sean— *or was that a dream—* foolishly into the woods in the dark of the night. *Follow him, he said... into the damned forest. I saw him sitting on the rock... but why did he attack me?* He opened his eyes for only an instant, then closed them again against the dart-like assault of the early morning sunlight, then lay, silently, waiting for the throbbing to pass, trying to sort out the muddled memories of the night before. *I'll ask Ian... no, Ian isn't with me... he's drunk and asleep by the campfire... Who is there? God, why can't I wake up?*

"How long do you think he'll sleep?" A voice, male and vaguely familiar, was asking.

"It's hard to say." Another answered, a woman, with a burr in her speech. "It be quite a knock on the head he took."

Melly? Is that you?

A young man speaking with an apologetic stammer joined the conversation. "I didn't mean to... if I'd known who... are you sure he's all right? Why doesn't he wake up?"

I am awake.

The woman answered in a motherly, reassuring tone. "Calm down, lad. How could you have known? And he did come up on ye from behind; now, didn't he... ye reacted as anyone of us might have done." A damp cloth was placed over William's eyes, blotting out the filtered sunlight.

Take that away, I can't see. Who are you?

"Is there any change?"

Ian?

"Not yet," the first man answered. William felt a hand patting his own. "This seems all too familiar somehow."

"What does?" the younger man asked.

"Him... sleeping there. Lookin' just as he looked last time I saw him, after his trial," the man replied, lifting one of William's hands. "I'll never forget the sight of him layin' there in the crypt all but dead... all mangled and bandaged." He set William's hand down gently. "But sound asleep, with the most peaceful expression I'd ever seen on him... as if he were simply taking a nap."

"I remember." Ian— *yes, that is Ian*— answered. "God grant it doesn't take five months to wake him from *this* little nap, as it did from that one."

"Amen to that," the man agreed. After a pause he said, with a slight chuckle in his voice, "When he does come 'round, it'll be quite the surprise for him to be seeing my sorry face lookin' down on him. I'm sure he never thought he'd see the likes of me again in this lifetime."

"Ewan," Ian began gently. "It isn't likely... that is... he may not know who you are."

Ewan?

"But he knows *of* me... doesn't he?"

"Oh yes, to be sure," Ian answered quickly. "God knows Simon has entertained him many an evening telling the tales of all your adventures together, and Will has laughed at them well enough. But to be honest, I don't believe he truly remembers any of those times or the people involved." He became quiet for a moment, then continued. "The last night we camped, he told me some of what he did remember. He remembers you as a lad, Duncan, and he remembers Edward, somewhat but not much else. Even Sean and Laurel seemed to be lost to him."

"No," Ewan replied, sounding skeptical. "Now, that I find difficult to believe."

"Believe it," Ian countered, slightly defensive. "I'm sure if Simon had not been with us all these years, Will would not have known him either."

"Settle down, Ian. I believe you. I'm just surprised is all... he's even forgotten about Sean?"

"He has— look, he's moving. Lass, quickly—"

The wet cloth that covered William's eyes was pulled away and he managed to turn his head to the side slightly. He tried to speak, but only coughed at the dryness in his throat.

"He's coming around," the woman said. "There now, open ye eyes... Duncan, hand me that cup there."

"This?"

"Aye, thank ye. Here, drink up..."

A cup was brought to William's mouth and he sipped a bit of water. "Thank you," he said, as finally the throbbing began to subside. He opened his eyes again, slowly this time, being wary of the sunlight.

"Will?" the man with the familiar voice called.

William blinked hard. After a moment, his vision began to clear. He looked from one face to the next of the people huddled around him and settled his sight at last on the man who was kneeling the closest to him. "Ewan?" He studied the face closely for a moment. The man's voice had certainly been familiar, but his face seemed to be that of a total stranger. Even so, William was certain, this was indeed Ewan. It was his old friend, the one Simon had told so many tales about. "Ewan!"

"Aye, Will. It's me." Ewan grinned. "You *do* know me!"

William tried, but failed, to grin back. "Aye... Ewan, yes I know..." He glanced around to the others gathered over him, then gasped, feeling suddenly light headed when he looked on the face of the youngest member of their band. "Sean?" He closed his eyes tightly. "I must still be dreaming."

"No... I'm not Sean."

He opened his eyes, cautiously peering at the young man. After a moment, his eyes went wide in recognition. "Duncan? Little Duncan Wilbrun?"

Duncan grinned nodding his head. "Aye! Only I'm not so

little anymore. I'm a sentry now," he said proudly thumping his chest. "As Sean was." The pride faded quickly, replaced by a pathetically apologetic frown. "Although I'm sure Sean would not have mistaken you for a bear and tossed you over his shoulder... some sentry I've turned out to be."

"A sentry." William closed his eyes for a moment, praying these people would not all disappear when he opened them again. When he did open his eyes, it was the woman he saw first standing above him with the wet cloth in her hand. *I know her.* She went to place the cloth on his eyes again, but he reached for it, moving it aside. She placed it on his forehead instead.

"You've a rather nasty lump," she explained, shyly looking away from him. "There's a balm in the water I used for the cloth, ye see... it will ease the swelling."

William stared at her face. The shape of the jaw, the little mole on her cheek, the kind smile, the little dimples on either side of her eyes... *I know her!*

"More water, little one," she said, as she pulled the cloth away, handing it to Duncan.

Duncan nodded, a ghost of irritation in his eyes, as he dipped the cloth in the little cauldron Annlise had filled with her special water. He squeezed it out, and handed it back to her.

"Thank you, little one." She placed the cloth back on William's forehead.

Little one? He's a grown man? He continued to study the features of her face as she ministered to his head. He closed his eyes for a moment, and heard her speaking, saying "There, little one..." Her voice sounded odd and strangely echoed somehow, and he opened his eyes. "Little one..." he heard her say, though he finally understood it wasn't her voice he had been hearing but a memory.

Run away, little one! Run away!

"Rebecca? Mum?" William reached for her hand as she attended the cloth again. "No... that can't be... who are you, lass?"

A patient, sad smile crossed her face. "No, Will, I'm not Rebecca. Though I suppose I do look like her a bit. I'm her sister, Annlise. Do you remember me? I was in service in Aberdoir. You and Sean helped me away from there one summer. Do you remember?"

William studied her face another moment, scouring his memory for an image Annlise and Sean together, but all he could call to mind was not Annlise but her sister Rebecca's frantic screams telling him to run away. "I'm sorry, lass. I remember very little about that time."

"Everyone... move back, give him room." Ian pulled Duncan and Ewan back by their shoulders as he assumed his traditional role of William's physician. "Can you sit up?" he asked, grasping William's left arm at the elbow with his right, sliding his left under the middle of his back. "Tell me when—"

"I can do it, Ian." He wrested his arm from Ian's grip. With little effort or thought of what he was doing, he propped himself on his elbow, turning himself onto his side. He glanced back to Ian and after a double take, stared stunned and appalled at the purplish bruise staining the right side of his friend's face. He suddenly remembering that he was likely the culprit who had caused it. "Oh, Ian. I'm sorry about that. I didn't mean to strike you that way. Are you all right? Let me look at that."

Ian stared stupidly, mouth half open as William bent his knees, and pushed himself up to kneel and rested one hand on Ian's shoulder, while gingerly examining the injured jawline with the other.

"Thank goodness. It's only bruised. I was sure I'd broken it, can you ever forgive me?"

"Forgive?" Ian stuttered, wide-eyes unblinking. "For what? I deserved... Will! Look at you!" He blurted, his face suddenly stretched in a clownish grin as he threw his arms around William. "How?" He pulled back examining him at arm's length. "I can't believe it. You're kneeling! How?"

William burst out laughing amazed at himself for not realizing that Ian could not have known of either the healing he'd experienced or the memories he had reclaimed. "It's a long story, my friend." He turned to the others, smiling. "But not as long as the tale I'm sure you all could tell. I can hardly believe my eyes to see you. Ewan and Duncan! Lad, you're a wonder to look at." He released Ian and knee-walked his way toward Duncan, who was still kneeling near the fire and embraced him. "You were no more than seven or eight when I saw you last."

"Aye." Duncan accepted William's embrace awkwardly and pulled back, shaking his head. "I don't understand."

"Don't understand what, lad?" William asked, unable to keep the smile from his face.

Duncan looked to Ian, apparently baffled by what he was seeing. Ewan and Annlise seemed equally bewildered.

"Will," Ian began, with the same stupefied expression on

his face, "how in God's name—"

"Kindred!" William blurted, dismissing Ian's half-asked question.

All faces turned to the edge of camp where Kindred, William's litter still in tow, had managed to wander to and stood patiently aside as if waiting to be noticed. "Kindred, come." She obediently approached him, lowering her muzzle to his shoulder, nickering into his ear. "Good girl. I'd forgotten all about you in my excitement." He stroked her head, smiling.

"You have a horse?" Ewan asked, as though he had never seen a horse before.

"Aye," William answered, still giving his attention to Kindred. "I do. This is Kindred," he said, stroking the white streaks in her forelocks. "We've got a lot in common," he laughed running his hands through his own hair, forgetting the white that had once striped his own black hair had disappeared when his legs had *awoken*— as he had come to think of it.

Ewan placed a hand on William's shoulder, turning him to look at him. "Will... it is you, aye? William Fylbrigge? The former Earl of Sutherland?" He set a suspicious glower onto Ian. "The *invalid?*"

Ian hunched his shoulders, relaying his own confusion and astonishment at what he was seeing.

"Of course," William laughed, "who else would I be?" He turned back to the horse, making a clicking sound with his tongue. "Down, Kindred." Without hesitation, the mare lowered herself to the ground. "Thank you, m' lady," William told her blithely, then moved agilely— for him— to her side.

He bent himself over her back, then mounted in the awkward but efficient method he had devised of half-tossing, half-pulling his leg over the saddle. "Up, girl." Kindred bobbed her head, as if in answer, then resumed her standing position.

The four astonished companions stood around him, stone faced, their gaping stares being almost comical to look at. Ewan took a step forward, examining the make-shift saddle and the finagled litter. Shaking his head in wonder, he looked up to William. "You have a horse and you *can ride.* But you set out through the woods alone in the dark, without so much as a rabbit knife in ye belt, *on your knees?"* He raised his hands palms up, then lowered them, his face lighting into a broad grin. "Well that's proof enough for me, then. You truly *are* William Fylbrigge."

"Proof?" William asked, amused. "How do you mean, Ewan?"

"The William Fylbrigge I knew so well back in Scotland *never* did anything the easy way." Ewan replied, then burst into hearty laughter, which was soon joined by all as they gathered around Kindred, at last giving William a proper welcome back into the fold.

Chapter 18

Mid October 1613
New France

"**L**AND HO!"

From within the galley of Ogham's ship, *Donas Faire*, Adrian Tearlach looked up from his meal at the sound of the crewman's call. "It's about bloody time." He wiped his mouth with his sleeve, then tossed his empty dish in the scuttle bucket and left the galley boy to clear away. He was about to knock on Garland's cabin door when it swung open and Peter Garland stepped into the narrow passage, narrowly missing a collision.

Garland stopped in his tracks, greeting Adrian with an expression of startled irritation. "Tearlach. I take it you heard the call. Seems we may step foot on dry earth again in our lifetime, after all."

"Yes, I was just coming to get you. I'm sure you're eager to see in what shape your new *dominion* was left to you." Adrian laughed sarcastically, then turned his back on Garland, hurrying up the stairs to the deck.

Adrian was eager to see the shores of New France himself. The band of a dozen mercenary hunters that Lord Ogham had so generously provided to his sojourn and the twenty sea-seasoned crewmen had grown restless in the past weeks. Keeping them from turning on him and each other had become a daily challenge. The presence of Lady Bryndah on board did not serve to quell the wave of malcontent among the crew by any means. When Adrian escorted her up the gangplank at the start of their voyage and saw her comfortably ensconced in the grand cabin within the stern castle, the men had protested vehemently, proclaiming it was a bad omen to have a woman on board— especially *that* woman. A few had tried to intimidate her, snarling vicious curses through rancid grins and making lewd threats of how they would make her useful as a distraction to their boredom during the long months of a sea crossing.

Bryndah, however, had proven herself to be uneasily intimidated. Even when one particularly lascivious sailor lured her on deck in order to make good on his threat to relieve his boredom. When he suddenly grabbed her from behind, bringing a dagger to her porcelain throat, she merely laughed and neatly produced a dirk from her delicate lace sleeve and handily planted it in the man's gullet. He crumbled, dumbfounded, to the deck while Bryndah stood bemoaning the stain his blood had produced on her silk gloves. When Adrian was informed of the attack by the first mate, his only reaction was one of mild irritation that the body had been left littering his deck. Bryndah apologized for the infraction with a demure curtsey, batting her eyes in mock contrition before she and Adrian tossed the unfortunate sailor overboard. That being done, Adrian informed the rest of the crew that Lady Bryndah was free to disembowel anyone else who dared cause her voyage to be less-than pleasant. The rest of her journey was thus free of further annoyance from the crew.

Peter Garland, on the other hand, made no attempt to

conceal his contempt for the Duchess of Lothian. He made only polite conversation when absolutely necessary, offering no more than a nod to acknowledge her presence should he meet her while strolling the deck or eating a meal in the galley. Bryndah, for her part, regarded Garland as nothing more than hired help. Adrian spent a good amount of his time keeping the two apart from one another, and assuring first one and then the other that each of them was crucial to the success of their mission.

"He's an insufferable bore!" she whined, one evening while she and Adrian dined in his private cabin. "And he still believes the whelp was innocent. Really, Adrian, I fail to understand why we just do not toss him overboard and be done with it. Surely we can bring the heathen back without his almighty blessing."

"I'm sure we could, m' lady. But our case against Edward will be stronger— irrefutable in fact— when Garland, himself, turns Fylbrigge over to Ogham. We'll have our proof that Edward knew the demon was guilty right along, and more— that he condoned, even encouraged, Fylbrigge to use his sorcery against Ogham. Then you can be sure that not only will your claim on the Fylbrigge coffer be secure but Drumoak, as well, will be as good as yours, my dear."

The toast was made, the calm restored— for that evening, at least.

The crew was placated with the stock of whiskey in the hold and the promise of monetary gain for completing the mission, leaving Bryndah to herself. If not for these, Adrian was certain, the crew would have mutinied out of utter boredom in the first weeks of the voyage.

When they set sail in early June, the navigator assured him the crossing would take no more than a month, six weeks at most, putting them on the shores of New France by mid-August. Adrian had entertained a moment or two of hope that they would actually arrive ahead of the *Lady Anne*. But, where the early weeks of the crossing had been blessed with a stout fair-wind and calm seas, in the third week, fair turned abruptly to foul. Twice they were blown severely off course taking weeks to right their way only to meet with another late summer gale that forced them to sail south, taking them eventually to Virginia instead of New France.

The last day of August found the *Donas Faire* anchored at Jamestown, her once-proud sails in tatters from the persistent storms, adding yet another delay to the voyage while repairs were made. This delay, however, had proven fortuitous. Only a day before they were to weigh anchor again, a fleet of scout galleons returned from a raid on New France. Five of the returning vessels carried a booty of furs, mast timbers, and even a few milk goats and pigs. All of which held little interest for Adrian, and even less for Bryndah, as there was nothing identifiable as "Fylbrigge" to be found among it all. The sixth ship, however, proved far more interesting as it was not booty that filled the hold, but human cargo. This ship had served as a prison for the few men who had survived the raid.

Putting aside their sparring for the moment, Bryndah and Peter Garland visited the hold together, on the small chance they may be lucky and find their common quarry among the prisoners, neatly bound and ready for delivery. But after an initial glance at the faces of the captured men did not reveal any who seemed remotely familiar, they left the unpleasant task of interrogation to Adrian. At first, Adrian gave little attention to the ragtag group of trappers and fishermen who were among the captives until his interest was piqued by one who had become delirious in a fever and started muttering something about his fate being the fault of that *damned Scottish demon* who had cursed them all.

Adrian attempted to woo the man into his confidence, pretending to be sympathetic to his hardship to elicit more information. When the man had only become more crazed in his fever, Adrian had lost patience with him and sliced his throat in full view of the rest of the captives.

"I won't be so kind hearted with the rest of you," he told them, cleaning the blood from his dagger, using the dead man's own shirt. "This man was obviously in a great deal of agony, and now... thanks to my *kindness*, he has found his peace. Is anyone else in need of *peace?*" It did not take long after that to learn what he already suspected; the man the delirious prisoner had referred to as the Scottish demon was a fellow named Philbrick, the village woodworker. The poor man had suffered some crippling injury years before but who had recently been lost in some mishap involving a bear.

"Philbrick, is it?" Bryndah laughed as she and Adrian toasted this first promising bit of information, "I should think he could have come up with something more imaginative than that."

Garland, though intrigued with the information, was less enthusiastic about continuing their journey, as his main purpose for making the crossing was secondary to the hunt for William Fylbrigge. Ogham promised him a governorship, however there seemed precious little left to govern in the wilds of New France.

"Adrian, what is the point? The man we were seeking is obviously not there any longer. I should think we would be wiser to cut our losses and return home. I find all this... *wilderness* distressing."

"We're going!" Adrian snapped, leaving no room for debate. "He's there. I feel it. I know it."

"So you told Ogham. I was skeptical of it then and I still am not convinced of it now! Even if this Philbrick person is indeed William Fylbrigge... they say he is already dead! What is the point?"

Adrian clenched his gloved fist into Garland's cape, pulling the man forward and leered into his eye. "You thought he was dead before and you were wrong."

They left Jamestown the second week in September. It took nearly four weeks, but now, at long last, on the tenth of October, the shores of New France were within sight. Adrian and Garland stood on the bow surveying the rocky coast.

"Nothing but trees," Garland grunted, looking toward the shore, his hand to his brow shielding his eyes. "Pointless."

"He's there," Adrian replied calmly, without turning to look at Garland.

"He's dead. Accept it. The most you can possibly hope to gain from this little excursion is a handful of furs and perhaps a native carving or two."

"How is it you are so blind— a carving?" Adrian turned to look at Garland, eyes wide in sudden inspiration. "Of course. That's all we need."

"Hmm? Now what are you prattling about?" Garland

yawned and turned his sight back to the shore.

"A carving! So what if he was carried off by a bear— I don't really give a damn, except it makes my purpose a bit difficult. All we really need to prove our case is evidence that he *was* here. That he does not now, nor has he ever, graced the crypt under Drumoak in blissful eternal repose."

Garland stared, a mystified expression on his face. Adrian threw up his hands in a frustrated sigh that the governor seemed so dull as to miss the significance of what he was talking about.

"The carvings!"

"Native carvings? Heathen tokens—"

"Not the native carvings!" Adrian rolled his eyes. "Fylbrigge's! He was known for his carvings. It seems he presented every lass from Cornwall to the Orkneys with some sort of carved trinket. Heaven knows I've seen enough of his little whittlings littered about the taverns and inns of Stonehaven like so much bric-a-brac." He raised a brow and leaned close to Garland. "And I would recognize the handiwork of that particular artisan anywhere in an instant."

Garland scoffed, laughing out loud. "Handiwork? Perhaps in his better days he carved like the masters, but even if he *was* here— and I am still not entirely convinced he was— I'm sure he did not spend his days carving bric-a-brac. You, of all people, should know his hands were hardly human after you were through with him. I find it difficult to believe he would even be able to hold his knife, let alone carve wood with it." He laughed, then turned back to look at the shoreline. "You won't find your proof here. We shall land to find nothing in Port Edin but trees and rubble. I shall be happy to order the captain to return us to Scotland, even if we are to go empty-handed. I've no want to stay here to govern a graveyard."

"Have no worry on that score, Peter." Adrian said. "We will most assuredly be returning to Scotland. But make no mistake... it shall not be empty-handed."

Chapter 19

"**I**AN?" WILLIAM NUDGED his companion, who was sleeping in an uncomfortable looking posture against a tree. "Wake up. It's near dawn," he said, keeping his voice low for the sake of Duncan, Ewan, and Annlise, who were still sleeping.

Ian raised his face toward the fading moonlight, then turned toward William, groaning. "I'm awake." He stretched, wincing and rubbing his arms. "Oh, what I wouldn't give for a hot bath and a real bed," he moaned to himself, as had become his morning custom. "Have you been up long?"

"For a few hours. I took Ewan's watch."

Ian shook his head, chuckling softly. "Will Fylbrigge on guard duty. I'd never have imagined that a few months ago." He looked away suddenly, clearing his throat.

William gave him a quick side glance, then tossed a few pieces of kindling into the campfire. The night Ian had fallen asleep drunk was a sore subject for both of them, but the look of grief in Ian's eyes whenever the conversation danced in that direction was all the apology necessary.

"Coffee?" William reached for the kettle that was perking on a rock within the ring of campfire he had been tending all night.

Ian yawned an affirmation, reaching for his cup.

"This is the last of it," William said, as he poured. "Not to worry though; there should still be a few sacks left in the root cellar from last year. Remember? Last fall, Melly's father sent enough for a battalion."

Ian nodded. "I remember. The ship arrived just after the house was raised. The most valuable treasure Edward sent wasn't the silks or gold, but the sacks of coffee beans and barley... and the casks of fine Scottish whiskey of course," he laughed quietly, adding wryly, "for *medicinal* purposes only, you understand."

"Absolutely!" William chuckled. "Purely medicinal."

"I suppose we should make the best of this last pot," Ian sighed. "Who knows if we'll ever get back to that root cellar for more."

William looked up toward the southwestern sky, scanning the tree tops, until he saw what he was looking for. He smiled to himself as he watched the silhouette of a large bird spread its wings and take to flight in the morning sky. "We'll be within sight of Port Edin today," he said, as he watched the bird kite in a lazy spiral above the treetops. "Trust me."

Ian followed William's gaze to the circling raptor. "Seeing signs, are you?"

"Something like that."

"I'd be content to see simple signs of life," Ian commented. "I was certain we would have come across someone by now. I simply won't believe that the raiders took the *entire* population of Port Edin, save Josephine and her friends."

"They didn't take us," William pointed out. "And they didn't take my family. They made it home. And so will we." He looked up again to the sky, then said, "He promised."

Ian gave a quick glance to the bird, then said quietly, "Well then, far be it for me to doubt. Today's the day."

William could see by the look in his eyes that Ian truly did hold doubt. In the week since he had rejoined his companion, it seemed like every conversation he had with Ian had been nothing more than a series of polite gestures of agreement, followed by a patronizing smile as though Ian were humoring a child— or a simple minded invalid. The trend had started that first evening while they reminisced around the campfire about their former lives in Scotland.

Ewan related his version of the infamous night of Willie Fylbrigge and his trained monkeys in a boisterously animated narration. His account was close to the one Simon had retold on Christmas Eve, however Ewan elaborated on something that Simon had chosen to leave out; the details about the tavern dancer named Cassandra, who had accompanied them back to camp, claiming she was owed money for the *service* she had provided to William earlier that evening.

"Ye were deep in ye cups that night, Will. Ye didn't even remember it in the morning— so ye claimed— but that lass was convinced you had pledged your entire fortune and ye hand to her that night, and she meant to have it. God only knows how she managed to convince Sean to let her ride back with him. But then, Sean never did miss an opportunity with the lassies. He always could catch 'em, but he was careful ne'er to get caught himself. Seemed like in every shire we camped near, at least one doe-eyed lassie was left calling after him as we rode out. Each one believing they would be the one to tame the rogue," Ewan laughed heartily, joined by Duncan and Ian.

Annlise looked up over the mending she was doing, pulling sharply on the thread with an air of disapproval. "I think you should have a bit more respect for the departed, Ewan," she said quietly. "You make him sound like a perfect cad, which he was not."

Ewan caught her eye, cleared his throat, then took a swallow of water from his tin mug and wiped his mouth. "Aye, ye right lass, he was a good man. I meant no disrespect, God bless him." His laughter waned and he grew serious. "Edward was fit to be tied when he heard Cass's claims that night. Had Sean not covered for ye, Will, Edward would have skinned ye alive."

"Sean covered for me?" William asked, surprised at Ewan's sudden change in mood. "How?"

"He told Edward *he* was the one, not you, who was owing Cass for her service, and that she was merely confused in her head," Ewan chuckled, making circles in the air with his finger around his ear. "If Edward had known the truth..." He rested a hand on his knee and leaned over, staring into the fire as he spoke. "He would have annulled your betrothal to your lady, right then and there. Old Sean saved your marriage that night. He swore the rest of us to secrecy and put you on the proper road to home the next day. He always watched out for you that way."

"He still does," William replied, casually staring into the fire. "I'll have to ask him whatever became of that dancer. He remembers it clearly, I'm sure." He looked up to see four pairs of astonished eyes staring at him.

"I think you're still rather muddled in the head from Duncan's attempt to save us from the marauding giant bear of New France," Ian quipped. "I'm sure you meant to say that *you* remember things clearly now... you were speaking of yourself and the memories you've regained. Right?" Ian asked, a curious tilt to his head.

William realized he must have sounded a bit daft, speaking of Sean as though he were still among the living. "No... I meant... I'm sure he *would* remember... if he was here with us."

Ian nodded, smiling over his cup, then cut his gaze toward Ewan and Annlise, who shared similarly odd expressions. "I'm sure he would, Will."

The others laughed lightly, exchanging more quick side glances. Annlise smiled her motherly smile, reaching to William's forehead and brushing the hair away from the bruise he had gained from Duncan's *ambush*. "Is that lump still a bother to ye? I'd be glad to prepare a good strong powder for you in a special brew, if ye wish," she offered.

William shook his head, moving her hand away irritably, as though it were a fly that had landed on his face. "The last thing I need is more *special* tea." He spoke far sharper than he intended, then smiled sheepishly when he saw her face flush and her eyes grow wide. "Please forgive my temper, lass; I thank you for your kind offer. Ian's right, my mind *is* a hopeless muddle but it was muddled long before Duncan mistook me for a marauding bear," he said, making light of the awkward moment.

Annlise smiled shyly, relaxing a bit. "I'll forgive your temper if you promise to tell me if you change that muddled mind of yours about that powder."

"Fair enough," William laughed, thus leaving the uncomfortable moment behind.

The next day, while William prepared his litter and

tended to Kindred, the others began the deliberation of which direction they should travel.

"I say we keep heading north," Ian suggested. "There is likely to be a ship or two that may yet still pass there and perhaps we can signal—"

"But Port Edin—" William attempted to interject.

"Think, Ian," Ewan said, tipping his forehead sharply with his hand for emphasis. "Should Edward think enough of us to send a ship back, it will come from dead on east. We'll be far more likely to spot it from the eastern most point than from the north."

"But Port Edin—"

"I think Ian is right, Ewan, look here," Duncan chimed in, opening a rolled up piece of parchment. "According to this map, it would seem a far easier trek to head toward the north shore. And shorter too. And like Ian says, ships still pass through this inlet here."

"Port Edin—"

"But Ewan's right," Annlise joined the argument, tracing her finger on the map near the representation of the eastern shore. "We'll be far likelier to see a friendly sail from the east than to the north.

"But it's at least a month's journey—" Ian began.

"The ships won't see us otherwise," Ewan countered.

"Folks—" William tried again, unsuccessfully to remind his traveling friends that he was there. "We need to head—"

"Possibly two months!" Ian argued.

"Not if we take this route." Annlise thumped the map again.

William took a long exasperated breath and turned to his

mare, who stood patiently aside while he loaded the litter she pulled. "Down, Kindred." The horse responded at once, lowering herself to the ground to allow William to mount, seemingly oblivious to the arguing humans around her.

"There'll be ships in the north, as well," Duncan contended, roughly rolling up his map.

By the time William was fully mounted, the arguments had escalated nearly to the point of shouting. After another futile attempt to make himself heard above their din, he put two fingers in his mouth, and loosed an ear-splitting whistle to get their attention. The four silenced at once, each snapping their heads to gawk at him. He bit his lip to keep from laughing aloud at their startled expressions.

"Port Edin is to the southwest," he stated simply. "It's no more than forty leagues. We can be there in a few days."

"Port Edin?" Duncan gasped. "Why, for pity sake, should we want to go back *there*? There's nothing left."

"Because, lad," William explained simply, "it's where we have to go. It's where the harbor is. And if Edward does send the *Lady Anne*, she will likely go there first; not to the north, and not to the east point."

"But…" Duncan began, then turned impatiently to Ewan. "We can't possibly go back there. If that group of women you saw in the native village really did make it back, others may have too. Goody Ashcrofte could start spittin' her venom to the few men who may be there to listen… they'll just drive us out again. We told you how they all turned on us at your *funeral* of all places. No disrespect to you, Will, but if they turned on us when they thought you were dead, how much worse will it be when you show up alive? Gads! They'll tear you apart!"

"Duncan," Annlise hushed him, gently.

"But..."

"Lad," William said softly, a ghost of a grin coming to his face. "We don't know that to be the case. I've seen what was left by the raiders and that alone makes me fairly certain that Goody Ashcrofte's gossip vine has grown far away from the likes of me. And who would she rally? The trapper men? Not likely. Those few fortunate trappers— if any— who may have found their way back will be far more likely worrying about getting their homes fixed in time for winter than in tearing apart the village cripple on the word of one misguided old biddy."

Duncan looked from one face to the next in a silent plea for either Ewan or Ian to take up his argument. Neither man had an answer for him. William could see their reluctance to agree with him etched in the lines of their faces, but after a moment, Ewan shrugged and picked up his traveling pack, and hung it over his shoulder.

"It's a fair argument Duncan makes, Will. True, there may not be many a soul left for Goody Ashcrofte to rally, but perhaps there were *some* men who escaped the raiders by fleeing into the forest and they'd likely to have made it back to Port Edin by now."

"But they all know me, Ewan," William argued. "They're my friends and—"

"You had friends in Stonehaven, too!" Ewan shouted, silencing William abruptly, his mouth closing with an audible click of his teeth in surprise. Ewan took a long breath, then softened his voice. "My point is only this, Will. On nothing more than that harpy's word, the folks you call your friends turned fierce on Melly and Seany. Perhaps you're right and they've put any interest in you aside in favor of rebuilding the settlement and moving on, but... the threat may still be there. Now, you know I'll stand with you and fight if it comes to that, but are you certain you want to risk that mob comin' after you that way?"

"Yes, I'm sure." William stared into Ewan's serious eyes, then to each of the others in turn. It was his turn to consider their argument, but it only took a moment for him to make a decision. Sean had assured him that Melly and Seany had gone home to Scotland. Ian assured him that was true. Scotland was where he needed to go and he needed to go back to Port Edin first in order to get there. And after everything he had endured thus far to be with his family, he would certainly not allow the likes of Goody Ashcrofte to stop him.

"Ewan, it's possible you're right. But it's also possible that the only *mob* we're likely to face is Goody Ashcrofte and her two old crones. I should think with you at my side that even *I* could hold my own in a fight against them." He laughed lightly, humorously, then stopped abruptly, his face reddening as inexplicably from the dark place in his brain, another lost memory suddenly found its way back to him:

"Ewan?" William asked as Ewan stepped in pace with him as they headed toward the foyer in Drumoak. "What else did they bring?"

"Surrender orders," Ewan answered quietly. "My lord, we should have followed your orders. I'm sorry."

"Water under the bridge, Ewan. Save your grief for later."

"I'm pleased to know you'll stand with me and fight,

Ewan. After all, it's not as though we're facing the hunters in the foyer of Drumoak this time. Is it?"

The color drained from Ewan's face and he turned away. "I've not forgotten. Not a day has passed since then that I do not feel regret that I stood aside when the hunters came to take you. But I was following orders. Edward *told* Simon and me not to challenge Tearlach."

"Tearlach?" William asked, mentally sifting through his memories for the face that fit the name.

"The lead hunter who was sent to arrest you," Ian answered for Ewan. "Do you remember him?"

William closed his eyes, wanting to better see the memory, yet wanting to push it back at the same time. The images rushed over him like a wave. He saw the foreboding figure of the hunter standing in the foyer, flanked by a dozen or so hooded men. Tall and dark, Tearlach's odd golden eyes stared unblinking from under the dark hood he wore. William drew his hands together, cupping his left within his right, absently rubbing circles with his thumb over the gnarled knuckles. He opened his eyes again, and answered quietly. "Yes, Ian. I remember Adrian Tearlach. Ewan, please forgive my anger. It was misplaced on you. I know you had no choice."

"You are more than justified in your anger, Will. I should have covered your back that morning in spite of Edward's order to stand down," Ewan said quietly, a look of genuine grief in his eyes. "It's you who must forgive me."

"'Tis naught to worry on now, my friend," William replied. "As I told you then; it's water under the bridge. You've got my back covered now, aye? That's what matters."

"Aye," Ewan answered, slowly placing his right fist over

his heart. "I'll not let you down again. I swear it on my life."

Duncan spoke up, mimicking Ewan's gesture of promise with his own fist over his heart, emphasizing his uncanny resemblance to Sean. "I am at your side as well, my lord."

William smiled, gratified yet embarrassed, to be addressed in such a formal way. "Thank you," he said quietly, crossing his arm over his chest in tribute to his friends.

Ian stepped forward. "As long as we're speaking oaths," he spoke with a forced cheerfulness, and tapped his chest with his hand. "You've got my pledge as well, Will. But I'll leave any mortal battle with Goody Ashcrofte on your behalf to these two stalwart and steady gentlemen. But you can count on Annlise and I to stand ready with ale and bandages." He gave her a mischievous wink. "Right, lass?"

"Right. Will be my pleasure." Annlise returned Ian's wink.

"Good then," William said. "It's agreed. We return to Port Edin."

The few days William expected the trek to take had turned into a full week. He suspected his companions were beginning to doubt his assertions that he was leading them in the proper direction. Truth was, William wasn't leading at all— he was following. Following the signs, as Ian called them. He retrieved the coffee kettle from the campfire and poured himself another cup. Ewan, Annlise, and Duncan didn't have the same liking for it that he and Ian did, so he didn't feel too badly about finishing that last pot between them. In the sky, far to the south, the echoes of the eagle rang through the trees. *Yes, I know, I'll get them moving after breakfast.* The raptor screamed again, tipped a wing, then circled away again.

Ian finished his coffee and held out his cup for William to refill it. "I suppose it's time to wake the others," he commented, but made no sign of moving away from his spot near the tree. "Then again, Ewan didn't get much sleep last night, perhaps we should let him rest a while. One day more or less makes little difference—"

"It has to be today, Ian," William said sharply, setting the kettle down hard on the rock. "I told you that already."

"For pity's sake, Will," Ian sighed. "We've been out here for months, what does one more day truly matter? All that lies in Port Edin is rubble and death."

"And four sacks of coffee in the root cellar!" He set a fierce glower on Ian. The eagle screamed again, far away, and he glanced toward the sound. He took a long breath and calmed the anger from his voice. "And a harbor. I know you don't understand it, but I *know*— as sure as I see you sitting there— that *Lady Anne* is approaching."

Ian scowled, chewing his jaw tight. He opened his mouth as if to argue again, then turned away, shaking his head. "You're right. I don't understand. What is it you possess that makes you so damned certain it's necessary for us to rush back to Port Edin?"

"Trust." William turned away, leaving Ian sitting silently near the tree.

A quarter hour later, Annlise, Ewan and Duncan were awake and preparing for another day's hike through the wild forest.

"Today's the day," William said again, quietly, as he mounted Kindred and took his customary position in the lead of the little expedition.

~

By noon, they were within sight of the broken remains of the gates of Port Edin. William called Kindred to a halt just short of the last hundred paces from the entrance, surprised to see a man standing, straight-backed and still, beside the shattered wooden panel that was once the gate. He held a musket on his shoulder and stared straight ahead, apparently unaware of the approaching group of wanderers. The man was unfamiliar to him, dressed formally in a kilted uniform, one he had never seen worn by any resident— or, for that matter, visitor— to Port Edin.

William looked back over his shoulder to where his companions were following several paces behind him and signaled for them to stop. He put his hand to his mouth, then motioned for them to retreat quietly, back into the concealing boughs of the forest. Kindred's footfalls made a crackling on some twigs in the underbrush, and William gave a quick look back to the strange sentry to see if he had heard. The man remained as he was, looking away from them.

"What is it?" Ewan whispered, when they were beyond the sight of the sentry.

"Did you see the guard?" William asked, leaning down from Kindred. "I don't know the colors he wears."

"Guard?" Ian gasped. "Are you sure?"

"Take a look... carefully," William told him.

Ian crept quietly to stand behind a large tree, just beyond the edge of the road. He craned his neck around slowly, then beckoned to Ewan to join him.

"Damn," Ewan said, when he saw the man.

"Do you recognize the colors he's wearing?" Ian asked.

Ewan nodded slowly, a knot twisting into his brow. "I do, but... it can't be."

"Ogham!" Annlise gasped, standing close behind Ewan.

He turned startled, shushing her with a hand over her mouth. She gaped beyond him to the man standing by the gate, her eyes wide with a terrible look of recognition.

Ewan lowered his hand slowly, then placed his finger to his mouth. "Go on back." He mouthed to her, then grabbed Ian's shoulder and pulled him away from the tree, heading back to where William and Duncan waited.

Duncan met them half way. "What's wrong?"

"We've got a problem," Ewan answered quietly, walking past him directly toward William. "We need to go back... there was a cave not too far back. We can talk there." Without waiting for an answer, and assuming the role of commander as was due his rank, Ewan led them back down the path they had just come from, hurrying them along, but signaling for them to remain quiet at the same time. A quarter mile or so of backtracking and they arrived at the cave, its entrance concealed with a dense veil of moss that grew from an overhanging balsam tree.

Duncan, Annlise, and Ian hurried in moving as far back as possible.

"Down, Kindred," William ordered. She lowered herself, obediently down to her stomach, her hooves folded beneath her as he dismounted. He paused long enough to stroke her neck. "Thank you, m' lady," he told her, then hurried along on hands and knees to the entrance of the cave.

"Duncan," Ewan whispered his orders with the air of a soldier. "Come here, where you can hear us, but are able to keep watch."

"Aye, sir," Duncan answered, in the manner that was appropriate for his rank.

"Do you mind telling me what's going on?" William asked, making his way to the back of the cave. He crawled to a large boulder where Ian gave him a hand, easing him up to sit. "Who is that man?"

"Lest I'm mistaken," Ewan began, his voice quiet but with a hard edge to it, "that's one of Ogham's hired dogs. I'd know the colors anywhere."

"Ogham?" William asked. "The duke from... where was it?" He closed his eyes, trying to bring the information he knew was there someplace buried in his head, to the forefront. "What duke was he?" he shouted unintentionally. "Kylkannen? Bannenvale?"

"Shh!" came a chorus of his companions.

"Sorry," he whispered impatiently. "I know I should know this, but right now, I don't have a desire to play coy and pretend to remember what you're talking about. Just tell me."

"Ogham of Lothlanne Castle," Annlise answered him, placing a hand on his shoulder. "Edward's primary rival. The one who..." She pulled her cloak close around her, as if to stave off a sudden chill, leaving her sentence unfinished.

"The one who what?" William grabbed her hands, turning her toward him. "What are we facing at the gates?"

"The one Thomas convinced to bring the charges against you," Duncan answered, from his post at the cave entrance.

"Thomas?" William shook his head, growing more impatient with himself, and with the half-bits of information he was getting. "Who on God's earth—"

"That loathsome snake!" Ewan hissed. "Don't you even remember *him*? Gads, Will. 1 know it was bad for you, but can't you even bring to mind the man who did his best to see you dead and gone? Your own miserable brother!"

"Brother..." William began, then stared in the dark of the cave at Ewan, silhouetted by the entrance. "Yes, 1..." In a rush, the dream he'd had, the night he had become separated from lan, invaded his head. And as clearly as if he was there, sitting and conversing in the flesh before him, William could see the image of Sean, telling him:

"No reason that you should remember him, I'd call it a blessing that you don't. But if you must know, his name was Thomas, Earl of Aberdoir. And that be all 1 care to discuss of him."

"Was? He's dead as well, then?"

"Long dead. Best forgotten."

"But Thomas is dead, Ewan. He's no longer a threat to me." William spoke quietly, in a determined calmness. "Long dead. Best forgotten."

"Aye, he's dead and no longer a worry," Ewan said. "But Ogham is very much a threat, Will. And that sentry is wearing his colors. 1 know the tartan. I've gone against it enough times."

"1 know it too," Duncan added. "He's sent scouts after—"

"Scouts?" William scoffed, not beginning to fathom why an old adversary would wish to send scouts chasing half a world after him. And how could he have possibly known to come to Port Edin, which he was beginning to think of as the *island at the end of the world.* "How could he know I'm here?"

"Perhaps we are jumping to conclusions," Annlise suggested. "Is it possible he's merely staking claims within the territory?"

Ewan rested his hand in his chin, pacing the sandy floor of the cave. "I suppose that could be true. There has been ample time since the raid for word to get back to England that this place could be theirs for the taking. Perhaps that's all it is. Ogham has made no secret of his desire to extend his reach to the New World." He looked up sharply to Annlise, a sudden inspiration making a statement on his face, "Lass, you lived in his castle, do you recall ever hearing him speak of ... expanding his realm?"

Annlise laid her palm on her necklace, in her customary posture of thought, her eyes half closed. "About a year ago," she began in a thoughtful, almost wistful tone. "A message was sent from King James. I was tending Ned in the nursery adjacent to Ogham and Lady Bryndah's suite when the page arrived. I heard him— Lord Ogham, that is— bragging. Aye, that's what it was; bragging."

She paused long enough to swallow, then continued. "Seems that he'd been granted the right of claim to some territory of his own choosing, to be settled in James' name, ye see. Who he entrusted the governing of his claim to, was to be left to his own discretion."

She closed her fist around the silver trinket as a deep furrow creased her forehead. "He was proud, aye. Boastin' to Lady Bryndah about his boon. But she mocked him, telling him it was a fool's compensation the king be givin' him. No more than a token gesture of goodwill that meant nothing. She laughed at him and... och, he were angered then. They fought, yellin' at each other in the most hateful way." She looked away, wearily shaking her head. "I'm ashamed to admit I gave little Ned a dose of sleeping powder jus' to spare him hearin' his parents fight," she said off-handed, then returned to her narration, pacing the sandy floor of the cave. "Lady Bryndah told the duke that he should simply sell the claim and be done with it. 'Take as much as ye can from some poor sot and fill your own purse', she were sayin'. Ogham would have none of that. He told her she must be daft in the head. A governorship in the New World would be far more rewarding monetarily and he was not about to turn it down."

Ewan drew a long, thoughtful breath and released it through a deep growl. "Then it's possible he's merely sent scouts to lay his claim. Their presence may just be an incredible coincidence."

Though he could not make out the details of Ewan's face in the dimness of the cave, William could hear the doubt in his friend's tone. "You're not convinced of that, are you?"

"Not entirely, no," Ewan admitted. "But I've no better explanation to offer right now. There is no way possible for him to know you're here."

"Well that should settle it then," Ian said, to no one in particular. "We can't go back to Port Edin, now."

"There is no other place to go, Ian," William said, rubbing his eyes with his hands. "That's where the ship will come. We need to be there."

"Why?" Ian shouted. "Did your signs tell you Ogham would be there as well? It's far too dangerous. It's time to rethink this, Will—"

"No!" William growled, nearly falling off the rock. Ewan made to catch him, but William shoved him off angrily, intent on confronting Ian. "Damn it, Proctor, I've told you over and again, I need to get into Port Edin!"

"Why?" Ian asked in loud exasperation.

"Because he told me I have to go there in order to get home!" William shouted, sending echoes through the cave.

Duncan turned from his place at the cave mouth. "Quiet!" he called, silencing them at once. Even in the dimness of the cave, William saw the confounded looks Ian and Ewan were sharing.

"Who, Will?" Ian asked, his voice far softer, more cloying; the sort of tone taken with the feeble minded. "Who told you?"

You will never understand? Though he couldn't see Ian's eyes, he knew the look in them would not be condescending, but concerned. He could hardly blame him— he was beginning to think himself daft for what he wanted to say: *Sean told me. Before he turned into an eagle. He's the one I'm following, you see.* Instead, he drew a long, steadying breath, and answered, "Akonni. When his tribesmen returned from bringing Josephine back to Port Edin..." he hesitated, uncomfortable speaking an outright lie, but felt it necessary at the moment. "He said he thought he'd seen the sails on the horizon... far to sea."

Ian exhaled and William could sense him relaxing. It had been a satisfactory answer.

"Then a ship *is* coming," Ewan said, a hopeful note to his voice.

"It could be any ship," Ian sighed. "Even another of Ogham's or worse— another raiding galleon."

Ewan grumbled under his breath and turned away. "Let's hope not."

After a pause from his place near the front of the cave, his eyes fixed on the sky to the south, Duncan said quietly. "He's right. *Lady Anne* is coming back for us."

"Lad?" William asked, surprised by Duncan's comment. *Do you hear him too?*

Duncan shrugged and chuckled turning to his companions. "At least that is what I choose to hope. Either way, we can't sit in this cave forever. Are we going or not?"

William half smiled to himself, dismissing the odd hope that Sean had been guiding his other brother as well. "We're going."

Ian shook his head, throwing his hands up in resignation. "Well, if we're going, then we need a plan. How do we get past the sentries?"

"There was only one, Ian. I suspect it would be easy enough to sack him," Duncan said. "He didn't look all that big. Ewan and I could take him down easily enough."

"That may be true enough, Duncan, but what of his companions who may be standing watch just inside the gate?" William said.

"Others?" Duncan scoffed. "I saw only the one scrawny sentry."

"Scrawny he may be," William said, patiently, "but there is no such thing as only one sentry. There'll be more inside the gates. And they'll all be equally armed. Your swords are no match for their muskets."

"Aye," Ewan agreed. "I would be surprised if they didn't take up residence in your own house, Will."

Duncan snapped his head around, a look of sudden inspiration lighting his face. "Do you suppose your arsenal is still there, Will? Hidden in the walls?"

"The walls were still standing last I saw them," William replied. "I didn't think to check the stores, but last I knew, there were at least half-dozen muskets." He slapped his leg frustrated with himself for his lack of foresight in not taking anything with him. "I suppose I wasn't thinking clearly. When I couldn't find Melly and Seany... or you, Ian, I saw no need to..."

"Don't blame yourself," Annlise told him gently, lightly placing her hand on his shoulder. "Ye couldn't know ye family had made it safe off the island and that we'd be needin' the muskets; now, could ye?"

William shook his head. "I suppose not."

"She's right you know, Will," Ian chimed in. "And besides, firearms are not your weapon of choice, are they? At least, I can't recall ever seeing a musket in your hands. Do you even know how to fire one?"

William chuckled in spite of himself at Ian's consoling pearls of logic. "No, I've never fired one," he admitted. "But if I had one in my hands, I could certainly *look* like I knew how to fire it. After all, I know which end the ball comes out."

"I know how to handle a musket. I'll be glad to show you."

All heads turned to Annlise.

"What is so astounding?" she asked, sounding annoyed, though slightly pleased with their stunned silence.

"You are," Ewan answered, with a tone of admiration. "Lass, ye be a wonder to me, more an' more. Where is it ye learned to shoot a musket?"

"'Tis only a matter of aimin' the thing and pullin' the lever," she answered. William could almost hear the blush in her voice. "A child could do it."

"Ye never held one either, aye?" William asked, laughing. When she did not return his amusement, he cleared his throat.

After a long moment, she answered flatly, "Never," then laughed with him, bringing to end yet another uncomfortable moment between them.

William resolved that once they were safely settled back in his garrison— and he had no doubt they *would* make it in safely— he would have a private conversation with Annlise, to see if he couldn't smooth the waters between them. Since his first meeting with her, she had seemed self-guarded and almost fearful of him. As though she were terrified to make him angry. William could not for the life of him think what it was about him that could so intimidate an otherwise stout-hearted young woman, who seemed far more self-assured than he could ever hope to feel about himself. Truth be told, he was beginning to realize that he held the same astonished admiration in her that he suspected Ewan was feeling.

"Well, I guess it makes no difference who can shoot or not," Duncan sighed, bringing the conversation back to the matter at hand. "The guns are back in the garrison and we're out here. And we can't just walk through the gates, now, can we."

"Why not?" Ian asked, suddenly getting to his feet. "We pose no threat to them. Surely other settlers have found their way back since these men have arrived. Why not us?"

Ewan paced for a moment, apparently mulling over what Ian had said. "Well, ye have a point there. We don't know for sure they're hostile just because they be wearing the colors of our chief rival. As Annlise said, they could just be here staking a claim for Ogham."

"And what do you think that guard will do when he sees the tartan you're wearin', Ewan?" Duncan snapped. "If we know their colors, they're sure to know ours at first sight. And they'd react the same as we would in their place. Attack first, then find out the reason for our presence."

Another heavy silence descended.

Outside the cave, as if to offer her own suggestion, Kindred nickered quietly, shaking her mane to rid herself of an annoying fly.

"E'e, Kindred, ela'tiek pugjig," William answered her absently in Akonni's language, too distracted by his own thoughts of how to get past the sentry to realize what he was saying.

"What?" Ian asked. "Did you say something, Will?"

"Hmm?" William looked up, then realized he what he'd done. "Oh. No, Ian. I was just telling Kindred we'd be going soon, to be patient." He shrugged. "There must be some way to get back into Port—"

"I didn't know you spoke the native language," Ian interrupted.

"Just a bit that I picked up. Perhaps we should scout around the perimeter to find a hole—"

"Just a bit? Will, that rolled off your tongue like you were born to it," Ian persisted, his voice taking on the giddy timber that William had come to know as his "idea" voice.

"What of it? I picked up what I needed to while staying with Akonni's people— what are you doing?" William pushed Ian's hands away as the apothecary began oddly grabbing at the buckskin shirt that Ah'Reehl had given him.

"Will! You're brilliant!" Ian shouted, circling around the rock where William sat, looking him up and down as if he'd never seen a man sitting on a rock.

"Ian!" Ewan hushed him. "Keep your voice down."

"What are you talking about?" William asked, completely bewildered with Ian's sudden excitement.

Ian continued his scrutinizing survey, circling the rock again, until William reached out and grabbed his hand to gain his full attention.

"Ian Proctor, will you please enlighten me?"

"Look at you!" Ian answered, a wild glee in his tone. "With your hair black and long past your shoulders, your native clothes... you need a shave of course, but don't you see? *You* can get us past the sentry. For certain, they'd know Ewan and Duncan's colors, but Will— or should I call you 'W'yiam'— you can approach them as a native."

William stared at Ian, barely able to see his face in the dark cave but still able to discern the look in his eyes. "You're daft, man. How many Mi'kmaq do you know of who speak with a burr? And I hardly know enough to—"

"And how much do you think that sentry knows of the language? You could fill your mouth with pebbles and babble, and he wouldn't know the difference. As for your burr... well it's not half as thick as Ewan's is anymore."

"But..."

"Ye right, Ian." Duncan left his spot by the entrance, taking the same tone of excitement. "I hardly hear it in him. And didn't we all mistake him for a native when I tossed him? You can do it, Will. You fooled us and we *know* you!"

"But I haven't got my razor," William protested.

"Use this." Duncan pulled his dirk from the holster on his thigh. "Annlise gives a right fine shave, and she can heal any cuts she makes anyway—"

"Cuts?"

"—and Ian, you can go with him." Duncan went on, ignoring William's objection. "Since they won't know you either. Then you can see just how many of them are there, and if they'll be much trouble to deal with. Once you're in, you can ingratiate yourself into the garrison on some pretense of wishing to speak to their leader. That will get us information, and may even give you an opportunity to get into the arsenal. Damned shame you haven't got your cleric robe with you. You could claim you've been off converting and baptizing the native heathens or some rot like that. They'd eat that tale right up."

"That may still work, Duncan. Excellent suggestion!" Ian said, seeming more enthusiastic now that there was a bit of theatrics involved. "Not all missionaries take the robe you know, and I can certainly assume that role quite readily, claiming my good friend W'yiam as my Indian guide through the forest primeval."

"That will get you through the gate, but then what?" Ewan asked, tempering Ian and Duncan's excitement. "How do the rest of us get in? And how do we get back *out?*"

"The same way we came out the first time," Annlise suggested, "through the hole in the barn wall."

"Aye," Duncan grinned. "Will leads Kindred to the barn stable, and we sack whatever guards we find and steal their uniforms. We get in, get Ian and Will, and get out through the barn again. We then send *Lady Anne* Edward's usual signal— two flaming arrows and we're done. You see? Easy enough." He crossed his arms, grinning, obviously pleased with himself for coming up with such a brilliant plan.

William shook his head, half smiling at the irony that it was the same sort of rash adventure he and Sean would have undertaken in their youth— though with far less foresight as Duncan's. *Pure Wilbrun.*

Ewan glared, not amused, and pointed out an obvious flaw in Duncan's plan. "They'll expect him to dismount, perhaps even insist upon it. And when he does... well, I can only imagine the cruel sport they'd make of a lamed Indian once his friend is away in the garrison. How do you intend to defend—"

"Do you have a better idea?" William asked with a frustrated growl. "I can't go in any other way than on horseback. I admit I'm not overly fond of the charade, but I do agree it's the best way. Let me take that dirk with me or better yet, one of the swords. I'll hide it under the horse blanket. I may not be able to fire a musket with any accuracy, but I can swing a blade if I must."

"Can you?" Ian asked quietly, his former enthusiasm turned to concern. "Your hands and shoulders are not so strong. You'd be as a rabbit attacking a wolf."

"Even a rabbit can deliver a vicious bite when it is cornered and angry enough, Ian. And make no mistake, where Ogham is concerned, I am far past angry." The tone in William's voice left no room for further debate.

Whether it was borne of the determination or desperation within him to return to his family, he wasn't certain, but in that moment and without preamble, the gentle wood-wright of Port Edin assumed the formal and authoritative demeanor that was due his former rank as the Earl of Sutherland. "Anyone have questions?" No one did. "Then that's our plan. Annlise, take Duncan's dirk. I'll be needing that shave if I'm to truly pass as a native. I trust you could offer a fine close shave without water, however there is a brook not far and we'll go there. Besides, I'd prefer you not do it in the dark."

"A wise thought," she replied.

"Ian," William continued. "You come with us to the brook and we can leave together from there. Annlise will come back here and wait with Duncan and Ewan. Keep out of sight, but be ready to flee if ye must." He paused, choosing his words carefully. "Ewan, promise me that should something go wrong, you three hightail it to the north. Do *not* come in after us. Is that clear?"

"No!" Duncan protested. "You cannae expect us to leave you behind *again.* Not after all we've gone through to bring you home. We'll fight who we must—"

"Peace, lad." Ewan raised his hand to Duncan. "He's given an order. Ye best learn to be following them."

"Aye," Duncan grumbled, then stalked away toward the cave entrance, muttering under his breath.

"Good lad," Ewan said, watching Duncan before he leaned close to William and spoke in a low, serious tone for his ears only. "If ye think I'll be sittin' on m' hands just waiting to know ye be slaughtered, ye be daft... *my lord.* I'll not have ye taken on my watch again." He extend his hand, offering a knight's elbow-to-wrist shake. "Your back is covered. Understand? I'll not be letting Edward down, lad."

William accepted his hand and matching Ewan's covert tone, he answered, "I appreciate that, Ewan, truly, but I mean what I say and I shall not have more blood on my conscience."

Ewan frowned and gave William's arm a squeeze in reply. "And I'll not be havin' *your* blood on mine. Now, ye heard me tell Duncan he mus' learn to be following orders... and I meant what I said. But Will, ye mus' remember somethin' here. I'm under Edward's orders to bring you home. Remember, I took an oath long ago to protect ye. I intend to make good on that oath. I will be right behind you."

"No, Ewan." William replied stubbornly. "Ogham's men will be on you in a heartbeat. Please... don't risk..."

"Are ye forgettin' ye wife?" Ewan growled, tightening the grip on William's forearm.

William stared, silenced by Ewan's sudden gruffness. "My wife?"

"Aye, Melly. Ye remember her? By now she's back within the walls of Drumoak with ye wee son on her lap, the two of them still mournin' ye death."

"But I'm not dead!"

"Ye will be if ye keep to this foolishness." Ewan's voice grew louder.

Ian and Annlise stopped their conversation and turned to look.

"Will, ye wife and ye son are needin' ye with them. Edward plans to name Seany as his heir; ye know that, don't ye?"

"No," William whispered. "No, Ewan, he can't. He can't lay that mantle on my son as he did me. It's a curse."

Ewan released his grip and backed away slightly, his expression softening from his anger. "Well, curse it may be

and trust me, I'm believing ye may be right 'bout that, but
there are those who would scheme against Seany to steal it
from him just the same. You know that far too well. Edward
is old, and it's a fair wager he won't live long enough to see
Seany grow into his manhood, which means the lad will be
wearin' that mantle far sooner than he should have to. He's a
child, Will. No match for Bryndah and Ogham and, let's face
it, Melly hasn't the head or the nerve to stand against those
two either. Seany needs you! And he needs you alive. And, by
God, that is the way I intend to bring you home. So don't ask
me again to leave ye behind."

William nodded slowly, not taking his eyes off the
silhouette of his friend, the reality of the circumstances
becoming painfully clear. "You're right, Ewan. Seany can't
stand against them. I need to get home. Cover my back as
you deem best, but please... promise me this— if something
does happen to me, you are to get Duncan out safely. He's my
brother's flesh, Ewan. I owe him that."

Ewan crossed his fist across his chest, nodding. "Clear."
He stepped back, without releasing William's wrist, helping
to guide him off the rock to the sandy floor.

"Time to go." Without waiting for a response, William
made his way on hands and knees out to where Kindred
rested on her belly waiting. He unhitched the litter from her
harness and unfastened the make-shift saddle. "I hate to ask
one of you to forfeit your blade."

"Take mine." Duncan unfastened the scabbard from his
waist and handed it to William. "It's not as long as Ewan's
and will be easier to hide. And it's not as heavy to swing."

William took the sword with a nod of understanding

in Duncan's attempt at diplomacy. "Thank you, Duncan. Blessed Mother grant I shall not have to put to test the strength of my arms. But if I do, I'm sure you're right that the lighter blade is best. Though I truly do not like the idea of leaving you without a weapon."

"Don't worry about that, Will. I'm fairly resourceful when I need to be. I've been known to strike a mean blow without a blade."

"I'm sure you have," William replied, unconvinced, but with little choice but to believe the lad. "Help me with this, will you? I'll need to be able to reach it easily, but it needs to be under the quilt, out of sight."

Once the scabbard was safely harnessed to Kindred, the quilt was draped over it carefully concealing the entire blade. The saddle made up for the slight budge made by the hilt. When saddle and scabbard were secured, William went to the litter and retrieved the leather satchel containing his journal and the wooden box he had taken from the dresser of his burned out bedroom, and tied it on as well.

"You keep the rest of this," he said, routing through the remaining articles on the litter. "There's a few provisions left and a spare blanket." He mounted silently, then signaled for Ian and Annlise to follow him.

Ewan took hold of Annlise's hand and turned her to face him. "Duncan and I shall wait for ye here. Ye take care, lass," he told her, then pulled her forward and kissed her lightly on the side of the face.

She blushed lightly and nodded, then took a step back and smiled. "Be well, Ewan."

~

"Just a bit more... hold still."

William flinched as Annlise scraped away the last of what was left of his beard, the rough edge of the dirk catching on the scar on his cheek. "Careful... it's a bit tricky there. I'm used to my wife taking care of this for me, you see. And it took her some time to get the knack. I believe she can take credit for the lesser scar near my ear." He half-smiled, trying to ease the tension.

"It would be less tricky if ye'd trust me, and relax," she said, tight lipped, while stretching the skin around the scar to smooth it as best she could. "If you keep talking, I'm likely to make a new scar to match the one ye wife left ye."

"I thought Duncan said ye could heal whatever cuts you make."

"I can," she replied, coolly. "And if ye keep talking, I'll be sure to prove it to ye."

"Sorry," he muttered, trying not to move his mouth as she carefully made a final pass on his cheek.

She stepped away from him, wiping clean the blade with the hem of her frock.

"Done?" He asked, running his hands over his newly shorn cheeks.

"Aye, best as I could do without a real razor," she said. "Ye face is still in one piece."

"Thank you." William smiled, still rubbing one cheek. "It's a fine job," he said, turning to Ian for inspection. "Well? Will I pass?"

Ian screwed up his eyes, tilting his head, scrutinizing William top to bottom. "You'd fool me if I didn't know you. Although the color of your eyes may be troublesome."

"There's little I can do about that, Ian. We just need to hope Ogham's men haven't come in contact with enough of the native people for them to find a green-eyed warrior out of place."

"Good point," Ian chuckled. "Let's hope that's the case."

Annlise frowned, as she packed up the dirk. "'Tis not the color of ye eyes that has me worried. It's how to explain yourself for staying on the horse. Have ye thought what you'll do if they insist ye get down?"

William glanced to Ian, hoping to see the light of inspiration on his friend's face. Ian only shook his head and shrugged.

"We'll think of something."

Annlise's face flushed suddenly, and she took a loud breath. "Ye are as reckless a man as I've ever known, William Fylbrigge."

"Reckless?"

"And stubborn! Why will ye not allow me to do what I was sent here for?"

"Annlise, there isn't time for another argument," William shouted, sending an unintentional echo through the forest. He swallowed his breath for an instant before speaking again in a far quieter tone. "I'm sure your talents are as impressive as Ian and the others have told me. But I will only tell you this one more time— the tendons were *cut!* No matter how much magic you possess or how much the Blessed Mother shines on you, you can't change that! Done is done."

"Done is done?" she railed. "Have you so little faith left in you, Phoenix, that you cannae allow me to try?"

"Phoenix?"

"Aye, that's what I called ye. And that is the name by which ye be known to the countless souls who've found their courage to stand up and fight for our right to worship God and Goddess by looking to your example. And I'm findin' it harder to believe ye to be the same man, whose memory so many of us have rallied 'round these past six years, in the hope of a new life. Our Phoenix, who in the name of the Blessed Mother, refused to surrender to the bishops and priests..." She took a breath and turned away, her shoulders shaking beneath the cloak she wore. "Ye cannae find it in ye to allow me to even try to *start* the healing? Are ye so afraid that I'll fail?"

William sat silently for a moment before lowering himself to the ground and moving toward his horse. "Down, Kindred" When the horse had obediently lowered herself to the ground, William reached into the pack behind the saddle and withdrew the satchel that bore his journal. He stroked the tooled eagle on the cover, then said in a nearly inaudible whisper, "'Tis not a fear that you will fail that prevents me from allowing you to cure me, Annlise. But a fear that you *won't* fail." He placed the book in the leaves on the ground before him and opened it slowly, turning the pages carefully as if it were a fine antique he held, and not his own journal made of leather and paper.

Ian crouched on the ground before William, placing one hand on his shoulder. "Why do you fear success?"

"Not success, Ian. Debt." He pointed to the pages of the journal before him. "The Blessed Mother and Father do not dispense their blessings for free. If I've learned nothing else from this book, it's that."

Ian looked where William indicated on the page. "It's merely your journal, Will. We've read it together many times... there's nothing in there about paying a debt to your Goddess."

"Look again, Ian," William told him.

Ian stared at the page, a confused furrow in his brow, as he impatiently shook his head. "All I see are the same entries I've seen for years... your arrival at Drumoak, the time the mare was ill, the pirate games you played as a youth under the cliffs of Drumoak... simple memories..." He stopped talking suddenly, the furrow deepening as he stared at the pages, his eyes growing wider by the moment. "It's changing," he whispered.

The entry William had chosen to show Ian was dated: 29 May 1606. A simple short poem that read: *Of all the meadows 'neath the moon, that God hath dressed in floral— No bird hath song, nor flower bloom, as fair and sweet as Laurel.* Ian had read it many times, and had quipped on more than one occasion that perhaps William should have made his occupation as a poet rather than a wood-wright. But the words were shifting, moving around the page as though they were liquid, until at last they stopped, and it became clear what was now written on the page: *By the light of the full moon, in the meadow at midnight, cut the chicory with a golden blade, while singing your prayer to the Goddess for her blessing. Use the blue blossom wisely, seeking to harm none. The laurels gained will then be worn in sweet victory, in the name of the Lady and the Lord... .*

Ian looked William in the eye. "How?"

William met Ian's unblinking stare square on. "The entries I made before my time here are all like this. The words are veiled by a charm of my own making... to hide them from all eyes but my own." A slow mirthless grin found its way to his face. "The only trouble is, I cast the charm so well that the words were hidden from me as well... until I remembered."

"It's come back to you then?" Ian asked, swallowing hard.

William nodded slowly, keeping his eyes on his friend's.

"All of it?"

William nodded again.

Annlise lowered herself to her knees beside William's open book, tentatively turning the pages, then blushed and looked away.

William placed his hand on her chin and guided her sight back to the book. "Please. Read it, Annlise," he told her quietly. "You, of all people, must understand the debt the Mother and Father demand for the blessings They bestow. I cast the charms far too often, relied on the chants and the spells far too heavily." He turned back to Ian. "Though Melly rightly called them *prayers*— and I accepted the blessings granted to me; my talent with music, my persuasiveness, Melly's hand in marriage... and especially the self-confidence I gained by use of this one special chant. All these things came to me by the whim and mercy of Olde Ones. Yet I gave little or no thought to repaying the kindness of the Blessed Lady." He gestured with a gnarled hand toward his feet. "But as you can see... She extracted Her price from me as She saw fit. Had She taken the price from me alone, I would not hesitate to allow you to use your healing charms for me now, Annlise. But you see, I simply can't allow you to earn a debt on my behalf as Laurel did."

Ian's eyes averted, a milky glaze forming at the mention of

Laurel. "No... Will, you can't believe that Laurel died for the sake of an impossible debt owed to your Goddess. She died because of the ignorance of the magistrate who believed her to be a witch."

William held a hand up. "Believe as you will, Ian. And allow me the same privilege."

"Ye truly believe the Mother would punish me for healing you?" Annlise asked, closing the book and handing it back to him. "Is that why She's given me the gift?"

"It's not mine to say for sure. But I am not willing to risk that for you."

"It's not yours to say; that be true enough. But I can't believe I stand to be smote fer using the gift." She stood up, brushing away the leaves that had gathered on her skirt. "And if truth be spoken, I believe it is not a debt to the Goddess ye be fearin', William Fylbrigge, but the simple fear that ye might be right about those severed tendons."

William stared at her, suddenly finding he had no argument for this accusation. "And if the fear proves true and you can't heal—"

"Then ye be no worse off than ye are now. But if ye allow me to try and we're given the miracle... then I'll gladly accept whatever debt there be."

William sat silent, mulling over Annlise's arguments, unable to find a flaw in her reasoning.

"Lass," Ian placed a hand on Annlise's shoulder. "I don't think you fully understand the extent of his injury. Joseph was thorough with his blade. Charms and chants won't help him to walk."

Annlise snapped her head in Ian's direction, her eyes

flashing. "Have ye no belief, Brother Ian? Were ye not reared on stories of healin' and miracles in ye own faith?"

"I believe in God," Ian answered defensively, his cheeks flaring suddenly scarlet. "And I do not dismiss your faith in your Blessed Mother or the ways of the old religion... but I also believe in common sense. I know the sort of damage that was done to him."

He's right... it's impossible... William looked from one to the other while they argued, torn between logic and hope. He glanced down to the book, tracing his hand along the binding, silently reciting his prayer for courage. Eyes closed, rocking slightly on his knees, he waited for the inner peace the prayer usually brought to find him. *... show me the way, remove my doubts...* Annlise and Ian continued to argue

Blessed Mother... tell me what to do? I wish no debt to befall Annlise... but there is no sin in wishing to be healed... is there? High above him, the echo of the scream of an eagle rang through the tree tops. He opened his eyes in time to see the regal raptor light on the highest branch of a fir tree. *Is that really you, brother?* he asked silently, feeling slightly foolish for the thought, but at the same time, finding a growing certainty within him that he had just received the answer to his prayer for guidance.

"Is the healin' ye see in him already not enough to convince ye there be a chance?" Annlise was saying, jutting her hand toward William, but keeping her fiery eyes trained on Ian.

"There's a logical reason for that! I just don't know what it is, yet," Ian retorted.

"Am I allowed a voice?" William asked, interrupting the quarrel. "Or are the two of you going to fight each other to the death on my behalf?"

Annlise blushed and looked away from both men.

He glanced back up to the eagle making certain it was really there, then looked to Annlise. "Lass, do what ye will. Perform your healing rite."

"Will, there's no time. We'll lose the daylight if we stay here much longer," Ian protested. "There are no miracles lurking in Annlise's box of herbs and simples that will get you on your feet."

William held his palm up signaling for Ian's silence. "Ian, you, of all people, should accept the possibility of a miracle, after everything you've seen." He extended a hand to his friend. Ian accepted it, as if taking a handshake, but before he could withdraw, William tightened his grip pushing the former monk's sleeve up passed his wrist with the other, exposing the marks encircling his wrist.

"You never told me how you came by these scars, my friend. I always assumed you would, one day, tell me they were gained the same way I came by mine; unjustly inflicted on you at the hands of a merciless captor for some imagined crime. And had I asked you directly, you would have let me believe just that." He paused, turning Ian's palm up examining the recently healed scars on his inner wrist more closely. "But I'd be wrong. Wouldn't I? These are the marks of a man who has lost his faith. More than once."

Ian tugged, self-consciously trying to wrest his hand back, but William held it firm. "Please, Will. It's all in the past, now. I've put that demon to rest, long ago. My faith is intact."

"Is it?" William asked, slowly releasing his grip on Ian's hand. "Good. Because I need your faith— and your help—

now, more than ever."

Ian withdrew, taking a step backward. "Do you truly believe she'll be able to make you walk? After all this time? What of that debt you were so afeared of only a few minutes ago?"

William closed his lips tight, sighing, then shrugged. "I believe there is no harm in trying, Ian. As for the debt, I will pray to My Lady and Lord that it be mine alone to pay."

Annlise stepped forward and knelt in front of William. "You've more than paid your debt, Phoenix."

William smiled and took a long breath. "What must I do for your ritual?"

"Relax," she answered, a slow grin finding her face. "Lie here on ye back in the soft leaves. I'll get my kit."

William lowered himself carefully as Annlise instructed and closed his eyes. "Are you still with me?" he asked, then smiled as a reply came to him in two voices at the same time; Ian's quiet, "Aye," and the reassuring scream of the eagle high above him as it took to flight.

Her ritual was reverent and formal and quite beautiful to William's mind, and he could not help but allow himself to be caught up in the song she lifted to the sky. Her words were of the old Gaelic tongue that he had not heard in many years; not since his childhood in Aberdoir when Rebecca had sung to him of the old ways. With the utterance of the first syllable of Annlise's song, the Gaelic was clear to him again, and the familiarity was comforting and seductive and whatever doubts he harbored that her 'gift' was merely superstition were banished from his mind. At that instant, he trusted. She lifted her song and prayed, her head thrown back, eyes fluttering closed in a near trance-like rapture, her right palm flat against her sternum covering the silver charm, calling on her Goddess and her God for the healing to come through. William lay still, transfixed by her singing and the soothing echo of her toning. In the midst of the echoes, he felt himself drift and he began to believe beyond reason, the healing would be complete.

As her song faded, she fell forward, weeping into her arms on the leafy riverbank, exhausted and near unconscious. William held his breath until the last echo waned, waiting for the wasp stings to begin in his feet heralding the miracle. But the stings never came and when the echoes were silent, his feet still hung dead at the ends of his legs.

They wept together for several moments before Ian joined and knelt with them. William would not have tolerated a declaration of defeat from his friend at that moment, though that is what he had expected. Instead, Ian had simply embraced the two of them quietly before turning away, busying himself by seeing the pack was secure on Kindred's back. It was then that William realized that Ian too, had believed— if only for the briefest of moments— the miracle would happen.

Chapter 20

Adrian Tearlach looked up from his journal to the young scout who was standing in the doorway of the room he had claimed in the garrison as his study. "Well? Speak, man. What have you discovered of this wretched place?"

The young man hesitated. "Little, sir." The nervousness in his eyes was enough for Adrian to know the news would not be what he hoped for, and the scout was aware of Adrian's habit of taking out his wrath on the messenger if the message was not to his liking.

"How little? Any people?"

"There are but a handful of old women and a few half-starved goats and cows left to the place." The scout risked a glance to meet Adrian's glowering stare eye-to-eye, then quickly averted his sight tensing his posture as if to brace himself for a temper storm.

"Women?" Adrian asked, intrigued. "How many?"

The scout seemed to relax when the storm did not come, his shoulders lowering slightly. "Three, sir. Old. We found them huddled in one of the small houses that hadn't burned completely." His brow wrinkled as he added almost to himself, "Curious thing. At first, they were terrified just by the sight of us, but then one of them... seemed *glad* to see us."

"Glad? How so?"

"She ran to me and... embraced me, sir. Praising God the whole time that she was at last delivered from... something I couldn't understand."

"Emotional French woman," Adrian sniffed, dismissing his former intrigue.

"Oh, she's not French, sir. By her accent, I'd say she hails from London."

"English?" Adrian raised a brow, his interest renewed. "The others?"

"I couldn't tell. They didn't speak, only gaped at us like bloated sun fish on the sand." The scout risked a subtle chuckle. "My thought is they're all three gone quite soft in the head with not a half-penny worth of wit among them."

"I asked not for your thought," Adrian grumbled.

The scout snapped to attention immediately, his eyes widening for an instant.

Adrian allowed himself a smug, satisfied grin at the scout's discomfort. "It is apparent to me these woman must have somehow managed to elude the raiders and have probably spent months cowering in that hovel defending themselves against the native savages. I should think it only natural they see us as deliverers in that light. After all, isn't that what we're here for? To deliver them from the demon?"

"Aye, sir." The scout answered, keeping his eyes straight in front of him. "Ye be right, sir."

"Of course, I'm right. I take it they've been secured and are awaiting my questioning."

There was no response for a moment other than the nervous crease which appeared again on the scout's brow. "No, sir."

Adrian slammed his fist on the desk. "Why not?"

The scout flinched. "I did not see the need. They were not who you sent us to look for... sir." His eyes darted to and from Adrian's, a timid hopeful smile coming to him. "But fear not, sir. They won't be leaving. Give the order and I shall bring them—"

"I gave you the order!" Adrian yelled, pounding the desk again. "I said I wanted every living soul in that settlement questioned, cataloged, and accounted for. I want to know of every dog, cow, rat, or snake that breathes air and every creature that doesn't! I want information! Proof! Do you understand me?"

"Y-yes, sir! Proof, sir."

"For pity's sake, Adrian, settle down. You're loud enough to wake the dead." Peter Garland entered the cabin with an imperious air, looking down his long straight nose to the scout as he walked past him. "I'm astounded you have yet to demand the interrogation of the barn owls to be sure they're not harboring any dead earls within their feathers."

"Proof will be found," Adrian growled through his teeth.

"Face it. There is nothing to be found here but ruin and rubble. We waste our time. Or is it the mythical phoenix you expect to find rising from the ash, reborn to prove his existence for your gain alone?"

"You try my patience, Garland." Adrian waved his hand toward the door, turning suddenly to the timid scout who stood silent, his mouth hanging open, stupidly. "Leave! Go back to the women and bring the one you spoke of back to me. I shall question her myself. Understand?"

"Aye, sir." The scout turned briskly on his heel and left the study quickly, closing the door behind him.

"You may wish to spend your life chasing after shadows," Garland said, yawning into his hand once they were alone. "But I am content to cut my losses and leave this godforsaken piece of ground and return to Scotland. It's clear to me there is no need for a governor on this rock in the ocean."

"You think yourself too important for your own good, old man," Adrian growled under his breath. "Don't delude yourself with the belief that I am obligated to allow you to return with me. I could cut your throat and drop you into the sea for chum with very little provocation and no one would be the wiser."

Garland put his hands on the table and leaned over it, meeting Adrian's eyes. "Without my seal and my witness, even if you *do* manage to find your proof, there would be nothing to corroborate your claim, now would there?" He turned his back, reaching for the doorknob, then stopped short when Adrian's dagger flew past his head and lodged in the door with a loud *thwack.*

"You are not dead right now because I did not wish to hit you with the blade. But make no mistake, Garland. You *are* expendable."

Garland casually plucked the knife from the wood, deftly tossing it point over handle, then back to Adrian. "If I were wrong, I'd be dead. You do need me." He turned, opened the door, and left without further harassment.

"We shall see about that," Adrian growled, leaning over the table, his eyes fixed on the door.

Garland walked away, side-stepping around the voluminous silk skirt of the woman standing in the corridor.

Bryndah waited for Garland to walk through the door and out to the porch, well out of earshot before coyly slinking up to the chair across from Adrian.

"I take it you were listening," he muttered, dipping his quill angrily into the ink.

"It's a small house, Adrian. It's difficult not to listen."

He merely grunted in response as he scratched the quill briskly over the page, writing: *12 October, arrived in New France. Many trees, few people. The scouts have reported Port Edin to be deserted save for three old women. No sign of Fylbrigge yet. However I have yet to search with my own eyes.* He reached again to the inkwell to refill his depleted quill but stopped, point poised over the elegantly gloved hand that covered the well.

"Are you to ignore me all afternoon?"

He sat back with a sigh, drawing the feathered end of the quill through his fingers. "What do you want?"

"It's been a long journey, and a lady grows weary with only clumsy sailors with filthy hands and self-important governors for company." She drew her silk covered hand to her face, tapping her temple with her index finger. "I was just thinking. It would be ever so pleasant to seek out more... *feminine* company. Don't you agree?"

Adrian allowed a shadow of a grin as he tossed the quill to the desk and closed the journal. "By all means, m' lady. Take an escort with you. Seek out the English woman first, my gut tells me she is our key to the treasure."

"I knew you'd understand."

The two stood at the same time and, leaning across the desk, they kissed. Bryndah turned and walked toward the door, then paused and looked back over her shoulder. "Soon, my love."

Adrian tipped his head slightly, grinning. "Soon."

It was near dusk when William and Ian left the protective shadows of the forest and came within view of the sentry who stood by the gate, William astride Kindred and Ian walking along side.

"There it is," William said, more to himself than to Ian.

"I see it." Ian took a long breath. "Are you sure you're up for this, Will... or should I say *W'yiam*?"

"Aye, Ian," he said quietly. "It's the only way to get home. That's where the *Lady Anne* will come. It's where he said I needed to go." William felt under the blanket for the reassuring presence of Duncan's sword, giving the hilt a near affectionate pat. He glanced over his shoulder back toward the woods to see if Ewan and Duncan were still with them, but he saw no trace of his friends. *They've already headed to the back of the barn... just as they were supposed to. Trust, Will.*

"Will... I know you've got your reasons for believing in miracles... and far be it for me to doubt you now after all I've seen..." Ian looked away, hesitating. "But how can you still place such faith in..."

William waited for him to finish his thought, worried that Ian was going to launch into another argument over the presence of miracles. However, after a few moments, it became apparent that Ian was embroiled with some inner battle that prevented him from continuing.

"Ian," William began, quietly; Ian did not look at him. "These past months— years— have certainly been more than a small test of my faith. If there is anyone who has doubted the wisdom of the ways of the Gods, it has certainly been me. But you're correct when you say I've got my reasons for believing in miracles. For trusting."

"Trusting what? Who?" Ian asked, an unfamiliar tone of despair in his voice that William had no ready answer for. "She failed, Will."

William reached for Ian's shoulder in a gesture of comfort. He wasn't sure which was eating at his heart more; acceptance of the lack of healing or the despondent pall in Ian's eyes. He would have liked to offer the perfect words of encouragement— for both of them— at that moment, but found there was really nothing for him to say. *He's right. She failed.* He took a breath and sat back on the saddle, turning his face skyward to scan the tree tops.

Ian followed William's gaze and spoke quietly. "Even though you're still forced to ride, you still hold fast to your visions and your faith. I cannot pretend to share your confidence that there will be a ship... or that we'll even be readily welcomed at the gate... but I see that you truly believe, without a doubt, that you're being guided. Don't you?"

William nodded slowly. "I do. Can't you?"

"To be honest, I don't trust anything I can't see." Ian looked away, toward the shadow of the gate. "But I trust *you.* And truth be told, I trust you far more than I've ever trusted myself— or God, for that matter. You've been a good friend, Will."

William smiled, again at a near loss for words. "So have you."

"Let's go then." Ian took hold of Kindred's bridle resolutely and led the way toward the gate. Her hoof falls became louder as the forest path gave way to the well-worn hard-gravel path, alerting the sentry of their approach.

"Halt!" The man drew his blade and brought it to the ready. "Who goes? Be ye friend or foe?"

"Please, good sir, stand down," Ian called back, with the natural cheerfulness that had won William over so easily on their first meeting in Stonehaven. "Thank God, I've found my way back! I was beginning to think I'd never be among my countrymen again."

Ian's performance was flawless. So easy was his delivery that, for a moment, William mused about how throughout his life in Port Edin he had never seen the apothecary in a somber mood. The easy way Ian was able to contrive his mood now made him pause to wonder how many time his old friend put on his cheerful front as part of a charade.

The guard seemed immune to Ian's infectious cheerfulness. He took several menacing steps forward, his hand at the ready on his sword. "State ye name, sir."

Ian came to an immediate halt, though the smile remained on his face. He gave William a quick glance, then turned his attention back to the guard. "My name is Proctor, sir. I'm the apothecary for Port Edin. Or rather, I was, until recent events."

The guard narrowed his eyes, looking Ian up and down. "Apothecary, ye say? A healer, ye mean?"

"Yes," Ian replied, his voice remaining casual, but his calm was belied by the flexing of his jawbone. "I've been the one taking care of the ills of the people here. I'm afraid I've been wandering the forest for months, lost since the raid. I was thrilled to finally find my way back to the gate... what's left of it. I can only assume you're here as a resettlement representative, sir?" Ian spoke rapidly, forcing a smile

"Ye in the way of healin' ills of the stomach?" the guard asked, dismissing Ian's question.

"Stomach?" Ian seemed taken aback, but maintained his performance. "Why, yes. I've been known to brew a remedy or two for woes of the stomach."

"Good. Ye be comin' with me, then." The guard jutted his chin toward William. "Who is this with ye? He a healer too?"

"Oh," he chuckled. "No, he's not a healer. This is W'yiam. My guide. I don't know what I should have done without him. He's the one who put me back on the road to—"

"Can't he speak for himself?"

Ian silenced, his customary nervous blush finding its way to his cheeks. "Forgive me, sir, and here I am wasting your precious time. W'yiam?" He patted William's leg, as if trying to gain the attention of someone who didn't speak the language. William understood— it was time to perform.

Ian extended a hand in the general vicinity of the guard. "Greet the guard."

William regarded Ian's face for a moment, feigning ignorance. "Kwe?" he said, shrugging his shoulders.

"The guard." Ian said slowly, as though speaking to a child.

William tilted his head and waved, smiling congenially as he delivered a much longer greeting in the Mi'kmaq language that rolled fluently from his tongue. "Hello, you bloated piece of swine dung," is what the guard would have heard had William been speaking English.

The guard screwed up his face, stepping closer. "Eh? What

ye be sayin?"

"He says, he's pleased to meet you," Ian explained. "I'm afraid he doesn't speak our language very well, sir. And I've only a cursory understanding of his, but we've managed to convey our thoughts to one another nonetheless."

The guard gave Ian a suspicious side look, then stepped closer to the horse, taking her bridle roughly in his hand. Kindred whinnied in protest, yanking herself away from his grip. The guard grumbled and reached for her again but William impulsively leaned forward, seizing the man's wrist.

Ian immediately grabbed William's arm, then the guard's in an attempt to pulled the two apart. "W'yiam, don't be rude," he said, forcing a smile through his clamped down teeth. "Let go of him. I'm terribly sorry, sir. He's very possessive about his horse. W'yiam... please."

William narrowed his eyes at Ian then set his glare on the guard. He squeezed the man's flesh for a moment before reluctantly releasing him.

"Savage has a grip like a vise!" the guard muttered, massaging his wrist.

William took a priggish satisfaction is seeing the ghost of his own hand showing pink on the man's flesh.

"Yes... his hands are..." Ian looked over his shoulder to William, a brief and silent question on his face that he immediately discarded before turning back to the guard. "Quite strong. I'm sure he meant you no harm, sir. He doesn't realize his own strength."

William grinned, crossed his arms over his chest, and sat back on the saddle as amazed as Ian at the strength of his own grip.

"Well I'll be takin' ye in to see the gov'na," the guard said angrily.

He reached for the bridle again, then hesitated as William made a slight lurch forward. They stared at each other for a moment, until the guard slowly, and more gently, took hold of Kindred's bridle. William made no move to stop him, but kept a warning scowl on him.

"The governor?" Ian asked, keeping his congenial air.

"Aye, that's what I said. I've orders to bring all new comers to meet him. And that would be the likes of you two."

Ian and William exchanged startled glances.

"Well, you hardly need to bring W'yiam to see your governor. He won't be staying. He was merely my guide to help me find my way back here. I don't think your governor would be interested in speaking to a native—"

"My orders are clear," the guard grunted, returning William's scowl with one as threatening of his own. "And he's not the first of his kind I've brought in. Though the other fellow was far better mannered, and had the decency to speak in our own language."

"Other fellow? There's another native here?"

"*Was*," the guard corrected. "Two in fact. *Both* spoke the language. And I can tell ye, the older one seemed to know his proper place and was not grabbin' at anyone. Even offered to help the cap'n out with a bout of bilious stomach he was havin'. The younger one made the mistake of raising his fist to the cap'n. Cap'n taught him his place, fer certain right then an' there. He ain't a man to cross." He gave the bridle an impatient yank and began to lead them toward the inner gate. "No more talk. Come with me now."

Ian reached for the man's arm and turned him to face him. "Please... explain what you've said. What did the captain do?"

The guard exhaled loudly, impatiently rolling his eyes. "What do ye think he did, man?" He made a slicing motion with his thumb across his throat. "The savage was attackin'. Cap'n laid him out where he stood with the other watchin'. Had the drink the old man give to him not settled his gut, he would have gotten the same treatment right then. But the cap'n ain't quick to throw away what he may find useful. And the old healer seemed useful for a time. Till he took to moanin' and wailin' o'er the other one. Made so much noise we had to put him down right next to the other." He pointed with his thumb toward William. "So ye best be advising ye friend here to mind his manners and not make too much noise."

"Thank you for the advice." Ian swallowed, and then forced his smile back to his face.

William reached forward, grabbing Ian's shoulder, turning him around, "Akonni?" he whispered.

"I don't know," Ian answered quietly. "But Akonni would be very likely to offer help if the man seemed ill."

William nodded his agreement. "Sosep?"

"Perhaps," Ian said, craning his neck to get closer to William. Keeping his voice as low as possible, he said, "We need to rethink this plan. You can't possibly go in—"

"Come on, we've not all day." The guard gave the bridle another yank. Kindred pulled away again with an indignant shake of her mane. "Stubborn nag!"

Ian moved away from William quickly and reached for the bridle before the guard had a chance to grab it again.

"Sir, it may be best to just send W'yiam and Kindred here on their way. I'm sure W'yiam has nothing... useful, as you say, to offer your captain, and it may be best not to... uh... annoy him."

The guard looked from Ian to William, apparently thinking it over. Ian risked a hopeful glance up to William.

William creased his brow and shook his head. "Mu! Uh... Akonni. So'sep..." He bit his lip resisting the impulse to blurt out in English that he would not leave until he knew for certain who, if the guard could be believed, had been slain by his captain. Ian was shaking his head in confusion, hunching his shoulders. In frustration, William grabbed the apothecary's shoulder and leaned as close as possible and took a gamble that the guard would not recognize the Latin that he was certain Ian would understand, "Ingressus, frater Ian." *I'm going in there, Brother Ian. Understand me, dammit.*

"What's he sayin?" the guard asked, thumping Ian's shoulder to turn him towards himself. "Can't ye make him speak in a human tongue?"

"Ingressus," William repeated.

"Uh... he says," Ian gave one last pleading message with his eyes. "He says he will... *please... get out of here.*" Ian mouthed the last part.

William held his ground and shook his head.

Ian turned back to the guard, abandoning his ersatz cheerfulness. "He'll lead the horse; you have no need to pull her. Come on. I've a remedy for bilious stomach I can prepare for your captain." Ian pursed his lips in resignation, then stocked past the guard toward the gate.

William kicked in gently, moving Kindred along behind

him. *I hope I know what I'm doing.* He surveyed the treetops quickly, hoping to catch a glimpse of the eagle, but could not see beyond the thick canopy of balsam that surrounded the stockade.

When they finally entered the village, a knot of bile found its way from his stomach to his throat at the sight of the two dozen or so armed men who mulled casually amid the ruins of his home. The pyre had been removed, a blackened circle of soot on the sand the only evidence of its existence. The splintered pile of charred wood that had once been the chapel had been hauled against the north perimeter of the stockade. A small shed built of new wood, its doors open to reveal an impressive store of gunpowder and weaponry, had been erected in the former chapel yard. Several more kegs were stacked outside the shed. The little cemetery, once concealed by the chapel building, stood stark and naked to the sky, most of the shrubbery and undergrowth having been burned away. A few of the wooden markers, though blackened with soot, remained upright, their inscriptions still visible. William suppressed an unexpected wave of grief that threatened to steal his nerve when he saw that in the farthest corner of the plot, the smallest of the markers remained pristine and untouched by the fire, the inscription "Philbrick" still plainly visible above an elaborate filigree of carved ivy.

"Fergus!" The guard shouted as they crossed the square. Another sentry, an older man with a less than friendly scowl on his face, stood leaning against the barn door turned and waved then casually walked over to join them.

"New comers?" Fergus asked, sparing only half a glance

to Ian and William, but seemed to take a keen interest in Kindred.

"Aye. Cap'n'll want to see this one. Says he's a healer."

"I can speak for myself, sir," Ian said, curtly, then turned to Fergus, his hand extended in greeting. "I am the former apothecary for this settlement. I'm pleased to meet you."

Fergus looked at Ian's outstretched hand, then dismissed it with a disinterested snort. "Ye may be useful," he muttered, still surveying Kindred, apparently failing to notice the man who sat on her back.

"I was takin' them to see the gov'na," the guard informed.

"Get back to ye post, Thomas. I'll take 'em from here."

"As ye wish, Fergus." Thomas replied with a shrug, turned on his heel and headed back to the gate.

His name is Thomas? Now there's a foul omen. William willed the growing churning in his stomach to end. *Maybe I should ask Ian for some of his stomach remedy. Sean, are you sure this is the only way home?* He scanned the sky quickly, hoping— yet not truly expecting— to see the eagle keeping watch from some inconspicuous perch, his doubts proven sound when he found no trace of the bird.

"Get down," Fergus grunted, finally acknowledging William's presence. "I'll be takin' ye nag." He reached for the bridle. Kindred backed up two steps, but he managed to grasp her. He looked up to William, for the first time speaking directly to him. "I said, get down."

William shook his head, feigning ignorance.

"Uh... Fergus, is it?" Ian tapped the man on the arm. "I'm afraid he doesn't speak the language. And if you please sir, I beg you allow him to keep the horse. It was a gift to him...

you see... ."

Fergus turned a skeptical eye on Ian. "Well it will make a fine gift for the governor now, won't it. We're in need of all the horses we can get and this one has just been given as a gift." He spread a rancid smile across his face. "And Governor Garland wishes to thank you." He turned quickly and slapped William's leg, then pointed gruffly to the ground. "Off now. By ye own power or mine."

"Mu!" William yanked on the rein, pulling Kindred away. His knee brushed against the hard hilt of the sword concealed beneath the blanket. For a moment, he considered drawing the blade and charging back through the gates to the forest. But there were far more soldiers mulling around than he had first realized, and it would be foolish for him to believe he could best the lot of them. And what of Ian? He couldn't very well leave his friend behind to fight alone.

Fergus lunged for the bridle and managed to wrap his hands around the harness, holding onto it with an unimaginable strength as Kindred bucked and struggled to get away.

William just managed to hold on by wrapping his arms around her neck, weaving his fingers into her mane. She reared twice, nearly throwing him off both times. Though he managed to stay amount, the sword became dislodged and slipped from the scabbard, falling to the gravel with a loud clank.

Fergus released Kindred at once, diving for the fallen blade. "What the—"

In a mix of panicky Mi'kmaq and Latin, William called to Ian to run. "Mu!... frater Ian, effugio!"

Instead of running, Ian dove for the sword, but Fergus was quick and twisted himself lithely, snatching it away from Ian's hand. Ian barely avoided a hoof to the head as he rolled away from where the sword had fallen. Fergus put one armor-booted foot on Ian's chest, then raised the blade threateningly above him.

William pulled hard on Kindred's reins, forcing her to rear, her front hooves beating wildly in midair, only inches behind Fergus's head. *Run dammit!* "Ian! Effugio!" he cried, desperate to draw Fergus's attention away from Ian. Fergus twisted around, keeping his foot planted on Ian's chest and raised the sword, two-handed above his head, this time setting his aim on Kindred. William managed to pull her back, just in time to avoid the strike as Fergus swung the blade defensively in her direction.

"Ian!" William called again as he struggled to stay mounted. Ian remained prone on the gravel, unmoving, under Fergus's foot.

The melee had drawn the attention of the other soldiers and they began leaving their posts, running to join the fray. In an instant, William and Kindred were surrounded. Kindred whinnied and reared again, tossing her mane to and fro as dozens of hands grabbed at her reins and bridle. William held on desperately, while feebly attempting to fend off the men with his fists and knees. The pack on Kindred's back loosened with her bucking and William was only vaguely aware that his possessions were being spilled haphazardly to the ground to be trod on by the frantic horse. He completely lost sight of Ian in the tangle and feared that he must have surely been trampled by the men, or worse, by the hooves of his own horse.

"Ian!" He called out, but was silenced quickly by a hand coming across his mouth from behind and a strong arm pulling him backwards off the horse and into grappling arms of a dozen armed men, before being slammed onto the gravel.

"Teach him some manners," a man, William assumed was the guard named Thomas, was yelling. He was answered with shouts of agreement and menacing jeers from the mob.

William flailed his arms wildly, trying to strike at anyone within his reach until he felt the sharp impact of a booted foot to his chest, and another, immediately after to his stomach. He groaned and lay still, while his vision slowly faded to gray, then to black. He lay near swooning, listening to the sound of dozens of mettle clad feet stepping around and near him, crowding, and kicking. He wrapped his arms over his head, and was about to call out in English for help, when suddenly the mob withdrew, leaving him lying, half conscious on the gravel, struggling to regain his breath. After what felt like several long minutes, but was really only seconds, he opened his eyes to see what— or rather, who— had saved him from being trampled to death.

"What's all this? Gentlemen, settle! Make way, let me through." The booted feet parted, making way for a tall, gaunt man, wearing the vestments of rank, his long black robe floating just above the ground as he approached. He stopped, his feet near William's head, as he looked down on him for a moment, then sniffed. "Oh, I see. Another wild savage." He shook his head, clucking his tongue then turned away, walking toward the last place William had known Ian to be. "Who are they?" he asked, his voice sounding oddly echoed to William's ear. And eerily familiar.

"This one claims to be the apothecary to this village. Just wandered in a bit ago." Fergus replied, while two other men hauled Ian to his feet and held him upright while his head lolled forward. Fergus grabbed his chin and shook slightly. "He'll come round. Weren't much of a blow I give him. Only enough to disarm him." He lifted the sword as proof.

Disarm? Liar. Ian wasn't armed.

"I see. Take him to the garrison and stay with him until either the captain or I have time for him." The gaunt man turned away from Ian, and set his attention on William. "And did this savage attack as well?"

"Aye, sir. He's dangerous. Took the lot of us to bring him down."

"I see." He put a toe under William's torso, rolling him to his side.

William groaned at the piercing pain in his chest. He instinctually wrapped his arms around his ribs, suspecting one or more of them may have been cracked.

"Gentlemen, if you would." The gaunt man motioned to two men. They flanked William, and gracelessly hauled him up, holding him with his arms draped over their shoulders. Each man was at least a head taller than him and, in the position he was held, only the very tip of his toes dragged on the ground. He squeezed his eyes closed, then opened them straining to clear his vision while trying not to cry out in English as each breath he took stabbed at his damaged ribs.

When his vision cleared, he was looking in the face of the gaunt man. A terrible wave of dread washed over him as a sudden and horrifying memory confronted him. He knew the face. It had haunted him in his dreams for years, though it was one of those that he could never pull to the fore during his waking hours. He knew the voice and the cold, droning tone of indifference as he gave his orders and the way he said "I see" that had brought the vagueness to clarity and he realized the identity of the man who stood before him. *And Governor Garland wishes to thank you,* the guard had said. *Garland? Peter Garland? God, please let this be a bad dream.* William carefully averted his gaze willing Garland to turn away, hoping that the man knew little enough of the native people that his green eyes would not betray him.

Garland surveyed William's clothing quickly, seeming disinterested in looking further until he glanced at his face. His brow creased and his eyes widened slightly. *Oh God, he's recognized me.* William steeled his jaw and forced himself not to meet Garland's direct stare.

"Is there a reason to detain the Indian?" Garland asked, almost casually over his shoulder. "Why not send him on his way?"

William looked up, surprised, then looked away before Garland turned back to him. *You don't speak English! Don't react... he doesn't know me!*

"Well he come in armed, didn't he? And he brung ye such a nice horse for a present," Thomas answered sarcastically. "Besides, we've strict orders to bring *everyone* to see the Cap'n."

"I see. Take him to the barn for now," Garland told the men, turning away. "Bring the other to my quarters. I shall question him first."

William watched him go, allowing a slightly painful

breath of relief. His next breath however, was sharp and caught in his throat as Garland paused and turned back, and took a step closer, staring for a moment. He looked as though he had something he wanted to say. The look of recognition returned to his eyes, but there was something else there. *Maybe he doesn't know me after all. Blessed Mother, please don't let him know me...*

"My lord?" One of the men began. "Is there anything more?"

Garland exhaled loudly, shaking his head, and at last, turned his back and began to walk away, giving his orders as he left. "Just water the horse and see that it's properly stabled. I'm sure the captain will be pleased. He's been bemoaning the lack of a proper mount since we got here."

"Aye, sir." They moved to follow Garland's orders as a third man took hold of Kindred and led her away ahead of them into the barn.

He didn't know me. William risked another painful breath of relief as he was turned and led away. He dared not glance over his shoulder to Ian, though he assumed he was being hauled similarly toward the garrison. *Ian is resourceful... he'll be fine. Ewan is behind us... he'll be fine... Blessed Mother, what have I led us to this time?*

"In ye go." The men unceremoniously released their grip, dropping William into a pile of hay in the stable. He landed with a thud, sending bright star-pains through his ribs. He scrambled to his hands and knees in a vain attempt to rush past the men.

"Hold on, where ye think ye goin?" One of the big men bent and picked him off the floor and carried him to the back of the stall, pushing him down against the railing. The man crouched in front of him, pointing a finger, and spoke as though he were scolding a child. "Sit! And don't ye move or fight with me. I've no use for ye kind what don't know ye place. So ye best be jus' sittin' back right here." His right hand suddenly raised, brandishing a long curved blade. "Or I'll cut ye so quick, ye'll be dead afore the first drop o' blood hits the floor." He laughed coldly. "You don't even know what I'm tellin' ye, do ye."

William stared at him, holding his tongue. It would not do for him to let on now that he understood every word. He looked at the blade only inches from his face and stealthily closed his hand around a fistful of straw. Keeping his eyes fixed squarely on the knife, he shrunk back meekly against the railing of the stall.

The man grinned and brought the knife to William's throat. "Good. You're afraid. You should be. You may live longer that way. Those two were braver than you and look at them." He gestured over a shoulder with his thumb, then pressed the knife firm against William's flesh, not quite cutting, but close.

William made a quick glance to where the man had pointed and knew that the blade at his throat was not an idle threat when he saw the still, dead forms of two native men, half shrouded under Akonni's hooded bear-skin cape.

"No!" William cried, then with a strength and speed even *he* was unaware he possessed, he pushed the straw into the soldier's face, scratching his eyes. The man fell back, dropping the blade, clutching at his eyes, cursing fiercely. William seized his moment and scrambled past on his hands and knees, grinding his teeth against the pain in his ribs. It was then he realized that, for the first time in longer than he could remember, his arms and shoulders felt strong and whole. His legs moved effortlessly, without the stiffness in the thighs that had been accompanying his crawling for the past weeks. *Annlise! You've done it!*

With a fury born of the new hope that burned from inside him, William planted his foot behind him and pushed off, an intangible yet certain belief that Annlise's ritual had been successful after all. He felt his toes make contact with the floor, the first sensations he had felt in years. In less than a heartbeat, despite the agony in his ribs, he pushed himself off the floor. Certain for the first time that his foot was soundly beneath him, he launched himself toward the stall gate, his left foot taking its proper turn after the right. Two steps, then four, he released a whooping cry of victory with each successive step.

But his victory was stolen from him before he was more than two paces away from the stall, when from behind, something hard and heavy came down on his head. He fell to the hay with a gasp. A second blow fell on him, and all he was aware of then was the sudden silence and blackness around him.

"Wake up."

A sharp strike to his cheek brought Ian suddenly back to himself. He slowly opened his eyes. The chair he was sitting in was familiar, the cushion worn to his own shape. It was his favorite chair that he'd spent many a winter's night sitting in beside the hearth fire, reading or conversing with his adoptive family. *Will's parlor.* He looked around, confused. It was the Philbrick parlor, no doubt, but the chair was the only thing about it that felt inviting. Melly's once lovely draperies hung in blackened shreds from the rods above the windows. The furniture, much of which William had spent months building in his workshop, was scarred and marked with burns from fallen embers. And though the soot and ash had been cleaned away, a heavy stench of burnt cloth and wood still permeated the room.

"Drink this."

A flask of liquid was shoved into his hand. Ian looked up to see a tall, thin, stern looking man glaring down his straight nose to him.

"It's only water. Drink it," the man told him, impatiently.

Ian took a tentative sip, then a larger mouthful when he was certain it truly was only water. "Thank you," he muttered, handing the flask back to the man, who began to seem familiar.

"My apologies for the brutality you've experienced. I assure you I bear no ill will toward you, sir." He sat opposite Ian in the chair where Melly had spent most of her evenings knitting or mending. He tented his fingers and half-smiled. "So tell me, how is it you came to be wandering the forest?"

"I explained before, Mr...."

"Forgive me. Garland. Peter Garland. I am your new governor." He extend a thin hand toward Ian. "And you are?"

A shudder of dread washed down Ian's spine as, at last, he recognized the man who sat before him. The last, and only, time they met was during William's trial. At that time Ian had been dressed in his cleric's robes, his hair cropped short above his ears and his face, clean shaven. Back then, he was known simply as 'Brother Ian'. He wondered if Garland would remember him now that his hair was long and his beard full. He hesitated only slightly before accepting a quick, curt, handshake.

"Proctor." Ian told him. "I— John. *John* Proctor." *No sense in revealing too much truth.*

"Mr. Proctor." Garland nodded, a momentarily skeptical lift in his brow. "I understand you were a resident to this settlement prior to the... well, unfortunate handling of the change of authority."

"The massacre, you mean," Ian said coldly. "Yes, I lived here. I was the doctor for the good people of this settlement."

"I see," Garland answered, unperturbed. "So you were familiar with many of the families who lived here?"

Ian nodded.

"Were you familiar with the family who occupied this particular dwelling?"

Before Ian could answer an armored sentry appeared in the doorway, carrying a bundle haphazardly in one hand. "My apologies, m' lord."

"What is it, Thomas?" Garland asked, glowering at the young soldier.

"I've got his belongins here, sir. We've searched them. No weapons. Only provisions, some clothes, a book or two. He seems to be what he says he is."

"Leave them and be gone," Garland ordered.

"Aye, m' lord."

Thomas dropped the bundle on the floor next to Ian's chair, spilling the contents. Ian caught his breath, then covered his reaction, hoping Garland did not notice when William's journal tumbled out of the pack, its front cover falling open. A smaller book— his own journal of herbal remedies— slid out, landing on top of William's. Ian casually bent, tidying the books into a neat stack next to his chair.

Garland reached down, picking up the smaller of the volumes and began randomly thumbing through the pages. "You seem quite good at your craft, Mr. Proctor. An impressive diary of remedies you have here." He paused in the latter part of the book. "Feverfew, white willow... ." He looked up, under his brow. "A good amount of native preparations. You've adapted well to this wild, untamed world. You even managed to befriend at least *one* savage."

Ian held his tongue, struggling to keep his tone calm and casual. "One has to adapt to survive, sir. With all due respect, I find the native people far less *savage* than those who descended on us this past spring."

Garland closed the book and handed it to Ian. "Perhaps." He bent, reaching for the other book, just as the door opened again. He stopped reaching, turning his attention to the door. Ian was grateful for the distraction. "What is it *now*, Thomas?"

"Best come with me, sir. There's trouble in the square... fight, sir. The savage attacked Fergus... we be needin' ye orders, sir."

Garland stood and followed Thomas to the door, then stopped. "Mr. Proctor, I shall ask you to remain here, guarded... for your own protection, you understand, until I return. Please, consider yourself my *guest* and make yourself comfortable. I shall return presently." He turned briskly, leaving the room, slamming the door behind him. There was no lock that Ian knew of on that door, but he heard the heavy voices and rattling of armor just beyond.

He took another drink of water, discovering his hands were shaking. Outside the window, he saw two more men patrolling the perimeter of the house. *Can't go out the window.* He tried to see the square, fearful of what may be happening to William in retaliation of his *attack.* The parlor did not look out on the square, and he could not see beyond the sentries anyway. Frustrated, he sank into his chair to think, his foot brushing against William's journal.

He picked it up, gingerly flipping through the pages. He'd never known until this day that the book had been charmed to appear different from what was actually written on the pages. As he turned the pages now, they appeared to him as they always had, neatly written in small script, a poem here, a drawing there. He allowed himself a false sense of relief that it all appeared innocent enough. *No magic in this book.* But when he turned to the page William had shown them earlier, his stomach quaked as the newly revealed words remained in clear view. And not just that one. He frantically flipped page after page, watching, mesmerized and terrified as the letters rearranged themselves on the pages. Soon every entry made prior to the crossing from Scotland had changed into an impressive and confounding collection of spells, potions, charms, and prayers to the Gods and Goddesses of the Old Gaelic religion. *A damning tome this would be. My God, Will, had this ever been seen before...* He turned to the page where he himself had begun writing entries while William was convalescing on the ship, lost in his coma.

4 October 1607
Mehlyndia has asked I keep this book for him while he cannot.
I shall do my best. ~ Ian

We are to sea for two days now and he has scarcely opened
his eyes but for moments at a time. But his sleep is natural and
untroubled, and this is a good sign. I am confident he should be
fully back to us in another day or so... .

Well I was wrong on that count. He flipped through his own
entries. None of those, of course, changed before his eyes.
The entries William had made since then, too, remained
static, unchanging on the parchment. The last entries
William had written were done recently during his time with
Akonni's people, chronicling the miracle of his healing and
his belief that he was no longer alone— his brother was with
him. *He believes... my God, who am I to doubt him after seeing*
all this? He fought a wave of emotion, reading Will's words.
The pain of losing his family, his anger, his desolation at the
loss of faith, yet he continued to write— for Seany:

Autumn, Date~ unsure. 1613.
Seany, it's been months since you trotted off to feed Dragon
and I left on that fateful trip into the woods. I write to you now
from a stump in the middle of this wilderness, alone and more
than likely near the end of my time. I don't know if this book
will ever find you but I'll try to be thorough and write as much
as I can in the hope that the day will come when you will read
it. First of all, son, please forgive your Papa for leaving too soon.
You know I meant to come back after only a day or two. I pray
that you and your mother got along well and the fates have been

kind in my absence. I miss you more than I can tell you.

My son, the day may come when you are confronted with tales about me that will seem fantastic in the telling, perhaps even frightening. I ask that you keep your heart and mind open, and believe me when I write this that I am not the demon they profess me to be. I only wanted to do what was just, and what was expected of me in the name of the Lady and the Lord...

The writing ended there, the script streaking off the page. Ian smiled sadly, realizing that Will had probably fallen asleep while writing. With a sense of grim resolution, he retrieved the ink and quill from the pack and opened to the end of the journal. His own faith that the book may someday make its way to Seany was far less than he knew William felt. But, for his friend, and so that someday Seany may know what happened at the end, he began to write:

12 October 1613
The new governor, a man named Peter Garland has arrived in Port Edin. He looked at me strangely, when I was brought to him, almost as though he knew me, though that would be unlikely as my appearance is vastly changed since last we met. I'm confident he does not know who I am, though it is only a matter of time until he does.

The door flew open suddenly and Ian dropped the book, his entry left unfinished.

"Come on, Cap'n will want to see you." An older guard picked Ian up gruffly by the shoulder and pushed him from the room. "Garland knows better'n to keep the cap'n waitin...

damned fool. Ye shoulda been brought in right away."

"There's no reason to be harsh, sir, I don't intend to fight—"

"Not yet! Are you daft? He said no interruptions." Another man, similarly armored, blocked the path of the one pulling Ian.

"He said he wanted to see all newcomers, no exceptions!"

"Yes, yes but not *now!*"

Using this slight distraction, Ian twisted himself sharply away from the guard's grasp and in a fool's effort, made a dash toward the door. He managed to turn the knob in his hand just before he hit the floor.

"Ladies, come in, please. Join me, won't you?" Adrian smiled invitingly.

"Go on, dear. Don't be shy," Bryndah cooed sweetly to the terrified looking woman who she escorted on her arm. "Remember, I'm right here... we're going to be fast friends, you and I. You've had a terrible ordeal, poor thing. All those months lost in the heathen forest. That's no place for a well-bred English lady, such as yourself. "

The woman smiled nervously, squeezing Bryndah's hand appreciatively with one hand, pulling her shawl around herself with the other.

"Please, dear lady, calm yourself." Adrian donned a look of empathy, speaking in a soft benevolent voice as he stood and graciously pulled a handkerchief from his sleeve, offering it to the woman as she lowered herself into a chair at the dining room table.

She released her talon-like grip on her shawl, accepting

the handkerchief, her face pasty white, her eyes wide and bulging within the sockets of her too-thin and pinched up face. She blew her nose with a grand honk. It was obvious she was frightened but Adrian was not as certain as the scout had been that she was deranged. During this interview, she had answered all of his questions clearly— if not longwindedly— freely offering what she apparently felt were unimportant details of the former daily existence of the good folk of Port Edin Settlement. Bryndah dabbed at the corners of her eyes with her handkerchief, shaking her head in well-rehearsed sympathy. It wasn't until he had asked her guest to elaborate on the demon she had mentioned to the scout that Adrian began to doubt her lucidity, as she began to ramble in some unintelligible twaddle about ghosts in the forest.

"I saw him, proud as proud is, right here before me! A hideous ghost in the woods... he looked at me... nay *through* me, I could feel his eyes burning me... those demon eyes!" She covered her face with her shawl, shaking with an inconsolable sobbing that could have moved even Adrian— had he not been at the end of his patience— to tears to witness.

He crouched down next to her, bringing his mouth close to her ear, and spoke again in a soothing susurration. "There, there sweet lady. You're away from that dreadful forest and those ungodly heathens. Now, Josephine— may I call you that? Or, do you prefer Goody Ashcrofte?"

She nodded, a shy curl on her lip. "Josephine, if ye please, my lord."

"Adrian, madam. You may call me as such. Drink your ale- that's fine English ale you know." He flashed a quick wink to Bryndah behind Josephine's back. She returned it in kind.

"You're very kind, my lo— Adrian." She peeked up sheepishly over her shawl, drawing in a long staggering breath. "I scarcely remember the last time I had *real* ale."

He patted her hand and offered her a warm smile before he took his seat at the head of the table. "Now, let us forget the unpleasantness in the forest for the moment, shall we? I'm fascinated to learn more of the family who lived here." He gestured toward the fireplace where a small wooden horse sat idle on its rockers, a stringed musical devise resting up against it. "A family named... oh what was it?" He creased his brown, snapping his thumb and forefinger. "Phillips... Flintbrick... ."

"Philbrick," she told him, then sipped delicately at her ale, raising a brow to him as she looked over her cup.

"Ah, yes. Philbrick." Adrian smiled, then leaned on his arm over the table, grinning as one of her friends might do before learning a juicy piece of gossip. "Tell me about the Philbricks."

"Can you see anything?"

Duncan looked back over his shoulder down to the bottom of the maple tree he had climbed in an attempt to get a clear view of the perimeter fence. Annlise looked up, biting her lip, flinching each time a branch creaked under his feet. "I see a lot of trees, but not much else." He looked back toward the village, squinting against the setting sun. He cursed himself silently for not thinking to take his spy glass out of his pack before he climbed the tree.

"Any sign of Will and Ian?" Ewan called up.

"No," Duncan answered. He looked up toward the top of

the maple, judging himself to be more than three-quarters of the way to the top. The branches thinned out considerably as he ascended, and his footing became less sure. The slightest breeze sent the tree swaying like a ship on a stormy sea. He set his foot in a notch and hoisted himself a bit higher, clinging to the trunk as it pitched and yawed in the wind. His left foot slipped, rolling off a narrow branch, nearly sending him plummeting but he righted himself right away.

"Careful!" Annlise cried. "Oh, lad, come ye down here. If ye can't see anything, there be no sense in riskin' ye neck to look."

"I'm all right," Duncan insisted catching his breath. *You've lost your mind, Wilbrun. Or are you, truly, trying to break your neck?* "I'm almost there." He worked his way up another four feet or so, all the while questioning the wisdom of his own insistence that he climb the damned tree instead of allowing Ewan to do it, as the older man had originally proposed. *I'm too stubborn for my own good.* He climbed higher still until there were no more branches large enough to bear his weight. "I made it!" His new higher perch rewarded him, at last, with a fairly unobstructed view of the fence just opposite the barn. "I see it!" He called down, excited. "The opening behind the barn is unguarded! Looks like we may just be able to get in the same way we came out."

"Good lad!" Ewan called, grinning, shaking a fist in a gesture of victory. "Come on down, now, afore Annlise worries herself into a palsy," he bellowed, laughing.

"I'll worry if I choose, Ewan McDonough. That's a far fall with a good hard ground below," Annlise retorted, twisting her apron in her hands. "Ye be careful, Duncan."

"I'm always careful," Duncan muttered, taking one last look past the village to the sea beyond. "Hold on, then!"

"What lad? Ye see somethin?" Ewan called.

"Can't be sure..." Duncan narrowed his eyes against the glare of the sunset reflecting on the ocean, "but it looks like... it is! Ewan, there's a ship comin!"

"A ship?" Annlise gasped spinning on her heel to look for herself. "I can't see through the trees, are you sure?"

"Aye! Be there, clear as day."

"What colors be they flying?" Ewan asked, a concerned grimace coming to his face.

"Can't tell for certain, Ewan, but... the sun is gleaming on the masthead... .and it looks like..." he shook his head in frustration that no matter how hard he squinted he just could not see the details of the ship. "I can't tell. It could be Lord Ogham, himself, for all I know."

"No." Annlise said simply, a strange trance-like cast coming to her face; she smiled oddly.

"What is it, lass?" Ewan took one of her hands in his.

"Don't you see? He said the ship was coming, he's been saying it for days. It's Edward's ship. I know it is."

Ewan grinned and pulled her close. "Aye, lass, I believe ye may be right." He released her slowly, then looked up to where Duncan sat in the tree. "Lad, come on down now."

Duncan waved, then began his descent. A sudden blustery wind took hold of the tree, thrashing the thin branches near the top whip-like against his skin and deafening him to everything other than the whining wail it made. He threw his arms around the trunk, and hugged it for a moment until the wind died. When the wind left his ears, the first thing he heard were Annlise's frantic cries to him from below.

"Blessed Mother! Come down slowly, lad. Watch your—"

"Wait! Hush!" Duncan called down. He froze, cupping his hand around his ear, listening for what he thought was the sound an angry mob. *Not again!* He held his breath, straining to hear more, when a cacophonic chorus of swallows took to flight from a nearby oak. "What the—" Duncan tightened his grasp on the trunk as the flock scattered, passing him on all sides, then up and away to the open sky. He followed them with his eyes, as they swirled cloud-like to the sky where he saw the likely culprit that had sent the birds winging; a lone golden eagle turning lazy circles, directly above the tree. He grinned and exhaled in relief.

"What is it, lad?" Ewan shouted.

Duncan was about to call down that it was only a flock of birds when again the chaotic sound came to him and this time, there was no mistaking the voices of shouting men and the agitated whinnies of a horse for sparrows. "Something's happening in the village!" He scrambled down the tree, haphazardly sliding down over small branches, nimbly planting his feet in the crooks of larger branches until he was low enough to leap to the ground, landing in a crouch only two paces from Ewan. "Fight of some kind... I heard them. Sounded like another riot. I couldn't see beyond the fence."

Ewan helped him to his feet. "How many? Could you tell?"

Duncan shook his head, still regaining his breath. "Hard to say... at least a dozen... maybe more. And at least one horse involved."

"Will and Ian," Annlise gasped, bringing her palm to her throat. "They've been found out!"

Ewan frowned, looking to Duncan. "Could you tell if it was them?"

"No... but it's a fair guess that she's right. Kindred is the only horse we've seen since we arrived. It has to be her."

Ewan nodded his agreement. He picked up Duncan's pack and tossed it to him. "Come on, then. We move now. Back in through the barn, then whatever it takes to get them out of there." He turned without waiting for an answer, leading the way back to the path to Port Edin— Duncan and Annlise following without argument.

"What about all that talk of following orders? I mean, I fully agree we need to move—"

"I am following orders!" Ewan stopped abruptly, spinning on his heel causing Duncan to nearly collide with him. "My orders come from Lord Edward... same as always. Only this time, I don't think Will is going to be upset with me for following Edward's orders over his. Do you?" He set a furious glare on Duncan. "Besides, I told him straight out I had no intention of leaving him behind. He's expectin' us, Duncan."

Duncan stared wide-eyed, stunned at Ewan's sudden anger. He had heard several accounts of the day William had been arrested, each version slightly different from the next, yet each containing one common element; Ewan McDonough, second in command under Sean in William's personal guard, stood down and allowed Adrian and his mercenary hunters to drag the man, whom he had sworn a death oath to protect, away bound and bridled from Drumoak. Duncan had never fully believed it had been that simple and that, surely Ewan and Simon had put up *some* sort of resistance. He'd always held to his own truth that they had fought gallantly, despite the odds, surrendering only when the last of Edward's guard had been bereft of their blades. But now, it was clear to him; Ewan *had* stepped aside. *No wonder he is so determined.* "Ewan, I meant no—"

"The daylight's waning," Annlise spoke up, ending argument.

"Aye. We need to get moving," Ewan answered her without taking his eyes off Duncan. "Any questions?"

"Only one. Why are we still standing here?" Duncan asked, a slow smirk curling the corner of his lip. "Let's go get Will and Ian."

Ewan's angry grimace softened into a grin as he slapped Duncan on the shoulder. "Good lad." He turned and resumed his determined march to Port Edin.

"He's not goin' to be able to answer any questions. He's still out cold."

"Mmm?" Ian turned his head slightly toward the sound of the voices that found him. "Who's out?" he began to ask, when another voice joined the first.

"Captain is getting impatient."

"He won't want to be seein' this one 'til he's done with that old biddy anyhow. And if this one still be out, then we just bring in the savage."

Savage? Will? Lying on his back, unaware of where he was, Ian listened carefully trying to identify where the voices were coming from. They sounded muted, as though the speakers were contained within a wooden box. He forced his eyes open, but there was nothing around him to see but blackness. He rubbed his eyes, then blinked them a couple of times just to be sure they were truly open.

"Won't get much from the Indian. Doesn't even speak the language. It's *this* one who the captain will be more interested in. And he's not goin' anywhere." The comment was punctuated by a loud thump that sounded like it was coming from a spot just above Ian's head.

It's not they who are boxed in... Ian flayed his hands out before him in near panic, half expecting to feel the confining lid of some sort of box above him. He sighed in relief that his hands only met with air. He felt along the floor to the wall, following it with his palms from corner to corner, realizing the box he was in was more likely a closet. He allowed himself a moment to breathe, slouching down opposite from the wall he assumed was the door. To his surprise, the panel he leaned on gave way slightly when he leaned on it. *This must be the door.* He quietly shifted toward the other side, then stopped, confused when he saw the sliver of light that shone through a crack in the panel. *No... this* is *the door... that's candle light.* He ran his hand along the side wall hoping he would find... *there it is!* His hand came to rest on a knothole in the wall. *I'm in Will's magic closet!* He pulled the knot to open the panel that concealed the rope that lifted the closet to the second floor, the wood squeaking against the hinge.

"Did you hear that?" one of the muffled voices asked. Ian froze, daring not to breathe.

"Hear what?" The other answered.

"I think the gov'na's *guest* may be comin' round."

Ian quickly laid back and closed his eyes to narrow slits, holding his breath for several long moments as the door creaked open and the closet was slowly illuminated with the approaching glow of a candle.

"Is he awake?" A man asked.

A rough-calloused hand took hold of Ian's chin and turned his head back and forth a couple of times. He fought the urge to grab the hand, forcing himself to submit to the inspection as he had no means to defend himself and was unsure of how many soldiers may be occupying the house.

"No, he's still out. Fergus mus've clocked him harder than he thought." The owner of the hand grunted, then stood and left the closet, closing the door. Ian heard the scraping of the latch hook on the outside of the door, the one Will had insisted be there to prevent Seany from playing in the closet.

Ian waited, not moving, the beating of his own heart echoing through his ears. *Calm down... they think I'm sleeping... good, let them think it.* As his eyes adjusted to the blackness, he could begin to see the flicker of candlelight filtering through a minute crack in the door. It was just enough to reveal the outline of the panel, which remained slightly ajar. Carefully, desperately trying not to make a sound, he got to his feet. *Damned thing always did squeak... lift the panel slightly... don't let it rub...* He lifted and pulled the panel open, relieved that he was able to swing it open silently. He reached inside the alcove, feeling for the pulley rope but only found an empty space in the hollow of the wall. A new fear was born in him that the rope may have been damaged in the fire or gnawed away by rats. If he could find it, would he be able to pull it silently?

Dear Father, let me have this one... please? Where is it?

When his hand finally found the rope, he wrapped his fingers around it tightly, testing the tautness. *Thank you,*

Father! There's no slack, it's still here. Pull... quietly... As he had a hundred times before, in the days when William depended on him to move him around the house, Ian grasped the pull rope, one hand above the other and prepared to lift the closet to the second floor. He had never taken notice of how loud or quiet the lifting mechanism was, as he had never had the need to do it silently before now. He made a short test pull, barely enough to move anything yet enough to turn the pulley and lift slightly. To his dismay, he heard the familiar whine of the rope on the pulley and groan of the wood. He released the rope, slowly easing the box back down. Though the sound was not terribly loud, there was no chance he could hoist the closet to the second floor without making *some* noise.

He stood silently, rethinking his plan. There was only one way to get out of the closet unseen; through the door on the second floor. His heart sank, realizing that the second floor door would also be latched from the outside. Another safety precaution William had taken for Seany's sake. But that hook was smaller and was designed to keep a five-year-old boy *out,* not a thirty-five year old apothecary *in.* With enough effort, he was certain he could break it open. *More noise.* He slouched against the wall, discouraged at his predicament.

A man's voice, drifted in through the back wall, where the dining room was. It was the first time Ian realized he could hear the conversations from both rooms within the closet.

The man in the dining room spoke with a refined, gentlemanly articulation, far more eloquent than any he had heard used by the soldiers. His voice had a cloying, non-threatening lilt, as he spoke to his guest.

"Dear lady, thank you for your most... *illuminating* visit."

Ian recognized Josephine Ashcrofte's pathetic voice answering.

"You mustn't think ill of me, sir. You must appreciate how difficult it is for me to... say these things. After all, the Philbricks were like family to me."

Family? Josephine, what have you done now? Ian cupped his hand around his ear trying to better hear the conversation.

"Ah, my dear, I understand. But truth is truth, is it not? And truth is always rewarded. Now, you must understand that I am thoroughly convinced that what you've told me is the absolute truth, but since the master of the house is no longer in residence... as it were... we will need certain proof to bring back to the magistrates."

"Proof? He built the very house you sit in!" Josephine replied, and Ian could just imagine the gossipy expression on her pinched-up face.

"I cannot bloody well bring a house back to Scotland!" The man snapped, impatiently, then silenced himself.

Who is that? I know that voice... he's playing with her for information...

"Forgive me, please, Josephine. I did not mean to be rude."

He paused, and Ian heard him cross the room to the buffet that occupied the space directly behind the closet. He poured a drink— Ian could hear the liquid hitting one of the pewter mugs and the thud of the carafe being placed back on the buffet.

"I must beg your indulgence for my ill-temper. This climate does not agree with my body, it seems. I've been bedeviled in my gut with cramps. It tends to make me...

unpleasant."

Bilious stomach... so that is the captain. But I know that voice!

"What sort of proof do you need, Adrian?" Josephine asked, meekly.

"Adrian?" Ian gasped out loud, then clamped his hand over his mouth, nervously looking over his shoulder to the door, but it was apparent no one heard him. *That's impossible... no one knew... how could he know? Father in Heaven, of all people...*

"Oh... something to prove beyond doubt that he was truly here." Adrian continued, "Something that will not be disputed, you see. This little carved trinket, for instance, would be perfect. The work is not as detailed as some I've seen in and about Stonehaven, but it certainly looks like Fylbrigge to me. But, that is only my opinion. There is no proof of the artisan who carved it. And even if we could prove it to be his work, there is nothing to prove that it wasn't carved years ago. You see my problem? I need something... dated."

Ian's stomach turned as it came to his mind instantly that the proof Adrian needed was standing unconcealed in the corner lot of the little cemetery behind the chapel. To his horror, he was not alone in his thought.

"There was a bad fever last winter," she began coyly. "Nearly every family in the settlement was affected." The chair scraped the floor, and Ian heard her footsteps approaching the buffet.

"What proof does this offer?" he asked, sounding more irritated than intrigued.

"The baby—"

Ian did not hear what Josephine was saying as the

conversation in the dining room was suddenly drowned out by the sound of the kitchen door being flung open, banging on its hinge. "Blasted savage, I should flay his gullet like a fish! Damn near blinded me, he did, tryin to run off! He didn't get far I can tell you, and I took care to see that he won't!"

The commotion of several chairs being pushed back and hitting the floor, and steel booted feet tromping the wooden floor made it impossible for Ian to hear what more was said. *Will! My God what did they do?* Ian seized the opportunity the noise provided to jump to his feet and, without a second thought, he pulled wildly on the hoist rope, unconcerned with the sound it would make, his only thought to find the hidden cache of firearms and get out to find his friend. He knew without thought, from habit, that it took only five hand-over-hand pulls to bring the closet completely to the second level. The pulley wheel had rusted with disuse and whined in protest at being called into service, the wood of the closet groaned and creaked as it was hoisted but Ian did not stop, reasoning the sound of the closet was louder to him than it would be out there and would be buried in the confusion anyway. He reached the top and pulled the clamp down onto the rope that prevented the closet from crashing back to the first floor.

Straight out, two steps across the hall to my old room... please God, let it be empty. He pushed on the door and as he expected, the hook was in place. He pushed with his shoulder and all his weight, and it easily gave way just as he hoped it would. *I'll fix that for you later, Will...* He pushed the door open; it was dark in the hall way. *Good! That means no guards.* He knew the house well enough to negotiate the rooms without a candle. He carefully left the closet, staying crouched, listening to the melee from the kitchen below. Moonlight flooded the hall through a gaping hole in the roof, providing him enough light to see his path. The door to his former room was blocked by charred debris but he managed to climb over and push the door open.

The room was in a shambles of fallen roofing and timbers, the walls blackened with soot. The full moon shone bright on the splintered remnants of the bed and dresser. This room seemed to have taken the brunt of the damage during the raid. Ian mused that if it had not been for William's funeral, he may very well have been asleep in that bed when the roof collapsed onto it. *I'll have to remember to thank Will for his timing...* He pushed the door closed behind him as best as he could, before intrepidly journeying into the treacherous terrain of his bedroom. Past the fallen armoire and over a shattered rocking chair, he placed his footsteps carefully as to not make any sound that may carry to the lower level. He knew it was only a matter of time before someone opened the closet in the kitchen expecting to find him there, only to find it empty. He half-laughed, imagining the dumbfounded expressions on the lunkheads who put him there. *Perhaps they'll think me a witch as well. But Adrian is no fool, and won't take him long to figure out how the pulley works... no time to ponder, Ian... find it! Where is the damned panel?*

He was startled by the sound of footsteps in the corridor on the opposite side of the wall. He crouched down behind the ruined armoire, listening.

"The attic door is at the end of this corridor."

Josephine.

"Watch your step, my dear, it's frightfully dangerous. I'd not like to see you tumble through a weak spot in the floor." Adrian chuckled.

Let her tumble clear to Hell! What is she leading him to?

Ian hesitated, undecided between finishing his search for the secret panel that led to William's cache of arms or to creep out of his hiding place to follow Josephine and Adrian. *And what will you do when you catch up with them? Get a weapon, fool, then follow.*

The door at the end of the corridor creaked open. "We're fortunate this end of the house is still intact," Josephine commented. "It should still be right at the top of these stairs. My dear husband, Ephraim— God rest his soul— was kind enough to carry it up here himself for her, the very day the child passed on, you see."

"Kind of him indeed," Adrian replied. "To spare a grieving mother the heartbreak of looking upon an empty cradle."

The cradle? Ian thought, as he listened to their footsteps and scraping of heavy objects in the attic above him. *How incredibly cold hearted.*

Josephine's muffled voice came through the ceiling. "The carving is crude, but still, I'm sure it is what you need."

Ian, jaw clenched tight in disgust over Josephine's duplicity, continued his search of the wall, running his hand along the wainscoting, feeling for the indentation he knew would open the panel. It only took a moment to find the proper spot. *Please let it still open,* he prayed, glancing at the crumbled wall and ceiling. It was more than possible that the panel would not open properly. He turned the indented piece of wainscot until he felt the latch on the inside of the wall release, then carefully pulled the panel open. He managed to open it about a foot before it caught on a beam that had fallen through the ceiling. The charred timber groaned, sending a hail of soot raining down onto his head. Ian stepped away quickly, fearing it would fall. After a moment, he put his shoulder to the door and pushed with all his strength, gaining another foot. More soot fell on him but he kept pushing until the space was wide enough for him to pass into the secret passage. He slid into the dark chamber just as the timber gave way and crashed to the floor.

"Damn!" He quickly pulled the door shut, and waited.

Less than a heartbeat later, he heard the clattering of armored feet tromping up the stairs, opening and closing the bedroom doors as they approached the room he was in. Ian heard them slam the door to the magic closet, shaking his head in wonder that no one had yet discovered his absence. The door to his own room squeaked open. Debris and broken furniture was pushed about.

"It's all right, Thomas," the intruder called out. "Just more timber fallin'. Surprised this whole end o' the building hasn't fallen yet." He was answered by another man from somewhere on the opposite end of the corridor.

Ian released the breath he hadn't realized he'd been holding onto when he heard the bedroom door swing shut again. It was completely black in the cubby behind the wall. He felt around in the pockets of his overcoat until he found the small tinder kit he always carried. He offered a hurried prayer of thanks that it had not been confiscated. He fumbled in the dark with the little kit, feeling for the flint stone and the filings that would light the little candle he carried. Setting the filings in the tin lid of the box on the floor before him, he felt around in another pocket looking for his hunting knife to strike the flint stone. "Damn!" He had not been so lucky with the knife as he had with the tinder box and was forced to abandon the idea of lighting a candle as he had no steel in which to make the spark. He carefully pushed the panel open slowly and listened. Satisfied the intruder had truly left, he pushed it open as far as he could, flooding the cubby with moonlight.

The moonlight seemed as bright as day after the complete blackness he'd been in. He could clearly see the object of his quest now; the muskets, neatly stacked in the cubby behind him. "Thank you, Father in Heaven!" He marveled for a moment that they were actually still there and miraculously untouched by the fire that had destroyed the room just opposite the wall where they lay. Even more miraculous, he realized he had put the tinder box down only inches away from a tin of gunpowder. "Thank you again!" He laughed nervously, realizing that had he been able to light his candle, he may have very well caused an explosion in the cubby.

"Now, let's see how prepared Will truly was. Powder, tamper, musket balls..." He fumbled with the weapon, cursing his ineptitude with it— he'd never fired a gun in his life— uncertain if the powder or the ball went first, or how much powder was needed in the pan under the flint. "This is useless! The best I could do is hit someone with the handle!" He tried again to work out the mechanics of the thing, his hands beginning to shake with frustration. Below him, in the kitchen, a grumble of surprised voices rose up and he heard the repeated slamming of the closet door.

"He's vanished!"

"Impossible!"

"Who left the door unguarded?"

"No one! We never left the room!"

"He did not just vanish into mist; find him!"

I'm found out. Ian grabbed a leather satchel that had been stored in the cubby, hurriedly stashed a handful of lead pellets and a horn of gunpowder into it, and slung it across his shoulder. Along with the muskets were two smaller flintlock pistols that he decided would be less unwieldy. He tucked one in the strap of the satchel and kept the other in his hand as he crept out of the cubby, navigating the debris along the floor toward the far wall.

Something hard crashed to the attic floor above him, followed by scuffling sounds against the wall. *They've found the cradle.* Ian held his breath straining to make out the conversation from above.

"No date! No signature... did the man take *no* pride in his artistry that he should leave every damned piece without a mark? Just more pathetic ivy and filigree!" Adrian shouted, his anger punctuated by a sudden loud crash of wood splitting against wood, which sent a shower of soot and dust down where Ian crouched. "I need damned solid evidence!"

Ian exhaled in relief, crossing himself nervously, stifling the half-crazed laughter he felt coming.

"But I can assure you, he carved it for Christmas last—"

The door slammed shut and Josephine's prattle was obscured by the sound of running feet and more shouts, this time coming from the stairwell.

"What's all the commotion?" Adrian asked.

"Cap'n... sir... newcomer." A breathless soldier had apparently charged up the stairs and Ian assumed by the echo of his voice that he remained in the stairwell while he addressed his captain.

"Newcomer? When?" Adrian demanded.

"He come in just before sunset. Said he were the 'pothecary—"

"Proctor!" Josephine's shrill gasp chimed in.

"The companion you told me of?" Adrian asked.

"We only had but the one apothecary, it can't be another. And thick they were together, too, I can tell you." Josephine confirmed. "Scarcely ever did I see one without the other close by."

"Where is he now?"

After a hesitant pause, the soldier answered, "He was locked in a closet in the kitchen, but... now... ye see, he's gone, sir. Vanished."

"Gone? From a locked closet? Was it left unguarded?"

"N-no—" The soldier was suddenly silent and Ian heard the unmistakable thud of a body rolling down the stairs, followed by a brief surprised whimper from Josephine.

Before he could hear more, the corridor and stairs became alive with clattering armor and tromping boots. No longer concerned with being quiet, Ian scrambled across the rubble to the trap door under the window that led to the outside. He threw aside the charred remains of the little rag rug that covered the door, and grabbed the ring that served as a handle, opening the hatch. He jumped to the ground, allowing the trap door to slam shut behind him, sending a sharp echo reverberating under the eaves. Ian had to dive behind the rain barrel when he heard approaching footsteps. Two guards rounded the corner of the house just as Ian gained the cover of the shadows. They patrolled from one end of the garrison to the other.

When the guards disappeared around the corner, he crept out of the shadow, clutching one pistol in his right hand tightly and feeling for the security of the other tucked into the belt of the satchel with the other.

The moon was brilliant, peeking out through a thin veil of milky clouds, casting an unearthly glow on the landscape of Port Edin. From his vantage point, he could clearly see two armed men flanking the open barn door, one of them alert, the other leaning against the door frame, arms crossed over his chest, his head nodding. The inside of the barn was illuminated with the orange glow of an oil lamp that hung from a rafter near the stall. A third man paced back and forth keeping a vigilant guard over a man clad in buck-skins, lying prone on the hay-strewn floor, his hands bound behind him, and ankles crossed and lashed together with a length of hemp rope. *Will! Dear God! Please don't let him be...* He watched closely for a moment, then nearly wept in a wave of relief when he saw William's arms move slightly and his hands open and close, grasping at his bonds. *Hold on, Will, I'll think of something.*

Before leaving the protective shadow of the garrison, he plotted his course; rain barrel to wagon, wagon to hay bales, then finally, to the back side of the barn, where he hoped the escape hatch was still blissfully unguarded and he would find Ewan and Duncan waiting ready to sneak into the barn. He would need to warn them about the guard at the barn door once he got that far. The sky was fairly cloudless, offering little protection from the moon's betraying light, but a small swirl of clouds born on a fast moving wind offered him the moment's cover he needed. He ran, light on his feet, slyly staying within the meager shadows point to point until he reached the hay bales. He abandoned any hope of reaching the back of the barn unseen when the clouds parted, flooding the barn in renewed moonlight.

Crouching breathlessly behind the bales, only yards from the guards at the barn door, he removed the satchel from his shoulder. The gun in his right hand trembled fiercely, nearly slipping from his sweaty palm as he clumsily removed the lid from the powder tin with his left hand. He had no idea of how much powder should go into the barrel or the pan under the flint, but he thought it best to err on the side of too much, rather than too-little and filled the barrel nearly half-way before jamming a palm full of pellets into the end. The sack containing the remainder of the pellets slipped from his hand, landing in the gravel with a muffled jingle.

The guard closest to Ian thumped his companion on the shoulder, startling him out of a doze. "You hear something, Duff?"

"Hmm? Where?" Duff yawned. "Oh, blimey, Fred, just when I was about to convince Nelly Dix to—"

"Come on, man, look alive." The guard thumped Duff again. "Ye still on guard duty, ye know."

"Guard duty!" Duff spat on the ground. "Would you tell me why it takes three men to guard one sorry Indian?"

Fred held up a hand, signaling Duff's silence, gesturing with a jerk of his head toward Ian's hiding place. "Thought I heard somethin' from o'er there."

Ian shrunk down as far as he could, remaining as still as was possible, watching through a gap in the bales.

"So go see," Duff grumbled. "I'll cover ye post"

"Right." Fred unsheathed his sword and turned toward the bale.

Ian shrank back as far as he could into the shadow, the pistol held tightly in his two hands as his shaking thumb slowly pulled the hammer back. Fred approached slowly, squinting his eyes, peering into the shadows and probing the ground and scattered debris with his sword.

"Captain's comin!" Duff called.

Fred spun on his heel and hurried back to his post.

Ian exhaled, lowering the weapon slightly.

Adrian strode to the center of the common, each hand clenching a pistol. The moonlight glinted off the muzzles of the guns. The menacing sneer and strange golden eyes had not changed in the six years since Ian had last encountered him, and the very sight of the man was enough to make Ian's blood boil in his veins.

"Attention! Every half-witted one of you!"

The guards snapped to attention, several coming out of cottages, some coming from the garrison, all going to the common where Adrian stood. Ian held a moment of hope Will's guards would leave the barn just long enough for him to slip in through the big doors. He crouched forward, ready to move at his first opportunity. Duff whistled to Fred, beckoning with his hand, and the two hurried together to the square. Ian slunk along the side of the barn, being careful to stay within the shadows until he was close enough to peer into the barn through the space between the open door and the jam. To his dismay, the last guard had remained at his post within the barn, though he now stood with his back to his captive looking out through the doors toward the square. Ian took some comfort in seeing that William had come around and had managed to roll to his side, his eyes trained keenly on the guard, his arms struggling against the bonds as he carefully sidled backwards toward the hay.

Ian felt around the ground near the foundation for something, anything, he could toss to divert the guard's attention. Almost instantly, his hand closed around a palm-sized stone. The guard stepped forward, stopping even with the threshold.

Come on, two more steps and you'll be out in the open... clear shot. Ian readied himself to hurl the stone, creeping as close to the barn as possible. He looked through the crack again, checking again on William, who had managed to back himself another couple of feet closer to the hay. The guard made a quarter turn and paced a few steps away from where Ian crouched. William lay perfectly still, following the guard's movement with his eyes. While the guard was turned, Ian waved his hand behind the crack in the door, hoping to get William's attention, but the guard turned around before William looked in his direction, forcing him to shrink back against the wall.

Ian was suddenly startled by a gunshot, fired by Adrian to the sky from the middle of the square. He fell against the barn, dropping the stone, and nearly losing his grip on his own pistol. He pressed his hand to his mouth to prevent himself from crying out.

"Garland!" Adrian shouted, then raised his left hand and fired the second pistol. "Garland! Come out here!"

Garland? Dear God. Ian stole a quick look into the barn, to see if William was aware of who it was who was shouting in the square. One quick glance gave him his answer. William was keenly aware and had stopped struggling, laying still as a stone, the color gone from his face, his eyes wide and fixed on Adrian.

The soldiers stood at attention, none seeming to dare to move as Adrian readied one of his pistols for another shot. "Garland! Do not make me wait!"

A moment later, Peter Garland, bearing a lantern in one hand and something that looked like a book in the other, strolled unhurried and seemingly unimpressed with Adrian's authority, to the middle of the square.

"You really should consider relaxing, Adrian. You'll burst a vein with your shouting," Garland said, simply.

"I've no more patience with you," Adrian growled, his teeth locked as he spoke. "You were to tell me when there were newcomers. Yet I find that two have come and I was not informed. My time has been wasted in idle prattle with an old woman when I could have been questioning someone more informative."

Garland's grin widened though his icy blue eyes remained cold. "I questioned the apothecary in the garrison before I was called away on some trivial matter. When I returned, he had been removed. I assumed he had been brought to you." He cast his eyes in an arc to the men who stood around him, then back to Adrian, raising a brow. "Apparently not. Ah, well. At least *my* time was spent more productively. I've made a most interesting discovering among the apothecary's belongings." He glanced to the book he held.

Adrian raised the pistol and pointed it under Garland's chin. Ian was astonished that the judge barely flinched, keeping his grin and stare cold and hard.

"You cost me my proof in not informing me, yourself!" Adrian pulled the hammer back. "The man has fled."

"Fled?" Garland clucked his tongue sarcastically. "Pity. He could have concocted a potion or something to make your disposition more tolerable. But I shouldn't mourn the loss of your precious proof too grievously, Adrian. All the proof you need is right here in my hand." Garland laughed, pushing the book into Adrian's ribs.

It was then Ian realized what Garland had in his hand when the light from the lantern fell on the cover. Even from the distance he was from the men, he could clearly see the embossed image of the diving hawk and the initials W.F. *No!* He crept forward as far as he dared and raised his own pistol again.

Adrian lowered his own pistol, looking at the cover. "Where did this come from?"

"I told you. It was among the possessions brought in by the apothecary." Garland cocked his head smugly. "I take it, you know what this is."

Adrian caught his breath staring at the book, a salacious hungry grin spreading under his golden eyes. He holstered his pistols and took the book from Garland, caressing the tooled cover like a lover. "Oh, yes," he replied, not taking his eyes from Garland. "Fylbrigge's jour—"

Before Adrian could open the cover, Ian closed his eyes

and squeezed the trigger. An ear-shattering crack of gunfire exploded from the over-loaded pistol, the backlash sending him flailing backwards, crashing against the barn. A muddy darkness crept over him. He had the vague sensation of hot liquid flowing over his face as he stared skyward. The last thing lan Proctor saw before the darkness swallowed him was the regal wingspan of an eagle, silhouetted by the full moon as it turned slow circles over his head.

Chapter 21

EWAN CREPT QUIETLY along the stockade fence at the gate side of Port Edin. A sentry paced the opening. Ewan watched for another moment to be certain there were no others. A moment later, a voice from within the stockade called out and the sentry responded with a wave of his hand.

Ewan made a soft trilling sound, mimicking the call of a night bird as a signal to Duncan, who was surveying the east side near the opening to the barn. *Only one at the gate. More inside.* He waited a moment until Duncan's return call echoed through the trees. *Two men, no way in, coming back around.* A moment later, a third call from the north— Annlise, *six.* Ewan sounded another signal and the three rejoined in a thicket behind a large bolder just west of the main gate.

"The two I saw seemed easy enough," Duncan explained. "But without my sword, I didn't wish to risk it."

"Wise choice," Ewan told him. "First thing we do is get you a weapon." He peered over the boulder, watching the lone sentry pace back and forth in front of the gate. "His will do." He looked up toward the cloud covered moon, frowning. "The wind is not on our side. Those clouds won't last long; we'll have to be quick if we're to stay unseen."

"Don't fear on that, Ewan," Annlise whispered, placing her hand over her necklace. "We won't be seen."

Duncan grinned, tapping Ewan's shoulder. "Trust her."

"I always do," Ewan replied with a wink.

Duncan nodded and crept out stealthily away from the concealing thicket, keeping a keen eye on the gate, Ewan following a pace behind. Suddenly two more men appeared from within the gate.

"Down!" Duncan gasped in a harsh whisper.

Ewan nodded but stepped on a dried branch that snapped loudly under his foot.

The three men at the gate turned toward the sound, one making a motion for the other two to investigate. Ewan shrank into the shadow as far as he could, then noticed Duncan's dirk shining plainly in the moonlight. *He'll be seen!* He dared not risk another bird call, as the sentries were approaching quite close now. Duncan stood stone still as the clouds moved away from the moon, revealing even more of him in its light.

Behind Ewan, Annlise muttered something under her breath in the strange language she used in her toning. She slowly crouched down on one knee and turned her face toward the moon resting her hand on her throat while rapidly repeating her strange chant over and over. The sentry was within ten paces now. Ewan watched helplessly as the man drew his sword and turned toward Duncan.

Ewan reached carefully for his own blade, ready to strike if he must. To his amazement the sentry— looking directly at Duncan— sheathed his sword, turned on his heel, and headed back to the gate, calling to his companions, "Must be squirrels."

Ewan exhaled, amazed at what he had just seen. *He didn't see him! He could have reached out and touched Duncan...*

but he didn't see him! He turned to see Annlise smiling at him, tipping her head slightly. "You're a wonder, lassie," he mouthed to her, grinning.

The second sentry approached, equally oblivious to Ewan's presence as the first was to Duncan's. He held his breath. As soon as the soldier was within arm's reach, Ewan knocked the man to the ground with the hilt of his sword. The sentry landed with a thud in the under duff. Wasting no time, Ewan took the man's sword and tossed it to Duncan, then took his musket and powder horn for himself.

Annlise hurried out from behind the rock and secured the man's hands behind his back with a strip of linen. She tied a second strip across his mouth to prevent him from alerting the others.

"Done," she said, checking the bonds one more time.

Ewan motioned for her to hurry. "Stay between us, lass. One more man and we're clear."

"He'll be lookin' after this other one in a moment," Duncan whispered. "Be ready to sack him when he comes by."

"Shh." Ewan warned, indicating the guard was coming back toward them.

"Who's there?"

Duncan raised his sword.

"Call out!" The guard insisted. "Friend or foe! Seamus, be that you?"

When no answer came, the guard doubled his steps, his sword at the ready. Annlise began her rhythmic patter again. This time, they were not so fortunate when the guard caught sight of the glint of Duncan's steel. In an instant, the guard's sword was arcing toward Duncan.

Duncan swung, deflecting the strike. Ewan pushed Annlise protectively to the side, then leapt forward, striking the guard from behind, affording Duncan the opening to disarm him with a well landed slash across the man's forearm. Ewan deftly retrieved the fallen weapon and tossed it hilt-first to Annlise. Duncan finished the skirmish, striking the man unconscious with the hilt of his newly acquired sword.

"Two down," Duncan grinned. "We may yet take this settlement back."

Before Ewan could agree, a loud crack shattered the silence, followed by an angry, bellowing call from the center of the settlement. A moment later, they heard a second shot and the sound of armored boots hurrying over the hard packed gravel.

The way to the gate now free of sentries, the three approached cautiously, peering into the settlement from behind the half-opened gate.

"Can you see?" Annlise asked.

"They're being called to order," Ewan told her.

"Any sign of Will and Ian?" Duncan asked, craning to look for himself.

Ewan shook his head, surveying as much of the settlement as he could from his position. "Come on, they're not watching the gate, we'll stay along the fence."

Staying within the shadows, they hurried along the inner stockade fence toward the little cemetery that was once in the chapel yard to crouch behind the stack of powder kegs that were stored there. From there, they could clearly see the open barn doors, the inside lit by lanterns and the sentries who stood guard there.

"What do you suppose they're guarding in there?" Duncan whispered.

"Not a what, a who," Ewan growled and carefully stood up to gain a better view of the barn. "We need to get over there."

"How? There are soldiers everywhere!" Annlise asked, pulling Ewan down behind the kegs.

Ewan shook his head, at a loss for an answer at the moment. There seemed no place within the square that wasn't patrolled or guarded, with more men spilling out from within the darkened ruins like ants from a long dead log. "It won't be easy."

"Ewan!" Duncan grabbed Ewan's shoulder excitedly, pointing toward the barn. "There, behind those bales."

Ewan squinted his eyes, unable for a moment to see what Duncan was pointing too. "What, lad? I don't... Ian!"

"Looks like he found the weapons."

"If we see him, then surely someone else can," Ewan growled, then with sudden inspiration he turned to Annlise. "Can you protect him from being seen from here?"

"I don't know... I don't think so."

Ewan shook his head, frustrated. "He's no soldier. I should never have allowed... wait, he's ducked within the shadow. Good, at least he has that much sense. Will must be in the barn."

"Blessed Mother!" Annlise gasped drawing her fist suddenly to her mouth. "No! It's him!"

"Who?" Duncan asked, forgetting to whisper.

"Shh!" Ewan warned. It was then he got his first look at the face of the man who stood in the middle of the square, pistols smoking from each hand, his face ominously illuminated by the lanterns carried by the men at his side. "Bloody hell! What is *he* doing here?" Ewan growled under his breath.

"Who?" Duncan asked again, much quieter.

Annlise's eyes were wide, fixed on the man. It was the first true look of fear Ewan had seen on her. "Adrian Tearlach," she whispered.

"Dammit! I knew it was foolish to let Will and Ian—"

"Done is done!" Duncan said, motioning for them to be quiet. "Let's just concentrate on helping Ian and Will, and worry about Adrian and his ilk after. How hard is that?"

"You don't know Adrian," Annlise said, still staring. Her hand found its way to her throat again, worrying the silver knot anxiously between her thumb and forefinger. "He's ruthless, Duncan. He'll cut ye down without half a thought if he catches site of ye, ye just don't know..."

Ewan put a comforting arm around her shoulder. "We'll be careful, rest assured. But Duncan's right, we need to first get to Will and Ian. They all seem distracted now and, with luck, we'll make it out before Adrian even knows we've entered the settlement."

"Mother grant that be the case," she whispered between clenched teeth. "I thought I'd at last seen the last of that black-hearted devil. If he sees me... we're undone."

Duncan turned her to look full at him, pulling her lower behind the kegs. "Are you saying he *knows* you?"

She stared, wide-eyed, tears beginning to shine in the mottled moonlight, before she answered, "Aye. Well. We are... *were*... betrothed."

"What?" Duncan and Ewan gasped together, then hushed

each other immediately. Duncan risked a peek over the kegs, then sighed in relief. No one seemed to have taken notice of them.

"*He* was the one?" Ewan asked, aghast. "Blast it all to Heaven and Hell!"

Duncan turned her to look at him. "Betrothed? I don't understand."

"Lad," Ewan began. "Ye recall I told you the story... when Sean and Will rescued the damsel and saved her from marrying a monster?"

Duncan nodded slowly. "But I was a child, and that was a fairy story."

"No, lad. Were nae. Annlise be the lass who ye brother... she be the damsel he rescued."

Duncan was silent, staring at Annlise.

"Why him, lassie?" Ewan asked.

"'Twas long ago... it was arranged... I had no choice!" She cried, knotting her hands into Ewan's sleeves, speaking between sobs so softly Ewan had to strain to hear what she was saying. "It was that vile Thomas of Aberdoir who arranged it... when I was in his service... Adrian is a hard man to have for an enemy but a right powerful ally should he find favor with ye. Thomas practically fawned on him to gain his alliance, promisin' him the moon, to go after Will. But, Adrian is not an easy man to win over, claimin' there wasn't enough gold in Aberdoir that would satisfy him... ."

"What changed his mind?" Ewan asked, gently.

"I was Adrian's price, ye see. He'd taken a fancy to me... the Blessed Mother only knows why... but he did. He asked Thomas to release me from his service, to wed him...

Thomas agreed, of course, and it was settled." She looked up into Ewan's eyes, then away, as though ashamed of what she would say next. "In the beginning... it seemed a miracle to me. I'd prayed for a way to leave that house... and Adrian, at first, was... attentive, charming, kind, even gentle."

"You loved him?" Ewan asked, incredulous, a sudden bile rising in his gut.

"At first... but it didn't take long before his true nature began to show. One evening, only days before we were to wed, he came to call, drunk, angry about some imagined wrong someone had shown him... he struck me, and I... ran from him, ran from Aberdoir manner and took refuge in the tavern in the town. That's where, Will and Sean waiting for me... Adrian followed me, but Will, Lady bless him, ran right out and created a diversion, telling Sean to take me out the back, where their horses were, and to run, promising to be right behind us."

"Sean got you away from him?" Duncan asked, as quietly as she had been speaking.

"Aye, we rode through the night, all the way to Bannenvale and found shelter in an abandoned barn." Her hand went again to her silver knot. "We stayed there for three days... mostly waiting for Will, ye see. Sean was frantic that they were separated, but he refused to leave me. We became quite close during those... three days."

"Adrian found you together, didn't he?" Duncan said, his jaw tightening.

"He found us lying together..." Annlise sobbed, burying her face in her hands. "Adrian vowed that Sean would pay for what he'd done. It was three years, near to the day, later that he made good on his threat."

"Annlise?" Duncan began tentatively. "Matthew..."

"He's Sean's son," Annlise smiled sadly, then dissolved again into tears. "Duncan, can ye forgive me? 'Twas all my fault Adrian killed ye brother."

Ewan pulled her to him, and embraced her tightly. "The bastard killed him on his own, Annlise. 'Twasn't ye fault, lassie. Tell her, Duncan... Duncan!"

Duncan— his sword clutched tightly in his hand, his face grim, eyes locked on the man who stood in the square— left the shelter of the shadows, brazenly falling into step with the other soldiers who were lining up in rank to listen to Adrian's order. His stride was so determined and steady that he blended unnoticed with the rest of the soldiers. Only the tartan of his kilt would reveal his true alliance but in the dark, the blue, black, and yellow of Edward's house was indiscernible from Ogham's brown, black and white.

"What is he doing?" Annlise cried. "He'll be found out!"

Duncan continued on boldly, cleverly remaining behind the line, unfaltering in his confident march until he reached the far side of the square. Ewan realized that Duncan had crossed the square in plain sight, completely undetected. He took a position near the open door, exactly opposite from where Ian was crouched behind the bales.

Another man, tall and lean, dressed in a regal dark cloak approached Adrian. He held a book in his hands; from his vantage point, Ewan could not see what book it was but it appeared to be of great value to Adrian.

"Oh, no!" Annlise clutched Ewan's sleeve with one hand, and pointed across the square to the other. "What is he doing?"

Ewan looked up in time to see Ian stand up behind the bale, his pistol held straight, two-handed at his eye level. If the shot sailed true, it would miss Adrian— who Ewan assumed was Ian's target— and more than likely hit the casks he and Annlise were hiding behind. Ewan grabbed Annlise by the arm and ran from behind the casks, just as Ian's shot rang from his pistol. As Ewan feared, the shot went afoul of its human target but found its mark planted squarely on the bottom most cask.

"Down!" He threw himself onto Annlise, diving to the ground just beyond the boundary of the cemetery, a few feet from the smallest marker.

Almost before the echoes of Ian's shot died, sparks and smoke arose from the cask and a second later, the earth shook with the reverberation of an explosion the likes of which Ewan had never experienced in his entire life. The sky was alight with flashes and flying debris.

Ewan lay sprawled protectively on top of Annlise, as smoldering wood and gravel rained down around them, obliterating any trace of the existence of a cemetery. Ewan glanced up in time to see the smallest— and until that moment, the only unscarred marker— become engulfed in flames, the name Laurel Philbrick morbidly illuminated in the fire. As the marker burned away, another name began to shine within a blazing filigree of carved ivy— Fylbrigge. Unnervingly, Ewan could swear that he heard the wood release a wailing shriek of agony as it flared, sending orange tendrils spiraling skyward. But then the shriek became human— and female. It was then he looked up and saw the shadow of the woman who stood just beyond the marker, her eyes furiously mirroring the flames, her long talon-like hands splayed angrily and drawn into frustrated fists as the marker crumbled to ash, as if it never existed.

"Bryndah... ." Annlise cried out, then became abruptly silent as Ewan collapsed from a sudden, sharp kick to his forehead.

"Who fired that?"
"It came from the barn!"
"Was he hit?"
"Where's the gov'na?"
"Everyone to arms!"
"Captain! Are ye hit?"
Adrian caught his breath and reached for the hand that was extended to help him. He pulled himself up, his ears still ringing with the echoes of the explosion. He coughed, grimacing at the suffocating smoke that filled the square. "Thank..." The man who had helped him up had seemed to be swallowed in the smoke and had left him. *Typical. Cowards.* Around him, shadowy figures of running men, some carrying buckets of water, others simply running around in a frenzied panic, all of them faceless in the haze.

The fire was spreading, carried on the falling embers from one thatched roof to the next, igniting one after the other. "Bloody hell!" He gathered his wits and made his way back toward the garrison, covering his mouth and nose with his hand. "Garland! Where are you? Answer me!"

"Adrian!" A woman's voice called to him. In the melee of the shouting men and growing roar of the flames, he was not certain if it was Bryndah or the old woman they had been wooing for information. "Adrian! This way!"

"Bryndah? Where are you?"

"This way!"

The voice came from behind him now, and he spun on his heel to go the other way. A soldier carrying a bucket of water crossed his path spilling it on him. "Fool!" He backhanded the man across the face, sending him sprawling, then lumbered back into the smoke in the direction of the voice.

A sudden whirl of wind whistled through the square, momentarily clearing the smoke enough for him to get his bearings. He had thought he was heading to the garrison, but now he saw he was truly facing the barn. The fire had reached the roof and small tongues of flames danced along the beams. The circle of cleared smoke, revealing the object he had forgotten in the confusion. The book lay face down in the gravel.

"Adrian!" The voice called again from behind him. He turned toward it, hesitated, the turned back toward the book, hurrying to retrieve it from the ground. The smoke swirled about, again concealing it from his sight. He closed his eyes and reached.

From within the blinding wall of smoke something sharp and fast moving struck his head as he clamored for the book. "What—" He flailed his arms against a second assault, this time coming from behind, and accompanied by an ear splitting banshee-like scream, knocking him to the ground. He skittered backwards, back into the strange smoke-free circle until at last his assailant was revealed. "Damned bird!"

The eagle dove again, dragging its talons along the

soft flesh of his cheek, tearing open a vicious gash. Adrian searched wildly for his pistol, but neither of his firearms were holstered. He rolled to his hands and knees, grasping a fistful of gravel, flinging it blindly as the bird descended on him again.

"Guards! Fergus! Thomas! Someone! Kill this damned bird!"

His cries went unheard in the surrounding chaos as the men were more concerned with escaping the fire than in fighting with a bird.

Someone called out, "Back to the *Donas Faire,* lads! Hurry!"

"No! Cowards!" Adrian shrieked. "Help me!"

"Adrian!"

He turned quickly, regaining his feet, instinctually covering his head with his arms against another possible attack from above.

Standing just beyond the veil of smoke, he could see it was Bryndah who called to him. She stepped into the circle, lightened by the moon and the glow of the flames, her elegant skirt pitted and tattered. "I've brought you something."

It was then Adrian realized she held one hand behind, as she spun and yanked a struggling young woman by the wrist into the clarity of the circle. The woman fell to her knees at Adrian's feet, crying, covering her face with her hands.

"Look up!" Bryndah grabbed a fistful of strawberry hair and turned the woman's head, revealing her face in the moonlight.

Her light blue eyes glistened with terrified tears as she stared up into his face. He knew her at once. He'd never forgotten the delicate lines of her face, still lovely, despite being twisted in fear. "Annlise Chase." The heartache he'd felt at seeing her again was short-lived and disintegrated rapidly into fury. He struck her sharply across the face with the back of his hand, sending her to the ground. "Why are you here?" he demanded.

Annlise sobbed, shrinking away as he raised his hand again.

"Think, Adrian!" Bryndah stepped forward, halting the strike. "Or were you unaware that Annlise is a healer?"

"What interest is that to me?" he hissed.

"She's your proof, you dullard." Bryndah laughed menacingly yanking Annlise back to her knees.

"Proof?"

"Think!" Bryndah yelled. "Why would my father send a healer if not to *heal* someone? Someone who must require a good deal of healing."

Adrian's eyes widened. "Yes." He looked sharply to Bryndah, smiling. "Excellent, my love." Another sudden strike sent Annlise to the ground, dazed. He knelt next to her, feeling her neck for a pulse. "For a moment, I feared I'd dispatched our proof prematurely." He lifted her limp body, cradling her gently for the moment.

"That would have been a pity," Bryndah snarled.

Annlise stirred, moaning, then blinked her eyes open. Adrian smiled and set her down on unsteady feet. "Ah, good. You're awake, darling. I've missed you." He laughed. "Now, be a good girl and go with Bryndah into the garrison."

Annlise swayed and nearly fell as Bryndah held her under one arm and bore her away through the smoke toward the house. When they vanished, Adrian turned back toward the barn. The roof was entirely alight now and the hay in the upper loft was beginning to catch. He hurried to retrieve the book again, then stopped in his tracks as the screech of the eagle split his eardrum again.

He looked up to the outline of the flaming barn, expecting to see the devilish winged creature coming for him again. Instead he was confronted by a man standing backlit by the flames, his sword raised. Adrian took a step closer, staring at the face of the man as his features flickered in and out of view with the smoke and glow of the flame. The illumination from the barn made the illusion of an unearthly halo around him that made it difficult to tell if the mark on his face was a scar, or some trick of the moonlight.

"Wilbrun," he whispered, disbelieving his own eyes. "It's impossible."

"Is it?" The man raised his sword higher and took a step closer.

"You can't be here!" Adrian pawed his belt, searching for the only weapon he thought he'd find; a small dirk. "I... I killed you years ago!"

"Adrian! Down!" Garland's voice came from behind him, sounding strained and wheezing in the smoke.

Adrian turned, too late to avoid the blow from a man bearing the crest of Stonehaven on his shoulder. A younger man, similarly garbed, pushed a battered Peter Garland to the gravel. Adrian glanced back over his shoulder. The specter he'd believed to be standing there before was no longer there. He chided himself for his foolishness, reasoning he must have mistaken this young man for his old rival.

The attacker looked away from Adrian for a moment. "Good work, Duncan."

Adrian seized the opportunity to feel for and finally find his dirk. In a flash, he was on his feet, surprising his attacker by planting the dirk into his side.

"Ewan!" Duncan yelled and raised his sword.

As Ewan crumbled to his knees, Adrian wrested Ewan's sword from his hand and struck him on the side of the head. He turned just in time to deflect Duncan's strike. Duncan rallied, swinging wildly with both hands, slashing high and low, Adrian meeting and countering every strike without fail.

"You're well trained, boy." Adrian jeered, stepping back, yet holding the sword at the ready.

"By the best," Duncan snarled, keeping his eyes fixed.

"Adrian—"

"Shut up, old man!" Duncan yelled, circling around behind the governor.

Adrian lunged forward and the two crossed blades above Garland's cowering head. Around them, the crackle of burning timbers rose to a near deafening roar.

Duncan thrust, cutting Adrian's forearm, then looked up toward the barn. The flames had completely engulfed the loft and smoke billowed orange from the open doors. "No!"

Seizing on Duncan's momentary distraction, Adrian growled and made a swift circular strike, entangling Duncan's blade in a clash of metal, sending the weapon flying from the young combatant's hand.

Duncan dove in a tumbling roll toward his blade, but Adrian was quick and landed the hilt of his sword neatly between his shoulders, knocking the young man face first into the dirt. Adrian kicked him hard in the ribs, then turned him to his back with his foot and brought his sword to Duncan's throat.

"I know who you are now, Wilbrun," he taunted. "You're no better match for me than your brother was. Poetic that I should finish you as well, isn't it? And profitable too!" He laughed and pressed the blade closer to the flesh, making a shallow cut just under Duncan's chin. "There is a handsome price on your head, boy. And I'll be sure to carry it to Ogham in a bloody sack as proof that I dispatched his would be assassin."

Duncan groped for his sword, Adrian kicked him again, and put a foot on his chest, poising his sword for the final thrust.

"Adrian! Look!" Garland groaned as the barn began to collapse in on itself.

From within the inferno like an avenging angel, the sound of clattering hooves and the frantic neighing of a terrified horse echoed above the roar. A half-breath later, silhouetted by an aura of orange smoke, a lone horseman emerged from the flame, his clothes and hair leaving smoking swirls in his wake. Adrian watched, transfixed for an instant as the ethereal rider charged toward him. He broke his trance in the last instant and raised his sword defensively, but it was too late to deflect horseman's the strike.

A second later, Adrian Tearlach lay dead on the ground, a child's wooden sword protruding from his throat.

"Easy, Kindred!" William clung to the mare's mane as she reared, kicking her front hooves wildly. "Steady, girl!"

Kindred at last responded to his voice and steadied. William brought her back around, out of the smoke, back to his fallen companion.

Duncan was at Ewan's side helping him to his feet. He retrieved Ewan's sword from Adrian's dead hand, reverently returning it to its rightful owner.

"Ewan! Is it bad?" Will called.

Ewan shook his head, holding his side. "I've had worse, I'll be all right..." The pained grimace on his face, split into a wondrous grin. "Will... glad to see ye whole, lad. I was certain we'd lost ye in the barn."

"I thought it myself, for a while," William replied. "Duncan, are ye all right?"

"Aye, just a flesh wound," he told him, rubbing the spot that Adrian had cut. A ghastly stain of blood darkened his tunic under his chin. He drew his hand away wet, but the bleeding had already abated. "Ye saved my life just then." He scowled at the corpse on the ground. "Bastard," he said, then pulled the wooden sword from its neck and wiped it clean against the dead man's own sleeve, before handing it back to William. "I always knew this would come in handy one day."

"Absolutely." William took the sword, absently tucking it into the buckskin sash that served as his belt. Garland coughed loudly, still on his knees not far from Adrian's dead body. William glared at him. "I'll deal with you later," he grumbled under his breath. Garland didn't seem to hear as he coughed louder at the swirling cloud of smoke around him. "Duncan, get him away from the smoke, but whatever you do, don't lose track of him, got that?"

"Aye." Duncan grabbed Garland under one arm and

hauled him to his feet. "Sorry for the inconvenience, Gov'na. But it's either stay here and choke, or come with me. Where do ye want him, m' lord?"

William made a dismissive wave of his hand, reminiscent of the disinterest Garland had taken in his own welfare all those years ago during his trial. "Near the beach. Perhaps one of his comrades will take pity on him and put him on a long boat."

Garland was seized by a violent fit of coughing as Duncan led him away.

"Will... Annlise is in the house..." Ewan groaned, holding his side. Blood trickled between his fingers.

William looked up toward the garrison. An invading rain of embers from the barn landed on the roof. The timbers began to smolder as if in sympathy with the rest of the settlement. "My God. Ian was in there, too! Are you strong enough to follow?" He turned Kindred in the direction of the garrison, intending to ride her right into the house as he had done before.

Ewan answered by dropping back to one knee on the ground, shaking his head miserably. "Ian's... not in there. Saw him... near the barn."

William looked at the barn, its skeletal remains ablaze and its collapse imminent. "He's in the barn? Ian!" William cried in near panic, kicking Kindred's sides turning her toward the barn, reasoning that Annlise seemed relatively safe within the yet-ignited garrison. The mare balked and reared, nearly throwing him. "Kindred! Forward!"

Ewan lunged, grabbing the rein that dangled from Kindred's bridle and threw his weight on the rope, halting her. "No... Will... it's too late. Ye can't go back there!" He groaned, his face contorted in pain as he wrapped the rein around his wrist. "He's gone... Will."

"No!" William cried. "Let go! I have to find him!" He kicked in hard and seized the reins from Ewan, but Kindred would not go any closer to the barn. The adjoining wood shop was now equally alight, obliterating all the clever innovations William had contrived that made it possible for a lamed wood-wright to operate the mills and lathes. His heart pounded wildly as he watched the fire claim, one by one, every structure, as if it had a mind of its own to utterly erase any trace of the existence of Port Edin and his own presence within the settlement. He squinted against the flair of the fire, scrutinizing the ground immediately in front of the barn, finding no trace of his friend amid the jumble of fallen timbers and smoldering planks.

Ewan rolled in the gravel, clutching his side and groaning. William looked from his wounded friend, to the fiery barn, torn between looking for Ian or helping Ewan. An explosion within the center of the barn, ended his indecision, as a ball of fire William swore was born in the depths of hell itself, burst from the grain bin adjacent to the barn, blowing the remainder of the structure to splinters. He fell from Kindred, losing his breath in a shock of pain from his damaged ribs as he landed in a heap next to Ewan. He barely escaped being trampled by a frenzied tangle of hooves as Kindred whinnied, then vanished in a wild gallop into the smoke.

"Damn!" William screamed when he'd regained his breath, more from anger with losing the mare than from the pain in his ribs.

A woman's high-pitched scream came from within the garrison.

"Annlise!" Ewan yelled. "I... I can't get there."

"I can." William ground his teeth, and pulled himself to his hands and knees. "I'll need your sword, mate."

"How are you—" Ewan gasped. He looked near to fainting but allowed William to take his sword.

William didn't answer Ewan's half-asked question, but set his eyes on the front porch of his former home. The explosion from the barn had accelerated the flames on the roof and the second story was nearly fully involved, the damaged timbers from the last fire being easily reignited. Getting to his knees, he staked the sword two fisted into the ground. *Blessed Mother, banish doubt... guide me...* Using the sword for support and straining every muscle in his body and with every ounce of determination he possessed, for the first time in six long years, William Fylbrigge got to his feet and stood on them.

His feet held him though they screamed with the same waspish pains that assailed his legs before. He planted the sword a few feet ahead of himself and miraculously, his feet followed.

"Let me go!" Annlise screamed from within the house. "The fire! We'll both be killed!"

William thrust the sword again, making more progress, and then again, faster this time. He mourned the loss of his mount as it would have made this quicker. Still, he was moving. "Annlise!" he called to the house. "Annlise! I'm coming! Can you hear me?"

"Please! Let me out!" her cries suddenly seemed muffled

and accompanied by a furious pounding. "Let me out!"

He reached the porch steps and climbed the stairs on his knees, then scrambled to the door, using the door handle and the sword as support. "Annlise! I'm coming!"

The door swung in before he'd had a chance to release the handle, sending him ungraciously to his hands and knees onto the kitchen floor, losing his grip on the sword. He groped blindly in the darkness of the kitchen, then froze when his hand fell not on the hilt of his sword, but on something softer, something made of silk.

"Let go," the owner of the silk grumbled in a throaty, threatening tone.

William drew his hand back, startled, and looked closely to what he had touched. The waning orange glow of a dying lantern barely illuminated his immediate surroundings but it was enough for him to see that he was kneeling at the foot of a woman dressed in a gown that was far more regal than he had ever seen worn by any woman in Port Edin. He walked his sight up slowly, an unnamable and unexpected wave of dread preventing him from looking up to her face as though the sight of her would rob him of his soul.

This is not the time for fear! He scolded himself, as something in the woman's voice opened the floodgates in his memory, drowning him in a deluge of ugly and incredible memories. Images seen only in nightmares of bon fires, beatings, and punishments endured as a child, crystallized in his mind. Memories so terrible he believed them to be only bad dreams, but now he knew had been real. Annlise's screams and frightened pounding melded with the memory of his own childhood cries of help to be let out of the suffocating coal shed behind the blacksmith's forge and then being freed by the nurse who had loved him— Rebecca. Annlise's cries echoed Rebecca's the last time he saw her as she perished in flames, crying to him with her last breath to run away. *Run away, little one! She was real... Rebecca! God, I remember... Mum... The dragon killed you!*

A claw of fingers tangled its talons through his hair and forced his face up to look at her. She held the lantern close to him, blinding him from seeing her clearly for a moment until she drew it back, and her face became clear to see. She was still hideously beautiful, the years not diminishing the heart-rending resemblance she bore to her sister— his wife. Her eyes caught the refection of the lantern and flickered with the flame, as they always did in his nightmares and her lip curled in to a malicious grin. "Hello, William. It's been a long time."

Don't let her steal your fire! Not now! No more dragons! He backed away quickly, pulling his head from her talons. The sword glinted from under the hem of her skirt. He reached quickly but she kicked it away, sending it clamoring into the cast iron legs of the oven. He went to grab for it, but she landed a sure strike with her knee to his forehead, sending him flailing to his back.

She stood over him now, still gripping the lantern, her smile widening into the same sickeningly distorted mask he remembered from his childhood. The last time he'd seen that smile was as the world faded from him at the end of his trial, when Garland had forced him to drink the poison. Her smile alone had been enough to accomplish what no other adversary had ever done: stolen his nerve and reduced him to a cowering child. Even while enduring the tortures in the tower, he had not known the same paralyzing fear her smile elicited from him.

"Let me out!" Annlise cried, and he knew now she had been locked within his magic closet.

Bryndah laughed, mocking Annlise's cries. "Let me out! Let me out! Just like you used to cry."

William stared, fighting down the instinctual fear. *She's mad!* Her laughter echoed throughout the kitchen, seeming impossibly loud.

She raised the lantern higher and held it above him. "What's wrong, William? Afraid? You always were a spineless boy. I see your years of cowering in this place have not changed that. I have little doubt why Mehlyndia has left you here to rot. She grew tired of you, didn't she? Did she finally realize what she sacrificed for the likes of you? Half a man—"

"Enough!"

In a heartbeat, before he even realized what he had done, William drew his knees to his chest and kicked out against her. She gasped, furious, losing her grip on the lantern. It barely missed his head as it crashed to the floor next to him. The oil from the lamp spilled out, and caught fire in the corner behind him. He rolled aside quickly, and was on his knees reaching for the only weapon he had left to him— the wooden sword in his belt. He held it tight in his right hand while groping for the edge of the table with the other to pull himself up.

Bryndah was quick and was back on her feet before he could get to his own. She pushed him back, her hands going for his throat. They rolled on the floor away from the spreading flame from the lantern. William had never fought with a woman in his life, but for Bryndah, he would certainly make this exception. She squeezed at his throat, digging her nails into the flesh at the back of his neck. He drew his free hand into a fist and swung, striking her cheek. She released his throat and struck him in the same manner as she rolled off him. Reaching for a small stool, she jumped to her feet. Holding the stool above him, she brought it down fiercely. But he was just as quick and moved just enough to avoid having his head bashed by the thick wooden seat of the stool as it shattered to splinters against the floor.

She wailed in frustration, reaching for another chair. William managed to gain his knees beneath him and skittered under the table, intent on reaching the closet before the fire from the lantern reached it.

"Coward! Come out and fight me!" Bryndah screamed, smashing a second chair against the floor, the pieces falling around him, acting as kindling to the spreading lantern flame.

To his horror, William realized that the fire from the second story had spread down the stairs, the flames licking the ceiling and mingling with the lantern fire.

"Will!" Annlise screamed and pounded from inside the closet. "There's... smoke... help me!" She was coughing now and her pounding was growing weaker.

William was beginning to see what Bryndah was truly doing; herding him away from the only way out of the burning house so she could flee the kitchen and leave them both there to burn. But incredibly, instead of wisely heading for the door, she turned and lunged toward him again, her fingers again groping for his throat.

William raised the little sword defensively in both hands, just as Bryndah came forward. He closed his eyes and thrust as hard as he could as she fell on him.

He opened his eyes and rolled her off of him. Her face wore a mask of frozen disbelief as her hands clawed at the wooden sword that impaled her between her breasts. Her eyes found him briefly and flared wide before they rolled back in her head. He tried to look away but found himself both fascinated and horrified by the flames that snaked along the floor, licking at the hem of her gown. *No one deserves to be burned alive... but she is already dead. The dragon is dead!*

"Will..." A weak and coughing Annlise called to him, her cries breaking the trance the flames cast on him.

He lifted the latch and opened the closet as quickly as he could. She tumbled into his arms still coughing. The smoke near the floor was thin, but the flames were spreading rapidly.

"Hold on, Annlise, the door is open... we'll make it."

Together, they crawled to the porch, to the stairs and back toward the place in the square where William had left Ewan. They found their friend just as an explosion from the center of the garrison sent the remainder of the building skyward, miraculously sailing away from them as the three huddled together in the center of the square.

"We made it," William gasped, coughing, clutching his companions. "Now, pray for rain."

"Aye..." Ewan squeezed William's forearm, "rain..."

"Rain..." Annlise whispered.

The three fell silent, none letting go of the others, as the wind began to change, clearing the smoke away from them.

The wind turned cool and fresh, the sweetest William could remember in a long, long time. The flames waned, and the silence of the night fell around them. Ewan passed out, clutching his injured side with one arm, his other wrapped tightly about Annlise. She lay at his side, her breathing steady and quiet. William rested his head on her back, exhausted and allowed the gentle breeze to lull him to sleep just as he felt the first kiss of gentle rainfall on his cheek. He smiled as he drifted into the black, listening to the waning echo of the call of an eagle and the rumble of distant thunder.

It was over.

Chapter 22

"**W**ILL."

William sat up quickly, looking around. The sun was just peeking over the landscape, casting a pink glow on the horizon. A jumble of blackened timbers that were once the buildings of Port Edin lay in smoldering heaps. He scanned the rubble slowly, searching for the source of the voice that had called to him. "Where are you?"

"We're over here." The voice came from the direction of the former barn, though he could not see anyone. He turned to nudge Ewan or Annlise, then stopped, startled to find himself alone in the center of the square. "Ewan? Is that you? Is Annlise with you?"

"Here, Will," a voice said, directly behind him, accompanied by a gentle tap on his shoulder.

William spun on his knees, gasping in surprise to see three shadowlike people standing behind him. He was certain no one had been there a moment ago. He relaxed quickly however, when he recognized the one speaking to him was Sean. *I'm dreaming again.*

Sean extended his hand and helped William to his feet, his form becoming clear and solid with the motion.

"Was it supposed to be like this?" William asked, still grasping Sean's hand. "So many dead?"

"You did what you had to do, Will," Sean answered.

"You've fought the dragon your entire life. You're free of her now."

William was unnerved to see that Sean's lips were not moving with his speech and his voice was coming from that place behind his ear again, rather than from his brother's mouth. "You're not really here, are you?"

Sean only smiled, then turned and gestured to the shadow standing to his left. It took a step forward and bowed its head. When it looked up, William was looking at Akonni's gentle face.

"It is as I was shown, W'yiam." The Shaman's voice was as Sean's, detached and hovering behind William's ear. His mouth remained fixed in a gentle smile, unmoving with his words.

"No. Surely, you were not meant to die, Akonni," William whispered, wanting to embrace the man, but somehow fearful that he would dissolve into mist if he tried to touch him. "Why did you come to Port Edin?"

Akonni placed his palm on William's cheek and smiled. "You needed me." He took a step backward and William nearly fell to his knees, astonished as the Shaman's features began to change, his face elongating, his hair growing into strands of jet black silk, punctuated with a shock of white coming from his temples. The transformation continued as he stepped backward and bent forward, his hands rolling into balls and then turning into hooves before they made contact with the gravel.

"Kindred?"

The horse bowed, nickering an affirmation, then reared with a joyous whinny, before turning from him and galloping into the mist.

"Kindred? Akonni? All this time? How?"

"Will." Sean tapped his shoulder. "How is not important. It is as it is."

William looked onto his brother bewildered, his vision beginning to blur with tears that were forming. He'd long ago abandoned trying to hide his emotions from Sean and he let them fall freely. "He told me to trust. I trusted. But he should not have died... for this."

"He chose his fate, Will. Same as we did."

"We?" William asked.

Behind Sean, the third shade stood with its head bowed as though waiting to be invited to join them. William's stomach lurched and he collapsed to his knees burying his face with his hands. "It's Ian, isn't it. God, please. Not him too." A gentle hand fell on his shoulder, but William refused to look up not wanting to see his friend in the company of these *ghosts*. But the voice that spoke was not Ian. It was a woman. Reluctantly, he looked up into the face of a lovely young girl with the large brown eyes and chestnut colored hair. She leaned forward, placing a soft kiss on his forehead.

"That's because I love you."

"Laurel." William stood, throwing his arms around the lass, embracing her like he'd never embraced anyone in his life. "Is it you? Are you truly with me?"

"I'm always with you," she answered, squeezing him tightly for another moment before stepping back.

"I have you back again... you and Sean..." He stopped midsentence, his eyes going wide as a revelation descended on him. "Have I joined you? Is that what this is? My journey is finally *truly* over?"

"No!" she answered quickly, then laughed. "No, Will. You're still among the living. And your journey has only begun, my love." She had never called him that in life, but somehow it seemed natural and right coming from her now. "And there are no longer any dragons in your path."

William turned away for a moment, his face suddenly turning hot. "I did not set out to kill anyone. You understand that, don't you?"

She placed her hand under his chin and turned him to her. "You saved two lives, Will. Duncan and Annlise would both be with us now, if not for you." She reached into the pocket of her cloak and withdrew an object and placed it in his palm, closing his fingers around it. "It's time to tell you about this."

He opened his hand and saw that he held the silver eagle badge. Confused, he looked up. "My eagle? I'm to give this to Seany, right?"

"When the time comes. But for now, you keep it." She took it from his hand and pinned it to his shirt at his right shoulder, then smiled and closed her eyes. Keeping her palm on his shoulder, she began to chant, "In the name of the Lady and the Lord, I ask Your favor fall on he who bears this silver blessed by Thee. As mine own tears doth bless this charm, let nothing earthborn cause him harm." She opened her eyes and stepped back. "That is the charm I placed on you all those years ago."

"You... charmed me?" he whispered, toying with the badge on his shoulder. "That no harm should..." He looked up quickly with a sudden understanding. "Elinor knew about this. That's why she was so keen to keep this on my shoulder... when I was sick and when I was on the ship... and you gave this to me before my trial... this is why Garland's poison didn't kill me."

Laurel nodded and stepped back. "The debt is paid, Will. You're free of it now."

"Debt?"

"The Lady and the Lord do not bestow their blessings for free." She winked, quoting one of Elinor's favorite lessons from their youth.

The air suddenly rumbled with distant thunder. Laurel turned toward the sunrise, her smile fading. "It's time to go."

"No, please don't leave me again, Laurel." He reached for her but she backed away, shrinking with each step, her brown eyes turning black before she reshaped completely before his eyes.

"I'm always with you." Her voice came to him from behind his ear, as the little mouse on the ground twitched her whiskers and scurried off toward a pile of rubble near the remains of the barn.

The thunder grew louder, shaking the ground where he stood. He turned to Sean, who still stood quietly to his side. "Must you go, as well?"

Before Sean answered, an incredibly loud crack of thunder exploded in the sky around them. The earth trembled beneath him, and he fell to his knees. Another explosion rocked the world and he covered his head with his arms, falling prostrate to the gravel, until the loudest and last grumbling peal of thunder sent him back into the sudden silence of the abyss.

~

Thunder? No, it's not thunder. There is no rain... the storm is over.

"Look! In the square!"

Sean? Are you still with me?

"Where?"

Laurel?

"There they are. All three!"

"God in Heaven! Ewan! Annlise... Will!"

"The ground is shaking. Be careful..."

"Will, wake up, lad. The ground is solid, don't ye worry." Heavy but gentle hands lifted William by the shoulders, rolling him away from the warmth of the body he had been lying on. "He must have heard the cannons," a man was saying. "Help me sit him up here. Will, can you hear me?"

"Have ye decided to stay?" William asked, sleepily, but the aches in his joints told him his dream had ended. The stabbing pains in his ribs reminded him of what had gone on the night before. "Annlise!" He tried to sit up but the pains prevented him from moving too quickly. "Annlise... where are ye, lass? Are ye well?"

"Will... settle down, lad. She's fine."

It was only then, William opened his eyes to see a familiar face looking down at him, a joyful smile stretching his cheeks under tearful eyes.

"Simon?" William rubbed his eyes.

"Aye... 'tis me."

William grasped his friend's forearms and pulled himself up. Ignoring the pains for a moment, he embraced Simon, tightly. "My God, I can't believe it. You must be a dream." He pulled away grimacing, clutching at his ribs. "But no dream ever hurt like this." He tried to smile but failed.

"And here 'twas me thinkin' I be dreamin' you!" Simon placed his arm around him gingerly, helping him to sit up. "I could hardly believe it when Duncan said ye were alive. It's a miracle." He looked around the square, shaking his head as he surveyed the destruction. "'Tis a miracle that any o' ye be alive."

"Aye, 'tis." William's thoughts turned to his waking moments. "Did you say cannons?"

Simon grinned, and answered. "Aye, we run the sots out o' the harbor. Weren't much of a battle, we just sent a few warning shots o'er their bow. They took to sea without a fight."

"Oh, sweet Mother..." Annlise groaned under her breath, rubbing her neck as she sat up.

"Lass, are ye well?" William asked, placing a hand on her shoulder?

Annlise nodded groggily, before fully opening her eyes.

"Simon," Duncan called suddenly, as he knelt over a still and pale Ewan. "He's hurt badly."

"Ewan!" Annlise hurried to where he lay, his face ghastly white, his eyes half open, staring straight ahead. His left hand clutched at his side, his fingers caked with dried blood and mud. She gently stroked his face and hair then placed her ear on his chest and listened carefully. "I can't hear—"

"Oh, no." Simon moaned as he knelt next to Annlise, placing his hand on her back. "Are we too late, lass?"

She looked up startled, then threw her arms around Simon's neck and embraced him, crying. Simon patted her back, allowing her to sob all over him.

"My God." William whispered, looking down on his friend. *Not another...* He felt the familiar shudder snake its way through his middle as he realized his own hands and clothes were also caked with dried blood and mud, left over from his battle with the dragon. *So much death... it wasn't supposed to be like this.* He reached to Ewan's face and gently brushed his hand over the half-opened eyes, closing them completely. He rested his hand there on his friend's eyes for a moment, offering a silent prayer for him. A moment later he pulled his hand away, having felt the faintest of movement beneath his palm. He looked closely, hopefully at Ewan's eye lids. "He's alive," William said quietly, half fearing if he spoke too loudly, it would be a lie.

"What?" Annlise turned away from Simon, wiping her face.

William carefully moved the leather tunic Ewan wore and placed his ear on his bare chest, and listened. "Yes! Annlise, listen!"

She listened, where William had, then burst into new tears. This time smiling, as she patted Ewan's face, calling to him, "Ewan... wake up. Ewan McDonough, don't ye be leavin' me now... wake up."

Ewan's eyes began to flutter.

"Ewan!" William called, squeezing Ewan's right hand. "Can ye hear us, my friend? Please... wake up."

Ewan squeezed William's hand, then moaned as he opened his eyes.

"Thank God!" Duncan cried, his voice shaking. He shouldered his way past William, taking his place beside

Ewan, cradling the older man's head in his hands.

William could see the relief in Duncan's face as he allowed two very unsentrylike tears to drop from his cheeks onto Ewan's face. William moved away quietly, allowing the lad his moment.

"I knew you'd be all right, old man."

"Suckling bairn..." Ewan moaned in response, then blinked open his eyes, looking on each face in turn. "Help me off this dirt, would ye, lad?" Duncan and Annlise helped him to sit up, right next to William. "We'll talk about followin' orders later."

"Absolutely." Duncan grinned. "Soon as we're to sea, ye can call rank on me and have me keel hauled if ye like. But right now, just catch ye breath."

"To sea?"

"Well, unless ye prefer to be walkin' home..." Simon hunched down in front of Ewan. It was the first time Ewan had noticed Simon's presence.

"MacHenry, you old sot!" Ewan grinned and reached out, then groaned, clutching at his side.

"Easy, friend," Simon said. "Ye just sit for a bit like Duncan told ye. Then I'll get ye aboard ship and I'm sure Annlise can take care o' that hurt ye got."

"She surely can." Duncan chimed in.

Annlise beamed through her tears, already fussing about the wound in Ewan's side. "Aye, I'll do m' best."

"I'm sure ye will, lass. I remember what ye done for my Prissy. And I thank ye dearly for that. She was well and strong last I saw her, and the bairn was growin' in her, right proper."

Annlise blushed. "I'm glad ye told me that, Simon. Thank ye."

Simon patted her shoulder, then stood up. "The tide goes out near sunset. We should be ready to sail by then. Duncan and I can take care o' getting what's left of the provisions from the root cellar..." he looked around scratching his head. "If we can *find* the root cellar under all this mess. We'll need the extra food for the trip home. I only provided what I thought I needed for the crew and the four I thought I'd be pickin' up here. I hadn't counted on the extra passengers ye see." He laughed, gesturing toward William. "And I never expected to see you at all, lad. But I'm sure I can scare up room for ye."

"Extra?" William asked, confused. "Even with me, there are only five—" He swallowed hard and turned away. "Four. We're only four, Simon. Ian isn't with us anymore."

Simon's face softened. "Aye. Duncan told me. I'm sore sorry about that, Will. Ian was a good man. And a good friend."

"Thank you... he was that," William answered quietly. "Looks like you have enough provisions after all. There's only four of us."

"Well, actually..." Duncan began, tentatively, "There are five."

"What do you mean?" William asked. Ewan and Annlise exchanged curious glances.

"Well, ye remember ye asked me to keep an eye on—"

"Garland!" William blurted. "I'd forgotten all about him."

"You're not telling me that *he's* coming with us?" Ewan asked, incredulously. "That black-hearted bastard? He's the reason—"

William raised his hand. "Peace, Ewan. Is that what you're sayin' lad?"

"Aye." Duncan said, giving Ewan a wary glance. "Ye see... while I was—"

"Are ye daft? Why should we take the likes of—"

"Ewan, please," Simon interrupted. "I think ye should hear what the lad has to say. Believe me, I wasn't eager to allow him on my ship either, but... well it makes sense."

"Where is he now?" William asked, before Duncan had a chance to begin his explanation.

Duncan looked to Simon, as if waiting for a cue.

Simon shrugged, "Go on, lad. 'Tis your idea."

"Mr. Garland," Duncan called, cupping his hands around his mouth.

A moment later, Peter Garland entered the square, coming from behind a pile of ruins he had apparently been standing behind, waiting to be called.

William's stomach tightened at the sight of the man. He walked confident and straight-backed, his hands folded neatly within the voluminous folds of his sleeves. He paused only a moment, glancing at the corpse of Adrian Tearlach, still laying where he'd fallen the night before, then proceeded to where they were gathered. As he neared and William could see his face more clearly, he realized that the expression the governor was wearing was more akin to contrition than arrogance. He kept his gaze on the ground and bowed his head slightly in greeting, then stood silently next to Simon.

"What's this all about, Duncan?" William asked.

"You asked me not to lose track of him," Duncan answered. "The only way I could do that was to stay with him on the beach. Once word was out that Adrian was dead, all of Ogham's sots made for their longboats and headed back to their ship." He spared a sly one-sided grin. "None of them seemed to mourn too terribly about it. Turns out, none them had any loyalty to him or Ogham, really. Mercenaries, the whole lot of them."

"Even the mercenaries didn't want you?" William chuckled ruefully under his breath.

Garland made no response, maintaining his stoic silence.

"Well..." Duncan cleared his throat. "That's not exactly true, Will. A few of them *did* stop to help him. Ye see, even though technically, they were working for Adrian— odd as it seems— there was honor among them. Mr. Garland, here, had earned the respect of a few of the men for not bending to him and Lady Bryndah. They actually *liked* him."

"Did they?" William rested his chin in his hand, growing a bit impatient with Duncan's narrative, but this last bit of information did seem a bit intriguing. And so what if a bunch of mercenaries liked Garland? Was he expected to change his mind about the man on that count? "Duncan, this is all well and good, but you must appreciate my... position." He gestured sarcastically to his legs, which were more stiff and sore than they had been in weeks. "This man literally held my life in his hands and he crumpled it into ashes. He had the authority to dismiss those ridiculous charges and set me free. He found me innocent of casting spells and that should have been enough. But he administered that damned trial by poison anyway."

Garland lifted his chin then and looked William in the eye, and said simply, "I see I was mistaken in my declaration of your death, Mr. Fylbrigge. It seems you did survive."

"That's where you're wrong, sir." William scowled.

"Everything that was William Fylbrigge died in that chair that day, when I swallowed your dose. The man you see here now is merely a shade of the former William of Drumoak. For nearly seven years I've been more dead than alive, not even knowing why. It took a second *death* for me to remember it all. So you see? You were not mistaken. You did kill me. Are you pleased?"

Garland met William's stare for only a moment, then lowered his eyes. "Mr. Fylbrigge, I cannot stand here and pretend to understand how it is you're here, or why. The dose *was* designed to kill you. That was my doing and I fully confess to you now that I doubled the nightshade for the test quite deliberately."

"What?" Ewan gasped, lurching forward. Annlise pulled him back. "Duncan, enough of this, see what kind of evil—"

"Let them finish," she told him quietly.

"Please, hear the rest, then make your judgment," Duncan pleaded.

"Finish it then," William said. "Tell me why you wished me to fail the test."

"Not fail, sir," Garland corrected him, a curious crease coming to his brow as though he was genuinely confused why William wasn't understanding. "I wanted you to pass. To prove you were innocent."

"Pass? But... for what purpose? Why bother if passing meant I was to die?"

Garland sighed and looked down. "Because I knew that had I dismissed it all, Ogham would have merely found another magistrate who would gladly accept his bribe and you would have gone through it all again. Believe it or not, Mr. Fylbrigge... I truly believed then, as I do now, that you were completely innocent. But... there was too much stacked on you, and... had I not taken that step, you surely would have endured a far worse fate at the hands of a less scrupulous judge. I believed... I acted compassionately." He looked William in the eye. "The best I could do for you was to spare you from the fire."

"Spare..." William shook his head, not knowing what to believe. "You felt no need to spare Laurel."

"Laurel?" Garland asked.

William ground his teeth. "The one who burned in my place, by *your* order."

Garland nodded sadly. "Ah, yes. The girl who disguised herself as an acolyte. Another unfortunate... mistake on my part, I'm ashamed to say. Believe me, sir, it has weighed heavily on me all these years as well, but the law being as it is... I had little choice. She confessed of her own free will. I find some consolation in knowing she died quickly, rather than having been tortured first."

A heavy silence fell among the group, each face eventually turning to William. He looked up to see them all looking at him, waiting for him to make the decision. He didn't know what he was to think. On one hand, he could easily banish Garland to the forest to let him take his chances with the wolves. The man had destroyed his life... *he wasn't alone. It was all of them... Thomas, Bryndah, the clerics, Adrian... Garland was only a pawn.* On the other hand, there had been too much death around him and he knew he could not knowingly send the man off to die, no matter what he'd been guilty of. This wasn't Adrian who was about to slay Duncan, or Bryndah who would gleefully allow Annlise to perish in a burning closet. He was just a man standing there, trying in his own pathetic way to apologize. Then he remembered the odd look Garland had given him the night before.

"You recognized me last night, didn't you?"

Garland nodded. "Oh, yes. And it distressed me to know what Adrian would do should he see you."

"Yet you were willing to turn me over... I saw you give my book to Adrian."

"Your book, sir. Not you. It was my hope he'd take it and abandon his search."

"Then for that, sir, I am grateful. Thank you." William said, quietly.

Another long moment of silence followed. William was running out of arguments for leaving Garland behind. He wanted to believe the man was lying to him, merely looking for mercy, but the look on Garland's face now, as well as the one the night before, told him otherwise. "What can you offer me now, besides your obvious contrition, should we allow you to sail with us?" William asked.

Garland glanced between Duncan and Simon, as though seeking help from them to find his words.

"Will," Simon began, "ye see, when we get back home, ye cannae just dance back into Stonehaven, calling out ye be home. You would be staked faster than lightning strikes."

"That's right, Will," Duncan added. "By law, you're only innocent because they believe you're dead. In order for you to go home— and have a life— the writ needs to be changed by the magistrate who wrote the original declaration." He gestured to Garland.

Garland tipped his head, one brow raised, a ghost of a grin growing on his face.

"You are willing to change the writ?"

"In return for safe passage back with you."

"What happens when we land?" William asked. "What stops you from running to Ogham, or Dunkirk, or the King himself, telling them I've bewitched you into changing it?"

"A fair question." Garland cast his eyes down, lifted his shoulders slightly, then lowered them. "All I have to offer is my word, sir."

"Your word? Forgive me my skepticism, but it seems you are merely wishing not to be left behind. Not that I blame you for that."

"As the young man told you, I was offered safe passage back aboard the *Donas Faire.* I refused."

"Why did you refuse?" William asked, narrowing his eyes.

"Frankly... I wanted no more voyages with harpies and pirates."

"Harpies?" William could not resist a grin. "You needn't worry on that anymore."

Garland surprised William with an unexpected grin of his own. "True enough, but I was unaware of Lady Bryndah's demise at the time. It was those other three that boarded I was not eager to share passage with."

"Other three?" Annlise asked. "What other..."

William suddenly laughed out loud at the realization. "Sweet Mother! Goody Ashcrofte and her gaggle have sailed with the pirates!"

"I believe that was her name, yes. Josephine Ashcrofte." Garland grimaced. "I've never met a more annoying woman in my life. Her friends were no better—"

"Ha!" Simon blurted, slapping Garland on the back, causing him to stumble a bit. "That's them, all right! I can't think of a better ship for them to sail on. Though I'm not sure who I should feel sorrier for, the gaggle or the pirates!"

"Yes, quite." Garland cleared his throat, regaining his composure.

"What d' ye say, Will. Should we let this sot sail with us?" Simon asked, as his grin slowly turned serious. "It's your decision."

William looked to Ewan, raising a brow.

Ewan shrugged, shaking his head. "Why not. We can always toss him overboard if he becomes troublesome."

"True enough," William agreed. Still sitting on the gravel, he extended his right hand. "Welcome aboard, Mr. Garland."

Garland accepted William's hand and shook it heartily, then withdrew quickly when William grimaced. "Forgive me. I should have realized..."

William drew his hand back slowly, staring at it as if he had never seen it. The newfound strength and dexterity he had found the night before seemed to have vanished with the dawn. His knuckles were as swollen and gnarled as they had been before Annlise's rite of healing. His shoulders and arms, again protesting with spasms and twinges at being called to reach. He glanced to his legs, startled to realize he had no sense of where his feet were in relation to the rest of him.

"Will?" Ewan spoke softly, still sitting next to him on the ground. "What's wrong?"

William couldn't find his voice to answer. He sat supporting himself by leaning on his left hand, the shoulder beginning its old trick of shaking under the strain. He stared unblinking at his knees, at the soiled worn places in the leather leggings, as an affirmation that they had worked for him. *Move!* He ground his teeth in his jaw, calling on everything within him to fold his knee. *It can't be gone... Blessed Mother, why?*

He felt a gentle hand on his shoulder and Annlise's voice, soft in his hear. "Will?"

He clenched his eyes shut and drew his hands into fists and growled, as ever so slowly, he was able to fold his left leg, then the right. He let his breath out, opening his eyes, blinking away the tears he refused to allow to show. "There."

"Will! Ye moved them!" Simon grinned, amazed. "Ye done it, lad! That was amazing—"

"Simon." Ewan raised a hand, signaling Simon to be quiet, then got to his knees, putting a supportive arm around William. "Relax, lad, you've been sleeping on the gravel all night and you're simply stiff. I'm barely moving myself. We'll get ye aboard *Lady Anne* and scare up a hot bath and ye'll be right again. They'll work again."

Simon shook his head, his smile dissolving into confusion. "What are ye telling him, Ewan? Are ye daft?"

Duncan pulled Simon aside, explaining in a hushed voice. Simon turned an astonished face on William, then back to Duncan. He returned to William and hunched down before him. "I'm sorry, Will. Duncan told me... I can hardly believe it. He said ye been getting along on ye own... on ye knees?"

William nodded, still concentrating on his rebellious limbs. He could feel the stings and spasms in his upper legs just as he had the morning he'd awoken in Akonni's lodge.

The knees responded only slightly to his command to move. He was aware of the sharp stones beneath his calves, but at the bottom of his legs, the feet that had supported him across the square the night before, lay as numb and useless has they had been before.

"Ewan's right," Annlise assured him. "It's just from lyin' here in the mud—"

"I walked."

"On ye knees, aye, we know ye done," Ewan said. "Ye will again—"

"On my feet!" William turned an angry eye on his friend. "I stood and crossed this square *on my feet*. Last night."

Annlise and Ewan exchanged confused glances. Duncan shrugged, palms up.

"Don't you believe me?" William asked. "I used your sword, Ewan... for support true, but still, I walked!" He turned his face away quickly, feeling the scarlet rise, furious at the notion that the miracle could be so short lived. He forced his knees to fold another inch, then dropped his chin, exhausted with the effort. "I walked."

"I believe ye, lad," Ewan replied quietly, though his tone was unconvincing. "Here, let me help ye—" He clutched his ribs, catching his breath, then shook his head apologetically. "I'm afraid I'm little help."

William abandoned his arguments, pushing his own anger and frustrations aside when he saw the pain on his friend's face. "Annlise, can you help him?"

She stood and, with Duncan's help, got Ewan to his feet. He leaned unsteadily on Duncan's shoulder for a moment, grasping at his injured side before attempting to stand on his own. He swayed a bit, Duncan catching him before he fell.

"Easy, mate."

"We need to get you aboard," Annlise said, examining the wound with her palms. "Duncan, can ye get him to the longboat?"

"Aye, I have him," Duncan answered.

"Good, lad," Simon said. "Get him comfortable, then get yeself back here. I'll need ye help finding that root cellar."

"Come on, old man. I have ye." Duncan half-grinned as he bore Ewan away.

"Mind ye breechcloth, ye wee bairn. Just walk," Ewan grunted in return. "Come on, gov'na, ye may as well come with us," he called over his shoulder to Garland.

Garland nodded and half smiled, a relieved glint in his eye as he followed them down the path to the beach where the boat waited.

"You should go with us now, Will," Annlise said. "I can make a hot wrap for ye muscles that will ease the pains for ye. Simon can carry ye down."

Simon knelt without hesitation, as he had for the years, and went to lift him. "Aye, 'tis a good idea. Ye'll feel like a new man aft' we get ye cleaned an' fed."

William pushed him away, angrily. "No, don't lift me. I'm not helpless!"

Simon backed away, looking stung. "I... my apologies, m' lord."

William sighed, disgusted with himself for railing at Simon that way. "Forgive me. That was uncalled for. Please, my friend, I do need some help here."

Simon shook his head, turning his hands palms up. "Will,

I'm not sure what to do for ye. I'd be glad to bear ye down to the boat, if ye let me."

The thought of being carried grated on William. He'd thought himself free of the need for such help, but it was also obvious to him that for the moment, he lacked the strength to re-train his knees to walk for him. *It's not forever. Just for today, right? I'll have months aboard the ship to regain my strength... just for today...* "Not jus' yet, Simon. I'd like to help ye find the root cellar before we go aboard. I think I've a good idea where it is under all this mess."

Simon nodded and turned to Annlise. "Go on, lass. Go take care of m' mate. Send Duncan back and we'll join ye when we're done, aye?"

She bent and placed a kiss on William's cheek. "Don't ye be fearin, Will. You'll see. Ye've not lost it."

"Thank ye, lass," William forced a smile. "I believe ye right."

She gave Simon a quick smile, then hurried to join the other men. William watched her run across the square and down to the beach. "She's in love, ye know." He said, looking up to Simon.

"Aye, I think ye right," Simon agreed. "But I don't think Melly will be pleased."

William laughed. "Not with me, lunk. With Ewan!"

"Oh." Simon winked and chuckled. "That be a relief."

"How is Melly?" William asked, staring past Simon to the sea, suddenly lonesome at the mention of her name.

Simon kicked at the gravel a bit, not looking at William. "She's well, all things considered. Settled back in her old suite in the castle. Spends her days at her drawings and looking after Seany. She puts on a brave face for Seany and Edward's sake. Last I saw her, it was pretty clear she's mourning ye fierce, lad. So is ye boy."

"Seany is well?" William asked quietly.

"Oh, aye. He's missing ye too, of course. But he's taken to Drumoak as quickly as you did. And don't ye know, Edward has already provided him with a pony of his own."

"A pony?" William smiled at the thought, though it brought him close to losing his war with the tears that were threatening. "Seany has a pony. That's grand."

Simon smiled to himself. "Prissy is expecting ye know. I'll be a papa by the time we get back."

"Aye, Ian told me that happy news. Congratulations."

The two grew silent for several minutes. William closed his eyes, bringing Ian to mind. *I'm so sorry, my friend. You should be here to celebrate with us.*

"Well," Simon sighed, breaking the silence. "I supposed we best be finding that cellar. If that pile over there was the barn, it won't be hard to find. The cellar door was just to the right of the big doors."

Simon frowned, his brow furrowed in a deep crease, as he looked at the imponderable jumble of charred timbers that was once the barn. He walked through the rubble kicking at splintered beams, turning over blackened boards. William sat in the same place in the square, knowing he wasn't being of much use, but still feeling that he couldn't leave the settlement until he was sure. It wasn't the root cellar that William was keen to find a trace of. After all, he reasoned, Adrian's party must have already found it and cleaned out whatever dried fruits, fish, and grains may have remained after the raid. Last year's harvest was all but drained before he, Ian and Ephraim had headed into the woods, and there had been no harvest this year to replenish it. *Simon must realize this... he was here when the raid came.* Still, Simon searched like a man possessed through the timbers to find the handle of the door that led to the cellar, and William knew then that Simon was not truly looking for provisions.

"He was near the doors, Simon." William called.

Simon looked over his shoulder, paused, nodded in understanding, and continued digging with a slightly renewed energy. He turned a plank and paused, as though he'd found something.

"What is it?" William called.

Simon picked up a blackened heap and brushed it off, then headed back to William. "This is yours, isn't it?" He handed William the burned and tattered book. The edges of the pages were singed, but overall, it was whole.

"My book!" He opened the cover carefully, blowing away blackened flakes of charred leather. "I thought for certain this was lost." He turned to the last page, looking up to Simon. "I've been keeping this for Seany. It's always been my hope that he'd read it one... day. There's a late entry," he said, as he read the words Ian had written only the night before, his voice catching in his throat. "Seems Ian was concerned about Peter Garland as well. He didn't let on who he was... faithful to the end."

Simon crouched down. "I'll find him, Will. We won't sail without knowing he be truly gone. I promise ye that."

"Thank you, Simon."

Simon stood and returned to his search. William put

the book aside, watching. His shoulders began to shudder, protesting at the way he had been leaning on his arm. He would have liked to have lain down, but feared the rest of his muscles may begin to fail him, as his legs seemed to, if he did. So he did his best to ignore the spasms, keeping his eyes fixed on Simon.

"They're all set. Annlise is getting a bed chamber ready for you."

William turned with a start. He hadn't realized Duncan had returned. "Thank ye, lad. It shall be good to sleep between sheets again."

"Ye've got company, Will." Duncan said smiling, pointing to the book on the ground.

"Hmm?" William looked where Duncan was pointing. "Well, hello there." He smiled, as from behind the big binding, the little oil drop eyes peeked at him, her whiskers twitching. He reached out his hand and the little mouse climbed into his open palm. "I'm glad to see you made it out, little one."

"Friend of yours?" Duncan chuckled, crouching down to sit next to William. He gently scratched between the mouse's ears. "Well, this is a brave little mouse, I must say."

"Aye, she is." William smiled. "She's a hero too."

Duncan cocked a brow, "Is she?"

William placed the mouse on his shoulder, then pushed up one sleeve. "I nearly forgot. I need to get this off." A length of rough twine was knotted tightly around his wrist, the end hanging in tattered shreds. "The other one fell off, but this one is rather tight."

Duncan gawked at the rope and the chewed end. "You're not telling me that... it... she..."

William raised his brow, grinning. "Gnawed right through it. How do you think I was able to get out of the barn? I was trussed up tighter than one of Elinor's roasted ducks."

Duncan shook his head, amazed. "Well then, this surely is one special little mouse." He retrieved his dirk from his belt and carefully cut the rope off William's wrist.

The mouse skittered under William's hair and across the back of his neck to his right shoulder. William pushed his hair to the back, to give her room, his hand brushing against something hard on his shoulder. "What... I don't believe it." He gasped, toying with the silver on his shoulder.

"Where did that come from?" Duncan asked, instinctually reaching for his own shoulder. Finding his own crest still in place. "For a moment I thought I'd dropped mine."

"No... this one's mine... it was given to me..." He retrieved the mouse from his shoulder, holding her in the palm of his hand. She sat up on her haunches, twitching at him. *I'll keep it for now, yes, and give it to Seany when the time comes.* He set the mouse down on the ground. She turned and hurried away toward the rubble, stopping every few feet to turn and look at him, before scrambling into the rubble, a few feet away from where Simon was searching.

"Did you see that?" Duncan asked, quietly, staring.

William nodded.

"Simon!" They both called together.

Simon turned, startled. "Duncan, come help me, lad."

"Go!" William said, as Duncan jumped to his feet, and ran to the place the mouse had disappeared under. Without waiting for Simon, he began tossing boards and broken timbers.

"Slow down, boy, I'm not holdin' a flame to ye arse ye know." Simon shook his head, as he joined Duncan.

Duncan ignored him, pulling piece after piece off the heap.

"I searched here, lad... there's nothing—"

"There!" Duncan shouted, as he tossed aside a piece of the door, revealing a blackened iron ring, peeking up through the gravel.

"I'll be damned. Ye found the root cellar." Simon chuckled, lightly. "It's not what I was hopin' ye found, but—"

"Help me," Duncan said, struggling with a beam that had fallen across the lid.

"Lad, slow down, we'll get there," Simon said, placing a hand on Duncan's shoulder. "The provisions aren't goin' anywhere."

Duncan grunted, still trying to move the beam away on his own. "Help me!"

"All right, all right." Simon grabbed the end of the beam with Duncan, and together, they managed to toss it off the cellar door. It landed with a splintering crash atop the rubble. Both men, stood back for a moment, catching their breath while the dust settled. A moment later, Simon's eyes went wide, as both he and Duncan dove for the brass ring, and together they lifted the door, and disappeared down the stairs.

William watched, holding his breath the whole time until Duncan's head popped up out of the cellar.

"We found him!" he called to William, with a triumphant whoop, running back to him. A moment later, Simon followed, cradling a disheveled and bloody Ian in his arms.

When Simon laid him on the ground, the apothecary blinked open his eyes, and smiled. William embraced him tightly, and finally gave up the battle with his emotions and cried, unabated and unashamed. *Thank you Laurel... God, thank you...*

Resurrection

Breathing sweet air again
I step onto moor and heath
Savoring the sun's first kiss
My feet come, unshod and blameless,
To worship sod and blade
O, joyous soul, to come
Again to dance upon the glen
I am home

Chapter 23

25 December, 1613
Drumoak Castle, Stonehaven Scotland

"They're so beautiful, Prissy." Mehlyndia beamed as she gently placed Prissy's newborn daughter in the bassinet aside her twin brother, covering them both snuggly with a soft lamb's wool blanket. "Such a sweet Christmas gift. Twins." She turned, wiping a tear from her face. "Simon shall be proud, indeed."

Prissy smiled from her pillow, still abed and weary from her long labor. "I wish he was here for the birth."

Mehlyndia dipped a cloth into a basin of warm water next to the bed, then wiped Prissy's forehead. It had been a difficult delivery with moments when it seemed both she and the babes would not see the dawn. The first bairn— the boy— seemed determined to come into the world back end first. But, after hours of Elinor's encouragement and skillful midwifery, little Simon Wynn MacHenry at last slipped onto the birthing quilt, announcing his arrival with a blessedly loud wail. It wasn't until he was cleaned and swaddled, that Prissy cried out that there was something more.

Elinor assured her it was normal and it was only the afterbirth that was to come. But even Elinor— who had birthed nearly every child in Stonehaven, if one was to believe her claim— was stunned to see the second little head peeking its way into the world. Fifteen minutes after her brother, Mary Rebecca MacHenry drew her first breath.

It was noon when Mehlyndia came to get her first glimpse of the twins. "I'm sure Simon would have been here if he could, dear."

Prissy nodded, her eyes half closed, dreamily looking toward the bassinet. "He'll be home any time now," she said, yawning. "I'm sure of it."

"Are ye awake, dear?" Elinor asked, peeking in from the door way.

"Aye, Elinor," Prissy answered. "Just barely."

"Ah, good." She smiled, entering the room with a bowl of fresh water and linens. She set them on the trunk at the foot of the bed, then tip-toed to the bassinet for a peek. "Oh, look at these two. So peaceful and calm. Fine and pink and full of life. As it should be." She tucked the swaddling a bit tighter around each, then went to Prissy, assuming her traditional role as family physician. "And how are you feeling, little mum?"

"Mum," Prissy smiled. "That's me, isn't it?"

"Aye, 'tis." Elinor chuckled lightly while she felt Prissy's head for signs of fever or cold. Satisfied, she nodded, tucking the blanket up a bit higher. "There are two gentlemen outside who would like to visit for a moment if you're feeling ready."

"I think that would be..." She yawned grandly. "... fine, Elinor. Just for a moment."

"Melly, dear, would you let them in, please?" Elinor winked, making herself comfortable on the edge of the bed.

"Come on in, Father." Mehlyndia ushered Edward in, leading a wide-eyed Seany in tow by the hand.

"I've come to welcome my newest subjects to Stonehaven, personally." Edward's eyes twinkled as he peered into the bassinet. "Congratulations, my dear. Well done." He picked up Seany and held him so he could see over the high sides of the bassinet. "Look there, lad. Isn't that a lovely sight?"

Seany tilted his head and wrinkled his mouth in bewilderment. "Which one is the lad? And how come they're so little?"

Edward set him down, laughing. "I'm sure I can't tell which is which either, lad. But I'll bet their mum can tell you."

Prissy yawned again. "Simon is on the left, that's Mary on the right."

Seany gave her a skeptical scowl. "Why is she bald, then? I thought lassies all had long hair."

"Seany," Mehlyndia scolded lightly, then grinned. "Sometimes babies are bald. Just like you were. She'll be beautiful one day, just you wait. Who knows? Someday, you might just take a fancy to this little lass."

Seany gave his mother a doubtful glance, then looked up to Edward. "Is it almost time for the feast, Grampa?"

Edward laughed, scooping the lad up in his arms. "More excited about Christmas than ye are about the bairn? Well, that can be forgiven I suppose." He set Seany onto his shoulders, holding his little feet. "Come on, lad, we'll leave Prissy to rest now. You and I have a lot of preparations to finish up. I'm counting on you and Matty to be my lookouts for any sightings of Father Christmas."

"I bet I see him before Matty does. He'll be too busy watching the pudding!"

"Absolutely," Edward chuckled, giving the boy's foot an

affection shake. "Then I shall charge you with guarding the pudding."

"Aye," Seany giggled. "I won't let Matty eat it all."

"Now don't you fill up on sweets all day, little man. You're to have a proper supper tonight. And please try not to get in Chase's way," Mehlyndia said, sternly but with a gentle smile.

"I'll be good, Mum." He grinned, showing off the brand new gap in his front teeth. "After all, I don't want to upset Father Christmas, do I?"

"A wise decision, Sean William." Edward said, then headed to the door. Pausing in the doorway, he turned, the twinkle in his eye dimming slightly. "Mehlyndia, I wish you'd reconsider and come down to join the festivities. All of Stonehaven has been waiting to welcome you home."

"I think it best if someone stays here with Prissy, Father. And I'm really not up, for—"

"It's been months, darling," Edward interrupted gently. "And it's Christmas. Geoffrey has even gone to the trouble of hiring a group of traveling mummers to perform for us tonight."

"Mummers?" Seany asked. "What are those?"

"Players... musicians or singers... I'm not actually sure which this group is. Geoffrey only just told me about them before I came up to see you. He said they arrived in town early this morning and would like to sing for their supper. And this being the first Christmas in seven years that I've opened the castle for the town, I thought it would be a nice treat." He looked up, pleadingly, under his brow. "You can't mourn forever, my dear."

"Melly, please go," Prissy said, squeezing Mehlyndia's

hand. "I'll be fine for a little while. Elinor will be checking in, I'm sure."

"Of course, I will," Elinor agreed. "It will do you a world of good, Melly. And you can wear that lovely new gown."

"Please, Mum?"

Mehlyndia smiled in spite of herself. "All right. I must admit, it will be good to wear a festive gown again." She stood and kissed Prissy on the forehead. "You really don't mind?"

"Go. Enjoy it. Save me some wassail. I'll be just fine," Prissy assured her, beginning to nod.

Mehlyndia made one more check on the babes, then accompanied her father and her son from the room.

By dusk, the great hall of Drumoak was alight with hundreds of festive candles and gleaming holiday vestments. Swags of evergreen boughs and holly garland hung from the windows and walls. The banquet tables were laden with platters and bowls of savory meats, breads, and other treats. Two massive evergreens flanked the foot of the grand stairs, both decorated with candles and sugared fruit.

At six-o'clock, Edward took his place on the first landing of the great stairs, Mehlyndia and Seany by his side, as he signaled to Chase and Matthew to open the grand doors of the foyer.

The people of Stonehaven filed in joyously amid the festive fanfare of Edward's herald trumpeters. The Christmas feast at Drumoak was legendary and for years had been a tradition in the village. When Edward closed the doors the year William and Mehlyndia left him, the town mourned with him. No celebrations took place during those long years and when Edward made the proclamation that this year, he would resume the Christmas ball, all of Stonehaven was abuzz with excitement.

There was speculation that Edward was to use the opportunity to formally name his grandson as his heir during the course of the feast. Some hopeful bachelors made wagers in the tavern that Edward would also offer his daughter's hand to the right suitor, and they were certain the duke would choose his next son-in-law that night. More than one hopeful young man— and a few not-so-young— pushed his way toward the front of the hall to bow for Mehlyndia. She acknowledged each with no more than a polite nod of her head. She sighed, fighting the impulse to turn and run back up the stairs to visit with Prissy or better still, run to the solitude of her own chamber.

Edward took her hand in his, giving her an encouraging wink. "You may have to become accustomed to being wooed, my dear."

"Father!" she whispered sharply. "I'm hardly ready to consider being wooed."

Edward placed his forefinger on her lips, his eye twinkling above a mischievous grin. "And I am hardly ready to allow you to be snatched away from me so soon, my dear. Rest assured, I shall not require nor encourage you to marry until you wish it."

She gave him a quick hug, then stepped back, blushing, unable to keep a pleased grin from her face, "I must admit I do find it flattering. It's good to know I can still turn a young man's head."

"Indeed, you can." Edward laughed aloud, then turned

to face the crowd, his arms flung wide. "Come in, come in. Welcome, one and all!" he bellowed joyfully from the landing.

"Happy Christmas, m' lord!"

"Blessed Yule!" they called, as they filed past, bowing or curtseying to the duke. As part of the tradition, many dropped scrolls bearing well wishes, or impossible requests, into a basket set next to one of the trees.

Edward would pick up each scroll, break the seal, and read aloud in a lofty voice. The scrolls were always anonymous, but part of the fun was for Edward to guess who the authors were.

"Let's see." He unfurled the first scroll with a flair of his wrists. "My guess is that this comes from a certain tavern owner."

Edward raised a brow over the scroll, giving an elderly man a wink. The man blushed and bowed slightly in acknowledgement, accompanied by polite chuckles amid the crowd. Edward assumed his proud stance and read the scroll.

"I believe it is Clive McGinty who requests that all flagons bearing the crest of the *Thistle and Lark* kindly be returned by those who stole— no that was crossed out— *borrowed* them from him. He promises amnesty for any who return the flagons full of the secret recipe heather ale from the *Hound and Fox* across town."

The room echoed with laughter as the tavern keeper blushed, shaking his head in mock confusion. "I'm sure I don't know *who* put that in the basket," he protested.

Edward pulled another scroll, still chuckling over the last. "Well now, this is interesting. This one has a seal on it." He grinned to the crowd. "Someone must want a grand favor from Father Christmas, aye?" He went to break the seal, then stopped, looking at it closely before he broke it. His smile faded and a crease furrowed his brow.

"Father?" Mehlyndia placed her hand on his arm. "What is it?"

"I know this seal," he said quietly, for her alone to hear, showing the seal to Mehlyndia.

She gasped lightly. She had seen it before as well, on a single document in her father's chamber. "The magistrate?"

The crowd had quieted down, all eyes now looking curiously at the duke as he hesitantly broke the seal on the scroll and opened the parchment to read. His brow knotted as he read, his eyes darting back and forth, then top to bottom. The paper shook ever so slightly in his hand. He looked over the scroll to the people in the hall. "Is this someone's idea of a cruel jest?"

Heads turned to each other, bewildered, the murmurs turning to a dull roar.

"It is not a jest, my lord," a deep and booming voice called from the back of the hall. "Go on, read it aloud."

The crowd parted, allowing a tall gaunt man to approach the stair. Edward's eyes went wide and his lips disappeared into a tight crease. "Explain yourself."

"I shall. But first, read aloud the proclamation. I assure you, my lord, it is quite genuine," the man said calmly, his head bowed respectfully.

Edward held the scroll high and cleared his throat. He glanced to the man again, raising his brow. The man smiled and nodded.

"In the matter of William of Drumoak, Earl of Sutherland..."

A sudden hush descended within the hall at the mention of the name.

Mehlyndia turned quickly, startled as Edward's voice began to crack. "Father?"

He shook his head and cleared his throat again, an incredulous smile coming to his face. He began again, more confident, and louder, "In the matter of William of Drumoak, Earl of Sutherland; Be it known from this day hence that all former charges be expunged from his name. This document hereby rescinds the declaration, dated 1 October 1607, stating whereas his exoneration in conjunction with his passing..." Edward skimmed through some of the more flowery prose, until he reached the bottom, and a single tear began to sparkle on his eye lid. "... hereby rescinded... he's free."

"What?" Mehlyndia gasped, echoed by the crowd.

Edward waved his hand to quiet them, looking at the tall man, then out to the crowd. "It's a pardon! A complete and unencumbered... pardon! His name is clean!"

Mehlyndia burst into tears with the cheers from the crowd.

Seany tugged on her skirt. "What does it mean, Mum? Is Papa coming home?"

Mehlyndia crouched down next to him, hugging him tightly. "No, darling, but it means, we don't ever have to call him Philbrick again."

"Oh," Seany sighed, clearly not understanding the grandness of the moment.

Edward quieted the crowd, beckoning the man to

approach him. "Mr. Garland... though I am grateful... I'm at a loss to understand why..."

Garland bowed his head. "It is simply the right thing to do. My only regret is that it has taken so long for me to do so. I beg your forgiveness on that count."

Mehlyndia gave her father a hug, whispering to him. "That is a wonderful gift. If only William were here to receive it."

"I know," Edward said, his voice failing him again. "Such irony. With this, he would be free to reclaim his title... and his life."

Someone near the door called out, "Mummers!"

Mehlyndia took a deep breath and wiped her cheeks quickly, turning her attention back to the festivities. Chase and Matthew were making their way through the crowd toward the stairs. Matty greeted Seany with a smile, slipping a cherry tart into his hand as he passed, giving Mehlyndia a wary glance. Mehlyndia raised her brow in mock reproach, then grinned at them. *Ah, well. It's Christmas. Let them have their treats.* "Go ahead, enjoy it."

Seany showed his toothless smile and broke the tart in two, offering half back to Matthew, who eagerly accepted.

A moment later, the doors swung open allowing a frigid burst of air to waft through the hall. The crowd parted as Geoffrey entered, leading a group of five players behind him, each wearing a gaily painted mask and shrouded within fur riding capes. The old luthier jaunted into the hall, as spirited as a man of twenty, dressed in a colorful harlequin tunic. He approached the foot of the stair, extended his right foot and bowed deeply before Edward. "My lord, it is our honor to provide you with tunes and entertainment this evening."

He spun on his heel and, with a flamboyant wave of his arm, motioned for the troupe to begin their performance.

Geoffrey struck the strings of his lute, playing a merry Christmas madrigal, while the masked players pantomimed confusion, looking to each other turning their palms up, pretending to search for something within their capes and pockets. The crowed chuckled appreciatively as they bumbled into each other in their make-believe quest.

"What are they looking for, grampa?" Seany asked, staring at them in rapt fascination.

"Just watch." Edward picked him up, giving the boy a better view.

Geoffrey began to sing the tale of Good King Wenceslas while the players continued their pantomime search of nothing in particular. Mehlyndia blinked back an unexpected assault of tears, as she remembered just one year ago when Simon, Ian, and Elinor had paraded through the parlor in Port Edin, singing the very same tune. *Could that have only been last year?*

Soon the players joined in Geoffrey's tune, singing loudly, and, to the surprise of everyone within the hall, extremely off key. The crowd became silent, offering confounded gapes and gawks and polite little snickers to the troupe, who seemed to take little notice.

"Good heavens," Edward said under his breath, covering his mouth with his hand. "I've heard sweeter music coming from the birthing stall in the horse barn."

"Mum! It must be Papa's trained monkeys!" Seany piped up, his little voice echoing through the hall, eliciting a burst of laughter from the crowd. Seany turned scarlet covering his mouth with his pudgy hands.

"Oh, Seany." Mehlyndia could not resist a giggle, even though she felt like crying. "I'm sure they're not *those* trained monkeys."

Suddenly, the outside doors swung open again, sending another frigid burst of air through the hall. The crowd silenced at once, all heads turning toward the door. The players froze in a comical tableau for a moment before running toward the door. They returned almost as quickly as they had exited. The smallest of the masked players assumed a lofty stance in the doorway bowing at the waist, before marching toward the stairs. Next, the four remaining players entered, bearing a chair supported by two long wooden poles. Seated in the chair, another masked man who was dressed in a long fur cloak with a garland of evergreen around his shoulders. A wreath of holly encircled his head, half concealed beneath his hooded robe. He held a wooden cane in one hand and small sack in the other. Geoffrey played a regal sounding march on his lute as the players bore this new character into the hall. The people applauded as the litter was lowered to the floor.

"Look! It's Father Christmas!" Seany called out gleefully. "I saw him first, Matty!"

The players lowered the poles and stepped aside, as if at attention. The seated player, looking through his mask, silently surveyed the crowd for a moment until they hushed. He hung the cane over the arm of his chair and made a beckoning motion to Seany.

Seany pointed to himself, his eyes wide. "Me?"

The man nodded.

"You best go to him, Seany. Ye can't keep Father Christmas waiting." Edward set him on the stair, giving him a pat on the bottom.

Seany approached the man timidly. Mehlyndia kept a watchful eye on him, ready to run to him if he became frightened. She bit her lip, resisting the temptation to embarrass her son by running after him.

Father Christmas opened his arms in greeting. When Seany was close enough, the man reached out and snatched her son in a sudden all-encompassing embrace, swallowing the little boy within the folds of his big fur coat.

"Seany!" she called out, horrified at the player's boldness.

Edward put a hand on her shoulder holding her back. She relented, but stared furiously at the man. *How dare he!* She would allow no more than another moment of this. If this man did not release her son, Christmas or not, she would step forward and pull him away. She watched, marking the seconds by the loud beating of her heart, waiting for Seany to squirm away, certain the lad must be terrified by now.

But Seany didn't squirm. Mehlyndia could scarcely believe her eyes when she saw his little arms suddenly fly up around the man's neck and clutch onto him as though he were afraid to ever let go. Father Christmas held on equally tight, burying his masked face in the boy's neck. The crowd was deathly silent, all of them seemingly caught up in the scene.

Mehlyndia hadn't realized she had descended the stairs when Seany was finally released from the man's embrace. He stood before Father Christmas, his back to Mehlyndia, listening. Father Christmas leaned forward and whispered something in the lad's ear, then placed something in his hands. Seany nodded, then turned back to his mother running to meet her. She dropped to her knees instantly, catching her son in her arms.

He hugged her for a moment, then stepped back. His eyes were red lined, but no tears were falling and Mehlyndia thought for an instant he looked far older than his six and a half years. Looking down to what Father Christmas had handed to him— a small leather pouch, and a folded piece of white linen— he simply handed it to his mother.

"What is this?" Mehlyndia asked, opening the drawstring on the pouch.

"A present," Seany whispered, then looked back over his shoulder to the seated man, his wide toothless grin finding his face again.

Mehlyndia unfolded the little piece of linen, trembling as she realized what she held. *This is mine... my wedding handkerchief.* She opened the pouch and nearly swooned as the silver eagle tumbled into her palm, landing atop the handkerchief, sparkling against the candle light around her. She looked up quickly, staring at Father Christmas. *He's sitting down... he's not walking... can it be?* She was about to call out but stopped herself when Father Christmas reached for the cane on the arm of the chair and her heart sank to the floor. *Of course it isn't. He never used a cane. Foolish fancy that was, Melly...*

She gathered her breath and got to her feet as the man planted the cane on the floor before him. Two of the players took a step closer to him as if ready to help should Father Christmas ask it. He grasped the cane with both hands, wrapping gnarled fingers around the handle, then ever so slowly got to his feet and stood there, leaning on the cane.

Mehlyndia took a cautious step forward, clutching the badge tightly in her palm. *He stood... it can't be...* She stared at the man's hands, then to his masked face, daring not to believe what her heart was telling her.

He glanced to the player on his left and, on his signal, the player pushed the hood back for him and removed the mask from his face while he stood holding the cane tightly in both hands. "Happy Christmas, Melly."

"William!" She ran forward, throwing her arms around him. "It *is* you!"

"Oh, no," he gasped as he lost his balance, sending the two of them falling backward into the chair.

"I'm sorry!"

Mehlyndia jumped off, drawing her hand to her mouth, laughing and crying at the same time. He reached to her, his eyes shining. She took his right hand gingerly, as he grasped the cane in his left and raised himself out of the chair.

"How?"

He grinned lifting a brow, then tapped the cane against his boot twice. Mehlyndia pulled his cloak aside, revealing William's most impressive new invention; a pair of wooden braces fitted from knee to ankle, then under his boot that securely supported his ankles.

He allowed the cane to fall to the floor as he embraced and kissed his wife, barely aware of the cheers that were thundering through the great hall... the great hall of Drumoak Castle, in Stonehaven as the people of Stonehaven welcomed home William of Drumoak, Earl of Sutherland.

Epilogue

William's Journal
May 1633

"**W**HAT IS IT, Papa?" the tyke asked, as his father set the ornately carved wooden box on the table before him. "Is there a secret treasure in there?"

"There is indeed," his father replied.

"Is it pirate's gold?"

"Oh, no, Willie, it's far more valuable than that."

The child's eyes grew wide in fascination, his lips drawn into a bow. He drew his hand along the carving at the top of the box, tracing the ivy tendrils and leaves. A small brass lock held it closed.

"It's locked, Papa."

"Oh dear," his father sighed then with a wink and a snap of his fingers, reached behind the lad's ear, deftly producing a small brass key, much to Willie's delight. "Hiding keys in ye ears again, lad?"

Willie clapped his hands, laughing. "Open the box, Papa."

The key turned easily with a bright click. The lock was removed and he set it on the table then rested a hand on his son's shoulder. "Go ahead, son. Open it up."

Willie grinned then lifted the lid, revealing the contents. His face melted almost at once from excited curiosity to confusion. "It's just an old book. There's no treasure here."

Sean settled in a chair and lifted his son to his knee. "Oh, now that's where you're wrong. The treasure is in the pages, Willie." He gently lifted the book from the box, setting it on the table before them. The tooled binding had hardened and darkened with age and wear. Small flecks of brittle leather dusted the tabletop as he slowly opened it. The time-stained pages, yellow and fragile, were burned along the edge. He turned to the first page and smiled at the crude little child's drawing there; a knight in battle against a fierce looking dragon. "There's a wonderful story in this book."

Willie tilted his head, curiously looking at the writing on the page that he was too little to understand. "What does it say here?"

The ink in the inscription was darker than the drawing having been written years later, the block letters formed by a slow and careful hand.

"It says; For Seany. May you read and understand all the things I wanted you to know. Life is a wonderful thing, my son. May you welcome every day with a prayer of thanks for the morning, an eager anticipation for the next, your memory of the day before always be sweet, and your dreams be ever free of dragons. "

"Is the story about him?" Willie asked pointing to the picture below the inscription. "Is that the dragon?"

Sean chuckled and nodded. "Aye, 'tis. He wrote in this book nearly every night." He sat silently, rereading the little inscription, remembering the first time he had seen it, all those many years ago.

"Who, Papa?"

"The Duke of Stonehaven."

Willie looked up confused. "But... that's *you,* Papa."

Sean chuckled lightly, carefully turning the pages. "The one who came before me, Willie," he said, quietly. "*My* papa. It's time you got to know him."

Willie nodded, and clutched his father's arm, pressing his cheek against his sleeve.

"Well then, let's start at the beginning when our hero was but twelve years old... 3 August 1600..."

Sean chose the passages he read to his son carefully, avoiding the darker times but elaborating on the more cheerful. The day would come when he would be sure to tell the whole story of his father's life to his son, and how he had shed the mantle of demon, becoming the much loved and respected Lord William, Duke of Stonehaven.

Willie listened quietly, asking a question every so often before falling asleep in his father's lap. Sean kissed his head, gently. "Sleep sweet, lad," he told him, then turned the pages, and continued to read.

13 October 1613

I will never again, in my life ever doubt the existence of miracles. Port Edin has just vanished from the horizon. I write this from the stern deck of *Lady Anne.* I'm coming home, son.

~William

25 October 1613

We've been blessed with a steady breeze and clear skies on our voyage so far. Ian is up and about, feeling much better. I've noticed he tends to retire early each evening, and he spends a good amount of time alone on deck. The wound on his forehead seems to be healing quickly, thanks to Annlise. Ian moans about being fussed over, but I suspect he is secretly enjoying the opportunity to be the patient for a change. Ewan is on the mend as well. His side pains him less each day, though I have noticed him affect a pitiful expression when Annlise comes to tend to him. He's not fooling anyone. And neither is she, as she takes extra care in tending to his aches and woes. The lass certainly has her hands full on this ship of invalids.

Simon does a lot of pacing, calculating to the best of his ability the weeks remaining until we reach Stonehaven. I believe he's announced his impending fatherhood at least four times each day. The others have taken to ignoring him, but I don't mind if he bends my ear with it. I miss my wife too.

Duncan seems to have found an unlikely friend in our guest, Peter Garland. I must admit, a more unlikely passenger I cannot imagine, but try as I may I'm having a difficult time disliking the man. Perhaps Duncan is the wisest of us all.

As for me, I take each morn as it comes. The stiffness in my hands has lessened a bit, and I've faith that I'll be back to my carving soon enough. I've faith as well, that it was not a singular miracle that I stood and walked that last night. I will not believe that what was given to me has been taken back so quickly. It's simply taking a bit longer this time to find my knees, but I'm confident I'll be at least back to where I was before the fire by the time we reach Scotland.

~William

15 November 1613

The weather turned foul in the night, and we have had to stay below. How do these sailors do this for years on end? We have each made at least two trips to the rail to purge our stomachs with the incessant rocking of this ship. The only good I can find in sea-sickness is the inspiration it has provided me to get my knees working again. I've gotten right good at kneeling over the rail.

~William

30 November 1613

Ewan and Annlise were wed today amid clear skies and calm seas. Ian performed the ceremony and Mr. Garland witnessed. I was honored when Annlise asked me to stand in for her father. Matthew is a lucky lad. Ewan will be a fine father to him, I'm certain. After the ceremony, a shadow crossed the deck from above. We are too far to sea for there to be birds, but Duncan pointed it out as well. No one else seemed to notice it. I'm certain that it was a clear sign that Sean approves of the marriage.

Having little more than the clothes on my back at the moment, in jest, I offered Ewan a gentleman's estate as a wedding gift. But the more I think on it, I believe I can make good on that gift. Annlise tells me Aberdoir was claimed by Ogham when he married Bryndah. But she's gone now. I believe my first order of business will be to reclaim it, and give it to the McDonoughs.

~William

1 December 1613

Ian has retreated to his cabin again. I wish I knew what it is that is troubling him so. I miss his laughter and quips over dinner.

The newlyweds have yet to emerge from their cabin, and I'm beginning to believe we will not see them until we land. Mother bless them both.

~William

4 December 1613

My knees will never be the same. This ship is nothing but wood and splinters and I find myself waxing nostalgic for the relative softness of the forest floor. Much as I hate to admit it, if I don't find a way to use these feet soon, I may have to resort back to that confounded chariot just to give my knees a rest. There must be a way to keep my feet under me properly.

~William

6 December 1613

Peter has been true to his word, and has scribed the writ that will assure my freedom once we land. I'm not as worried about the civil courts, as I'm sure Edward has some sway there, as I am in facing a mob who believe me to be a demon. There is not a writ in existence that will change rumor-poisoned minds. I fear it may become my life's work to live down the reputation.

~William

10 December 1613

Miracles come in many shapes. Today it came in the shape of a wobbly table leg that has the annoying habit of folding under at inopportune times. Today it collapsed just as I was about to win a game of chess against Peter. With his assistance I managed to brace the thing together in such a way to keep it from folding on its own. When we were finished, the table stood more sturdy than it ever has. It was Peter who suggested a similar solution may work on *my* legs. I must think on this more.

~William

23 December 1613

Oh, what a day! The braces work! I need a cane, perhaps two, to keep myself upright but by the blessings of Mother, I can stand on my feet again!

I put my new legs to work at once, and stood among my friends upon the deck as we approached Stonehaven and I looked upon Drumoak with my eyes rather than in a dream.

Sweet Blessed Mother, I'm home!

~William

25 December 1613

My sweet son, you are asleep on my lap as I write. I cannot express my joy. Sleep peaceful, lad.

We landed at dawn on this Christmas day. Simon and Ian put to shore first to make sure my way was safe. They came upon Geoffrey, my old teacher and friend, first. It was his suggestion that we enter the castle in the guise of mummers which gave Peter the opportunity to drop the writ in the wish-basket. (It never occurred to me, that my companions could be so unmusical!)

Seany, I'm sorry to have kept you waiting all day. You don't know how badly I wished to storm the castle walls and find you and your mother the moment we landed, but it was necessary to wait until Edward made the writ public. Now I'm free to be with you openly—civilly at least. I still face a challenge with the bishop.

This has been quite the Christmas! The gifts are too many to count, especially for Prissy and Simon. Twins. I'm thrilled for them.

I've met Matthew, my nephew. I'm glad to know you and he have become fast friends, Seany. I'm sure the two of you will be as adventurous as his father and I were in our youth. For your papa's sake, though, please be more careful than we were.

~William

31 December 1613

As I feared, Dunkirk has begun his campaign against me. He sent a warrant in the name of the church to Edward earlier today. Edward dismissed it of course. However, Dunkirk is insistent, claiming the church does not recognize Garland's writ as exoneration, as it did not come from a member of the clergy. A second warrant arrived within an hour of Edward's dismissal, this time delivered by a squad of hunters. I was gratified when Edward called his guard against them. Ewan crossed blades with the bearer of the warrant.

Edward assures me Dunkirk has no authority to carry out his warrant. Still, it would be to my benefit to obtain absolution from the church. Dunkirk may have no authority, but he is quite good at rousing the superstitious rabble into a frenzy. Without an absolution, I fear the good folk of Stonehaven will turn on me again.

~William

3 January 1614

I'm becoming more adept with the braces. Using a cane in each hand for support, and with Melly and Seany cheering me forward, I managed to cross the entire length of the great hall this morning on my feet. It only took twenty minutes. It's a start.

The stairs are another matter. I'm perfectly capable of getting up them on my knees, but Edward seems to think that it is undignified for an earl to go crawling about like a cat. Ian told him about my magic closet, and Edward had carpenters in the castle within the hour. I drew out a crude illustration of how it should work, and they went straight to work. I'm not sure I like the crank handle they used—it looks like it would be more at home in a prison—but it does the job, and the Earl of Sutherland can maintain his dignity when retiring to his room.

I rather like the portrait of me in the hall, however the plaque below it has to go.

~William

4 January 1614

Ian seems more himself again. When I commented to him that I was pleased to see he was cheerful again, he replied simply that inner peace does that for him, and that he was no longer struggling for an answer, and that he'd made his decision. He didn't tell me what that decision was... but I've a hunch I know.

~William

5 January 1614

Dunkirk's hunters returned early this morning with another warrant, this one signed by the Archbishop. Edward had little choice but to allow them into the foyer. I sent Melly and Seany to our chamber and had her bar the door. Prissy and the twins went with them, and Simon stood sentry outside the door. Ewan and Duncan rallied the rest of the guard, and they barred the hunters from going any further than the foyer. The bearer of the warrant read the wretched thing loud enough for it to echo through the whole castle, proclaiming that even Edward had no authority to dismiss an order from the Archbishop. I'm ashamed to admit I had a moment of real fear that Edward was going to surrender me when I was summoned to the foyer. Thank the Blessed Mother I was wrong.

I was determined to face them on my feet, so my arrival to the foyer was slow. By the time I arrived, they had retreated, and were marching in formation away from the castle, and Edward was shaking hands with a cleric who was standing with his back toward me. Grateful but confused, I asked what had happened. That was when Edward showed me the scroll; an absolution signed and sealed by a member of the clergy.

The cleric removed his hood, and Edward introduced me to the man who had just given me back my freedom. He called himself Father John de Baptise, formerly known as Ian Proctor, of Stonehaven abbey. I hardly recognized him with his hair shorn and his beard gone.

William

30 April 1614

Aberdoir was reclaimed handily with minimal bloodshed. One of Ogham's men was killed, and two of Edward's guard suffered minor injuries. By sunset, Ogham's banner came down, and the flying hawk of clan Fylbrigge was raised again.

Edward has left it to me to place an earl of my choosing in that estate. After a brief discussion on the importance of lineage, I informed the duke that I believe the estate should be left to someone of my father's bloodline. Therefore, I have named my brother's son as Earl of Aberdoir, his foster-father, Ewan McDonough to act as his regent until he is of age to assume the role.

Lord Matthew Chase Wilbrun Fylbrigge of Aberdoir celebrated his ascension with a honey cake and an imaginary dragon hunt with Seany.

~William

31 August 1614

It took seven years, but today, on the anniversary of our wedding, Lord and Lady Sutherland have at last taken up residency in Sutherland manner. It's lovely here, overlooking the sea. The demon tales do not seem so prevalent up here, which suits me well. I've been out and about in the little town here, meeting the good people who live here. For the most part, they are seafarers and farmers. Simple folk. Good folk.

~William

25 December 1614

We're back to Drumoak for Christmas. Neither one of us will admit it, but I think Melly and I would be glad to stay here... Sutherland is beautiful, no doubt. But it's not home.

~William

31 December 1614

I find it to be enormously handy to have a priest for a friend though I still cannot bring myself to address Ian as Father John. I asked him if he'd taken the vow solely to provide my absolution. He assured me that was not his only motivation, though it was the thing that sealed his decision. He helps now with the heather path. I cannot help but realize that I am not the only one who should be called 'Phoenix'.

1 January 1615

As a surprise to us all, Edward and Elinor exchanged vows this evening quietly and privately. Father John and I both officiated, joyously. Though the marriage will likely never be accepted by King or Bishop, given that Edward did not seek blessing from either. It shall be necessary for the couple to live quietly, and not flaunt the union publically. However, Ian blessed the marriage in the name of God, and I blessed the fasting of their hands in the name of the Blessed Lady and Lord. They are doubly blessed and no less married than the king and queen for those who count most. The bride is glowing, and the groom has not looked so content in years.

After the ceremony I was more than pleased to provide music. It's so good to sing and play again.

~William

4 January 1615
Melly has painted a new portrait of me to hang on the wall of not-so-dead nobles. She meant well, I'm sure, and posed me free standing upon the stairs. But I do not live my life as a lie, and after a bit of an argument, she relented and added my canes to the portrait.
~William

23 August 1616
Melly has given me a daughter. Born in the small hours, blessedly healthy. We have named her Cyslie Anne. She's the most beautiful thing I've ever seen. Seany is beaming with pride, proclaiming himself to be her protector for life. After all, he says, that's what brothers are supposed to do.

Prissy is expecting another little one almost any day. Sutherland manner will be full of children, it seems, and nothing pleases me more. In honor of Cyslie's birth, and because I simply wished to do it, I've given Simon and Prissy an estate south of here, a small barony they have named "New Edin," God bless them.
~William

12 February 1617
Quentin left Drumoak this morning for a visit to Aberdoir, with the happy task of helping to welcome Ewan and Annlise's new son, Colàn, into the world. What wonderful news. As I knew he would, Ewan has taken his role as regent seriously, seeing well to Matthew's education and overall well-being.

The lad will make a fine and just nobleman when he comes of age. I am pleased to see Aberdoir flourishing again.

Sean, your son is in good hands.

~William

16 February 1617

Quentin has sent a request to Edward that he be allowed to stay in Aberdoir with Annlise. Of course it was gladly granted, though I can tell Edward will miss his company. I should like to do something special for the chamberlain in gratitude for everything he's done in his service. After all, if not for Quentin, Duncan would have never made that trip to Port Edin. And lest I forget, I should make mention of my own gratitude for the gentleman. Without him and Rebecca, I would surely have never survived my childhood in Aberdoir. I've spoken with Father on the subject, and he has agreed to provide a stipend for Quentin, ensuring him a gentleman's leisure for the rest of his days.

~William

15 April 1617

Father has withdrawn from many of his public duties, asking more of me in months of late. I'm pleased to oblige, as I feel I know very little about the roles of government, and welcome the opportunity to learn. But I fear my education may be in haste by necessity. I believe he is dying. He protests my concerns of his health, assuring me that he is merely wishing to slow down a bit, and seek a bit of well-deserved relaxation with his wife. It pleases me to see the two of them so happy though Elinor, too, shows signs of worry.

~William

14 September 1617
Edward was laid to rest in the tomb that once bore my name. Ironic. I'll miss him dearly. I was with him when he passed at sunset last evening. At sunset tonight, I assumed his title. God grant I do him honor.
~Lord William Mastin Fylbrigge of Drumoak, Duke of Stonehaven

5 June 1624
Melly has taken ill. I've called for Ian, as he is the only apothecary that I trust, now that Elinor has passed. I don't know what I will do.
~W

6 June 1624
She passed early this morning. I've no strength to elaborate.

29 May 1626
Cyslie looks more and more like her sweet mother every day, and is my pride and joy. She has begun her music lessons, and shows quite a lot of promise with the lute. I was delighted to hear her play a verse of Greensleeves that she tells me she learned just for me as a special birthday present. Annlise has agreed to teach her the skills of her craft when she is a bit older, and Ian shall see to her reading and other tutoring, just as he taught Sean before her. It pleases me greatly to know she will be taught with gentle hands. It should be such

for all children.
~William

2 August 1626

My son was wedded to Simon's daughter, Mary, today. During the ceremony, Cyslie gifted her brother with a song of her own making. Both the groom and his bride were delighted. I've never been so proud of my children. Good heavens! I've become a father-in-law. Imagine that.

At the conclusion of the ceremony, at long last, I formally placed the crest of Sutherland on his shoulder and named him earl of that tenant.

~ I've done it, Laurel, I've given the eagle to my son, Blessed Mother grant it not be the burden on his shoulder that it was upon mine.

~William

1 October 1628

A grandson was born at dusk. Sean and Mary have named him for me; William the second. He's so beautiful. Melly would be so pleased.

I still miss you dearly, my love, but the eagle has assured me, it won't be long now before we're together again.

Sean my dear son, I want you to know that no father could be more proud, than I am of y

Sean traced his finger over last entry, the last letter drifting off the page as the quill dropped from the hand that held it. He closed the book quietly and placed it reverently back into the ornate box.

"I'm proud of you, too. Sleep sweet, Papa."